THE HASSAYAMPA KING
SECOND REVISED EDITION

BOOKS BY THOMAS PREISS

EVERYTHING COMES AND GOES—
PICTORIAL ESSAYS FROM THE DESERT

CHILDREN'S TITLES:
THE BOAT UNDER THE BOAT
THE OTHER SIDE OF THE WINDOW

Cover photo by Elisabeth Ansley

THE HASSAYAMPA KING

SECOND REVISED EDITION

BY

THOMAS PREISS

PERALTA PUBLISHING

POINT ARENA, CALIFORNIA

THE HASSAYAMPA KING
A PERALTA PUBLISHING BOOK

ISBN: 978-0-9798620-4-5

Library of Congress Cataloging in Publication Data
PERALTA PUBLISHING Tombstone, Arizona
PRINTED IN THE UNITED STATES OF AMERICA
9 8 7 6 5 4 3 2

Tombstone, Arizona

Permissions can be found on page 434.

For Mary Lynn

The son asked—"Who are you?"
The father replied—"I am . . . loved."

Acknowledgements:

I want to thank **Christina Wernette, Kirk Mobert, Sam Parsons,** *and* **Lillian Ross McFarland,** *for your interest and energy in the telling of this story. I could not have made this revision without you.*

A special note of thanks to **Saundra Brewer,** *for your tireless enthusiasm and experience—I will always be grateful.*

Mary Lynn Preiss—*for whom I owe my insignificant life. It is your eternal love, and support of this project that continues to push it out into the world. I love you and thank you with all of my heart.*

The soundtrack for the story.

Use your music service, and listen, while you read:

- Led Zeppelin – Thank You
- Simon and Garfunkel – Kathy's Song
- Simon and Garfunkel – For Emily, Whenever I May Find Her
- Creedence Clearwater Revival – Born on the Bayou
- James Taylor – Country Road
- Neil Young – Down by the River
- Neil Young – The Old Laughing Lady
- James Taylor – Fire and Rain
- Dobie Gray – Drift Away
- Jackson Browne – For Everyman
- Cat Stevens – Morning has Broken
- Cat Stevens – Father and Son
- Bobbie Gentry – Ode to Billie Joe
- Bread – Baby I'm-a Want You
- Neil Young – After the Gold Rush
- John Lennon – Imagine
- Neil Diamond - The Last Thing on My Mind
- Led Zeppelin – That's The Way
- Elton John – Bennie and the Jets
- Paul McCartney and Wings – Band On The Run
- Joni Mitchell – Blue
- John Denver – I'd Rather be a Cowboy
- John Denver – Rocky Mountain High
- Michael Murphy - Wildfire
- Paul Davis – I Go Crazy
- Don McLean – American Pie
- Cat Stevens – Into White
- The New Christy Minstrels – We Need A Little Christmas
- Bob Dylan – Desolation Row
- Led Zeppelin – Babe I'm Gonna Leave You
- Led Zeppelin – Dazed and Confused
- Led Zeppelin – Ramble On
- James Taylor – Sweet Baby James
- Simon and Garfunkel - America
- Peter Gabriel – San Jacinto

- The Band – The Weight
- Nick Drake – Pink Moon
- Thin Lizzy – Cowboy Song
- Pink Floyd – Time
- Fleetwood Mac – Landslide
- Bob Dylan – Knockin' on Heaven's Door
- Suicide Is Painless – Theme from the movie and TV series M*A*S*H
- Gordon Lightfoot – Song For A Winter's Night
- The Carpenters – Bless the Beasts and the Children
- Joni Mitchell – Two Grey Rooms
- Dave Mason – Can't Stop Worrying, Can't Stop Loving
- Glenn Miller – Moonlight Serenade
- Bruce Springsteen – Devils and Dust
- Heart – Love Alive
- The Who – Side Two of Live at Leeds: Magic Bus and My Generation
- Neil Young – Cortez The Killer
- David Crosby – Cowboy Movie
- David Crosby – Laughing

Chapter One

THE roofless front porch, eroded from the seasonal exchange of heat and rain, emanated the mild reek of wet cement. Small patches of sand collected in depressions caused by the weathering. Mitchell's shoes, hand-me-downs from his older brother Brent, rested in those depressions. Using the heel of the worn, black, Converse shoes, Mitchell pushed the sand to and fro, around the circumference of each gap in an absent-minded way. Because they were once Brent's shoes, he hated wearing them.

Wear them he did though. On this first morning of summer vacation in 1967, his nine-year-old bare feet still lacked the seasonal toughness that comes from a summer's worth of scampers across sidewalks and streets hot enough to simmer the bellies of red racers, which thrived in the oleander stands that separated houses in Mitchell's neighborhood.

It was still early. Temperatures in Phoenix, Arizona were normally cool until about 8:00 a.m. Early mornings for Mitchell, as he sat in the front yard meant reprieve from the insanity inside the complicated walls of his home. It meant that for a while, before the land mines started popping inside, he could look out, away from the front door, and believe that whatever he didn't see, didn't exist. This notion, in tune with the cooing of doves, the drone of small, single-engine airplanes high overhead, and the changing shade of two deciduous trees in the front yard, provided a momentary escape from his chaotic young life.

He closed his eyes. The bruise below the right one still smarted. It was puffy to the touch. He pulled the collar of his thin white tee shirt over head and reclined back on the porch. The blue sky appeared through the fabric. He was reminded of the corn flakes he had for breakfast; his breath trapped under the veil of the rag he wore.

He knew not what he liked or disliked about anything. He stared at the sky and found that when he did so his young mind lost the sharpness of reality and went numb. Life had already overwhelmed him. One day at a time Mitchell lost his young life to the dirty tricks of family secrets and alcoholic dysfunction. He didn't call it dysfunction. He had no name for what happened around him. He was simply an unwilling participant; aware only of what was just ahead, of what was exactly in front of him. He was aware that *he* was the moment in front of him; that he sat outside himself; not wanting anything to do with the *he* that was part of the home looming behind him.

Multi-colored tulips lined a walkway leading to the porch where he sat. One of the flowers died the year before, was dug up, and the hole left by having done so now held a wooden croquet ball. Its smooth top popped just over the rim of the hole. Two blue stripes encircled it and prompted a memory he wished to forget. *Brent put it there,* he thought. He forced Mitchell and his two younger sisters to play. After knocking Mitchell's ball into the tulip hole, out of play, he knocked Mitchell "playfully" in the face with his mallet, right under the eye. Mitchell touched the bruise again and shuddered at the thought of another day with Brent as a playmate.

Mitchell tried to bust him. Tearfully, he went into the house looking for help from his mom or dad, but they, too, suffered. They wagged pointed fingers at one another with claims of too much beer or too much nagging. There were strong comments about money, his older sister Julie and her boyfriend Garth, and words about a Catholic brother from the St. Francis parish spending too much time in their home. As he listened, Sorber, Mitchell's father, became furious over news of a pool party Ada, Mitchell's mother, had thrown two days before. The pool was full of fellow St. Joseph's Hospital nurses, skinny dipping and kissing one another. Mitchell remembered watching Ada put both his younger sisters on the laps of the nude nurses who floated on inner tubes, kissing one of them as she did so. The scene struck him hard, curdling some part of his heart. He could not take his young eyes off of one nurse in particular. She was engaging to look at, and, as he peered through the curtains, her shapely figure unwittingly became a part of his young psyche.

Mitchell sighed. He decided not to tell his parents about Brent's stinging blow to his face. He hoped the black patch beneath the eye would say enough. It went unnoticed by either parent.

He stood up on the porch and fetched the ball from the hole. He collected his mallet and played out the game he was kicked out of the evening before. With that done, Mitchell put his croquet ball back into the tulip hole just so; he was terrified of disturbing the exact position of the wooden ball. He wanted to leave it precisely the way Brent had left it.

For a brief moment, he stood on the "T" where the sidewalk on the street intersected the walkway to the porch and wondered which way he would go.

Walking east on Orange Drive, he left the boundary of his front yard and driveway. Two lots down the street stood an enormous house with a massive backyard where most of the neighborhood games were played. There were several secret entrances to the yard, including a long tunnel that burrowed under the overgrowth of an ancient stand of oleander. One either walked over the branches above the tunnel or crawled through it. A clearing in the corner of the massive backyard, where the two lines of oleander met, hidden away from the street, was where the neighborhood kids hung out.

It was in this clearing, the day before, that Mitchell ran into David Barnes. Mitchell shuddered again in memory. Barnes had taken his pants off, exposing himself, and wanted Mitchell to do the same thing. Mitchell, overcome with shame, ran out of the oleanders into the open heat of the afternoon sun. Mitchell heard Barnes begging him not to tell anyone. He would not even tell himself. Soiled inside, Mitchell ran through his house, passed the fighting, into the backyard, and dove deeply into a pool built there the year before. He let out just enough air to float to the bottom. He looked up at the sky, through the blur of surface water, longing for something safe around him. At that moment he saw Ada standing at the edge of the pool with a razor strap in her hand, pointing at him to get out of the pool. He slowly rose to the top, gasped for air, and began to cry. Ada grabbed his arm, yanked him out of the pool, and began whipping him with the strap. Mitchell's senses shut down but not before he saw his two younger sisters already crying—having suffered the same fate moments before. Ada was prone to wild, emotional outbreaks designed to keep her children under her control. They dreaded her.

The pool bottom memory and subsequent beating of the day before faded. He saw Barnes headed toward him. Mitchell cringed when Barnes waved. Rather than face him he walked across the street, ignoring Barnes' wish to talk. He hoped that by not seeing Barnes, he would not exist. As he moved back toward his house, shame-filled memories of putting hand lotion on his mother's breasts surfaced. She made him do it often and the sensation of touching them aroused and humiliated him simultaneously. He looked up and longed for the blue sky to take such thoughts and memories away, to make them disappear.

In part the blue sky—and what was before or after each moment—what encircled each memory, was not recognizable to Mitchell. He dismantled his life as he lived it; burning bridges as they were built, especially ones that might travel from his head to his heart. By doing so, he was unable to grasp his worth. He confused courage, loyalty, honesty, friendship, and love with cigarette smoke, fists, razor straps, and depravity. In that dark state he made it from one day to the next. In that fog he walked the life of a troubled boy from a troubled home.

Mitchell made his way to the opposite side of the street from where his home stood. He faced the two trees and stared, fumbling in his pockets for his Boy Scout pocketknife.

He re-entered his yard and without remembering how, made a well-rehearsed ascent into one of the trees; hands here, feet there, swing this way while pushing that. Once in position, Mitchell pulled out his knife and carved his initials and the date into a branch and above them a self-portrait of himself in the shape of a stick man. He carved a nose, mouth and eyes in the stick man's head, and when done, he imagined the stick man's eyes turning cross, looking back at him in anger. The mark on the tree marked him, and connected Mitchell to something more permanent and darker than the bruise under his eye.

The "M" for his first name and the "W" for his last were cut in deep and long incisions. The green bark was easy to slice with his knife and released a faint, tangy odor when opened up. The sap was sticky and stained his white tee shirt. The "6" and the "7," carved under the initials, were smaller and rounder. They were harder to cut because of the angle. They were not as deep and did not ooze sap like his initials had.

Mitchell looked at what he had done to the tree, sad that he hurt it. He watched his initials fill with sap, as the tree began to heal itself. The sap from the stick man and his initials filled the numbers of the year. He watched as the mark of his initials blurred the mark of a date. He watched his bleeding initials symbolize his borderless life, unaware that he had allowed the moment in the tree to define his existence.

Chapter Two

JULIE and Garth appeared as silhouettes at the front door. Out of the corner of his eye Sorber saw the young couple standing motionless, waiting to be invited into his home. Sorber's stomach turned. He puffed hard on his L&M cigarette, hoping to quell the animosity rising in his gut. The cigarette did not help.

He took another long drag, put his feet up on the sofa, and tried to enjoy a new program on television. Unfortunately for Sorber, what unfolded as a screen play on the set of *All in The Family* mirrored what unfolded at his front door; his daughter and her conscience objector, hippie boyfriend continued to wait in silence for Sorber to respond.

Mitchell watched his father shuffle uncomfortably. Archie Bunker mimicked Sorber's unease. Finally, Sorber's eyes narrowed, and then slowly turned from the television to the front door. There stood his precious daughter: tall, thin, pretty, with long blonde hair, and the smartest girl in her high school graduation class. Next to Julie was the antithesis of Sorber's hope for his daughter: Garth was also tall, and thin. He too had long blonde hair.

"Which one of you is my daughter and which is the ungrateful hippie?" Sorber blasted as he rose off the sofa and out of the room, turning off the television as he went. "I won't have that goddamn hippie in this house."

Julie's tears flowed. Rebuffed, she and Garth turned and left.

Mitchell got up from his well-camouflaged corner of the room and quietly turned the set back on. *All in the Family* disturbed him. Archie Bunker and Sorber both yelled about God and country. Gloria Bunker and Julie, with their blonde hair ablaze, shed lots of tears. Michael Stivic and Garth looked different but their complaints were identical. The show always ended on a high note, however. Lessons were learned. Tolerance was displayed. There was no ongoing rage. There were no sickening violations of body, mind, and heart. Mitchell turned off the television knowing only that he did not like the show. It did not make him laugh. It made him sad.

Mitchell heard more arguing coming from the back of the house. This time it was Brent's turn. "I'm with Dad on this He's a Jesus freak, for crap's sake!"

Mitchell peered around the corner and down the long hallway toward the yelling. Even from this distance Mitchell could see spittle hanging from Brent's bottom lip. "He lives downtown, in a piece-of-shit purple dump full of hippies, and he protested against our army in Vietnam! I don't want him in this house, either!"

Mitchell shut the arguing out and returned to his hidden spot on the floor of the television room. He thought of his father's WW II service medals, which he adored. He thought of a banner Garth and Julie painted when they first met that proclaimed 'peace' and 'love.' He thought of the words, or lack of them, spoken by both sides. Although he was too young to comprehend hypocrisy, he knew something did not add up either way. If Mitchell were able to make social distinctions, both in the home and outside it as well, he would see foundations crumbling.

Mitchell didn't make such distinctions. He did long for a normal family life. What he saw on television and in other homes in his neighborhood proved such places did exist. It was his misfortune to be a member of a family too weak to stand the friction of social unrest. Add the bitter whirl of alcoholism, and the strange, controlling, rage his mother and brother exhibited on a regular basis, and his hope for a normal family vanished.

The fighting fed Mitchell's moment-by-moment wish to get out of his house as often as he could. He learned quickly that when the arguing was at its loudest, Brent and Ada did not notice him.

There was nothing he could do about it. He found solace in his friends and in the outdoors. Amid the raised voices, he went out the front door unnoticed. *Perfect*, he thought.

Two streets north of Orange Drive, on Oregon Avenue, Mitchell found his friends, Dalton and Presley. They lived across the street from one another. Mitchell was safe where his friends lived.

"Beetle!" Dalton said, calling Mitchell by his nickname. "How about a game of Horse?"

"I'd like to, but first I've got something I need to tell you guys," Mitchell said. "I just found out we're moving."

Dalton and Presley were shocked.

"They're puttin' up a freakin' 'for sale' sign in the front yard right now," Mitchell said. "Here's my new address." He handed each a slip of paper with an address scribbled across it.

"Where the fuck are you going, Beetle?" Dalton asked.

"Prescott," Mitchell said. He took one of the slips of paper back and read out loud: "rural route 2, lot 45 B."

"What the hell is a 'rural route'?" Dalton asked.

"Bumfucky Egypt is what a 'rural route' is," Presley said.

"When?" both asked Mitchell at the same time.

"As soon as the house sells," Mitchell said.

The boys walked slowly and quietly toward Mitchell's house, needing to see the 'for sale' sign themselves.

As they moved through the streets back to Orange Drive, an ominous feeling of change stirred between them. Suddenly they were faced with the reality of certain words becoming a part of their friendship: of using phrases like 'used to be' and 'remember when,' in the context of their dialogue with one another. Nothing would ever be the same without Mitchell. The move was hard for them to accept.

⋐⋑

The U-haul truck had arrived. The driveway filled with boxes. While Brent and Sorber loaded the refrigerator and other appliances, cussing loudly as they did so, Mitchell snuck off to meet his friends in the oleander hedge one more time.

Mitchell was sadly aware of the moment before him, and of the ground he and his friends had played on for years. He took note of the identifiable features of his friends: Presley's crew-cut hair, and the mole on Dalton's shirtless stomach. Change was at hand. Mitchell thought life was unfair. He was loosing the best parts of his world and for what?

The thirteen-year-olds faced one another. This last meeting in the oleanders was a good-bye. This tender moment between Mitchell, Presley, and Dalton, was ripped apart by the loud voices of a raging

Brent and an angry Sorber, who swore and shouted at one another when an appliance box tilted off the truck ramp, and crashed onto the cement below.

Long after, as men in strange, high-tech times, they would recall the breezy summer evenings of their youthful years; how Phoenix cooled at night in May and June, and the clockwork timing of the monsoons in July and August, when the storm's wind and rain washed away the heat of the day. They would remember the Markgraf Pharmacy on the corner of Uptown Plaza and the *Playboy* magazines on the bottom rack, oddly in reach of their young and curious hands. In ritualistic fashion, the boys caught each new edition for years, expertly unfolding the center page so that all three could look without the cashier noticing. The memories that started with 'remember when,' and 'used to be,' were, with a handshake and a 'good-bye,' officially underway.

Chapter Three

SIAN looked coldly upstream on the Hassayampa River, south of Prescott, Arizona, toward Mitchell, her awkward smile expressing caution as she studied his face. She was leery of him. Her knowledge of Mitchell's actions that fateful night overwhelmed her. She could not figure him out. She wanted to know who Mitchell was, shutting out gossip from mouth and media as to the truth about him.

Sian sat in the back of the courtroom everyday during Mitchell's trial. She watched him intently, registering his reactions to gruesome crime photographs, and when the verdict was read. Just before the jury foreman stood to reveal their decision, Sian observed Mitchell turn toward the courtroom's tall windows, and joyfully stare out into another temperate, bright, Prescott afternoon. She wanted to know what he felt at precisely that moment.

Sian walked the perimeter of the courthouse lawns and nearby neighborhoods during breaks in the trial, thinking about Red's life. She struggled with the irony of learning about her mother's life and whereabouts through her death. The trial's testimony caused disturbing nightmares. She would wake up in the middle of the night gasping for air, and found that her subsequent tears and longing, for the mother she never knew, helped her fall to sleep again.

When the trial ended, she decided to stay in Prescott, as many visitors do once the town's charms sink in. She rented an apartment above a record store with views of the courthouse and its lawns, and gained employment as a waitress at the nearby Dinner Bell Café, just a short walk from her new apartment along the banks of Granite Creek. While working, she overheard gossip about Mitchell from locals. At one table in particular sat a couple of opinionated old timers who had the pulse of the town in their on-going debate:

"He's insane! How could anyone, I don't care what's been done, do what he did?" Jess asked.

"I could," Hartley said. "If I had found what he found, I probably would've done worse. The man is my fucking hero."

A hero, Sian thought. She had never known a hero. She had only known jackasses in her young life. She knew now that she got her looks from her mother, looks that had not been a blessing but a bane that caused her much heartache.

Sian enjoyed walking along Granite Creek. Afternoons were favored; the warmth and light from the sun scattering the shadows of tall willows relaxed her. She found solace on the creek and soon learned that the back entrances to both her apartment and the café opened onto the banks of the creek. She liked the fact that she could walk to and from work along a creek bed and often did. Frequently, upon arrival at her apartment, she would hear unfamiliar music coming from the record store. She would stop and listen. Through the cracks and snaps of old vinyl albums, Sian would wonder if her mother had heard and liked the songs. She wanted desperately to know her mother and the thought regularly occurred to her of approaching Mitchell, of introducing herself to him.

Prescott's courthouse square had routine. It was this routine that helped her cope with life's chaos. Each day of the week had its characters and events assigned to them. Regulars kept the doors of the café open. Sian began to appreciate how the seasons changed in Prescott, and what effect it had on the lives that made downtown Prescott home.

Sian was keenly interested in the lore, real or imagined, of Prescott and went to the Sharlot Hall Museum in pursuit of stories that made their way into photographs or written word. The pioneers were of special interest. She could imagine herself a woman living at that time. Of special note to her were the many references made about pioneer graveyards and the stories of how the occupants arrived at their final resting places. Life was a fleeting thing to Sian. Time had accelerated since the trial, and to see a person's life condensed into the chemical inlay of silver compounds on paper made her close her eyes and dream of other lives that had gone before her. She wondered which of those had visited the store below her apartment, who had gasped for air walking the hilly Carleton Street, and why they had decided that Prescott would be a good place to hang a hat.

From the outside looking in, Prescott was gorgeous. Its air, in the new millennium, was still clean. Its community and business leaders had created a vibrant economy without spoiling the town's heritage. It showed promise on all fronts and endeavors. As an outsider, it was shocking to Sian that people had less than hopeful outlooks on another day spent among the town's charms. Yet there they were, from one morning to the next, from one afternoon tea to the next, from one late-night cup of decaf coffee to the next; the town's many broken souls, medicating their cracks in the ambience and good food found at the Dinner Bell. Sian not only listened to their conversations and observed their body language, she would sometimes interact with guests, giving her opinions when asked, or not.

What none of the town's residents knew was that Sian was related to the recent events that shook their town; the brutality of that night going far beyond the comprehension of most sensibilities. It was her private secret and prayer, her rope to a past, and her hope for a future. She cringed when people, men in particular, talked about Red's breath-taking beauty. They would make rude comments while looking at Sian's mirrored loveliness, never making the connection that the two might be related. Sian helped that by never wearing anything tight or revealing. She was modest, but smart too . . . no one needed to know that she looked like her mother.

Sian had a spiritual pulse which reinforced her innate common sense, sizing up each moment of her day much the same way her mother had. Sian was a character-driven woman and wondered where she got it. That thought had the same conclusion; she was the way she was because her father wasn't. Her father reminded Sian of the brutality revealed in Mitchell's trial and she often thought that the series of events that led to Red's death began when Sian's father kidnapped her, killing the babysitter, so many years ago.

Her father squandered time and money. He took shortcuts and burned bridges, finding jail time a better companion than his role as her father. She spent many a year in foster care, and as she grew older, became the product of disdain and lust. Foster mothers were jealous of her; foster fathers were attracted to her. Yet these trials made her a stronger girl, then woman. She did not diminish into the statistics of broken foster care systems. She learned about faith when depravity abounded. She learned about love in its lack, about courage when filled with fear, about friendship among enemies, and about loyalty to her own life.

"To thine own self be true" were the words written on what was intended to be a tip, a coin left behind by a customer in a rum-induced fog. It was an Alcoholics Anonymous chip, the flip side imprinted with the Roman numeral "X." With sadness Sian realized that the possessor could no longer bear the weight of it. She cupped her hands around it, and then rubbed each side with her thumb; wanting to make the sanity it represented her own.

The AA tenet meant something to her. She could see herself in a better light since moving to Prescott. She saw a future brighter than what had been lived before. She was becoming something greater than the fearful beginnings her life had endured. Most of all, she was becoming more like her mother every day, in deed and thought, without realizing it.

She looked out the front windows of the Dinner Bell one morning and saw the old, familiar pickup truck and its owner drive by. She followed his profile, framed by the driver's-side window, illuminated by the high morning sun, as it made its way through one Dinner Bell window to the next. Others looked and pointed too. It was Mitchell coming in on a rare town visit for supplies. Sian walked slowly to the front of the dining room, following the truck's tailgate down the street and wondered about him—Red's husband—her mother's widower. She turned back toward the restaurant's dining room, her eyes staring at the floor in thought.

"Do you know who that was?" asked a guest.

"Yes, I have read and heard about him, almost daily, right here in this café," Sian responded, not looking at the person asking the question. She walked toward the kitchen window, removing herself from the ensuing buzz that followed the sighting.

Walking to the pass shelf, she looked at Mike, the cook, and a line of sweat that banded across his brow. She wondered what it was that made men do what they do. *Why?* She thought, as she stared at Mike's glistening forehead. "Why don't you ask him?" she stated below her breath.

"Ask what?" the cook replied.

"Oh, nothing, Mike," Sian said. She walked away from Mike and the pass shelf, toward a table, food in hand and delivered it, asking for any other wants or needs before departing to her next task.

Why don't you ask him, she stated in her mind.

The thought was ridiculous. Drive out to Mitchell's house and ask him why men do what they do! *What are you thinking, he's a nut job,* she thought. *He was also my mother's husband,* she continued in mild daydream. *And he doesn't look like a nut job; he looks like a decent man. Yet looks are deceiving, are they not?*

Looks are very deceiving, she thought again, but eyes are not and Mitchell's eyes, in the courtroom, stated something very different behind them than that of the violence he displayed. She suspected this was one of the reasons the jury showed mercy.

At once she decided that she would do it; she would ride out on her next day off and introduce herself. Butterflies flew at the thought. She was afraid of what she would find. The opposing personas of good and evil, so present in one man, was overwhelming to her, but the thought remained and the plan was put into motion.

The plan became an obsession as her work week ended. On a Saturday night, as the last check was dropped on a week's worth of waiting on tables, Sian began the task of closing down the dining room, getting it ready for the following Sunday morning shift. She was done for the week; the dilemma of following through on her decision was underway.

All manner of fear manifested. The thought of driving out to Mitchell's home raised her heart rate. She dropped things and bumped into the corners of tables. She appeared absent-minded, forgetting simple requests by surprised regulars, as she was normally very attentive. Yet the will to know her mother, to understand her life, in order to better know her own, was in place. Walking home beside Granite Creek, listening to water tumble north along the creek bed, Sian kept her mind's eye fixed on Mitchell's face and what would come out of his mouth when she saw him.

⁂

Mitchell was pulled from another daydream by the chorus of female singers that backed up Neil Young on his song "The Old Laughing Lady." Their collective voice gave some part of his brain a jolt, snapping him out of the daydream about a girl, a younger version of his wife. He felt sometimes that he was going crazy. His home was too quiet and her footprints, found everywhere, left him sad and often bewildered. He had not adjusted to life without her. He had not considered his place in his own life as a widower. He couldn't let such a notion come in.

The Sea Man walked along a barbed wire fence that ran in a north–south direction, from horizon to horizon. It had become a symbol of where he had been, and where he would go, and beheld gratitude in his heart for this insight—that had lately been revealed to him.

Chapter Four

THE U-Haul rumbled up to the corner of Camelback Road and 21ˢᵗ Avenue, east of I-17 in 1971 Phoenix. On that corner sat a Sambo's Family Restaurant adjacent to a Dunkin' Donuts. Mitchell's parents used both sugar factories as bribes to get the kids in the VW bus and on their way to points north of the Valley of the Sun.

Mitchell, with younger sister Emma, sat on the passenger's side of the U-Haul cab. Brent was driving. He was in control.

"Tell Mom you guys want Dunkin' Donuts," he said. "If you don't, I will bust you both right in the mouth."

Emma, seated center on the moving truck's bench, held in her lap the dead weight of dread, living only with the hope that she could blend into the seat's vinyl leather grunge well enough to be missed when Brent fired.

Mitchell watched Brent's thin lips move, making words that had no meaning, only tone. The young passengers did not respond, only trembled, much the way a puppy would under the thumb of a heartless human being. Both Mitchell and Emma had talked about Sambo's, and their excellent Tiger Butter served with pancakes the night before, and like any child anticipating a simple thing, found a moment of joy during their last night spent in the nightmarish family home on Orange Drive.

Upon exiting the truck, and with the roar of I-17 muffling spoken words and hidden feelings, the young brother and sister recited Brent's wish for donuts. Ada looked at them with an unfocused glance, and then turned her disgusted gaze upon the mess known as her son Brent. He looked away from the menace that was his mother; his black heart pinned under the load of her anger, sexual exploitation, and many undiagnosed mental abysses—all of which were now his to keep. He had been the target of Ada's unpredictable behavior since birth. With Sorber all but giving up as a husband and father in the face of Ada's erratic conduct, the younger kids were now the target of that evil as it passed through Brent.

Ada sent a dozen donuts to the VW bus and another dozen to the U-Haul. Everybody loaded in again and both vehicles made the turn north onto I-17. By the time Carefree Highway was intersected the numbers weren't pretty: Brent ten donuts, Mitchell one, Emma one; Brent five slugs, Mitchell three bruises, Emma two.

The resentment that boiled in Mitchell toward Brent grew. Emma cried as she usually did when Brent hit her. Mitchell stopped the tears a year earlier; not from shame but from fierce determination not to give in to the pain. Mitchell wanted to slug the bastard back. Each time another bruise was pressed into his skin, Mitchell envisioned his fists blasting Brent to Mars. It was going to happen someday, but it would not be today. With deep bitterness and an even deeper breath, Mitchell lifted his head to see a landmark approaching; a roadside rest known as Cordes Junction. It had a mom-and-pop soda stand, gas, and bathrooms for those in need of such services.

"You two assholes stay in the truck," Brent ordered, wanting to veil Emma and Mitchell from Ada. They obeyed. Mitchell rolled down the U-Haul window and was overcome by the rush of cool, thin, richly scented high desert air that rolled over the Sycamore and Black Mesas surrounding Cordes Junction.

He peered out to the morning horizon. The high desert air lifted his spirits in an unfamiliar way. Mitchell closed his eyes and inhaled deeply through his nose, and again the scent of the air elevated him. Although it was summer, the air had a spring-like feel to it, and in it Mitchell sensed unanticipated excitement for what living in Bumfucky Egypt might bring to him.

From Cordes Junction, the U-Haul and the VW bus made a right turn onto State Route 69, an old highway that traveled from the interstate to Prescott.

As the truck headed out, Mitchell stared into the side-view mirror and saw the trucks and cars on I-17 moving away from him, getting smaller and smaller, soon to disappear behind the hills surrounding Big Bug Creek. He saw the trucks and cars on I-17 as part of his old Windsor Square neighborhood, so familiar, yet so far out of reach. He knew there was no going back to what used to be just one day ago. Like watercolor upon canvas, the hills washed I-17 away, and he sighed, as what could no longer be seen, didn't exist.

Mitchell shifted his focus to the road before him. State Route 69 was observed in heavy silence, as the cold, pale towns of Mayer, Dewey, and Humboldt came and went. This added a sense of despair to the odd excitement found at the roadside rest in Cordes Junction.

The gradients of hills and grassy steppes slowed the U-Haul to a crawl. Ponderosa Pine appeared in heavy swaths rolling away to the south.

The truck crested the last hill at the east end of Prescott and picked up speed, giving Mitchell the sensation that he was being pushed into a place that held no appeal to him. Local landmark Thumb Butte, with its rocky top shaped like a hand flipping the town a bird, sat high on the western horizon. The landmark spoke to Mitchell saying; "Welcome to Prescott, now go home."

Mitchell remembered his friends. He recalled riding his bike to North Mountain Park in Phoenix, climbing the trails found there, and thrilling to the uncontrolled acceleration of his bike speeding toward the picnic tables far below. Mitchell looked down Gurley Street, Prescott's main thoroughfare, and found the side streets and buildings lining it to be rustic and run-down. Motels and small restaurants flew by his window, and then an armory next to a field filled with both ball players and spectators. The U-Haul made its first stop in Prescott at the intersection of Mount Vernon and Gurley. Mitchell looked south up Mount Vernon Road to find the street lined on both sides with decaying Victorian homes.

The light turned green. Thumb Butte reappeared at the top of another hill, and as the U-Haul followed the crest of the hill downward, Mitchell saw something quite unexpected: Prescott's town square. It sat in the middle of town with a stately courthouse and a park full of large American elms. Mitchell was surprised to see the square burgeoning with activity. The lush green trees, thick enough to walk on from tree top to tree top, contrasted with the brown Sonoran suburbia he left earlier in the day.

Brent kept the U-Haul in second gear as it ascended and descended the steep grades of Gurley Street. A traffic signal abruptly changed, forcing him to hit the brakes hard. The load in back was mercilessly rearranged. Brent detonated. He cussed loudly, clubbed the steering wheel, and attracted the attention of bystanders.

Mitchell was oblivious to all of it. He did not notice the movie theater, or the old buildings, or the unexpected changes of traffic lights. He had spotted a girl. She had jet-black hair reflecting sunlight, and a soft, white cotton shirt tucked into blue jeans. Mitchell's staring rested on her exposed feet, which were fitted comfortably into beaded sandals. When he looked up his gaze found two sets of eyes peering back at him: a young girl and an older woman. Mitchell self-consciously looked away, but found the visual memory of the young girl's bright, black hair remained with him.

The light changed. The truck lurched forward into the intersection. The passenger-side mirror framed the girl. Mitchell observed a silver-colored bracelet on her wrist similar to one Julie often wore. It bore the name of a soldier missing in action in Vietnam. Mitchell waved to her in the mirror, and, to his astonishment, she waved back, receiving an immediate reprimand from the older woman.

An indescribable fever revved in his heart. The moving truck made a left turn, removing the girl from view. He wondered who she was. There was both joy and desperation in him, as chance had simultaneously sparked then snuffed out a flame of virgin fervor in his heart.

The remainder of the drive through town offered Mitchell those things that a young member of a wildly dysfunctional family might endure, including the sight of Emma's continued blending into the truck's bench seat like a chameleon. There was more of the abusive language that brought Mitchell's shallow breathing to a complete standstill. There was resignation and then anger in his heart as well as in his hidden clenched fist. He saw far too many bars in Prescott and knew what that meant to his father's chances of sobering up.

There was an unexpected left turn off of Highway 89A, a road that led to Ponderosa Park, a Prescott subdivision where their new home was located. Brent had followed the VW bus into a motel parking lot.

At once a shouting match had erupted between Sorber and Ada. A local bank refused to release the house to his parents and they decided to stay one night in a motel south of town while the bank changed its mind.

Mitchell's family spent eight nights at the motel. Hell was had. Bitterness and embarrassment swayed into and out of the motel room's front door. The area's neighbors picked up on the sideshow and gawked at the family when they visited grocery stores and gas stations.

He knew something was wrong, but Mitchell's resilience while family horrors played out was growing. The presence of Granite

Creek, which ran beside the motel, and his revisiting the classic tales of *Tom Sawyer* and *Huckleberry Finn,* offered further reprieve.

For eight days he sat on the cold Granite Creek rock, watching the shade of tall pine trees fall across the pages of his books. Mitchell was again enchanted by the Samuel Clemens stories and began to see himself as part of the gang. He let the cold creek water run over his bare feet. He let his immediate surroundings speak to him through the subtlety of his senses. He made simple associations with the elements, finding in them what would someday become a voice of understanding in his heart as a man. His sense of touch showed him how hard a smooth piece of granite could be. His eyes watched the dance between water and rock, and understood that each would bend the other in the passage of time. His ears heeded the wind in the trees, and in their silent standing heard their purpose in life. The high azure heavens had the scent of the day attached to it, invigorating his young heart into action.

Huck Finn and the boys had elected Tom Sawyer First Captain of the Gang. Mitchell closed the book with a vision of himself as that captain. It was that vision that helped Mitchell loose himself on the rock and water of Granite Creek. Tom and Huck had become his good friends, and for eight days theirs adventures ran up and down the banks of the creek.

On the eighth day it abruptly ended. A crack from overhead, a crack that sent his friends running for the cover of the woods, a crack known only to him as his mother's voice, angrily called for him to come back to the motel; it was finally time to finish the move.

ॐॐ

Brent, Mitchell, and Emma re-entered the truck. Mitchell leaned into the door and peered through the window toward the mountain tops. He saw the rapid change of shadow and light in the trees. Closing his eyes to the moving pictures, Mitchell's heart was engulfed with despair. He looked over at Brent. He, too, was subject to the rapid changing of shadow and light. Again despair pulled at Mitchell, his mind's eye moving him through a slide show of his life. He leaned back in the truck, removing any view of his brother and succumbed to an urge to quit.

Quit what, he thought to himself. The many countenances of his family members passed through his memory. They were faces of rage, of drunkenness, of lust, of confusion, and fear.

He sat up in alarm as the truck's left-turn signal snapped on. The truck rumbled onto Forest Service Road 63, a dirt entrance to Ponderosa Park, and climbed up steep grades and around tight banking curves. Suddenly, in front of a startled Mitchell, rose the Bradshaw Mountains.

The truck stopped. Mitchell got out and walked east of the road toward a small hill. At the top, Mitchell took in the view of the woods that were now his home. Hope kindled. Though not fully aware of it, the hope building within was the voice of the woods calling him to be still, to be quiet, and to find rest between the breaths of those things that haunted his young life, and the woods that might change his fear-filled heart.

CR&

Unloading the U-Haul into a cabin in Ponderosa Park was a continuation of the same angry madness that filled the truck days before. Cussing, bruises, denials, and rage marched on. Brent found more opportunity to hit his younger brother and sisters. Ada and Sorber found more opportunity to tear each other down as poverty was now their lot in life.

Where does the blame rest for such displays? The younger siblings found no answers; the question was beyond their ability to ask. The fact that Ponderosa Park was filled with streams, pine trees, wildlife, flowers, ravines, gullies, abandoned mines, antiquated barns, and buildings pulled at their young minds. Mitchell thought about Forest Service Road 63, and how it continued south after they turned up a hill toward their cabin. He wondered where it would take him. He wondered about his new address and the rural route where he now lived. He looked at the cabin and its weary feel. He found a gully full of interesting items including a rusted-out Model 'T,' and several balding tires.

Mitchell plopped down, finding a perfect curve in the rocky outcrop at the top of the gully to cradle his back. It welcomed him. The sun and shade played on his face. He closed his eyes, taking the scent of the thin air into his lungs, thinking how good it smelled and how right it was to be a part of it.

He sat up again, took a rock, and in a high arch launched it toward the rusted icon. A loud tin clank echoed up from a direct hit, startling the dogs and his parents who were watching from the porch above. Mitchell stood, hustled back up the path to the house, and went to work unloading what they brought with them from the Valley of the Sun.

CR∂

The younger children picked spots in the back patio, an open-air, screened-in room perched out among the trees. Mitchell took the spot furthest from the back door of the cabin. Emma took the other end, and Dana, the youngest, took the middle, which left her with only the slightest chance of having any kind of privacy. Brent wasn't going to live with his family in the cabin. He had joined the Army. He would sleep in the living room the first night and then be taken to the Greyhound Bus station on Sheldon Street in Prescott at midnight the following day. He would be traveling to a far away place called boot camp where Mitchell hoped mean things would happen to him.

As the U-Haul was unloaded and the house began to fill with familiar things, the kids worked to unpack and set up the patio, partitioning the area with dressers and sheets hung from the ceiling rafters to give each a sense of having a room of his or her own.

Mitchell unpacked the last of his things, pulling two items from the bottom of a box: a scrapbook containing autographs of Thurman Munson, Joe DiMaggio, Johnny Unitas, and many others, and a radio that his dad had given him. He put both items on the floor near the head of his bed.

There was daylight left. Mitchell headed back to the gully. Brent and Sorber left with the truck, returning it to a gas station in Prescott. Mitchell watched Brent pull away, and was anxious for his older brother's final departure the following day. *Good riddance,* Mitchell thought to himself, not grasping that Brent's behavior toward him was a product of his family's arrival in hell, long before Brent had reached the age of accountability.

The crack of a raven added to the notion of a new world becoming Mitchell's home. He felt a twinge as he thought of his friends, now far away yet close in memory. He recalled the summer before, when he and Dalton went to Litchfield Park, Arizona, to a pro-am golf tournament. He remembered how excited they were at the prospect of seeing in person all of the day's great sports heroes. All was not well on that day. He had waited with Dalton for an hour to get one particular autograph and when his turn finally came, Mitchell could not recognize the hero's name or face. Unfortunately for

Mitchell, he asked the man what his signature said. "Get your fucking mother to read it," was the sports legend's reply.

Dalton and Mitchell left the crowd that encircled the celebrity, with Dalton shaking his had in embarrassment. "Its Joe DiMaggio, you dork." Mitchell looked at the autograph and said "Who?"

Mitchell laughed out loud at the thought. His sisters joined him on the porch, at a loss for something to do.

"Do you guys want to go exploring?" Mitchell asked. They didn't answer; they just looked silently out at the woods.

"Hey Mom, can we go exploring?" Mitchell asked.

"I don't care," she said. "Don't be late for dinner; it'll be ready as soon as that worthless father and brother of yours gets back."

◈◈

It was quiet around the dinner table. Nothing was said. The younger siblings cleared the table, then washed, rinsed, dried, and put away the dishes. They walked three short steps into the living room, and found spots on an old rug to sit on.

They soon discovered that unlike Phoenix, which had five television transmissions, there was only one in the mountains: NBC. *The Tonight Show* theme song woke Mitchell. He had fallen asleep after the dinner chores were done. As Johnny walked out on stage from behind the curtains, Mitchell walked into the back patio and headed for bed. Climbing in, he reached over the edge and found his father's radio.

The familiar radio stations in Phoenix were also no longer available in his new mountain home. KRUX and KRIZ were just dips in the radio static as Mitchell tried to pull them in. But to Mitchell's surprise, two other stations from other states were to become as familiar as friends: KOMA from Oklahoma and X-Rok80, from El Paso, Texas, were very clear, but only at night.

Night was when he needed the radio. The music abated his fear of the woods, as the only thing between his bed and the wilds of the forest was a window screen. When his sisters went to sleep and when he heard his mother lock them out of the main cabin for the night, he would turn on the radio and listen. Through the AM radio resting in his hands, Mitchell would become a part of the larger world. It would remain on all night; the music fading to static when the sun came up; that static becoming an alarm to get out of bed and discover what the forest would offer his endless boyhood energy, and joyful childhood imagination.

Chapter Five

MITCHELL crumbled to his knees. He felt tortured by the embodiment of Red, walking toward him, cautiously so. The cold waters of the Hassayampa encircled his legs, from knee caps to ankles. It shocked him for a moment, paralleling the icy blood running through his mind; coursing through his present thought; unearthing the past.

He threw his face in next. Under the shallow water he screamed. Angry at the intensity of his hallucination, he let out massive amounts of air, then inhaled . . . for a moment purposely . . . to drown what had become a quiet, veiled place of belonging in his mind. Betrayed by the vision, he shot up, back onto his feet, coughing wildly, cursing her loss, kicking the water this way and that, damning his own never-ending want of everything that was Red. He looked like a selfish, spoiled child; his face crimson; his tantrum leaving him drenched. He wrung the water out of his hair, beard and eyes, only to see Red still standing there, looking at him incredulously.

"What's wrong with you?" Sian asked. "The whole town thinks you're crazy. Are you crazy?"

Mitchell stood still, not understanding what was before him. "No, I'm not crazy," Mitchell said. "I feel crazy right now, seeing you, hearing you . . . who are you?"

Sian looked at Mitchell now with some kindness. She saw a man still under a cloud. "I'm Sian."

Mitchell heard her voice again, his mind looking at Red, though seeing someone not Red at all. "You are Sian?" he asked.

She nodded.

"Red's Sian?"

She nodded.

"But how . . . what . . . you are?"

She looked down at the water they were both standing in. In longing and in sadness she stated: "Yes, Red's Sian."

Mitchell fell back, his hind end hitting the river bottom hard. He was aghast at the detailed reflection of Red in Sian. Confounded, he turned to his side and pushed himself to his feet, stumbling to the banks of the Hassayampa.

"You are Red's daughter," Mitchell whispered, feeling his lips mouth the words, water draining from his mouth and beard. He stared at Sian, unable to put his next thoughts together. The presence of Sian was too much of a shock to Mitchell. She was the absolute mirror image of her mother. Painfully, Mitchell was forced to make sense of the apparent phantom of his wife. He shook his head again and asked "What the hell . . . is going on?"

"What do you mean?" asked Sian.

"Crap's sake, woman, you look just like my deceased wife," Mitchell said. "You look exactly like your mother."

"I know. I saw photos of her in the newspaper," Sian said.

"You sound like her," Mitchell spit. "What the hell . . ." he said again to the sky above him. "You look like her, sound like her, do you smell like her, too?" he asked the general area around them.

Sian didn't respond. She suddenly became keenly aware of how tricky this meeting was for both of them. Respect grew for him in his honest display of emotions and the confusion they caused him. In this quick, personal exchange, Sian watched the inside of a man work itself out into the open and was fascinated by the way Mitchell acted upon what he felt. It was raw and honest. Nothing was censored. His emotions came out like the tongue of a frog on a fly. It was ugly, heart-wrenching stuff and zapped Mitchell, throwing him inside the dark and stench-filled rucksack of his recent past.

Tears flowed from Mitchell. Sian was shocked by them and cried her own. He for his wife; she for her mother. Flashbacks of that night flooded his focus and he stood up again, kicking at the water and cursing the air. Gone was the magic of routine recently set in place. Mitchell suffered again the actions of others, and of his own. Sian put her face in her hands to find no solace, nor justice. She had missed her mother all her life and found now only another's anguish in her search to know who she was.

"I'm sorry," she said. "I shouldn't have come. I didn't mean to cause you more harm." She looked up from her hands to see Mitchell facing away from her. She took note of his straight back and broad shoulders, his unkempt hair hanging past them.

"No, it's okay," Mitchell said. "It's a shock to see you, but I can handle it if you just give me a little time."

Sian moved to the water's edge too, finding a rock to sit still on. She needed to steady herself. Mitchell overwhelmed her. He stood larger than life to her, through her understanding of him via media stories and gossip. All of it was no longer second-hand hearsay or journalistic conjecture; Mitchell was an intense man with expression emanating from each breath, and she admired him immediately because of it.

He moved to the water's edge, sitting on a rock about ten yards from Sian. He rubbed his scalp, whipping water from his hair while doing so. He wiped his eyes, cussing silently under his breath. His love and desire for Red had burst forth; he shuddered in isolation. Another inhale, another *son of a bitch* exhaled. From a distant track Mitchell heard "Thank You" playing as background to what blasted before him, letting the Led Zeppelin lyrics pull another tear from his trapped heart.

He looked up slowly to Sian, whose face was turned to the water flowing by. He let himself take her in, gingerly, yet felt still another shock of memory and emotion when he saw her nose in profile.

Sian looked up. "Why do you stare?" she asked.

"So many times I rested my forehead on that nose," Mitchell said, pointing toward Sian. "I'd take a deep breath and find faith in life, because she loved me."

"How did she love you?" Sian asked.

"She loved me," is all he could state at first. He took a deep breath and exhaled it into the view of the Hassayampa flowing down stream.

"All of me," Mitchell continued. "I was an arrogant, selfish bastard. She took all of it and turned it around in the light of her love. She made me see myself as God would see me. She showed me my own lost and stolen light, as if I were being loved by an angel."

Sian was moved. She understood Mitchell's description and tried to make it part of the view she formed of her mother's life. Her heart reached into a time long past, sadly grasping at a mother's love, asking for it to touch her infant skin. A tear came as she buried her head into her mother's bosom, taking comfort from so many hard moments. Sian reached up to touch her mother's face. Mitchell saw the intimate dream unfolding and turned away, giving her space alone with her longing.

Quiet stretched across the Hassayampa. Time passed with the water as it moved over the stones and roots without reckoning. Mitchell was peaceful. He too stared out into the unfocused past, held sharp by the same longing at the end of Sian's fingertips. A mother's daughter and a wife's widower found mutual ground in a shared loss; one made of grace, the other of lack.

Quiet moved between them, amplifying the bubble and tumble of the Hassayampa. Song birds chimed in, reminding Mitchell that life takes very little note of grief, moving on in anticipation of the moment ahead. Survival is like that. Wildlife is like that. The forest scene around the two humans beckoned them to let go and move on.

The quiet continued. Mitchell breathed deeply. Sian heard it innately and took a deep breath, too. Collecting his emotional heart, Mitchell felt the presence of Red's daughter close to him as fate moved forward, defining what the day ahead would entail. He would have to look squarely at her, and accept his personal experiences with her mother, when he related to Sian. He would need strength to give Sian what she sought in him without seeing his beloved in her. She looked at Mitchell with longing for her mother in her eyes, followed by more tears.

Mitchell stood up on the bank of the river. He moved toward Sian who stared past him. He came close and slowly put his hand out to her, silently asking for hers. Sian's gaze focused first on Mitchell's eyes, then on his hand suspended in front of her. Moments passed. Through her peripheral vision, she noted his hand remained motionless; its gesture intact. Turning toward him, she slowly put her cold wet hand in his, letting him pull her to her feet. He carefully wrapped her arms around her. She sobbed in Mitchell's chest, her open hands now wrapped as fists in pain upon it. His mind battled newly awakened memories. His arms held Red, his nose happy to breathe in her scent again. *Who could it be if it were not Red*, his body asked, as his mind cried out for God to help him find the role fate was asking of him.

Sian continued to sob; the sound now mixed with the songs of the wild world around them. Her loss now became Mitchell's as his eyes filled with compassionate grief for a daughter who found her mother too late.

Sian felt Mitchell's strength and allowed comfort to envelop her. She relaxed in Mitchell's arms, feeling exhaustion overcome her. Mitchell let go his support of Sian in degrees, allowing her at any moment to disengage. Sian backed up a step and half and looked down to the water flowing by. Mitchell stared at her red hair, at the curls, at its matted length past her shoulders and again fought off the physiological reactions he was experiencing. He too took a step and a half back and followed Sian's eyes to the Hassayampa. Then he turned from her and returned to the spot on the bank where he sat before.

Sian sat down, too, and drew a deep breath.

"You hungry?" Mitchell asked in an attempt to reform their thoughts.

"I think so," Sian stated, cautious about where the question was going.

"I live just around the bend. I'll give you something to drink and make you a sandwich if you'd like."

Sian thought for a moment about what it would mean to walk into this man's house. *My mom's house! I would see her life and what she built,* she thought. Sian looked at Mitchell and stated softly, "Okay."

They walked toward the road. Sian pointed to her car and Mitchell accepted the offer to ride with her back to his cabin.

"Where do you live, Sian?" Mitchell asked.

"I live in town and work at the Dinner Bell Café."

Mitchell knew exactly where the café was but found it surprising to learn of her employment there. He was surprised further that she lived in Prescott.

Sian turned her car up the short drive to Mitchell's cabin; her mother's home. In the small clearing she stopped, remembering scenes described inside the Yavapai County Courthouse. Mitchell looked at her as he got out of the car taking note of the concern on her face. Without saying anything he thought, *she has to make her own peace with what she knows of her mother's death.*

He walked out onto the property, toward the old oak that held Red's ashes in its shadow. He glanced back as Sian got out of her car still holding the door, unsure if she was truly ready to visit what was in reality a museum of her mother.

She looked toward Mitchell, who appeared to be lost in thought as he walked about the property, moving ever closer to the old oak. He motioned for Sian to come. She stared at the movement of his arm and hand toward her, knowing what he wanted. She shut the car door, put her hands in the jean pockets, and walked across the property toward him. She looked at everything but the oak yet knew that it was significant to the man who stood next to it.

Sian saw the inscription carved in the old oak; her mother's initials below Mitchell's.

"This is where your mother's ashes are," Mitchell said, pointing to the ground.

Sian looked down at the ground. "I know, I went to the memorial. I followed everyone out here and stood out of sight beyond those trees," pointing to a stand behind the cabin. "I watched as your friend dropped them to the ground. I cried."

Mitchell reached out and put his hand on her shoulder. "So did I. I couldn't reconcile her death until after the memorial. I had a pretty rough time of it." He removed his hand from her shoulder.

They stood quietly. Simon and Garfunkel's "Kathy's Song" came to mind, and Mitchell turned to walk toward his home. The song's mention of grace, while observing Red's ashes, pushed him to the edge of tears again, and a second display of such, in front of Sian, was too much to ask of his masculine heart.

"Where are you going?" Sian asked.

"C'mon," he stated over his shoulder. "How 'bout that sandwich?"

Again Sian hesitated, not so much from any reservation she may have had about Mitchell, but of entering her mother's home for the first time.

She turned toward the cabin and began tracing Mitchell's footsteps. She looked down at them and then back up to Mitchell's clean but un-kept hair, falling down to his neck and shoulders. Mitchell opened the basement door and went in, leaving it ajar for Sian. Slowly she entered and was immediately wrapped tightly by the atmosphere of the downstairs room. Her eyes adjusted and saw the stairs that led up to the main floor of the cabin.

From upstairs she heard Mitchell rummaging through kitchen cabinets and drawers. She stood frozen in the spaces of her mother's home. With her eyes closed, she breathed in the life left behind. She reached out for the staircase railing—her eyes still—touching her mother's fingerprints for the first time. Her hand clutched tightly around the railing—she looked down—put one foot in front of the other, and ascended the stairs into the open, incredible light of the A-frame cabin. She saw the thirty-foot windows first. Then the prism suspended at the apex. Her eyes darted about the large open room taking in each of the rainbows cast there. Some were large and brilliant, others as shadows of colored light—all crossing the designs of other objects. There were pictures of Mitchell and Red, of lighthouses, and watercolor scenes of the areas surrounding Prescott. Her gaze rested on a very feminine blanket resting over one end of a sofa. *She is still here*, Sian thought, letting a tear fall. She walked over to the throw and put part of it between her thumb and fingers, compressing the softness into her senses, touching the very fabric that kept the chill off her mother on a winter day. Sian closed her eyes; her heart sang for her mother. She lifted the blanket and put it to her face, glancing up to view the inside of a rainbow now shining in her teary eyes. She began to cry out loud, her shoulders convulsing up and down exactly as her mother had done, throwing Mitchell off again as he stood in the kitchen watching.

Mitchell moved toward Sian, his heart breaking again. Standing behind her, he reached out with both hands, wrapping them around her shoulders. Her convulsions stopped but the tears did not. Sian fell back into Mitchell, the blanket still in place upon her face. He held her again without reservation, for the second time on this sad day.

The joy and great sadness that was now Mitchell's to feel, at will, moved him in and out of consciousness. He was both aware and unaware of Sian's presence; her physical outline moving back and forth through his senses. He was mesmerized by both the sorrow and happiness that loving his wife had brought to him. He closed his eyes and could remember no more, his mind shutting down hard on the moment before him.

He looked about the floor of the
desert, and found its raw beauty essential to his
peace of mind. There was the Saguaro, and the
green grass that was laid out like a garden in
Eden—for as far as his eyes could see, and the
renewing wildflowers—their symmetry and
rainbow colors taking to the bend of the earth
around him. These creations of nature kept
him in the moment.

Chapter Six

"I'M going to work. Mitchell, you're in charge," Ada said as she popped her head into the patio early one morning on their second week as residents of the woods.

Changes had come during that time. Brent was whisked away, joining the Army. Sorber found field work in the Small Business Administration and left for rural areas throughout the Southwest.

Mitchell felt a huge sense of relief. With the doors and windows open each morning to the forest, Mitchell's quiet routine outlined his life. There were no landmines hidden under foot. He no longer had to question the motions and feelings of a young boy's day. He had become a part of the living, as if he had come out into the open air, when previously he had only known corners and cracks of light that held a continuing presence of dread. The day after Brent left, Mitchell stepped slowly onto the front porch, and in the morning light extended his arms and hands not only to practice a morning stretch, but as an expression of freedom. That first stretch in the light of the sun and in the absence of fear gave Mitchell a feeling of new life. It was evident in his steps, in his choices, and in his thoughts and speech.

Nothing brought the point home for him more, however, than sitting at the head of the kitchen table. In a chair recognized as Sorber's place, or Brent's when Sorber was unavailable, Mitchell's position in life had elevated. Looking across the table at his sisters, where he once sat with them shoulder-to-shoulder, represented a rite of passage. There was room now to rest his arms and hands. He made his presence known in his home, whereas doing so just a couple of weeks earlier meant an endless series of humiliating blows.

Mail began to arrive with his name on it. Mitchell received a cordial letter from a girl he had a crush on at Madison Park School in Phoenix. Marie told him about her vacation; a trip to Slide Rock in Oak Creek Canyon, outside of Sedona, Arizona, and said she promised to write again soon. Don, who by the 8th grade could neither read nor write, scratched out a barely legible announcement of the passing of a mutual friend, Ricky Coe, in a car accident. Mitchell remembered Ricky jumping on board the sky ride at Legend City, a local amusement park, with a girl. This forced Mitchell to ride in the next car with Georgia, a girl his age, who was enjoying a scoop of rapidly melting ice cream. It was an awkward situation for Mitchell, who lacked Ricky's confidence with girls in sky rides or on dance floors. With Ricky's vocal encouragement from the car ahead, and at nearly thirty feet above the ground, the sky ride was where Mitchell encountered his first kiss. Forever sealed in this memory was Georgia's frosted lips, laced with the flavor of butter pecan.

"Mom?" Mitchell asked, when Ada answered the phone in the pathology lab at the Yavapai County hospital in Prescott where she worked.

"What's wrong?" Ada asked, alarmed at the call from home.

"Can you pick up some butter pecan ice cream?" Mitchell asked.

"What's with you and butter pecan ice cream?" she responded. "And why are you thinking about dessert at nine o'clock in the morning?"

"I don't know," Mitchell lied.

"We'll see," she said, followed by inquiries about chores. While his mom was going over the list of things that were to be done by mid-morning, Mitchell heard a click and a whisper on the phone, then a startled but muffled "oops," followed by another click. *The party line*, Mitchell thought to himself.

Mitchell didn't respond to Don's letter because it was sent without a return address. He had written to Dalton and Presley giving them his new telephone number, and first impressions of his new home. Calls came in from both friends, and plans were made for them to come up the following week.

He did write back to Marie, thinking he would get another letter from her, but it never came. Mitchell's long walks back to the cabin from the mailbox were burdened by a lack of worth. This passed quickly. The cabin and the woods were showing him otherwise. Mitchell did not filter the events that shaped his parents' lives. He kept them "as is." He was not concerned about their validity. The woods were enough.

Mother Nature had begun to make sense to Mitchell. He was exposed to the warmth of the sun, to the calm of the stars and the songs on his father's radio, to the smells of dirt on his fingers and tree sap on his toes, to the hope of being a boy, to the joys found in just one moment of living, and those found in the next. In the evening the setting summer sun shone brightly through the front window, landing on the red brick fireplace and on Mitchell's face, as he relaxed in the absence of fear.

✥✥

On a Saturday morning, a 1962 International Harvester Scout, now Ada's sole mode of transportation to and from her chaotic life, sat parked on the side of the cabin where the heating oil tank and chimney were located. With his back to the gully, Mitchell sat in a chair that was once next to the pool in his home in Phoenix. It had a comfortable rip right in the center, allowing Mitchell to hunker down enough to rest his head and extend his feet.

"Stop slouching," his mom said from the living room. "When are they supposed to get here?"

"Any minute," was Mitchell's response.

He sat quietly, feeling excitement grow into all of his limbs. The three friends were about to be reunited again after several weeks of separation.

Evan and Marjorie, Dalton's parents, along with Dalton and Presley, finally arrived in Evan's truck. Mitchell stood up immediately. The dogs started their barking dance. Everyone in the truck waved at Mitchell. Anticipation had overflowed into wide grins. He wanted to bark and dance too. Emma and Dana came out, and although they did not know Mitchell's friends very well, shared in the happy moment.

The new arrivals were taken aback by the poverty before them. It was apparent to Evan and Marjorie that things had taken a turn for the worse.

The initial shock turned very quickly to a spirit of adventure as Mitchell gave Dalton and Presley a quick tour of the immediate surroundings. The parents gathered on the porch. Ada served coffee as Evan and Marjorie remarked about the undeniable beauty of the woods. It was Ada's saving grace to have the natural setting become the focus of conversation rather than the living conditions.

Mitchell didn't notice. He didn't realize or care that their status had gone from upper-middle class to poverty. From his first moment at the top of the gully, when the spirit of the wild called him, he never looked back.

It only took a few minutes for the same spirit to catch Dalton and Presley. The parents could no longer see their children. They were already gone out of sight, and into the gully.

"Is this your front yard?" Presley asked.

Mitchell had abandoned the notion of boundaries soon after moving into the cabin and said, "I guess it is."

"This is awesome," Dalton said. "Hey, look at the old car." At once all three boys scrambled for rocks and began to pelt different parts, making it an immediate game of skill. Dalton took top honors when he knocked a tail light off the rusted bumper.

Each found a spot to sit. Mitchell's younger sisters joined them, and pleasantries were exchanged. Watching his friends talk to his sisters made Mitchell realize that he was lucky to still have his friends, that time and distance did not end their camaraderie.

"He's gone," Mitchell said.

"Good," Dalton and Presley said in unison.

"The bastard might die, you know," Dalton said in reflection, as the confusion of the Vietnam War temporarily pulled the focus away from the view of the gully.

"Yeah, well, it just feels so good not to be hiding from him all the time! I get to say and do what I want now, for the first time," Mitchell said. His sisters nodded in agreement.

"So, what's around here?" Presley asked.

"I found a mine shaft," Mitchell said, pointing to the hill behind the cabin.

"Let's go check it out," Presley said.

"Have you thrown rocks down it?" asked Dalton. Mitchell had. The rocks had taken his imagination with them, as they bounced mysteriously in the dark, forbidding hole.

Before the hike to the mine began, all were called back to the cabin; Evan and Marjorie were headed home. The boys got their gear out of the truck. The parents made their cordial good-byes, leaving instructions regarding manners. The truck honked once, and waves were exchanged. The boys walked around to the back of the cabin, into the patio, and tossed everything onto Mitchell's bed.

They resumed the trek to the mine above the cabin. The dogs darted about. Ravens checked the boy's movements from high overhead. The day continued on; as did the boy's friendship; unfolding amid the magical shadows, and stunning light, of the woods.

Chapter Seven

SIAN awoke on the sofa to starlight flickering through the tall windows, her mother's blanket wrapped snugly around her. From above she heard a quiet melody flowing down from Mitchell's loft. It was a song she had heard in the record shop below her apartment in town. "For Emily, Whenever I May Find Her" was rich in the same lost hope she felt before Mitchell laid her down on the sofa. She had collapsed in Mitchell's embrace, falling into teary-eyed slumber. *Mitchell put me here*, she thought. She heard his voice moving softly between the lyrics of the song, not able to discern what he was saying. Her eyes moved about the room, again noting the placement, texture, and colors of objects that had made up her mother's life. A shadow moved across the ceiling; it was Mitchell moving about the loft—it was the same kind of shadow cast by the same lamp during the night of terror, but Sian would never know this. She was comforted by his shadow and his voice. *He is a very different kind of man*, Sian thought, as she reclined on the sofa. *My mother was lucky to have found him.*

In the morning, Sian sat up, curious about the night that had been placed upon her like a lid on simmering soup. She stood up and in the reflection of the tall windows saw Mitchell looking down at her from the loft.

"You're up," he said. "You must be hungry."

"I guess I am, can I go out onto the patio?"

"Right through that door," Mitchell said, pointing to the front door leading out to the balcony.

Mitchell watched her go through the door. Flashbacks of brutality came and went without much consideration. Seeing the door fly open and the evil jumping off the balcony lost its opacity, as did most of the memories of that night, save one. Mitchell still did not know what to do with the memory of Red lying on the bed, so he did nothing with it. He let it lie dormant in some part of his mind that was insulated from day-to-day living. It was still there, in full color, in full detail and smell, in full three-dimensional form real enough for him to step into it at will. But he had taught himself not to.

Mitchell made his way downstairs into the kitchen finding items to prepare a nighttime snack for Red's daughter. He looked out the front windows and could see her outline standing on the balcony.

He continued to fight the dichotomy of memory versus moment. Sian's stance, looking out beyond the trees, blended too easily in his mind with Red doing the same thing. She returned from the balcony and looked at Mitchell.

Silence created meaning in the moments that passed.

"Is it hard to be here?" Mitchell asked.

More silence.

"I'm missing something I never had," Sian said. "I'm discovering my mom."

"I've got so many pictures of her," Mitchell said, pointing to a corner of the kitchen filled with headshots. "She was my favorite subject. On my computer downstairs you'll find an endless array of headshots with all manner of lighting and shadow. She loved the camera—wait—that's not what I mean. She loved me, and it shows in the pictures I've taken of her over the years."

Mitchell thought of the very first photo he had ever taken of Red. He remembered the look she gave him through the view finder in which a decision had been made to finally take him to her bed. He had caught that moment on film and every other fiery red, white hot, honey-colored part of her soul as well.

"Photography is a hobby of mine too," Sian said.

"What do you like to photograph?" Mitchell asked.

"The faces found at the courthouse are my usual subjects," she said. "What time is it?" Sian asked, suddenly realizing she had lost track of it.

"It's a little after eleven," he said.

Sian looked surprised at the time and how the entire day and now half the night had been spent in Mitchell's presence.

"I should go," Sian said. "I can't believe I stayed here this long. I just wanted to see you face to face, to meet you. I never imagined I'd stay this long . . . ."

"You should stay," Mitchell said, interrupting her train of thought. "It's late. You can have the bed and I'll sleep on the sofa. We'll get an early start in the morning for whatever tomorrow brings."

Sian thought for a moment then said, "Okay. I've got some things in the car I should get."

"Okay," Mitchell said and watched her walk downstairs, opening and closing the basement door. He began to look for bedding to use on the sofa when he saw headlights pierce the tall windows, illuminating the ceiling. He looked over the edge of the balcony railing to see her tail lights moving through the bush toward FR 63. He was stunned to watch her leave without saying goodbye. Mitchell was sad for Sian, realizing that the day had been an overwhelming experience. He too was spent, emotionally and physically.

"For Emily, Whenever I May Find Her" returned to his mind. He wondered how long he had been standing there with bedding in his hands. He could not recall why he held such items in the first place. His experience with Sian on this day seemed more like a dream to him than reality, and, had not the energy to give it another thought.

He was grateful for this comprehension, which stated that he existed outside the confines of three-dimensional squares—ones he had created in his life over the years. Although not ungrateful for his job, home, church, bank, and grocery store—he found more of the moment when it was unencumbered by walls and ceilings, and the associated responsibilities to them. He understood that God was not necessarily inside, but outside those walls, and the maze they formed.

Chapter Eight

IT was early in the summer season for rain. June usually found the days bright and the nights dry. The three friends were surprised to see the morning sky grow dark on their first day together since Mitchell had moved away.

Rain soon filled the gully, cascading over the rocky outcrop. Behind them, a tree was split in half by lightning, teaching the boys right from the start that lightning had a smell and thunder could not only be heard, but felt, to their bones. Hair stood on end, ears rang, including Ada's, who heard her son and friends cuss at the shock of the event. For the first time, the boys heard thunder roll away from them rather than toward them.

The summer rain in the mountains gave Mitchell a growing appreciation for the natural work of the elements. His life changed because the topography changed. He was in direct contact with the components of Mother Nature herself as he often sat between the rain and the ground it sought. The back patio let in every shade and light, every nuance in temperature; as the day progressed, so did Mitchell. He became an antenna to the natural world, not by design or agenda, but by an innate calling. He was a part of his day where just weeks ago in another life he could not remember the moment before or anything after. Now he existed. Now he occupied space.

Dalton and Presley saw this change in him. Although Mitchell's demographics changed and his family had less, his friends could see that he now possessed more of himself. He had associations to things that he knew nothing of before.

Mitchell hightailed it to the gully below, dogs in tow. Dalton and Presley ran after him feeling for a moment the same change in themselves that was obvious in Mitchell. The rain came alive. They let out rebel yells as they chased the dogs, who were chasing Mitchell, who was chasing the rain that was dancing to Creedence Clearwater Revival's "Born on the Bayou," heard from a car passing by at the bottom of the hill.

The boys looked at one another. In them was a sense that they were moving through a door to an unknown world. This unfamiliar feeling brought both excitement and trepidation. But the rain had soaked them from head to toe and washed away their reservations about the elements of the woods. What was collecting in rain-soaked pockets and water-logged shoes was the sense of knowing that they were boys, and that they were acting as such for the first time, in the woods.

⚜

The following day began with a long look around. Mitchell, Dalton, and Presley were quickly out the door, making their way to the bottom of the gully. The morning shadows were as tall as the Ponderosa pine would let them be. Heading south on FR 63, they happened upon a cattle guard, a curious thing to city boys. Presley held a portable cassette tape recorder with James Taylor singing about what stretched out before them.

The cattle guard marked the boundary from private to federal land, and would require careful footing to traverse the three feet of railing to dirt on the other side. The cattle guard marked the entrance into adventure; a world of thought and movement written by Mark Twain himself.

The treetops rose high above them. The sky, capped with a cirrus ceiling, wisped into many things. The boys smelled a forest floor warming up to a summer sun. They looked hard to see what the bend in the road and the day ahead would bring; great anticipation flowed through them.

Mitchell's dogs, Jenny, and Caesar, learned quickly that the cattle guard was no match for them. They found another way around it. Their tails still sported an overhead arch and a nonstop wag. Their noses vacuumed everything in sight and they pranced toward the same wild call.

The air, thin but cool, crisp, and clean, made it difficult to get up any steam, especially for Dalton and Presley, who had only been with Mitchell in the mountains for two days. The acclimation process was slow but would not stop their arms and legs, and with one jump over the cattle guard, the boys found themselves on government land.

Washboards lined both sides of the road and were difficult to maneuver even on foot. The dogs were gone; distant barking clued the boys to their whereabouts. Before long their adventure brought to them a spur, a fork in the road. They took it and regretted the choice immediately. A startled bull charged toward them. In terror the boys ran for a large rock that placed them safely out of reach.

Once resumed, the smaller side road brought them to Indian Creek, a seasonal tributary to the Hassayampa River. Turning to follow the creek downstream, they spied many dark, wood-framed doorways and entrances into the hillsides. The abandoned mines fascinated them but common sense prevailed, and journeys into the centers of the earth were left to their wild imaginations.

At once all three boys were stopped by a sharp cliff-like drop. Over the edge each boy stared. Below them was a waterhole, fed by the year-round coursing of the Hassayampa River

Fascination stepped in. Separate attempts to scale the cliff down to the playground were attempted in vain. Presley changed that. He jumped. He screamed as he sailed through the air. Mitchell and Dalton joined his wail in utter disbelief. The icy water cracked around his body and enveloped him completely. Presley resurfaced, eyed his friends with joyful foolishness, and leaped up with mighty ruling hands, claiming the waterhole as his own. Presley then watched his friends fall through the air, engulfed in the same foolish joy, joining him in the cold, crushing beauty of crystal clear mountain water. It was a triumphant moment for the three friends and propelled them further into a day that indoctrinated them as citizens of the Prescott National Forest.

Each soon found the waterhole's edges; smooth gray granite, spotted white and blue, as cradles of temperate sunshine and rest. Each spun daydreams or napped.

The remainder of this first day out on their own in the forest brought other firsts; they viewed with gruesome curiosity the work of a large, black and blue tarantula wasp disabling the large, hairy spider, then yanking on the prey toward the wasp's lair, which nested its young. On their way back to the cabin the friends met a boy who would become known to them as Huntington Beach Bob. HBB had grass. Without asking, he gave to each member of the waterhole brotherhood a joint. Accepting such an item was a fateful moment for Mitchell.

෨෨

Strangely renewed of spirit and strength, they bid farewell to the pothead and sped up the remaining distance to the cabin. It was odd to be a part of such a small family; odder still to find the home empty of fear but not chaos, for Ada continued her erratic behavior, leaving the children alone often. It was lighter in the cabin. The setting sun illuminated every corner of the tiny home, and Mitchell saw that he came home to a place that looked almost normal.

"Hey," Mitchell said as he entered the front door first.

Dalton and Presley said "Hello," in unison.

"Where the hell have you three been!" was the parental response.

"You weren't supposed to leave us here all day by ourselves," Emma said, mad that Mitchell had done so. Both sisters threw fits. They tried to convince Ada that leaving them behind that morning constituted a breach of older brotherhood.

Ada told everyone to be quiet; she was in a sour disposition. As dinner was placed on a 1950's era kitchen table, the mood was subdued.

The older boys washed up in the bathroom for dinner. Dalton and Presley passed their joints to Mitchell. He took them into his corner of the back patio and stashed them in a secret wooden box.

During dinner, as the orange glow of sunset filled the cabin's main room, the boys shared stories of a most exceptional day.

Dessert was peanut butter cookies. The older boys agreed to take the young ones with them on their next outing to the waterhole, which would begin in less than 12 hours, immediately following a cereal box breakfast and chores.

Dinner was done. All reassembled in the main room. After a game of speed Monopoly (where the properties are dealt out like cards in a seven-card stud game), the boys decided to take a walk. The decision was communicated through a complex code of facial expressions and body talk. They existed inside each other's heads and often functioned as a single thought. One brain, six arms, thirty fingers, and three different ways of farting during a monopoly game, as a decoy to ward off attentions to rents owed. Beans for dinner always carried a further utility than just displacing hunger.

At last, with the Monopoly game over, they set out for a walk, taking with them Mitchell's secret box. They stepped out into the evening. The front porch of the cabin held them above a cool forest floor. Its westerly view showed the arc of dusky blue changing into a black starry night.

Mitchell went back in and grabbed a sweatshirt, a flashlight, and a book of matches. He told his mom that they would be back after a walk around the neighborhood. Everybody wanted to go. The dogs went, but the sisters stayed behind; the bedtime call had been made.

Dalton carried Presley's tape recorder. He had replaced James Taylor's *Sweet Baby James* with Neil Young's *Everybody Knows This is Nowhere*. As the first tracks played, the boys made their way toward the steps of a nearby, unoccupied cabin, nervous but excited about smoking the joints.

Mitchell pulled his secret box out of his pants pocket. He slid open the panels in a combination to reveal the chamber that held the marijuana cigarettes.

For all three of them, the first time stoned was initially uneventful. They smoked all the joints, coughed a lot, and thought they felt something, just not sure what. But then something did happen. In the starry night above, with the cool summer air around them, and a sense of exhaustion taking over, the tape recorder began to play a song they heard many times before, but not quite like this. As the song "Down by the River" began its methodical rhythm guitar, so did the three friends begin in unison their first stoned groove of any song. Hands strummed the air, feet tapped the wooden porch, eyes closed to the mental picture of chords and the colors they carried with them.

There would be countless more joints and songs to follow, but on their virgin voyage over a higher ground, "Down by the River" became and remained their flight song. Presley made a comment about how ridiculous they looked bobbing their heads back and forth and playing make-believe guitars. Their "highness" turned to silliness and laughter took over the trip for the next several minutes.

They headed back into the cabin, and straight for an already strapped fridge. Trying not to laugh only made them laugh more, and before they woke Ada, each grabbed a handful of peanut butter cookies and headed back outside again. Giddy and a little headachy from the weed and laughter, they sped downhill in the dark to the gully. Finding their way to the perch in the dark was surprisingly easy.

The air was light and crisp. With the Big Dipper as the focus of conversation, a unanimous decision was made to secure more weed from Huntington Beach Bob.

Exhausted, they made their way to the back porch, where sleeping bags and the all-night radio station from Oklahoma City put to rest the feet and hands of three young boys on a summer night.

Mitchell reached over the edge of the bed, turned off the radio, and felt for the cassette player. He pictured the control, rewinding the tape to the point where "Down by the River" might begin. He hit it perfectly. Through the screen the stars, bright on their own life, dotted Mitchell's tired imagination. The strumming began. The sound of the acoustic guitar closed Mitchell's eyes, fading the starlight to black. He would fall asleep with Neil's words as a lullaby, choreographing the movement of a dream that found him joyfully gliding headfirst over the lengthy arch of a rainbow.

Chapter Nine

SHE is a beautiful girl, Red said.

"Where have you been today," Mitchell said out loud. "And beauty has got nothing to do with it. She is the exact duplicate of you and I've never felt more flabbergasted with emotion than I was today out on the river."

Not physically beautiful, Mitchell, which she is, Red said. *She is a good soul. She's one of us.*

"I feel like it was all just too much for her," he said. "Kind of like much of her life must have been so far. I imagine she's had a tough life. I could feel it when I touched her today."

She has not been given more than she can handle, and has grown through each hardship, enriching the self-love God gives to us all. She is God, more so than most, Red said.

Red had become less an apparition outside of Mitchell and more a part of his own soul, a place she had also occupied while alive. The conversations were had as thoughts and had become a key part of Mitchell's well-being. It was as if their relationship had evolved even further than it ever could have before her death. They were no longer separated by skin, but had become one in mind and heart, and had brought Mitchell closer to the universal comprehension of spirit: closer to God as he understood Him to be.

I guess it's my turn to see her, Mitchell thought. "I can brave the staring and sit through some lunch at the Dinner Bell Café."

Chapter Ten

BUZZZZ. Hissss.

Hissss. Buzzzz.

Both sounds registered in Mitchell's semiconscious mind. The radio's hiss was Oklahoma's KOMA, its signal becoming static with the advance of the morning sun over the earth's horizon. The buzz emanated from a wood beetle; its pincher feet stuck in the back patio's screen covering.

He opened his eyes. Reaching up, he freed the beetle with his fingertips. As he sat up, the intense sunrise filled his mind, and he blinked to focus on the wooded view outside. He hurriedly kicked the blankets off his body. The sun's light and heat had made quick work of the previous night's chill.

Hunger chimed in simultaneously from every back patio resident, and Mitchell laughed out loud at the sight of sleeping rolls flying off in the ensuing charge for breakfast.

The children found the cabin empty. Ada had left sometime in the night. A deep breath passed through Mitchell followed by the hunt for cereal, milk, bowls, and spoons. Once at the table, Emma and Dana made deals with the boys to get food. The deal: to admit who was the boss of whom.

Mitchell thought about Ada's words concerning Sorber and Brent. "I hate it here," she had said, not making an effort to hide her feelings about Prescott and her husband from the children. "The bastard dragged me up here, promising some kind of better life, but I'm not better; I'm worse. I'm glad he's gone, both of them for that matter; they're worthless to me. Sorber's a worthless drunk and Brent's a coward. They've done nothing but embarrass me, and I just don't think I can take it anymore." Her words shamed Mitchell. Her words tunneled into him. They would make a precarious home inside his red chest cavity, latching onto a rib as a weight next to his heart, creating an imbalance that would haunt him forever.

He shook his head clear of the thoughts and stated plainly that it was time to hike back to the waterhole. On the way Neil Young's "The Old Laughing Lady" was heard from the cassette recorder and took hold of Mitchell. The music mixed with the sights and sounds of the forest; a moment referred to often in the days of his life to come.

When the song ended, Mitchell asked Dalton to play it again. He obliged. Presley asked why he wanted to hear it again, and Mitchell said he didn't know. "It has something to do with being out here."

The "something" would be the song's ability to grab Mitchell at any time in the years and decades to come, and yank him back to the very country road under his feet and to remember with brilliant vividness every detail of that moment; days of sunlight and elevated air, nights of distant dreams, and the calm of ballads sung by a man Mitchell would never know, but who seemed to know him.

The music and lyrics of Neil Young would become a large part of the foundation of friendship between the boys. Their leaderless lives needed an anthem. Their courage to live fully needed a voice. While responsibilities and the great characteristics of life, those of loyalty, compassion, honesty, and perseverance would come into play, there would always be a song by Neil that would lock their hearts in a face-to-face memory of who they were, walking toward the light of the sun, shining brightly down on a waterhole.

ॐॐ

How they lived their lives, on this fine summer day, would be considered reckless in the decades to come by an overprotective generation of parents. What these boys took, when they were made responsible for one another, was an opportunity to develop many things.

First was a sense of direction. They became supremely confident in their abilities to place landmarks as reference points, and to navigate through canyons and ravines, not losing their sense of where they stood in relation to where the cabin was. Their internal clocks developed into finely tuned tools. They became familiar with the angles of shade and sensed deeply the day growing long. Time moved through the rhythm of their bodies, becoming the light and shadow that moved across the bark of trees.

By summer's end, the boys would have new strength and conditioning. Their coordination and confidence in traversing a ledge over a cliff or balancing themselves walking across a long tree bridge grew quite large—their bodies full of what makes a boy stay a boy. The use of these expanding instincts to survive the wild would throw an eternal wake of self-assurance across the length of their lives. Giving up became a ridiculous notion. Effort ruled to the end of the day, when a tuna fish casserole awaited their ravenous appetites. Giving time to one another was the lesson learned.

They became reflections of Mark Twain writings. It was a magnificent place to be a boy. It was a rope swing over water. It was a canopy of stars under which eyes peered out from a hole in a sleeping bag. It was a sense of self, undeniable in the face of a world fettered with adult calamity. It was the faith of a boy walking hand-in-hand with the grace of nature. It was a perfect setting, a summer wind held at bay by a long-sleeved shirt. There was nothing more required. Mother Nature had them right where She wanted them to be.

As the gang made their way down the dirt road, the boys discussed girls, sports, and pot. Emma and Dana cared not for such topics. Emma was twelve and was lost in the theory and refinement of music, lying on her bed in a constant study of her guitar and violin, playing repeatedly James Taylor's "Fire and Rain." Dana's eight-year-old mind was building her own unique foundation for life. All continued to survive a horribly chaotic and reckless family, and now all three walked down a country road toward a waterhole with not a clinched fist, beer can, or shameful feeling in sight.

A new way back into the waterhole was discovered by Presley and all followed him into the path of another approach, soon dubbed the "back way."

Mitchell hung back a moment. He was caught up in the thought of flying. A bird of prey circled above, riding a thermal lift of air. The bird soared up and up, then dove back around to catch the thermal again. All was quiet except for the delight heard downstream, where Emma and Dana experienced the waterhole for the first time. Mitchell was glad. He was lighthearted. The deep blue sky was too bright to bear and he closed his eyes to the silhouetted grace of the bird losing itself in its own silent existence.

Mitchell put his arms out as if to mimic the circle of flight above him. The thermal simultaneously caught his arms and hair, blowing them upward in a demonstration of quiet freedom. Gentle confidence grew within, that his childhood would find its redemption with his waterhole friends and sisters. The dull cloudy fear of rage, arguing, and fists was leaving his heart. Yet tears flowed. Why he would grieve the departure of such wretched things confounded him. But grieve only for that moment he did.

Now there was another way to live. There was now only rock, water, and shade to consider. There was now only the passing of the sun and the thought of what was north, south, east, or west of where he stood that filled his day.

Mitchell was suddenly relieved. The thermal had returned and pulled the hair on his head straight up. It pulled on his spirit too. He opened his eyes, wiped his tears, and tested his ability to run downhill full speed to the waterhole, passed his friends and sisters who had gathered at its edge. He leaped as hard as he could, yelling as loud and clear as any savage, enduring a perfect belly flop into the water.

"Son-of-a bitch!" Mitchell exclaimed, trying to grasp for the air that was knocked out of him. He thrashed about, kicking and screaming at the top of his lungs. The gang laughed but questioned what he was feeling.

Mitchell friends and sisters were right to suspect something had just unfurled in him. He pointed skyward. Everyone turned to see the bird of prey playing in the wind. Mitchell's spontaneity and the winged embrace of wind high overhead was contagious.

The thermal, a gift from Mother Nature, had accomplished its intention; lifting the waterhole children into boundless childhood joy.

Chapter Eleven

MITCHELL walked out to the shade of the old oak. Sitting next to the tree, he found the carving he had made of his and Red's initials. He outlined them with his fingers. He yawned and then put his back against them, against the tree, and felt the sunlight warm his face. He stared into the sky, still finding his childhood focus of the color blue, taking note of his thoughts slipping into an infinite gaze of time and space.

৵৵

Sian stood in the shade of Prescott's courthouse. It was late summer. Angles of shade were changing. She took note of such and its affect on the subjects of her photos; the faces that had made downtown Prescott a part of their lives: cops, drug dealers, judges, patrons, city officials, school children, thinkers, bums, and, in particular, widows, who visited the square as part of their daily medication for loneliness. At least that's the way Sian saw them. Perhaps her own solitary existence was the inspiration fount in her large zoom lens. It was what she looked for. It was the success she enjoyed in the analog creation of her subjects. They were lonely beyond words. She often cried as she saw the pictures come to life in the chemical trays of her dark room.

She would find one redeeming quality about the often thin, frail looking women; their eyes seemed to be set with steel under their hat brims and brows. Almost unanimously, their eyes were a contradiction to the remainder of their physical existence. It was the photo she looked for; the paradox where life had left all signs of living, save the gaze.

The good ones would be blown up and tacked around the west-facing window of her upstairs apartment. It was through this window that the Arizona Pioneers' Home could be seen, with its residents making their way from its large porch to the grounds surrounding the courthouse. From this window Sian would make her quiet associations with death. *Death is a lonely door*, she wrote in white ink across one of the photos. *Merciful death, please come*, across another. *I'm ready*, written on a third. For all of the subjects in the large black and white photos, death was their next and last event. Sian saw gratitude for another day in some and spite in others.

ॐ

She was photographing a widow who sat alone on a bench. Through her viewfinder she noticed a trio of boys talking. Sian raised the lens slightly and brought them into sharp focus. Sian noted their attire; blue jeans were worn halfway across their bottoms, exposing underwear. Tattoos and skin piercings were prevalent. One of the boys didn't even bother with shoes; his socks were shockingly filthy and stained. It was not so much their appearance that unnerved Sian but their eyes as they glared at the widow. Sian sensed rage in them. *Why are they angry?* she asked herself. To her alarm, the boys started to walk toward the widow, who was unaware of their approach.

Sian pulled the camera away, looking around the courthouse for others who might be witnessing the event. Returning the camera to her eye, she began to snap photos. As the boys moved closer, Sian's alarm grew. They taunted the widow cruelly. To her surprise a fifth person entered the scene. Like oil on water the three boys backed away from the new figure now standing in front of the widow. Not a word was spoken by this man, who stood between helplessness and rage. It was Mitchell.

Sian continued to snap photos of Mitchell and the old woman. He sat down next to her. Without looking, Mitchell mouthed, "Are you okay?" The widow did not answer. She remained unaware of the boys' malicious energy. They regrouped across the street and began yelling obscenities. Mitchell stood up, silencing the volley. He looked long and hard at the boys, who represented the cruelty that had become the backdrop to his life. Backed by his stare, Mitchell raised his hand to the boys and pointed at them. They scattered down the street, disappearing out of sight.

Sian watched the hold Mitchell had on the townspeople. They looked on with interest and fear. Mitchell, Sian observed, was a monster to some and a hero to others, causing everyone to keep their distance from him. He wanted to be left alone, not because he was crazy or a recluse, but because he was not ready to make room for anyone in his life. Sian guessed, rightly so, that his mind was still filled with her mother.

Mitchell returned to his old pickup. The steel on steel clap made by the door slamming shut echoed down the street. He vanished as quickly as he appeared. She sat down, leaned against a tree, and let her compassion for Mitchell grow.

That evening, Sian developed the photos she had taken earlier. She stared at Mitchell's haunting defense of the old woman. Suddenly, a feature from one photo leaped out at Sian, stealing her breath away. She put her hand up to her neck and rubbed it, feeling a cold chill slide down her back. She bent closer, toward the feature in the photo, which was magnified by the developing solution in the tray. Revealed there, in stark shades of shadow and gray, were the undeniable stains of dried blood on the shoeless boy's socks.

"God is here," the Sea Man said out loud, to the fence and wildflowers as he walked toward his home—empty now that his wife had passed away.

Chapter Twelve

MITCHELL had fallen asleep again. He woke to the smell and taste of damp granite warming to the heat of the summer sun. He was exhausted, yet it was the best feeling he had ever known. He pushed himself up from the rock ledge lining the waterhole. He was puzzled by the naps. That made two so far. Looking down, he saw impressions of granite in his skin. Squinting, he looked around the waterhole. He was a touch disoriented. It was too quiet.

He was suddenly startled by voices downstream and Presley appeared through the reeds.

"You in hibernation, Beetle?" Presley asked, displaying his highly tuned ability to read deeper into a moment than most boys his age. "Beetle" was a product of one hot afternoon basketball game, where, dog-tired by the end, Mitchell had fallen asleep. His mouth hung open, giving his friends the impression of a bug; hence "Beetle."

"I guess so Presley," Mitchell responded. "I don't feel tired, just very relaxed."

"Well, relax later, Beet, you gotta stay with us. We've decided to go exploring in the canyon downstream, and you need to keep an eye on the little ones," Presley said, so matter-of-factly that Mitchell knew exactly what his next move was going to be.

Presley was as close to being a cowboy as Mitchell had known. It was Presley who introduced Mitchell and Dalton to hunting and fishing, even if it was just for doves and quail on telephone lines or crawfish in irrigation canals. He knew how to ride horses and rope cows and his entire home, inside and out, was decorated with antiquated farm tools and equipment. Presley's father was president of the state's dairy union and instilled in Presley a farmer's ethic about life. At an early age, Presley knew how to get up very early and work very hard.

Dalton and Mitchell thought Presley's life cruel. They believed Presley's dad was too hard on him, often convincing Presley at times of the same thing. Yet it seemed Presley always bounced back, learning what it was his dad wanted him to learn, and applying it to the task at hand.

Dalton's father was similar to Mitchell's. They worked hard for the first two-thirds of the day and drank hard for the rest. Presley thought his friends' lives deplorable for suffering the humiliation of a drunken father on a daily basis.

Gone were their fathers on this day.

For Mitchell especially, his two friends had become his family. In Presley, Mitchell found examples of what it was to be a man. In Dalton, Mitchell found acceptance.

Mitchell stood up and joined Presley in looking south as the Hassayampa River made its way toward a slot canyon. The river, which flowed year-round, added depth to the boy's friendship, its waterhole had become their sacred place, worthy of every effort yet to be, in the summer of 1971.

The day was still young. One by one, they sized up the approach of water rushing into a slot canyon, and the best way to stay in it while getting through it. A new adventure had begun.

Chapter Thirteen

THE day progressed. Walking knee-deep through the river in a slot canyon, they arrived at a point where the granite walls gave way to slopes growing up both sides of the river with room to move on both banks.

Hunger grew. Sandwiches wrapped in wax paper were gone in a flash, then peanut butter cookies. The long shadows of trees told them it was time to go home and they obliged.

Getting up and facing the walk back through the canyon, Presley looked up the slope to see a side road about one hundred feet above.

"Let's head up to that road, you guys. Our feet can dry out, and we can get home quicker," Presley said.

There was some mumbling among the gang, finding reasons for going back the way they had come. Presley's reasoning prevailed, however. They began their ascent out of the river's bottom. The hike up was deceptive. It was steeper than first assessed, but they arrived, after much teamwork, in getting everyone safely up to the side road. Looking back down, Presley decided he would never go that way again except as a last resort.

"Hey, guys, look!" Dana said, pointing to a green metal fence and gate that blocked access to points any further south. They walked forward a short distance, around a small bend, to see a full blown abandoned mining operation, complete with decrepit wooden buildings, rusted vehicles, a mine hoist three stories tall and, lastly, prompting a gasp from the older boys, a beautiful woman with long blonde hair, walking toward them, carrying a shot gun.

Her dogs were barking. "No one ever comes out this far, so when they bark, I look," she said as she approached the gate. "What brings you this way?" she asked.

"The river," Presley responded, eyeing both the gun and the woman's hair.

"We live in Ponderosa Park," Mitchell added. "We discovered the waterhole yesterday and the canyon below today. We've been exploring the Hassayampa. I'm Mitchell, these are my sisters Emma and Dana, and my friends Presley and Dalton."

"I'm Nikki. My father owns this land. I'm the caretaker. Between rattlesnakes and javelina, I can never be too careful," she said, as she patted the stock of her gun. "So you discovered the first waterhole, huh?"

"The first waterhole!" Dalton exclaimed. "How many are there?"

"Lots," Nikki said, "But the best one sits on my property. C'mon, take a look!" she stated, as their interest sparked.

They took Nikki up on her offer. She continued her introduction: she was the daughter of Arizona Governor Jack Williams. She lived in seclusion away from the constant attention received by the press. The gang did not really care who the governor was. What was of primary interest was another waterhole; second was Nikki. The boys stared, tongue-tied, while Emma and Dana had questions galore about the mine and its setup.

Nikki led the kids back to what would later become known simply as "Nikki's Waterhole." There was only one way to get to it: by walking directly down the middle of Hassayampa River. The second waterhole was located within the confines of another granite slot canyon. To get into the waterhole, one had to dive or jump into it from the top of the waterfall that fed it. Getting out was made easier with a rope strung from the top down to the pool, and footholds carved out by centuries of use.

The boys spent the remainder of the day there. Nikki left after showing them the way. On their way out they knocked on her rustic cabin door to say thanks and goodbye. She invited them back anytime, and would be gracious when the boys returned.

Day two drew to a close. Hunger, and a long walk ahead, with an even longer climb up the hill to the cabin, and to a sun setting in the west, awaited them.

When Mitchell entered the cabin, the sun's orange rays were ablaze on the red brick fireplace. He remembered the bird of prey and the thermal that lifted him earlier in the day. He stood in the middle of the living room and considered his silhouette on the wall; the sharpness of his shadow remained a visual confirmation of the growing awareness of who he was, or, at least, becoming.

Chapter Fourteen

IN a mood, helped along by Jackson Browne's "For Everyman," Mitchell contemplated the world's condition on two levels: spiritually and economically. He thought of the rat race created by Madison Avenue and how readily the society in which he belonged swallowed it all. He thought of the kindergarten through graduate school mentality, where a child is expected to spend twenty years of his life studying other lives, rather than making a study of his own. He thought of Madison Avenue's success in selling this mentality, and its ability to hurl one toward a predetermined existence, which resembled a cow-chute, designed to minimize risk thereby reducing creativity—key ingredients necessary for all the great leaps of human effort. There are and were exceptions to such statements, but on the whole, if a life does not hang from a limb, it will never reach its potential. He thought of how this notion fit into the theme found in the old man's journal—a book he had found in the floorboards of his cabin; the book he presently held in his hands, and in particular, a phrase discussed within; *the current of the expanding universe.*

The sun's light, streaming down from overhead, closed Mitchell's eyes. The bright blue expanse above, an endless ceiling for the waterhole where he quietly sat, gave him the impression of rest—the sound of the Hassayampa bubbling over rock and root made it so. He leaned back and thanked God for the risk he had known in his life; the word "life" being his last thought as daydreams replaced his thoughtful social commentary.

~§~§~

"Your fucking hero was at the courthouse scaring all the townsfolk yesterday," Jess said as he sat down across the table from Hartley.

"I believe the only townsfolk he scared yesterday were some punks gettin' ready to harass an old lady," Hartley said. "They say he appeared from nowhere and stood between the woman and her tormentors. The punks took off, screaming like babies with soiled diapers. I heard one of the punks is related to that *family.*"

"Which family?" Jess shot back. "The ones buried in Odd Fellows Cemetery or the one driving around in that beat up piece of shit truck?"

"Will you get over it!" Hartley said emphatically. "He's paid his price. Leave him be. He has to live with a lot more than you and I will ever have to. No doubt insanity is part of dealing with the things he endured that night."

The patrons at the Dinner Bell listened to the old-timers. So did Sian, who was busy winding down the breakfast rush. She was shocked to hear that the ruffian in the photos she took yesterday might be related to the evil circumstances of the night in question.

"What cemetery are you talking about, Jess?" Sian asked.

He was about to describe the cemetery when his jaw dropped open. Standing at the door was the very man he despised. Jess watched as Mitchell moved closer to the cashier and a sign that stated to Dinner Bell guests to seat themselves. Mitchell looked about the room, taking in each set of eyes and their motionless response to his presence. He moved toward a small table next to the east wall, and sat down. Immediately the couple next to him shot up, leaving their meals untouched and their bill unpaid, galloping for the front door. Hushed voices were scattered about. Mitchell slowly looked toward Sian, who stared at the ground, shocked to realize he was there.

"I can't believe he shows up here," Jess said to Hartley, who was all smiles.

"Good for him," Hartley said. He sipped his coffee, stood up and walked over to Mitchell's table. While Mitchell stared hard at him, Hartley put out his hand in a greeting. "It's nice to see you here," Hartley said. "Welcome."

Mitchell said nothing, but did shake Hartley's hand while watching Jess leave the restaurant in a tuff, feigning the welcome, saying "if that creep is allowed to eat here, you've lost me as a customer." Jess stormed out of the Dinner Bell.

Mitchell's eyes deflected the comment. "Don't mind him," Hartley said. "He's got his opinions."

"As it should be," Mitchell said. Hartley sat down for a moment to hear Mitchell state loud enough for all to hear, "And I could give a rat's ass what any body thinks of me."

"This I know about you," Hartley said. "Well, have a nice day," returning to his cup of coffee on the other side of the room.

"You, too," Mitchell said, now looking around the room for Sian. He found her still standing near the kitchen pass shelf, eyes cast downward. She was overcome by the amount of energy Mitchell generated when he entered the dining room. The room was hushed. When she looked up, she saw each patron with at least one eye on Mitchell and heard the conversational tone rising. She remembered that no one knew her recent interaction with Mitchell yet fear rose that he would reveal his intimate knowledge of her life.

He would not. He treated her as any other patron would; hardly noticing her as they talked but would glance at her as she walked away, acknowledging her beauty.

Mitchell sat with his cup of coffee, waiting for his breakfast, staring out the front of the restaurant and the passing of cars and trucks on Gurley. The restaurant slowly began to thin out as the breakfast hours ended. Mike began to prepare for lunch and Sian got busy changing out menus and refilling salts, peppers, and sugar caddies. Mitchell watched her work, observing Red's work ethic shine in her daughter. Mitchell sighed.

Soon another waitress brought Mitchell his breakfast. He remembered every occasion that Red had ever waited on him, making Mitchell feel as if he were truly a king. He remembered his beloved. She bestowed upon him a light that illuminated his dark life, revealing all in an accepting spiritual posture of unconditional love.

"How are you today?" Sian said softly, as she stood in front of him.

Mitchell bit the corner of his lip and stated under his breath, "Well, you know, it's still quite strange seeing you here, Sian."

"Sorry I bolted the other night," she said.

"Not to worry, it was a tough day for both of us."

"I photographed you with the old woman at the courthouse," Sian said.

Mitchell looked up, surprised. "You photographed me?" he asked.

"It was odd, Mitchell, you came out of nowhere and scared off those punks by just standing there," she said.

"I didn't like what I saw."

"People were talking about it this morning," she said.

Mitchell looked out the front door and shook his head to end the conversation about the old woman. Sian moved away from his table to continue her side work. She said goodbye to Hartley, who had been studying her interaction with Mitchell. Hartley waved goodbye. Mitchell nodded in response.

The restaurant now stood empty. Mitchell looked around, taking in the homegrown ambience, noticing for the first time that tables in the back held a view of Granite Creek. He walked to the back and watched the creek trickle past the café. Sian joined him.

"I walk along the creek to and from work," she said.

"You do?" Mitchell said.

"I live close by," she said. At once the ruffian they both knew well walked by the café, kicking rocks into the creek. He looked angry.

Mike noticed Mitchell and Sian talking while not facing one another. He thought this was odd and after Mitchell left he asked Sian if she knew who Mitchell was.

"Yes, I know," was her short response. "Do you?"

"Yeah, he's the crazy husband of that woman who died out there in the woods."

Sian shuttered in silence. "I'm sure there is more to it than that," she said guardedly.

"Like what," Mike said. "She's dead, and he's walkin' around town like he owns the place."

The conversation ended when the café's first lunch customers arrived. Sian repressed her pain and got back to work, oddly wishing Mitchell had not left. She looked with longing toward the windows where he had stood. She took a deep breath and faced the coming lunch rush.

He tried again, this time not thinking of the house where he resided. "God is here," he stated again. He felt the mechanisms of his body amp up. His senses were heightened. "Good," he thought. Visually more stunning than the moment before, the desert colors increased, brilliantly blending into one another, becoming intermittent brush strokes, as if from

an Artist's palette, and by an Artist's hand.
Every unimagined saturation of color burst
forth..

Chapter Fifteen

RETIRING earlier than usual to bed, all five explorers found their comforts. Ada closed and locked the back door and turned off the patio light. Dalton asked why she had locked the door and wondered what to do if he needed to use the bathroom. Everyone looked at the screen door to the patio. He thought it cruel to make the girls go outside to do as nature intended. "Does she do that a lot?" Dalton asked. "I guess so," Mitchell said. "I don't even notice anymore."

An endless starry night waited. The night sky camouflaged the thinness of the screen mesh. Demons departed and Mitchell thought the moment magical. Only the breath of slumbering younger sisters and whispers from Dalton and Presley were considered. He searched his father's radio for the sometimes faint, yet sometimes very clear signals from stations located in the direction of a full moon rising. The faint signal, like the distant stars, lulled him to sleep. Into his dreams came many songs. "Drift Away" being the first. He loved the song and every night made an effort to hear it again. He dreamt of other lives, of other adventures and wondered what it was like to live in the towns from which the signals emanated. It was this quiet connection to something beyond his limits, as a thirteen-year-old boy living deep in the woods, which captured the moments just before sleep. He wondered what the three friends would do with their lives and where they would go. His connection to Dalton and Presley tunneled into him and as "Drift Away" became his last thought of the day, Mitchell dreamt of a girl with jet black hair.

Ada had left early for work. The sound of the back door being unlocked opened Mitchell's eyes. He sat up, seeing the dawn spread over the hills behind the cabin. After listening to the Scout shutter down the hill and away, he slid out of bed and went into the cabin's main room. He put the new Cat Stevens album on the Magnavox hifi, turning it up to wake up the back patio.

"Morning has broken," the song said.

"Beetle, turn that shit off," Dalton commanded. Emma and Dana echoed his sentiments, minus the cussing. Mitchell ignored them and let the words to the song wake everybody up. He liked the song. It gave him hope and when he heard the last lyric sung; "God's re-creation of the new day," he was akin to its writer.

"Who's that?" Presley asked.

"It's Cat Stevens' new album, *Teaser and the Firecat*," Mitchell responded, now making his way toward the fridge for the day's gallon of milk. Putting it on the table, Mitchell announced that the milk had to last the whole day and to water it down if need be. The stampede for food was underway.

Before long, Cat Stevens' previous release, *Tea for the Tillerman*, floated through the small cabin as fine background music to get a day going in the right direction. One song from the album gathered heavily in the older boy's minds. "Father and Son" pulled at Dalton, Presley, and Mitchell. Each thought about the day they could leave their fathers' homes. Each was bitter about their fathers' hypocrisies. Quiet became a staple at breakfast.

"My dad never lets up," Presley said abruptly. "Day in, day out, week in, week out, he's always expecting me to do the same things with the same attitude, which are his things and his attitude. I don't want his life. I don't want his house. I don't want his religion. I don't want to know him; I want to know who I am."

"I don't know my dad at all," Mitchell added. "He's either at the bar, gone on business, or putting up with my mom's constant bitching. I'm invisible to him; I'm growing up without him."

"I'm kind of in the same boat you are," Dalton said, catching Mitchell's honesty. "My dad is always at Jay's Bar. The only time he says anything to me is when he wants me to mow the lawn or pick up the dog shit." Dalton had decided to use the word "shit" as often as he could.

"Yeah, but your dad makes me laugh," Presley said to Dalton. "He's funny when he is drunk."

At that remark Mitchell thought how sad his father was, sitting alone in the corner of the family room in the house on East Orange, or in anger defending himself in a fight with Ada. Mitchell thought of Presley's dad, who in Mitchell's eyes was a good one compared to his own; he was never drunk and ran an orderly household.

"At least your house is not filled with insane fights, beer, and cigarette smoke," Mitchell said to Presley.

Presley was not sure if Mitchell really understood what it was like living with his dad.

Dalton offered his own take on Mitchell's home life, citing how cool it was that every Friday night his dad would open up the house for happy hour, turn on the hifi in the living room, and then play his drums with the jazz music from the stereo. To Dalton, Mitchell's father seemed happy when he was drunk.

"Your dad can really play those drums, Beetle," Dalton offered to Mitchell, realizing Mitchell's blind side to his father.

As true friends, they not only listened to one another, but offered personal perspectives of each other's assessments, making their bonds stronger. This honesty gave each son a pressure release valve, comparing their fathers with those of their friends, realizing that things are not always as they seem. The bond between them increased that morning. Stepping out into the morning, into the crispness of the day, they found the sunlight and shadows of tall Ponderosa pine illuminating that which was not voiced at the breakfast table—the summer was changing each of them and how they related to the worlds their fathers had created.

Mitchell yawned, breathed deeply, and wanted to yell as loudly as he could. He wanted to let the forest know he had risen from a perfect night's sleep, the kind of slumber that only a boy, busy his entire day in the woods could have, and that he was ready to do it again.

The conversation at the breakfast table lingered. Something inside him said that any more consideration of his parents this day would be inappropriate, for the worries of their world were not his. He walked outside after breakfast with the rest of the crew.

The wood that his home was made of smelled of red dirt and brown pine needles. Anything not immediately within reach of Mitchell's hands or senses faded into the bright sunlight. His joy was found where his feet now rested. It was the occupation of his heart by the spirits of boyhood daydreams. His fingertips knew familiarity with the tops of trees and the softness on the edge of clouds. His hands glided with ravens overhead. His ears heard the wind reciting what he had not heard before. The wind presented the possibilities of a fearless boyhood imagination. Gone now the dark memories. Mitchell looked at the ravens. His hands followed their flight, lining up in perfect formation with the birds. With a deep breath, a breath that filled his boyish heart, Mitchell found himself becoming what the woods allowed him to be. He wondered how his life could go from a well-to-do neighborhood and a tortured existence, to poverty and complete joy in less than one month. He guessed a riddle was solved by asking the question, but it didn't matter to him. He believed the pain of the past was shed. He was free.

"Beetle," Dalton shouted, "snap out of it!"

"What are you talking about?" Mitchell asked.

"You were staring at your hands and dancing, Beetle, you weirdo," Dalton stated matter-of-factly.

"Where do you go in that head of yours?" Presley asked.

"Isn't it nice around here with Brent in boot camp and both parents away at work?" Mitchell responded.

"It's awesome," they both said simultaneously. Dalton added, "What was wrong with Brent anyway?"

"I don't know; it's not my problem anymore. He's the Army's problem now," Mitchell said.

"I think it might be the way your parents treated him," Presley said.

"I don't know why he was always so pissed off, but I do know that it was worse when it involved just Mom. He really hates her. There is something about Mom that really upsets Brent," Mitchell said. "I'm not sure what it is though," feeling a twinge of shame for not sharing with his friends his mother's insistence that he apply lotion to her breasts. Mitchell guessed correctly that Brent suffered a worse fate with his mom when it came to those kinds of things. Mitchell was unable to let himself imagine what "those kinds of things" might have been.

"Well, thank God, Brent's in boot camp and not here," Dalton said.

"He wouldn't like it here," Mitchell said. "I wasn't going to take his crap anymore."

Dalton and Presley looked at Mitchell as they tried to decipher his tone. They heard resolve in his voice. They had watched Mitchell suffer the indignities of his older brother for four years. They believed him when he said the beatings were over.

Mitchell wasn't sure if his resolve had come before or after Brent left. He knew now that he was not going to give up his newfound place in the world. Mitchell spoke out of the blue saying, "It is worth dying for, guys."

"What's that, Beetle?" Dalton asked.

"Stopping Brent in his tracks next time I see him," Mitchell said.

"How are you going to do that?" Presley wanted to know.

"I am going to fight back," Mitchell said. "He'll pay a price for taking a swing at me or my sisters. Living in fear of that asshole is not the price I should have to pay to live here in the woods. I would rather face him than hide from him; it's the only way to go now, guys."

Chapter Sixteen

AFTER a strenuous hike up to the lookout tower on Mount Davis, Mitchell sat back in a chair on his porch and imagined what words might have been exchanged after he left the Dinner Bell. He shuddered at the fear he had built in the townspeople because of his actions. The azure heavens, swept with slow moving bands of clouds, drowned his fearful thoughts. Sian came to mind. His compassion for her was substantial. Her life to date had been unkind. His last thoughts, before the heavens claimed him, were of Sian's face, which became Red's.

❧❧

Sian closed the door to her apartment, leaned against it, and sighed. She closed her eyes and thought of the discussion between Hartley and Jess about the ruffian at the courthouse. She dropped her backpack on the floor, kicked off her serving shoes, and stretched her ankles in every direction. She was physically exhausted. Slowly she undressed, put her uniform in the laundry hamper, and stepped into a hot shower. She let the heat of the water into her skin. She thought of nothing but the water dropping over and around her; through her hair and down her face, onto her shoulders and breasts, cascading down, over her buttocks to her feet, and finally into the drain, taking with it the harsh realities of the day. Harsh as in ugly-hearted customers bent on making Sian's shift miserable for reasons that remained with those customers when they left. Yet there were kind moments as well— when Mitchell came in. *When Mitchell came in*? She asked herself. *Why is that a kind moment?*

She did not know. She was comfortable with him and sensed no judgment from him. It was because she and Mitchell shared a deep cut into their own souls and found solace in each other's company. They shared their pain without saying a word.

Sian awoke from her shower dream. She stepped upon the bathroom floor and dried herself, patting down the different parts of her body. Making a hole in the fog, she peered at her reflection in the bathroom mirror, and this time did so without questioning who she was; she was becoming her mother's daughter. She put on a light bathrobe and moved out into the open room of her apartment. Looking around, she saw the photos she had taken earlier in the week.

She stared at the boys whose menacing looks toward the old woman turned fearful in the presence of Mitchell. She looked closer at the eyes of the one boy who stood out as the leader of the other two, the one whose socks were stained with blood. It was the same boy who walked below her at the café, when Mitchell had come in to see her. She moved into her makeshift darkroom, placed the negative of that photo in the enlarger, and zeroed in on the boy's eyes. As the enlarged eyes came to life in the chemical tray, she was astonished by their piercing quality. She had not realized the boy saw her photographing him. She backed away and to the right of the tray. From this view she studied them. In fine detail she beheld angry rage within; vicious in their intent, but she was not moved by them. They did not scare her. She had known evil and knew that fear only comes from a lack of understanding. Suddenly in his eyes she saw sorrow as well. In the face of these eyes her only impression was to find out more about the boy—to learn his name and connection to the horror of that fateful night.

She set aside the day and pulled close to her the moments spent in her mother's home with the man who lived there. She wrapped her fingers around an evening tea, letting the silence in her apartment, and her solitary existence, define her, as she fell into a deep, safe, sleep.

And again: "God is here." He heard the earth sing the day's presentations. His walking momentum rose. His physical systems sent messages of elation throughout his body—a spiritual connection to God, as Mother Nature, was complete.

Chapter Seventeen

BOBBIE Gentry's "Ode to Billy Joe" strummed easily out the front door. The summer sun was high overhead. Mitchell leaned back on the front porch, his head in the crack between two two-by-fours. He couldn't resist following the story in the song, visualizing a bridge high above him. He pictured his mother standing there, contemplating the end of her life.

Presley and Dalton had resumed the game of hit the tin roof on the barn below, started the evening before. They used the Louisville Slugger to blast stones out over the small valley in front of the house. Dalton was up, seven to five, over Presley, who was growing like a weed and not quite as coordinated as Dalton.

Weed, Mitchell thought.

At that moment Huntington Beach Bob turned the corner at the top of the long dirt driveway. He looked shyly at the gang, unsure if it was okay to come down onto the property.

He and Mitchell exchanged waves.

"Hey, guys, look who's here," Mitchell said to the batters.

They stopped to consider Bob's presence, remembering the marijuana he had given them earlier in the week.

"Hey," was all Bob said.

"Hey," the gang responded.

"Is your mom home?" Bob asked.

"They're never home, but my sisters are inside listening to every word you say," Mitchell stated.

"Oh, so how did you like the grass?" Bob whispered when he arrived on the porch.

"It made us cough," Presley said.

"It was alright, I wasn't sure what I was supposed to feel," Dalton replied.

"It made me laugh," said Mitchell. "Do you have anymore?"

"Do you guys want to buy a lid?" Bob inquired.

"How much is a lid?" Presley asked.

"It's about a three-finger sandwich bag full," Bob answered, showing the boys three of his fingers together, "about 40 joints worth."

"No, I mean how much money do you want for a lid?" Presley asked.

"Ten bucks," Bob replied, pulling the lid out of his pocket.

"What about rolling papers?" Mitchell asked. "Do you have any?"

Bob reached into his other pocket, producing a small white carton of *Zig Zags*.

The boys looked at each other. Presley was reluctant; he had his dad's voice in his head. Immediately Dalton and Mitchell wanted to purchase the weed and convinced Presley not to worry. Dashing into the cabin, the boys threw together the money. Mitchell sold a baseball card to Dana and raided the pennies in his dad's Droste's Cocoa tin piggy bank. Emma and Dana wondered why they needed money out in the woods, but let it go after they were told it was none of their business.

Having bought their first bag of weed, the gang proceeded into their corner of the back patio, took the contents out of the baggie, and dumped it into a shoe box lid. Seeds rolled to the bottom corner, creating an impulse in Presley to plant them. After learning the hard way that stems don't go with rolling papers, they sifted them out, too.

Each took a shot at rolling the weed. Mitchell caught on first and was designated the official joint roller. He spent the rest of the afternoon rolling joints to master his craft. He took the final product, counted twenty-six, and put them into his secret box. The gang elected to wait until after dinner to get high. They lacked confidence in their ability to hide the smell and blood shot eyes. Visine and gum would soon become a permanent part of the boys' gear.

Buying weed introduced the gang to several things: first, the illegal possession of a narcotic, which would never cross their minds; second, how to maintain a supply; and third, how not to get caught. They crossed a line—one that was not fully considered. They had put into motion a future that would greatly shape Mitchell's destiny; a future that would make him look long and hard at difficult lessons;

lessons that could have been better managed had leadership been present in his young life.

Finally, the weed brought countless moments of laughter, thoughts, and conversations that would not have otherwise been enjoyed. The boys claimed the term "pothead" as their personal references, and were happy to do so.

The summer moved on. June, then July, and the start of the Arizona monsoon season, then August, and the sad realization that a summer, written about in C. S. Lewis's *Birches,* was about to end. Out in the woods—with their boyish bodies and spirits at play in the Hassayampa—with Neil Young's heaven-sent anthems spurring them on—they grew into an appreciation for life that would have otherwise been lost.

☙❧

School was upon them. Dalton and Presley would return to familiarity at Madison Park Elementary with their teachers, coaches, and students. The thought of his friends leaving crumbled Mitchell. Prescott Junior High was seen only once by Mitchell on his way through town in a U-haul. That spec of time in the truck was a part of some other life, one he had forgotten, until now. Saying goodbye, for a second time that summer, was beyond his ability to cope.

The boys left in the same truck they arrived in three months earlier. Their parents had come up twice to see them—both times refusing to leave Mitchell and the waterhole. Considering Ada's circumstances, Evan and Marjorie offered to send checks to cover room and board for Dalton and Presley. Ada accepted their help bitterly.

Mitchell turned on the tape deck, cued to "Down by the River," and played the song while the truck's tailgate, and the back of his friends' heads, faded from view. He said goodbye to a time in his life that brought him closer to himself. When his eyes closed that night, when he remembered the sound of breath in his sleeping friends, he knew he would be okay.

The truck was gone. Mitchell watched the dust it made dissipate. The sun hung low on the western horizon. He looked at his feet and how they had grown. He moved to the far end of the front porch, and perched them securely on the railing.

The sun setting, despite the sincerest of prayers that it would not, was taking with it a summer of sweet memories—the kind that would begin and end at the foot of a tree—the kind that were sealed in water and rock—the sweet memories of nights that cradled much needed rest for the bones of weary boys.

The setting sun, first orange, then red, was reflected in a tear that had stopped mid-cheek on Mitchell's face. He missed his friends and guessed that by now they rounded the courthouse in Prescott, on their way back to Windsor Square, and the *Playboys* at the Markgraf Pharmacy. He remembered the secret passages of his old life that ran through backyards and fields. He thought of his friends living their lives without him. The tear was cold and held in it the last colors of a summer season in change. As the evening came, as it compressed the horizon's deepening hues, Mitchell wiped the trail of the tear clean from his face. He said goodbye to his friends and what he had shared with them in the Prescott National Forest.

Chapter Eighteen

THE school bus ride was a meditation of sorts for Mitchell. It was December of 1971. The frozen temperatures and the slide down the hillside from his house to the bus stop each morning wore out the seat of Mitchell's pants.

He liked the back of the bus. There was more swing in the back seat as the bus negotiated the curves to town. It was safer, too. He was having trouble with other kids and did not like the idea of looking over his shoulder on the bus or at school.

The school was just a stone's throw from the town square, now dead in winter's grip. The school was home to all kinds of kids: cowboys, Indians, hippies, jocks, but on a better note, there were also girls.

One in particular caught Mitchell's eye. She was the one standing on the corner upon his first arrival into town in the U-haul. She was fair-skinned, as most tans paled in the dead of winter in Prescott, Arizona. She had jet-black hair, wore glasses, and had a laugh that made Mitchell laugh when he heard it.

Lynn was leery of Mitchell. At first she was uncomfortable with his staring. A hard crush could be seen in his eyes. He filled his school day snatching views of her from different vantage points in classrooms and halls, mapping out her every move, obsessing over her, and calling her on the phone too many times. He would have been accused of stalking her, but that notion had not entered into the culture yet.

However harmless his intent, the constant attention had worn her parents' patience thin. They finally demanded that Mitchell call Lynn only on weekends and only once per weekend at that.

Ouch, Mitchell thought, when he got the news from her mother, who then let Mitchell talk to Lynn one more time before making him wait until the weekend to call. It was Monday and the news crushed Mitchell's romantic heart, which was something he did not know he had until he laid eyes on her at the start of the school year. During the fall semester, he convinced her to meet him at the Christmas dance, held in the girl's gym a couple of weeks before Christmas vacation started. Embarrassed by his feelings and that he was attending a school dance with a girl he liked, he did not bother to tell Dalton and Presley about her. They would find out anyway during the upcoming Christmas break and would have a ball with the information, laying it on thick, using every conceivable dig they could come up with. Mitchell would show Dalton and Presley a picture of her, but they would not be impressed. Mitchell was, though, and saw Lynn in every thought he had.

All of these moments were ahead, as he waited at the bottom of the stairs for Lynn to arrive at the Christmas dance. It was Friday night, December 10, 1971. It was cold. The country was falling apart. Nixon was off to China, Brent off to the North Pacific, Ada off into the arms of another man, and his friends hunkered down in the old neighborhood. Yet Mitchell was on fire. He was jetting through the emotions of a boy waiting for a girl at the Christmas dance.

It was a night he would never forget. Lynn wore a white dress. She was like an angel to him. He was embarrassed by his feelings but could not help himself; he was a boy in love. They danced twice. One fast, one slow.

On his way home his mind continued to race around her presence; *I will never forget either one of those songs,* he thought, playing the slow one, "Baby I'm-a Want You" in his head as he recalled how close she was to him. He remembered the smell of her hair and the tenderness of her cheek, and how his whole world had become the minutes he got to hold her in the darkened gym that night, regretting the seconds that had passed waiting to ask her to dance.

He had fallen in love. He was elevated into the wonder of the world, and of his life's possibilities, unbound by circumstance or fate, undaunted by time and what seemed an eternity until he saw her again. He was unashamed of how much his life became the tenderness he found near her, when he held her waist at the school Christmas dance, on a cold December evening.

David Gates' songs would become audio transcripts of how he felt for her. His songs gave Mitchell understanding of what love could be even in the face of an affectionless family. The girl became the soul of the boy, something perfect and beautiful in the dead of a long winter where the basics of survival in a penniless world had risen to the top. She was everything his young heart knew to hope for.

Chapter Nineteen

MITCHELL sat near the front window on Christmas Day playing a game of War with Presley. Dalton was poking the fire with the Louisville Slugger, now notched hundreds of times by a summer's worth of hit-the-rock. Emma was on her back, lost as she often was in the playing of her guitar. Dana, who was currently the object of everyone's attention, was standing outside, foot deep in snow, holding a ruler to the ground so Presley could record the Christmas winter wonderland with his Kodak Instamatic. The cabin was hushed and serene.

Sorber and Brent had come home for the holidays. On one side of a roaring fire sat a somber Sorber. Mitchell would look at him now again and for unknown reasons, had to fight off swells of tears. The sight of his father made him sad beyond his young years. On the other side of the open red brick fireplace sat a stoic Brent, unnerved by the changes Mitchell had gone through since leaving for the Army six months earlier.

Twenty-four hours earlier, when a cold front and snow started to blow in from the west, an exchange took place on the porch between Mitchell and Brent. To Emma and Dana's disbelief, their brother stood his ground with Brent. When the usual round of bullying began, Mitchell belted Brent in the face, knocking him off his feet. Brent looked into his younger brother's eyes and saw no fear, only blind anger. He sat up from the crushing blow to hear the conditions laid out by Mitchell. Through quaking tone Mitchell stated "I will kill you if you touch me or them ever again," pointing to Emma and Dana, speechless as they watched their brother take control. Brent stood up, bleeding from his lip, and walked off into his hard world, never to touch Mitchell or his sisters again.

The successful confrontation was the first of a handful of gifts Mitchell received during the next twenty-four-hour period. It was the moment when he turned fear into an asset rather than a debt, allowing him a claim that every boy looks for growing up—that of being a fighter rather than a coward. Mitchell could not help himself as he turned to his sisters, who were laughing out loud. He could fly.

From nowhere and back again came the passing memory of carving a stick man in a tree.

By seven o'clock, with Mitchell's Christmas Eve in full swing, complete with cabbage head hors d'oeuvres (a comical looking centerpiece using a whole cabbage, tooth picks, and small, cut chunks of meat and cheese placed randomly around the vegetable) and lime punch, he went outside to check on the progress of the falling snow. Standing on the edge of the property and looking back at the cabin, a classic Christmas picture unfolded before him. The snowfall had covered the Christmas lights Mitchell had put on top of the cabin: a peace sign nailed to the roof of his home. When his father saw it earlier in the day, he began to do his best Archie Bunker impersonation, making everyone laugh with the kind of warmth that does its best to hold a family together.

The snow covered peace sign, its colors glowing under the blanket of white, illuminated a colorful halo over the living room window, which held Mitchell's family together within its frame. With a newfound sense of dignity, he saw his family doing its best to be just that—a family. The Christmas tree filled the window and a fire glowed behind it. Best of all were the rosy cheeks of his two kid sisters, moving freely about the living room, no longer having to walk upon egg shells.

Poverty knocked hard. A can of peanuts and an orange were the gifts he found under the sparsely decorated Christmas tree. Explaining these gifts to Dalton and Presley was, for just a moment, embarrassing. But his friends moved on quickly to the winter wonderland that had been bestowed upon Mitchell the night before.

He looked across the couch at Presley who had grown two inches since his last visit, and smiled at him and Dalton, remembering something he had not been able to share with them from the day before.

Using eye and hand signals to communicate a rendezvous, the boys grabbed their jackets and gathered in Mitchell's corner, behind the closed back patio door. In the cold night their breath was as thick as cigarette smoke.

"I did it, guys," Mitchell said to them quietly.

"Did what, Beetle?" they asked in unison.

"I hit Brent," Mitchell said.

They hit the floor as squeals and hushed laughter threatened to reverberate throughout the house. Mitchell made them stop before it got out of hand.

"How?" Dalton whispered.

"When?" Presley asked.

"Yesterday, when he came home," Mitchell said. "He went right into his usual routine, and I hit him so hard he fell over. Then he got up and walked away. I told him that if he laid one more hand on me or my sisters, I would kill him. Afterwards, I started to laugh, I couldn't help myself. I felt like I was high."

"Well, it's about time, Beetle," Presley said.

"Is that why he's got a fat lip?" Dalton asked, laughing out loud.

"Shhhhh," Mitchell said, feeling pride at what it meant to stand up against the misery his brother had dished out over the years.

"I'd like to take a pop at him, too," Dalton said. "The bastard hit me, too, you know."

"Go ahead, I dare you," Mitchell said.

Laughing together, the boys agreed that what Mitchell had done was good. The vindication against the abuser and being together for Christmas vacation made Mitchell's world better. Snowball fights, snowmen, Christmas cookies, and a joint brought up the hill from Phoenix would make the Christmas at hand a good one.

✄❧

Earlier in the day, Mitchell had taken the broom down to the rocky outcrop overlooking the gully and swept it clean of the foot-deep snow. Within minutes, the sun had baked the rocky outcrop dry and the friends sat together, removed from the presence of Mitchell's family.

The sun shown brightly overhead. Still in the thirties, the air froze his nose and ears. Cupping them with his hand helped, but putting them squarely in the face of the Christmas sun was better. Mitchell thought it remarkable that even in the grip of winter, with snow covering everything that could be seen, his rocky outcrop could warm up and provide comfort to his legs and hind end.

As he sat on the outcrop with his friends, a new feeling grew within that would be hard to explain. There was regret in his heart for what he did to his brother the day before. He felt bad about drawing blood from his lip and watching him walk away, alone. By hitting Brent, Mitchell had become like him, and this thought did not sit well.

The lack of presents weighed heavy on his mind. The can of nuts was already gone; he had shared them with his friends. The thought of being poor chilled him.

"He deserved it," Dalton said.

"Beetle, you did what you had to do," Presley said.

"I still feel that I need to go one step further in putting it to rest, guys," Mitchell said. "I feel that I need to say, 'I'm sorry' to him."

"Beetle!" Dalton exclaimed. "How could you think you owe him an apology after everything he did to you?"

"He creamed you every day since I've known you," Presley said.

"It's all true," Mitchell said, "but not apologizing makes me just like him."

"Do what you gotta do, Beetle, but I think it's a mistake. I think he will just start whaling on you again," Dalton said.

"I can see what you're saying," Presley said, "but you are a bigger man than I if you do this."

"The other thing that's bothering me is the can of nuts I got for Christmas," Mitchell said.

"Don't let it bother you too much, Beetle. You've got other things here that I only dream of having in my own backyard," Dalton said. "I don't know what's going on with your dad and mom. My mom said that having a roof over your head and food on the table was a luxury at one point in her life, and sometimes things go sour for people for no reason at all. It just happens."

Mitchell nodded his head in agreement. What had gone sour with his family he could only guess. He looked down from a bone dry and warm rocky outcrop, surrounded by an endless sea of snow and thought the moment to be a rare one. He looked over to his friends who had offered him kindness and generosity. He looked back up at the cabin that held quite a different Christmas.

The New Christy Minstrels could be heard from the cabin. As he sat on the gully's top rock, he was growing into a new reality, one that came only by way of facing fear and trusting others. It was a reality that required a level of maturity, one that arrived through the filters of experience to say that what matters most is what he found inside himself.

❧❦

Christmas Day was drawing to a close. The sunset, reflecting starlight off the snow, sent the colors of a prism across the cold little valley.

As the sun dropped behind the hills to the west, the boys retired to the warmth of the cabin's main room. Brent was absent. He had left without saying goodbye. Sorber had taken him as far as the highway where he asked to be let out. Sorber had obliged.

Mitchell's apology went unspoken, yet the intention remained intact, and Mitchell felt right about it. At the end of his Christmas Day, his poor home and family seemed to be okay. There was a fire in the fireplace, a Christmas dinner to be enjoyed, and a gracious spirit moving through Mitchell—a feeling not often known by a boy in such conditions.

Chapter Twenty

WEEKS had passed since their last meeting but neither Mitchell nor Sian could stop thinking about one another. Both were consumed with the implications of their presence in one another's lives. For Mitchell, it was possibly a chance to make right the wrongs perpetrated upon his wife by protecting her daughter. For Sian it was the fascination of her mother's life in Mitchell's. She felt a kinship to him. This could only be so if through the years of marriage, the husband and wife had become the keepers of each other's hearts. This was clear to Sian; Mitchell had her mother's heart cradled within.

Sian stopped her thoughts about Mitchell to resume her research in the many microfilm slides available at the Sharlot Hall Museum—slides that focused on late nineteenth and twentieth century coroner's inquests. Her fascination with the old widows in Prescott's past brought her there, where she remained during those weeks since she had last seen Mitchell.

After some study, she was curious about a clue that would be revealed every ten years or so in the reports about a bloody sock print. From the late 1890s to the mid 1950s, she would see this curious item pop up. It would not appear again until the testimony she heard during Mitchell's trial, when a sheriff's deputy, first on the scene after Mitchell's 911 emergency call, described seeing just such a print on the floor where her mother was killed.

The names involved in each case were different, but the malevolence described therein was not. Sian's stomach would turn as she read the eyewitness testimony of cruelty perpetrated upon one human being by another. She felt the evil move through the microfilm as it advanced through the years in the form of a blurred, bloody sock print, its last impression made as it snuffed out her mother's life.

She was not ready for such an interpretation of evidence, and part of her mind reached for a logical conclusion that would not connect the microfilmed events and her mother's death via a supernatural hold. On this, her last trip to the museum, she hung her head low as she moved out onto Prescott's main thoroughfare. The sun had lost its moment in her heart, the sky its blue shimmer above her. Life's darkness covered her mind as she looked up, shading her eyes with her hand, straining to find both the sun and sky to lift her, but they could not. Her mother was taken by an evil that now filled her mind—an evil that overpowered her.

She looked around her distrustfully as the memory of foster fathers and boys surrounded her. She sat on a street bench and huddled her arms and legs in front of her in an effort to ward off menacing advances from within her own mind. She began to shake while tears appeared within in her eyes, blurring faces of her past that she had not thought of for some time. She realized that she had lived with the same evil her entire life; sexual and verbal abuse that became bloody sock prints reflected in her tears.

She frantically wiped the tears away as her eyes spit her young memories forth. Smells came next. Skin, alcohol, burning metal, and cigarettes, all became the smell of lust for her hair and breasts. She caved in and became the object of evil's desire, feeling nothing but contempt for her own life as the summation of her years clearly showed. She was reduced to short-term release for all manner of darkness in the minds and pants of men, young and old. There was nothing left but the cold floor on her back, her hair matted against her neck and forehead, discarded until the next time when alcohol, burning metal, and cigarettes became her skin—again.

She sat on the bench for hours, alarming passersby. Some recognized her, like the old timers Jess and Hartley who were just leaving the Dinner Bell. They said hello but when she did not respond, they approached closer and asked, "Sian, are you okay?"

She looked up slowly, revealing a vacant stare to them, giving nothing that they could discern as an answer to their question. For a moment Sian did not recognize them. She was lost in her mind, unable to find a way out of the grip her past had on her. Slowly she sat up on the bench, lowering her legs to the ground and allowing air to enter her body. She rubbed her eyes and said, "Yes, yes, I'm okay."

"Well, you don't look okay, young lady," Jess said sweetly.

"I just . . ." Sian couldn't put her thoughts together, unable to tell the truth about where her mind had taken her.

"C'mon, let's get you inside the café and get you some coffee," Hartley said.

They each gingerly took an arm and helped Sian up from the bench. Slowly they walked the quarter mile down Gurley Street toward the café with Sian between them. The walk helped Sian get her bearings and move away from her previous life, and as she looked around at the town and her two companions, she realized that she was at the receiving end of their compassion and not under the wickedness she had endured as a child and teenager.

She stopped suddenly, alarming Jess and Hartley.

"Gentlemen," she said, "I'm okay, thanks to you. I don't think I want to go in there on my day off. I'm sorry for my display back there, but sometimes life has a way of catching up with me."

Jess and Hartley got it, having moments in their lives that didn't add up to any accounting of justice or fairness. They looked at each other and then at Sian and agreed that going into the café on her day off didn't make sense.

"I think I'm going to head home," she said.

"You sure you're okay?" Jess asked.

"I am, thank you."

"Okay then, we'll see you when you work next," Hartley said.

They released Sian's arms and watched her move away from them, suddenly realizing her beauty and her attempts to conceal it from them, and everyone.

At once Sian turned back to them and asked "Do either of you know the names of the boys who were run off at the courthouse the other day?"

"Just one, the leader, name of Zac," Hartley said.

Sian mouthed the boys name—lost in thought again as coroner's inquests flashed through her mind. She waved goodbye and turned to go.

"She is a beautiful girl," Jess said. "I'd not noticed before."

"Yeah, me neither," Hartley said. "Interesting that you and I are just now noticing that for the first time."

"Why now?" asked Jess.

"I don't know, maybe she was just a walking coffee pot before now," Hartley said. "Now we see she has feelings and can be hurt like the rest of us."

"Good point, Hart."

The old-timers turned their backs to her and resumed their trek into the day.

Sian stopped and turned around to look at two people who cared enough to ask if she was okay and was grateful for that, but she still carried the overwhelming sense of evil that veiled and pocketed itself about town. She longed to see Mitchell. She felt safe with him and understood that Mitchell had faced down that evil and on one sad night long ago had slain it with his bare hands. She headed for her apartment, for her car keys and purse, and would find her way toward the Hassayampa River.

⨯⨯

Mitchell stirred on the sofa. He sat up and shielded his eyes from the bright afternoon sun. He had fallen asleep and was disturbed by a dream that Sian was in some kind of trouble and by the vision of the bloody foot print next to his wife. He put his face into his hands and rubbed his temples. Standing up, he walked upstairs to the loft to finish a task he had started before the unusual nap in the middle of the afternoon.

"God is here." Tears came. The Sea Man was as joyful, and as sad, as he could remember.

Chapter Twenty One

MITCHELL could now run the frozen sidewalks that led from the junior high school to the steps of the Yavapai County courthouse blindfolded during his lunch break. His brown bag lunch, consisting of a bologna and cheese sandwich, was stuffed into the large pocket of his parka. His breath, reflected in the light of a cold winter sun, kept cadence with his feet moving one in front of the other, toward the warmth of the granite steps on the east side of the historic building. It was here at lunch time that he spent a moment or two with Lynn. He knew now that she liked him. She looked for him the same way he did for her in the school halls.

He learned where Lynn lived on Highland Street. He memorized her telephone number, unaware that both her address and phone number would remain bits of information kept in storage, readily available, for the rest of his life. He learned the exact distance in feet from her doorstep to his, along with each angle in the road, and the size and color of the trees on both sides of it. He looked for the same landmarks, and shadows cast to and fro, from his house in Ponderosa Park to hers in Prescott. On Friday and Saturday nights he would focus every amount of energy found inside him to see her alone, away from the eyes of parents. He had fallen in love and was alive because of it. His entire life was planned out with her, talking often of what they believed in and what made sense in their world. Neil Young's "After the Gold Rush" became an anthem of their shared angst. They designed their futures in a world they knew would be unavailable, as it would surely crumble under the weight of their parents' generation and its wars and pollution. How odd it was for them to be so clear in their conviction at such a young age. They knew the steps they would take regardless of what was said by friend or foe.

As Mitchell's breath slowed and the sight of his favorite spot emerged from around the corner of the courthouse, he saw Lynn waiting for him. She smiled, making him smile in return. He treasured the spell she cast upon him. It blocked everything out save the warmth of the sun from his senses, acknowledging only her. He sat down next to her, no longer hungry. Her hand took his. He closed his eyes and as the bright day reddened the windows to his soul, he wondered briefly how he would explain to Dalton and Presley his feelings at that very moment.

Lynn began to talk. Everything she said was music to Mitchell. It was not necessarily what she said, but how she said it, that endeared him. She spoke about her older brother, of draft age, and her worry that he would be sent to Vietnam. The war disturbed Lynn deeply. She prayed to God every day for peace. She told Mitchell that the world John Lennon sang about in his song "Imagine" was her world and that there was nothing she wanted to give to him more than what was found in the refrains of that song.

On that note—when, on that day; breath could still be seen at the lunch hour; when the Superior Court judge could be seen through his office window; when Lynn's friends watched her from the Dent's Ice Cream parlor across the street—she leaned over, kissed Mitchell on his cheek, and presented to him an item that was very near to her heart: an MIA bracelet bearing the name of WO William Dunlap. The bracelet had belonged to her brother, who gave it to Lynn, who now gave it to Mitchell as a token of their shared longing for the world imagined in the Lennon song.

Mitchell and Lynn were officially going steady, declared so by a gleam in the judge's eye, as he watched the two carry on below him, perhaps remembering the tender moments on the steps of his youth. They stood up, kissing one another once before she ran off to walk with her friends back to school. Mitchell stood alone looking at her, feeling nothing but the sun's heat rising in his heart. He was loved.

⌘

Hunkered down in his corner of the freezing back patio, Mitchell contemplated the day. The floor was worn and in need of restoration. Mitchell found it easy to pick pieces and splinters from it while his mind idled from one moment on the courthouse steps to the next, cherishing the slices of time when he found his worth in the eyes of another.

He leaned his head back against the wooden walls, noticing for the first time that it was snowing. In his hand he held the MIA bracelet, rolling it between his finger and his thumb. He acknowledged the connection between wanting something to happen in his life and getting it. He wanted Lynn to be his girlfriend, and it came true.

He noticed this connection in many other things in his life, like a choice he made to play Pop Warner football and actually playing it, or wanting Dalton and Presley to visit and then having them come. He was aware of an ability to procure things and events in his life by wanting them. He remained unaware of any other mechanisms that might be in place in the process of watching his hopes become reality.

Mitchell still could not believe Lynn made such a public display of her affection for him. He was amazed at his possession of the MIA bracelet as he watched his reflection roll through the shiny silver surface.

Sitting upon the worn wooden patio floor, Mitchell could feel family members moving about the cabin; their footfalls vibrating throughout the poorly built structure. He again sensed change of his position in his home. Having a girlfriend added a new dimension to his thoughts about who he was. Mitchell filled the thin and vacant parts of his soul with the time he spent with Lynn. He had come full circle in his young life, reaching that side of himself that he never knew, yet could now own through the eyes of another. He found warmth in the possession of it. He found joy in the memories attached to it. It made him feel different inside, as if he was real to the world.

It did not occur to him to question who he was before the moment on the courthouse steps. He suddenly believed many things; things that he should have known about himself, and the world, long before he found himself as the hope-filled wishes of another.

Chapter Twenty Two

MITCHELL sat on the front porch with his younger sisters to the left of him and Huntington Beach Bob on his right. Out of the corners of both eyes he saw three pairs of legs swinging to and fro under the porch and back out again. They seemed to be moving a mile a minute, like playing cards pinned to the forks of bicycle wheels.

From the radio in the background Neil Diamond's sad tune "The Last Thing on My Mind" was heard. Mitchell thought of his brother, now stationed somewhere in the world, and he wished things stood different between them – a wish that had come and gone as circumstance encircled unkindness around their hearts, separating them forever as their lives unfolded.

The four looked out onto the valley before them. Spring had sprung, not only in the trees and mountains, but in their legs as well. Anticipation to run and jump and sink their bottoms into the icy waters of the waterhole began to grow. A desire to move their feet forward into action, toward a country road lined with adventure, toward a glass blue sky that held no border, flowed through their limbs. Life renewed, and the call of the wild was upon them.

Mitchell leaned back onto the warmth of wood, basking in the morning sun, and closed his eyes. The smell of spring spun in his heart. His breathing increased as the spirit of boyhood reawakened from the very dead of winter. He heard the wind in the tops of the trees ebb and flow as if reflecting in its own way the ocean tides as they cascaded over sand and stone. It stirred him. He sat up holding the palms of his hands together. Dropping his hands to his sides, he lifted himself off the porch and pounced down onto his feet as if part bobcat. With arms outstretched, his listened to the tempo of the song and began to spin slowly around with his head up and eyes to the vault of blue sky above, finding another consideration of forgiveness for Brent. He remembered a game of croquet and a mallet that struck him in the face. A moment of anger threw his spinning out of balance. He took a deep breath, lifted his head to the sun, put his arms to the wind, and gently began to spin again to the soft sounds emanating from the AM radio.

He wanted the words of the song to speak to him. He wanted to stop hating his brother. The song ended yet the lyrics lingered. He wanted the burdened memories to end. He wanted the joy of being a boy in the woods; to bury past hurts in the dirt. He no longer asked why his brother tortured him—the reasons didn't matter. What mattered was being a part of this season of change, allowing the sun and wind to be his friends again.

ဆာ

The summer sun roasted the boys out of bed. It was too hot to sleep in the direct sunlight on the back patio, so all five of them got up and moved into the cooler living room. Because yesterday used every ounce of energy they had for exploring, and because they crawled into bed from exhaustion shortly after dinner, they got more than eight hours of sleep by sunup the next day.

Dalton and Presley had returned for the summer. All sat around the table. Mitchell held up his head with an unmannerly display of elbows. He knew how much his mother detested slouching or elbows next to the food he was eating. He daydreamed that he swam in a giant bowl of Cheerios, gulping milk and cereal while doing the backstroke to keep cool.

They began to spend nights at the waterhole. Camp fires and joints became icons of their second summer in the woods. Each turned the crackling of a campfire into distant lullabies; followed the slow movement of the stars through the tops of the silent trees, and each watched the campfires grow dim in quiet contemplation. Concentration slipped beyond their reach; senses bubbled downstream, leaving them each night to their dreams, pondering the mysteries of boyhood among the mercies of Mother Nature.

ဆာ

Unsettled in sleep, Mitchell awoke one night with no idea what time it was. He turned his head from side to side eyeing his fellow campers. They seemed isolated to Mitchell. His thoughts passed through the empty halls of his school at night and how foreign they felt to him after the sun went down. The waterhole, its water bubbling through the granite shapes in the wee hours of morning left Mitchell with the same impression of unfamiliarity. He rolled his head back to see the brilliant Milky Way shinning brightly overhead in a moonless sky. The arching light peered into Mitchell. He sat up in the sleeping bag, leaned back on his locked arms, and was astonished. He noted the shadows thrown about him and gasped at the sight of them. *How extraordinary this is,* whispered a voice inside. *I am a shadow caused by the light of the Milky Way.* His first impulse was to wake his friends. *They would want to see this,* he thought.

A yawn broke in two the thought of waking them, and he succumbed to the need of sinking into his sleeping bag. Mitchell fell into a state of half sleep, dreaming of things watching him. He could discern figures that were etched in wood. Expressionless and unthreatening, the stick men blended into a memory of his father as he sat in a dark room at midnight, his cigarette ember retracing the arc-shaped stars of the Milky Way.

Sleep finally pulled Mitchell from the edges of his tired imagination.

Chapter Twenty Three

SUMMER rolled into July and August. Morning slipped across the sky. The boys stirred. One threw a pillow at another while a third demanded room service for three—corn flakes and sliced banana with at least one gallon of milk. Emma and Dana yelled from the kitchen to get out of bed and eat while the milk was still cold.

On this fine, long summer day Mitchell found a letter on the table from Lynn. Dalton and Presley went berserk. They tried to tackle Mitchell and to get the letter away from him.

Mitchell went outside with his treasure and found a place that would grant no passage to unwelcome eyes. His friends were aware of someone named Lynn—but not a *girlfriend*. She had left Prescott with her family for the summer, leaving Mitchell's heart to fight off the frost of being left behind.

Lynn's letter enlivened Mitchell. She wrote of missing him, of her father's cruelty in not allowing her to call him, and for limiting the use of letters over the summer. Lynn also wrote that her father believed she was much too young to feel the way she felt for Mitchell. The letter was discouragingly brief.

Talking to her on the phone or meetings on the courthouse steps for lunch were the only reasons why he wanted school to start again. He closed his eyes to remember moments on the granite steps. He remembered her making him laugh and talk about so many things. This was a part of him that his friends and family knew nothing about. He was different with her. She defined him and gave him added self-worth. As he closed the letter and put it back into the envelope, his heart gave in a little bit to the loneliness. It was difficult for Mitchell to believe she loved him and that she would come back to him.

He stood there just inside the shade of the cabin. The bright summer sun looked for his face, but Mitchell moved further into his home's shadow. He looked at the letter and the envelope that wrapped around it, understanding that love could be folded over and put away.

Suddenly, he was ambushed by Dalton and Presley, who jumped from the front porch in his direction, causing him to bolt out from under the shade of the cabin.

He stuffed the letter into his pocket, refusing them access to it. Their objections remained loud and long for most of the day, but Mitchell did not give in. He was not ready to share Lynn with his less-than-empathetic friends, who would be unmerciful in their boyish assessments of Lynn, however playfully so.

The interest in Lynn's letter subsided. On this afternoon, the boys continued their summer living along the Hassayampa, skipping rocks, climbing old oaks, and cooling off in the liquid magic of the waterhole.

If asked, the river would have responded with a kind word about the sight of them among her elements, making a day out of what was in front of them. Their daily outings had given them a rope from which their memories could swing—a rope that the river was happy to give them.

Chapter Twenty Four

THE beauty of White Spar Road elevated Sian. Her thoughts of Mitchell standing in the Hassayampa, wailing about like a madman in the water, still filled her with surprise, and now some amusement. She was happy to be on her way—to his home—to his world and the comfort she had found there.

In her relationship with him to date, the phone had not entered into the equation. Showing up unannounced at entrances to cafés and the banks of rivers had defined them. It was an unorganized association that gave both a jolt whenever one would think of or see the other. Yet as widower and daughter, they remained true to Red; an easy and relaxed respect that was never second-guessed. Red was the reason for the jolt they shared, for their keen interest in each other, and for the sheer pleasure they shared in seeing one another.

Music filled the cabin. Mitchell was in the loft doing a mental dance to the music with his hands, as he changed out the sheets on the bed—a task once done by his beloved and now done by him when necessity called for it. The song, "That's the Way," by Led Zeppelin, bounced off the roof panels and filled the area around his home, lifting Mitchell as his hands moved with the song.

Sian pulled up in front of her mom's home, opened the car door and set her feet on the ground, stopping short to register the strumming of the guitar and the song's lyrics. Her thoughts were pulled back to a place that was not of her experience, but her longing. She instantly melted into a place of make believe, where she saw her life as more than the sum of skin, alcohol, burning metal, and cigarette smoke.

"Hello, you," she heard Mitchell say, looking up to see him on the porch. Questioning her expression, Mitchell asked "Where are you?"

"It's the music," she said. "It's this music you are constantly playing out here. It takes me to a better place in my mind. I feel safe there, or is it here that I feel safe?"

She is safe, he thought to himself as he looked at her. "Hopefully you feel as safe everywhere, as you do here, and what a nice surprise to see you," Mitchell said.

"Its good to see you too," Sian said. "I was at the museum again today and . . ." She stopped.

"What's going on?" he asked.

"Can I come up?" she requested.

Mitchell's mood darkened. An alarm was now sounding in him but one that was more of concern than caution. He walked back into the cabin and stood at the top of the stair well watching Sian ascend to the main floor. They hugged one another then moved together toward the sofa, where each sat at opposite ends facing one another.

"Mitchell," Sian began "I found something odd digging around in the archives at the Sharlot Hall Museum."

Mitchell cocked his head sideways, noting stress around Sian's eyes.

"Have you been crying?" Mitchell asked.

"I have been," Sian admitted. "I can get engrossed in evil thoughts and then fall into a hole where I feel I can't climb out. I fell in there today after reading some old coroner's inquests at the museum. It's why I'm here. I needed to see you and tell you about what I've found."

Mitchell was now feeling more than just concern for Sian. "What is it; what's going on?"

"It's about Mom's trial, Mitchell," she said.

It was strange to hear Red referred to as "Mom," for Mitchell, but the term further endeared Sian to him.

"What were the years covered by the inquests?" Mitchell asked quickly.

"Late 1890s to the mid 1950s," Sian said.

"And what you are about to tell me comes from these archives and has something to do with my trial?" Mitchell asked, trying to get his head wrapped around what he was about to hear.

"Yes," she said. "Are you sure you're all right talking about this?"

"I guess I won't know how I feel about what you are going to tell me until I hear it," Mitchell said.

She looked at him sadly, then said "There are bloody sock prints found at four murders over this sixty-five year period of time, then nothing until your trial, where the same clue was entered into evidence during your proceedings," Sian blurted out quickly.

Mitchell's concern grew. He let himself move gently back in time to the night he lost his Red and remembered making such a mental note of just such a mark on the floor of his bedroom. He remembered the trial and photos again. He rubbed his temples and stood up, moved over to the windows and looked out. He took a deep breath and let the veil of his memory reinforce itself. He remembered the bloody, soiled sock and how it appeared on the ground the night he lost his mind.

"There's more," Sian said with regret in her voice. Mitchell looked at Sian. "The ruffian you scared off, the one we saw walking along the creek a while ago, in the photograph I told you about, he's not wearing any shoes, just socks and they are soiled with dried blood. I've learned his name—it's Zac."

Sian watched him, regretting the decision to share with Mitchell her discoveries. She could see the lines of pain around his eyes grow.

A pause floated between them. "Sian, I'm okay," Mitchell said, reacting to her concerned expression. "It's always tough looking at the facts. They've got colors and smells attached to them that can make me spit if I let them. I'm tired of this pain."

Mitchell continued: "I've got something I need to tell you, too, and I just now realized it's time. I think of your mom constantly. I believe she is in a place where there's no pain, where she's at peace and is filled with the presence of heaven. I believe she has no memory of what she endured here and wants me to know what she knows. I want more than anything to know that kind of peace."

Sian listened intently to Mitchell, who sat down at the other end of the sofa. She looked sad. Mitchell extended his hand out across the back of the sofa toward her. Without looking she put her hand next to his. He gently laced their fingers together. Traveling the distance between Sian's heart and her eyes, a tear appeared. Mitchell's lip quivered, and the rich sadness pulled them together again. He saddled Sian's shoulders with his arm and she found comfort resting her head on his chest. He held her tight and felt her pain come through again. He thought of the bloody sock print next to the bed and the sheets he changed moments ago and how one moment was not much different from another.

Sian's sadness subsided. Mitchell rearranged himself into a more inclined position at the end of the sofa and Sian followed suit. He was growing contented with Sian's presence in his life. Her demeanor began to fit his in an all too familiar way. She was finding a place in his life that was separate from the beautiful life he had with his Red. The fact that Sian was Red's daughter disturbed him less and less. His thoughts about his wife helped him to relax next to Sian, letting the relationship focus more on the development of friendship.

Mitchell put his other hand down on the end table and rested it upon the old man's journal. The times he and Red would read and discuss its contents sailed through his mind. He remembered the talk he and Red had about the notion of a prodigal father in a son's life, and the call that was made of the Sea Man, in the old journal, to do the same for his father.

Time passed. Sian fell asleep on Mitchell's chest while he continued thinking. He was unveiling a sense of gratitude to God for Sian and her timing in his life. The ongoing question of his worthiness, of Red, and now of Red's daughter, followed his gaze through the tall windows, and was filled with humility when suddenly, Sian stirred. She sat up on the sofa—a touch embarrassed by her continued habit of dozing in front of him. She, too, was sensitive to her close proximity to Mitchell and wondered about its appropriateness.

Mitchell sensed this. To calm her, he handed her the old journal.

"What's this?"

"It was written by the previous owner of this place," Mitchell said, pointing the ceiling of the cabin. "There are some amazing things expressed in it about God."

Sian shook her head then yawned. "Sorry about the naps. I'm not sure what kind of spell is cast here when I come over, but I don't mind it."

"I don't mind either, Sian," Mitchell stated. "I think I'd like to tell you that this is your home, too. Kind of like your birthright, I guess. Your mother helped me to build this life. She helped me convince the old man who wrote this journal to sell the place to us.

She made this cabin our home. Now it is your home, too, if you want it to be."

Sian was surprised by his offer. She had never had a home of her own—always the odd ball out. To have a place to call her own as her birthright stunned her.

"Wow," she said. "It's hard to imagine this, Mitchell. I've . . . I'm . . . I don't know what to say."

"Take your time, Sian," he said. "I'm not going anywhere."

Mitchell rose from the sofa. Sian turned forward toward the tall windows. Mitchell walked outside, inhaled the cool air, and sensed the perspiration created by the contact between them, evaporate. He looked skyward while sensing the very last minuscule drop of sweat become airborne; leaving a tingling sensation that lingered in his mind.

Sian opened the book. She noted many pages that had been dog-eared and saw her mother's fingers making the creases. She randomly opened to a page and read:

> *"God is here," he said. Tears came. The Sea Man was as happy as he could remember. His breath came alive. He stepped up his pace and felt his heart catch up with his breath.*

Sian closed the journal on her finger marking the page she just read. She saw Mitchell standing outside and joined him.

"What do you see up there?" Sian asked.

"Often your mother," Mitchell said. "Right now just the clouds."

"Is God here, Mitchell?" she asked him.

"He is," he stated simply. "Its like nothing I've ever read about God. I am leaning very close to the understanding that Jesus is my brother, and the Holy Spirit has left the Catholic altar to become these trees and the breath of every living thing I see."

"It's so simple," Mitchell said as he retrieved the old journal from Sian. "Like so many, I've struggled with religion. This book has given the name "God" to the peace and joy of the Hassayampa River. I still struggle with my fears—the biggest being any phrase that starts with 'what if?' "What if I had come home just a little earlier that night?" The question opened a bottomless, endlessly black crack of irony in both of their minds.

Mitchell sighed. "I wonder if I'll ever stop missing her."

"I don't know if you'll ever stop missing her, but I think it might be less sad as time passes," Sian said.

"I know you're right," Mitchell said. "I am less sad, but I long for her everyday."

Mitchell thought again of Sian's presence in his home and why she came into his life when she did. *Was there a further intention for Red? Is Red Sian?* He asked himself. *Is she a reincarnated version of Red?*

Sian saw the questions pass in Mitchell's eyes but had no answers. She thought again of the journal's message; *God is here.*

She looked around, making a connection to the notions that God could be right before her. The spirit of God could be in the creation of a forest, of seasons, and the water that flows through them.

"I feel different about everything when I am with you," Sian said. "I have thoughts that I've never considered before every time we are together."

"Like what?" Mitchell questioned, sensing Sian's closeness.

"I've never thought about God," she said. "I have too often thought of evil, and see it as the largest part of humanity."

"Your experience so far in life dictates that notion," Mitchell said. "Life's been ugly. But when do you and I begin, or continue, our journey on *The Current of the Expanding Universe*—as it is so often referred to in the journal? This is the reason for our living, Sian, to travel on this . . . *Heaven's Highway*, for lack of any better term, and put to task our response to life. Let's hope we can create our interpretations of life in good ways."

Sian thought of the night Mitchell lost his mind. She had her images of what unfolded and was too familiar with the circumstances that surrounded his soul that night. "What did you create that night?" Sian asked guardedly.

Mitchell said: "I think that we have no choice but to protect our world from evil. Our response to evil must be one of protection and prevention, but not necessarily one of justice. I wanted justice that night, and I took it. I failed to protect or to prevent. Evil travelled on the night your mother was killed, unencumbered, into the universe, and into our society, even into our hometown—Zac, in his filthy socks, tormenting the old woman."

Mitchell thought of the last time stick men had appeared to him. He thought of their crossed eyes, turned downward toward him and how often they had appeared.

"Sian," Mitchell said. "I have, throughout my life, had visions or imaginings of stick men peering at me with angry expressions. The first one I ever remember seeing was one I carved into a tree when I was young. I imagined that the eyes I drew became cross. I am, right now, realizing these imaginings could very well have been the symbol of evil in my life. I think evil passes through all of us in one degree or another, but in some it has never found a home. Your mother was one of those rare individuals, Sian. She was naturally good. She gave. She uplifted others with her love. She made me a better person. I think that you, too, may have the same propensity for love and for uplifting the world just by your presence in it."

Sian was touched by Mitchell's words. She had never imagined any man seeing her in such a light. Yet there he was, admiring her as someone who was worth defending from evil, and worthy of his praise.

Their conversation brought about a sense of peace. Mitchell stood viewing the woods and all of its creation—it was a growing understanding that what was before him could very well be God in his physical form. Sian let go of her earlier darkness, her mind idling on the rhythm of guitar and voice heard when she arrived earlier in the day. It had been playing over and over again yet the repetition went unnoticed until now.

Mitchell went in to turn off the stereo. When he returned, Sian was gone.

He stopped. Suddenly, the moment stood white and still. Nothing moved. From deep within him, to the stretch of the curving earth, beyond the blue heavens, there existed the calm, smooth, motionless passing of time.

*The Sea Man looked skyward to
mentally record what preciously remained before
him..*

Chapter Twenty Five

THE summer ended. Dalton and Presley left for home and their first days as freshman at Central High School in Phoenix. Mitchell resented going back to a "junior" high school. Although ninth-graders were considered big bosses of the campus, he still wished he could say he was in high school.

Lynn was the only redeeming quality about Prescott Junior High School. She would be there, in the halls, and at the courthouse for lunch. Football would start again as well. It would be Mitchell's fourth year. He enjoyed the game and was good at it, but wished he could play with Dalton and Presley at Central High.

Leaves began to change. The fall colors were a noted attraction for Prescott as the trees around the courthouse ignited with oranges, yellows, and reds in an awesome display of harvest time.

Letters came and went between the boys. Calls resumed between Mitchell and Lynn. A sense of familiarity grew as Mitchell started his second academic year as a resident of the woods and student at PJHS.

On his way to meet Lynn at the courthouse during the school lunch break, Mitchell was walking alone in front of a record store when something nailed him right in the middle of his bottom. It felt like a knife and shocked him for its brutality. It caught him off guard, reminding him of the same brutality he had suffered at the hands of an older brother.

He turned around quickly to ward off any more jabs and saw, standing directly behind him, an ugly boy wearing a cowboy hat and boots. Mitchell had seen him around campus before but had taken no note of him. They stared at one another, and as they did, the cowboy walked away mumbling something about Mitchell's long hair.

Mitchell stood for a moment longer in shock. He considered, when the cowboy kicked him, his hate, not only his own, but that of the cowboy's as well. It was an angry, vile hate, one that made Mitchell want to vomit. He closed his eyes hard. His mind presented to him the face of a stick man in the compression of blood vessels in his eyelids. He opened them and as he turned to face the back of the cowboy, who walked away with Mitchell's dignity, rage grew in him. He yelled obscenities and succumbed to impulses only his cells could remember. He wondered why he did not fight back. Old fears stung him at the instant of contact between him and the cowboy boot, and the spell of his old life, a life he had forgotten, had come full circle again.

Mitchell crossed the road angrily, walking on the courthouse side of Montezuma Street. He yelled at the bastard walking indifferently down the other side—oblivious to the crushing blow he had delivered to Mitchell.

Mitchell didn't know what to do. He decided to find Lynn and tell her what had happened, yet at that thought, shame overcame him—it came flooding back. His body had not forgotten.

"Hey," Lynn said. "What's wrong?" she asked, with much compassion in her voice. This kindness settled Mitchell's anger.

"Nothing," Mitchell said, reassuring her with a smile. Lynn talked about her morning at school and her family, and while Mitchell listened, the shame of not fighting back returned. He knew not how to break free from the hesitation he displayed; a character flaw he would keep secret, even to himself.

Talking to Lynn on the phone later that night helped but walking to the other side of Ponderosa Park to borrow a neighbor's phone kept Mitchell bound to his humiliation. His parents had lost their access even to a party line, and Mitchell rued the sound of his knock on the neighbor's door. On this night he could not reconcile his life which started with a kick from a cowboy boot and ended with a sad realization of being from a poor family living in a dilapidated one bedroom cabin. Hearing her voice however, lifted him above his dark thoughts.

⤜⤛

The hour approached midnight. He was obsessed over the assault in front of the record store, and his anger over it burrowed itself ever deeper into the cracks of his soul. His young mind did not understand obsession. He was hypnotized by the things his muscles and nerve endings could not forget, and the spike of energy his body received via the cowboy boot raised the tide of recall even greater than it was earlier in the day.

He did not know just how unprotected he was as a child—his was an over-used sense of fight or flight—which he faced regularly— by the light of day—and by the large dark plains of his dreams at night.

112

He needed a leader—a father who demanded respect and forthrightness from him—in the form of effort and honesty. A leader would have made Mitchell stand up and face his fear and by doing so, feel less alone. A father, who was himself fathered well, would have given Mitchell the tools to realign what happened to him on this day—into an event that would serve him later in life as a man. He was to come home and cry, through both humiliation and pride, and show the leaders in his life a black eye and a bloody nose—as trophies in his effort to defend himself.

He wondered where the courage he had displayed with Brent had gone. Mitchell did not know that sticking up for himself was his right and duty. When the spike of brutality hit, he was to turn without fear, and with courage and rage return the blow as hard and as quickly as he could. The shock of the lunch-time incident reconnected who he was as the target of fists and spit—rather than the boy on the Hassayampa River who knew who he was under the light of the sun.

On this night he held only his emptied vessel of dignity, and the disgrace of his poverty-stricken home. As he lay on his bed in the cold back patio, he sank slowly into the middle parts of his dysfunctional family—into visionless and soundless submission.

On this night he would lose his rope to a different kind of life—he would push it out of sight and then forget where it was stowed, instead reaching for a joint. He would begin a life of absorption, making the words and thoughts of others the borders and boundaries of his soul. He would put under his thumb the thumbprints of all other life, screening it with the blue smoke of marijuana.

On this night he accepted the beatings he endured as a child as the mark of his leaderless life. He collapsed under the weight of nothing to sink his teeth into. His wings were clipped, and he found his rounded back embracing yet another toke of another joint, blowing the tell-tale smoke through the patio's screen.

A vision took him into the main room of the cabin to see his father drunk. Through Mitchell's own bloodshot eyes, he accepted his father's state as the vision of himself in the days to come.

He found his place on the family totem pole and accepted his position in his father's life as his own. Horrified angels and ecstatic demons looked on through the living room window as any hope of changing the course of men in his family was extinguished.

Mitchell's legs grew numb. He heard the *Tonight Show* theme song from the living room and woke from his staring into the unfocused high of the drug. He realized his father was gone and wondered if he was really there in the first place. He was alone in his thoughts. He heard Ed McMahon introduce Johnny Carson. Exhaustion pushed him into a fitful night of sleep.

In early November, the nights began to turn from cool to cold. Mitchell opened his eyes. The cold had waked him. The orange glow of the alarm clock presented the time as a secondary feature to its illumination—Mitchell found more comfort in its color than in the information it provided. He rolled over onto his back, and heard his sisters sleeping. He was no longer stoned.

The Milky Way could be seen through the patio screen, silhouetting the tops of ponderosa pine—his soul silhouetted by Lynn's face. These were the colors of his night: Lynn's brown eyes, the blue of midnight, and the face of an alarm clock. These—the familiar things of his life. But changes were taking hold. Gone was the magic of the past summer; hope had become numb; the wind had gone; the river could no longer be remembered. He took a few more hits of a half smoked joint.

Survival simply became something he did. He slept. He barely considered school, save Lynn. After talking to her on the neighbor's phone he would stop off at Huntington Beach Bob's and smoke or buy his grass.

He faltered. He learned how to slide by; to be less than ordinary; to blend into the dust of the day. Mitchell was in a maze of no return, where each turn only took him further away from not only an exit but a reason to exit.

He closed his eyes to the glow of the alarm clock. The orange light faded to other things. A tree appeared, ancient in its design of branch and leaf. Its shadow fell upon the face of a young boy. Around him yellow and blue mixed with the innocent tones of a boy's skin.

Mitchell was dreaming. The scene was of a young life unencumbered of dark, heavy, distant things. The boy was absorbed in his own daydream. He could smell the salt of innocence on his skin. It was a picture of how things could be or must be. His hands and his knees were in the air. His mind belonged to the grass, and the breeze, and nothing but the strength of the tree could get into the world of the daydreaming boy.

But the dream turned over. The blues and yellows in the light of the day became orange and red in the dark of night. The tree was lifeless. The boy was joyless. Everything was upside down including the boy. His hands and knees were now dug into the ground, and pain was flowing from every part of him. The salt on his skin burned. He could not see what was happening to him but knew something was. He had no words for it, no comprehension that such things, whatever they might be, were possible. He was shocked, as if stabbed over and over again.

Mitchell woke to a silent scream. He was drenched in sweat and completely exhausted. He had lost a fight, and his mind faded to black.

He got up and faced the window over his bed. He breathed deeply the night air and this rhythm calmed his mind. He reached for his secret box. Without turning on the light he found it and his lighter.

With the light of the Milky Way high overhead, Mitchell went out into the night. He lit a joint and smoked it. Inhaling deeply and exhaling slowly, he watched the trail of smoke disappear into the night.

For several minutes he sat in the easy chair of his marijuana high. It warmed his temples, and turned his thoughts back to the scene of a young boy under the shade of an ancient collection of branches and leaves.

Mitchell made his way back to his bed. He had not been missed. His sisters barely stirred. Their sleep was deep, or at least it appeared to be. He was alone again with the glow of his alarm clock.

He thought of Dalton's family—and of Presley's—of their homes across the street from one another, ninety miles south of where he lay—of the streetlight that glowed in front of both homes like a beacon of normalcy. The orange universe found in the face of the clock was Mitchell's normalcy, and it's mesmerizing warmth lulled him back to sleep.

≈⚬⚭

The next morning rose without the aid of a sunrise. Ada unlocked the back door; its click the signal for the children to come into the warmth of the cabin's main room. Dana had entered first and grabbed the day's gallon of milk out of the fridge. Groggily, Mitchell made his way to the breakfast table. Ada had left without saying goodbye, leaving the front door ajar, letting the cold of the morning into the cabin.

Emma and Dana ate quietly as Mitchell sat down at the table.

"Where did you go last night?" Dana asked.

"What were you dreaming about?" Emma added.

"Couldn't sleep," Mitchell said. "I had a bad dream."

"About what?" Emma asked.

"I don't remember," Mitchell said honestly, still fuzzy from the short night's sleep and the extra pot he smoked in the middle of the night.

"You smell funny," Dana said, looking over the top of her cereal boxes.

"Don't worry about it, okay, Dana," Mitchell retorted.

"You shouldn't be smoking that stuff," she said. "It'll make you go crazy."

"You don't know what you're talking about, Dana, so just shut up about it," Mitchell said.

Quiet returned to the table as the three hid from one another behind the several cereal boxes on the table. Each had built a fort around his bowl to hide his face and to read the entertaining material.

As long as he remained a member of the family breakfast table, under the roof of his father and mother, Mitchell would remain distant from himself, finding no laughter in the heart that he held as his own. The colors of his childhood faded with the potent aid of joints stashed in his secret box, which symbolized many things that remained veiled in his heart.

Chapter Twenty Six

TWO years had passed in Ponderosa Park. Mitchell had grown in size, as did his general attitudes toward the country's political and social upheaval. Resentment about living away from his friends in Phoenix had grown too. Mitchell lobbied daily for a move back to the old neighborhood, and a chance to play football with Dalton and Presley at Central High School, the reigning state champions.

Ada was ready. She missed a lover—a pathologist who had moved from Prescott back to Saint Joseph's Hospital in Phoenix. She was tired of the hard life in Prescott. The winters blew too long, the loneliness apparently too strong, and now the prospect of becoming a pathology assistant at Saint Joseph's Hospital was a reality. Before Mitchell would know it, he and his sisters would again be living on Orange Drive.

In the two years Mitchell had lived in the forest, writing letters had become a favorite pastime for him. He enjoyed the banter between his pen and his friend's, and enjoyed the anticipation created while waiting the arrival of return letters from them.

There was one sad thing about moving away from Prescott—leaving Lynn would be hard. He knew he could keep their love alive by writing to her. A promise was made by both to stay close and in love through the U.S. postal service.

It would be unkept.

The move was under way. Mitchell suddenly realized his loss. He walked out onto the edge of the porch and looked down at the rocky outcrop. A memory of the boy he'd become appeared as a phantom of the rocks below him. The ghostly image looked despondent—Mitchell perceived great longing in the image not to leave what he had found as a boy in the woods. In bitterness, Mitchell's twin-self turned away, climbing over the face of the rocky outcrop, out of sight, where he made his way to the road, cattle guard, and the waterhole beyond.

Mitchell was leaving something very intense behind, something that he had no idea was his to keep—to fight for—to protect—to hold for the rest of his life—his boyhood spirit—which now refused to leave the woods. Mitchell let him go.

He looked only at the days to come. Dalton was getting a car. The intoxicating notion of freedom found in a 1964 Ford Galaxie 500 was foremost on his mind.

In another U-Haul, and as a last trip through Prescott unfolded, a sad twist of providence was presented. Lynn waited for Mitchell on the corner where they first set eyes on one another. The truck stopped at the courthouse so Ada could visit a bank. Mitchell took the chance to say goodbye one more time. Lynn gave him a drawing she had made of the Earth. Inscribed in her handwriting was the phrase; "it's the only one we have." He looked longingly at the drawing and then at Lynn, noting her jet-black hair shining in the summer sun. Their goodbye embrace would be their last.

Mitchell turned away from Lynn, as tears streamed from the corners of her eyes. It was odd for Mitchell to see someone cry for him. He walked toward the truck and noted that it was smaller than the one they used moving into Prescott. They had become less of a family in the woods. He looked over to the courthouse steps and saw his spirit again begging Mitchell not to leave. The image looked at Mitchell with dismay, as if it knew what the future would hold for the boy in his movement toward manhood.

Mitchell could not look any longer. He was beyond what he had become or so he wanted to believe. He was more than the elements of the woods. He wanted the city life and the options and stimulants of the city lights. He wanted to scramble through the charge of teenage years with his teenaged friends. All three were about to turn sixteen and stood poised to use the new wings that driver's licenses offered them.

Mitchell's woodland spirit and his young girlfriend desperately reached out for him. Mitchell's sadness in saying goodbye to both melted. He turned away sharply, and with a large smile on his face, climbed into the U-haul truck for brighter, warmer times that would be found down the hill, in the Valley of the Sun.

Chapter Twenty Seven

"Beetle, wake up," Dalton said through a crack in Mitchell's bedroom window. On a hot August morning, cracking windows was a necessary step in cooling desert homes that used water coolers as a means for comfort.

"I can't believe you aren't out of bed yet," Presley stated. Mitchell rubbed his eyes and sat up, right into the blasting rays of a summer sunrise. "We gotta go," his two friends said in unison. "We are going to be late for the start of Hell Week."

Mitchell rushed out of bed, threw on his workout clothes, slammed down a bowl of cereal, and in five minutes was in the Galaxie with his buddies, headed south down Central Avenue from his new address on East Orange Drive in Windsor Square. Ada's new job and Sorber's paychecks meant that rent could be paid.

They faced a moment that haunted them all summer—Hell Week at Central High School, under coach Rich Lane, was steeped in a winning tradition based on the "old-school" ethics of self-sacrifice and team work.

Hell Week, also called "three-a-days," meant the players showed up three times a day for practice. The boys would be on the football field just after sunup, and would still be there after the sun had gone down, in the heat of the monsoon season, learning and relearning the basics of playing the game.

Hell week was hell! It was an intimate experience for every boy as each got to know his part in playing the game. They grew familiar with the smell of their sweat-soaked helmets, and what their bodies were made of in the blocking and tackling drills that started as soon as they stepped on the field. They learned the details of the field; how the grass grew and how freshly watered desert dirt smelled, and tasted, and how to pull both out of their skin and mouths when necessary. Bruises were a part of the experience, not remembering how they got any of them. Slow and stiff were their limbs in the morning at the start of each day's drills. Exhausted were their bodies at day's end, riding home in the Galaxie to dinner and to bed, using the last bit of energy to fall over and go to sleep until the alarm clock rang again the next day.

Hell Week gave the boys a sense of what the world would expect of them, providing leadership through example. The coach wanted one hundred and ten percent out of every player all the time. He wanted honesty and detailed attention paid to the rules of the game—courage in the face of fear—perseverance when bodies and minds would rather quit—loyalty paid to the team through team work, giving to the total effort of the team that which would have served the individual better. He wanted every player to use his noggin! Thinking everything through was the order of the day, and if you weren't "Johnny-on-the-spot" every minute of every practice, you paid the consequences by running the bleachers at the end of six hours of practice.

Football gave the boys more of the same character needed when they navigated the Hassayampa River—the experience of doing something beyond what they thought they could do—made them stronger. Going through it together was what Mitchell needed the most; to belong within the circle of his friends.

The game became Mitchell's life. It was made of boundaries and strict expectations in behavior and attitude, using the time-honored methods that fashioned the great football heroes he watched on television.

When each day was done, Mitchell walked with the broad shoulders of accomplishment. He held his head high with his friends, who also walked with the same sense of achievement. It was more important to know what they knew in their hearts about themselves than what the world thought of them. Their success in surviving Hell Week would sit quietly with them in the days and weeks to come, bringing camaraderie with every other team member.

Hell Week mustered from the boys a call to courage every time he was assigned to block or tackle one of the older, stronger monsters of the team, which consisted of many players returning from an undefeated season, and a state championship the year before. Mitchell was blown away by the seriousness of the older players, who would humiliate the younger players when they did not give their very best efforts, but would build them up again when they got it right in their seasoned eyes.

No one on the team thought of himself as football royalty. On the first practice of Hell Week Mitchell found out why. Coach Lane was angry at the write-ups in the local press about *last season's* accomplishments while at the same time extolling unearned accolades on *this season's* players, who had become state-wide sports media darlings.

"Bullshit," Lane ranted. "It's what we do today that matters. Don't let me hear anyone on this team brag about what happened last year. The only thing this team has going for it is how hard you practice here today. Right now I want to see you and you (pointing at Mitchell and Dalton) over here. Line up across from Segur and Abney. I want to see you two pummel these all-state offensive tackles. All-state my ass!"

Terrified, they lined up across from Segur and Abney (who, at age seventeen, were the size of college and pro offensive tackles). The tackles were pissed. Dalton and Mitchell strapped on their helmets and flew into position straight across from the giants. The two younger boys were warned not to be hotdogs—playing the drill straight with no fancy footwork.

Coach Lane was impressed with the younger boys' efforts in blocking the seasoned gridiron players, even though the younger players picked themselves up out of the grass, squashed like mashed potatoes at a Thanksgiving Day feast.

"That's the kind of play I want to see out of every one of you, especially the starters," Lane yelled. "If I don't see it, you'll be sittin' on the bench come game night, got it!"

ഏ൴

Hell Week had ended. The boys were walking side-by-side, back to the showers, when the giant feet of Segur and Abney came up behind them. "You guys ready to do this again on Monday?" Segur asked, in a voice that sounded like an old man.

"Yea, were ready," the trio said together.

"You did good out there this week for being punks," Abney said. "But Monday is another day. Don't let up; play as hard as you can."

"Okay," Mitchell said.

"We won't" said Presley.

They watched quietly as their heroes walked ahead of them. Looking at the backs of the all-state tackles, in awe and respect, the boys wanted very much to rise to their expectations. Segur and Abney, now silhouetted by the setting sun, knew that surviving Hell Week was just the beginning—the sophomores had a long to way to go before they proved themselves.

⊰⊱

The hot, wet, monsoon season moved south into Mexico. The undefeated football season marched on for Central High School, and football weather had finally arrived in the Valley of the Sun. It was mid-October, 1973, the Bobcats were eighteen and zero, a win streak that now spanned three seasons.

Coach Lane was beside himself—the media had worked the Arizona sports scene into a frenzy over his team. He could not say enough to the press about leaving his team alone. "Eighteen and zero means nothing this Friday night!" was the only quote the reporters got out of him—forbidding the team members to talk to the press.

There was much to talk about. Records were being set. The very finest high school football was unveiled as one memorable play rolled out after another—drama and alertly-played football impressed the sellout crowds. The wide-eyed young friends remained three feet ahead of the intoxicating wave called a *winning* team.

⊰⊱

Social unrest was found in the form of Central High student body protests, which spilled out onto Central Avenue. Signs were carried. Traffic was stopped. Arrests were made. As in many cities across the country, the students were upset about Nixon, abortion, equality, and wanted more than just a cease-fire in Vietnam.

Fads were a part of student body life too, including long hair and streaking (running naked through public places). The friends loved that the front office would play "Bennie and the Jets" and "Band on the Run" every day over the loud speakers. Listening to the songs made them feel a part of the social change. As their hair grew so did their interpretations of what social unrest meant.

In the midst of rioting and streaking, Mitchell found a job scooping ice cream at the Carnation Ice Cream Restaurant on weekends. His two pals and many other members of the team would often come into the store to ride him and the hat he wore, while begging for free ice cream.

Mitchell found a good routine that fall. The football team and its coaches gave him leadership and stability; the school's student body provided direction on how to feel about a changing world.

Sorber was still gone. Ada was still out there somewhere trying to maintain her hold on youth, and beauty. He did not notice either. His focus was football and friends. The songs of Cat Stevens, especially "Father and Son," which had made its way into his heart, no longer echoed within. There was no one home to give Mitchell advice. There was no one to tell his gridiron tales, something that was the focus of every other football family at Central High.

◈◈

On Monday morning, November 19th, Mitchell, Dalton, and Presley walked quickly toward Coach Lane's office window. The sun's rays had not yet risen above the reach of Camelback Mountain's shadow—casting apprehension in Mitchell's mind. It was cold. Mitchell kept his hands in his pockets, watching his breath turn to smoke as he walked next to his friends.

The highly anticipated playoff season was about to begin and the boys were anxious to know if they were suiting up for Wednesday night's game between the Central High Bobcats and their arch-rival, the Camelback High Spartans—a team that they had beaten earlier in the season.

Tribute for the team's success during the regular season continued. The local papers called Central High's kicking team the most prolific in the country, as Darrel Getman kicked punts in excess of seventy yards during the season and Leif Pitman's field goals sailed longer than most NFL place kickers, completing a fifty one yard field goal two weeks earlier and a fifty yard field goal during the last regular season game. The offensive execution, the defensive shutdown of opposing teams, the blocking, tackling, and the head's up play made the team invincible.

"Guys, can you believe we're going to suit up for the game," Dalton said, as he pointed to a list taped to Lane's office window. "Were going to play Camelback for the regional championship."

"Awesome," Mitchell replied as the butterflies immediately settled into the lower parts of his insides.

The team spent the next two days watching eight millimeter films of the Spartan's offensive and defensive plays. Coach Lane was thorough in his preparation for victory in the playoffs.

Wednesday morning arrived. Dalton, Mitchell and Presley arrived on campus earlier than usual to let themselves become absorbed in the excitement of what the winter day ahead would bring.

They wore their game jerseys all day, proud of their work on the field during the regular season, and grateful to Coach Lane for his recognition.

A pep rally was held in the school gymnasium. The starters were recognized as was the exceptional play of the special teams unit, known by Coach Lane as the "Kamikaze Squad," led by a nut named Pierce Gorman, who spent more time airborne on the field during play than he did on his feet, launching himself into opponents in a successful effort to build fear in the opposing team. There were Pete Maloney and Adam Bedeau, starters since their sophomore year, returning from the state championship team. The regular season highlights were too numerous to recount.

The rally ended on Coach Lane's usual cautionary note. A twenty two game winning streak, an endless list of achievement and effort, meant nothing compared to what was before them on that evening. He recited the Lord's Prayer before letting the students return to class.

The day unfolded slowly. Mitchell could not concentrate on studies or eating. The game took precedence over everything.

Game time had arrived. Hoy Stadium at Phoenix College was filled with eight thousand people who had come to watch this high school football game. The boys were overwhelmed by the attention the team got as they ran out on the field. The bright lights made them self-conscious of their movements. Warm-ups were done. Last minute coaching adjustments were made.

Central was set up to receive the first kickoff, and true to form the team saw Gorman become airborne, flying by the openings of their face masks, into the shoulder pads and headgear of an opposing player, knocking him to the ground and setting Central up to score a touchdown on its first possession of the night.

The boys looked up at the scoreboard and saw the score seven to zero, just as it was supposed to happen. Mitchell looked into the stands and saw a sea of faces, except two - his parents. He waved at Dalton's and Presley's parents, who were sitting together.

When he turned back toward the game, a subtle change in the momentum of the play had occurred. In a heartbeat, the impetus of play seemed to be a half step behind what it was just before scoring the first touchdown. The game slowed to a standstill at times. The score at the end of the half was Central ten, Camelback seven, on a Pitman forty-one yard field goal.

One more score was made that night—by Camelback. In a second half that rolled by in slow-motion—as if the team were lulled to sleep by its own successes—Central lost its bid for a second straight state championship, losing to Camelback fourteen to ten. Camelback would go on to win the state title—giving little consolation to a Central High School team that had elevated itself far above the norm during the regular season.

The boys rode a dark and sad bus back to the high school. The loss was hard to take. Watching the tears flow from the likes of Segur and Abney left an indelible mark on Mitchell. He'd never forget the sobs coming from under the jerseys of his gridiron heroes, who had pulled them over their heads in shame and defeat. Behind his heroes' heads, Mitchell saw the silhouette of Camelback Mountain standing tall above the diminishing city lights, feeling his own elusive spirit disappearing with them.

There was a solemn mood in Presley's house when the boys walked in. They were stoned to the tips of their senses and stunk like fast food. Abney, who was dating Presley's older sister Sarah, was there. She consoled him as best she could. He looked over at the sophomores coming into the house, stood up and told them that they need to get the trophy back next year and walked out into the back yard with his girlfriend.

Although they had taken the loss to heart earlier, all three friends put the loss in perspective as they came out of the locker room an hour earlier. Presley had said "I think we need to drown our sorrows by eating turkey all day long tomorrow." Thanksgiving dinner was on between one and three o'clock at each of the boy's homes. They planned on dining at all three tables.

"It was quite a ride, wasn't it, guys," Presley stated.

"I'm amazed by it," Mitchell said. "I will never forget running out onto the field tonight with the team defending a state title."

"The loss is hard to take," Dalton said. "I wish we would have beaten them tonight."

"It was like we got caught up in the glory of the moment rather than doing what we did so well all season," Mitchell said. "I waved at your parents, and when I turned back, something about the game's momentum had changed."

"Sorry your parents weren't there," Dalton said.

"I don't care," Mitchell said.

"It kinda sucks," Dalton said. "Did they know that it was a playoff game?"

"I doubt it," Mitchell said. "but it was nice to see your parents there."

They were tired. It was time to call it a night and get ready for football and turkey in the morning. Mitchell watched Presley walk into his house, leaving the front porch light on as Abney was still alone with Sarah in the back yard. Mitchell declined an offer by Dalton to drive him home. They said goodnight, and Dalton walked into his dark living room, closing the red front door tight behind him.

Mitchell stood alone under the street lamp for a moment, stoned and feeling okay. He raised the collar of his flannel jacket up around his neck and put his hands in his pockets, turned, and headed home. The street lamps caught Mitchell's imagination as he walked. They were tall and yellow and camouflaged by the aged growth of a neighborhood a half century old.

On Thanksgiving Eve, Mitchell realized again the model for living was found in friendship and felt gratitude. As he made his way west on Colter, then south onto Second Street, he saw the street sign for Orange Drive. He turned west on Orange but stopped in mid-step. He did an about face, and headed to his old address. He didn't know why. It was cold, it was late, yet the urge to see the home he lived in for so long as a boy was strong, and in a matter of ten minutes he was there. He stood facing it, asking why he kept coming back. He looked up to the cold winter sky and could not find an answer. He turned west, took a deep breath to let go of the fragmented memories, and walked briskly back to his home and a long, hard, well-earned sleep.

Chapter Twenty Eight

THE holidays came and went. Mitchell saw his days as a sophomore at Central High as a time to coast, leading him to conclude that time could be killed without consequence. The face of time showed itself to Mitchell in both the arrival and departure of its light on the day—this take on life wrapped as insulation around those things that were important only to him; self-service replaced duty to family. He continued to slip away from what small hold his family had on him.

Spring brought change. An announcement by his mom brought Mitchell's world to its knees. His father called from Mississippi. He got a job in Reno, Nevada, and they would be moving there when school ended.

Mitchell was stunned. The news swirled through him—the ground beneath his feet gave way, like a sinkhole, and he fell into a cavern of loss—the greatest being the momentum his young life had created as a member of a football team that required more from him than anything he had known.

Another U-Haul was parked in his driveway. Placing his belongings inside the truck disturbed him deeply. Presley and Dalton stood beside one another and waved goodbye as Mitchell watched in the rearview mirror what was familiar to him disappear. The noise on I-17 filled the cabin of the truck. *This is fucking bullshit,* Mitchell thought. Ada stopped at Dunkin Donuts but Mitchell refused to look at her. His heart was sick.

❧

The overnight stay at the Circus Circus in Las Vegas brought little optimism to Mitchell. On a slow walk through the massive arcade, he found it filled with the lives of families connected in a way Mitchell didn't understand. He walked through the lobby of the hotel, out onto the Las Vegas Strip. The desert had cooled, and the breeze blowing through Mitchell's hair lulled his eyes closed. He saw his life at Central High fading into memory and bitterness, that turned to moisture behind his eyelids. It stung him. A cab pulled up and parked on the curb behind Mitchell. The song "Blue," by Joni Mitchell, played on the cab's radio. The lyrics gave him a shelf on which to place his despair. Her voice faded as Mitchell turned toward the lobby, and the cool desert breeze, now a cold wind, encased his heart.

The quick stay in Vegas ended, and the long US 95 to Reno presented itself as the horizon of Mitchell's life. The truck rumbled north and west along the Nevada–California border. Cars sped passed the U-Haul. Mitchell was now familiar with governors on U-Haul carburetors, limiting the truck's ability to build up speed. The AM radio found nothing in the giant expanse of the Nevada desert, and its static was the perfect accompaniment to his view of the road ahead—a road that pulled him further away from those things he held dear.

Leaving Las Vegas eleven hours earlier, Mitchell rumbled the truck into Reno. Looking for an apartment on Harvard Way, he could not stop looking at the grand and intensely beautiful Sierra Nevada mountain range, realizing with surprise just how close he was to Lake Tahoe. He kept his eyes toward the snow-capped peaks longing to see what the setting sun saw on the other side of the crest of rock towering above him.

Reno was an odd place to Mitchell. It was known as a gambling and divorce town where one had all night to do both. It was stuck in its own adolescence, unsure what to do with its potential and its past. Self-acceptance would have done Reno good. Instead it seemed to choke on its own self-loathing—second guessing the course it had taken as it hitchhiked its way on the backs of short-term decisions with long-term consequences. "Welcome to Reno" the sign said and in graffiti below it were the words "Now go home." *Where have I seen that before?* Mitchell thought.

Reno represented his parent's lives to date. His dad would again find solace in the neighborhood bar where he would drink his beer, paid for by his uncanny luck at the quarter slots. His mom would find comfort in her Old Grand Dad iced tea—the numbness paid for by a suicide attempt two months after their arrival. Life had gotten the best of both of them, and together, in their pain, turned their hopeless shoulders to each new day.

Mitchell's attempts to reconcile his parents' actions would start on the 395, south of Reno, where he often saw a man walking the length of the highway, smiling and waving at every car that passed by. It would end on a giant rock that jutted out from the side of Mount Rose Highway. The rock was comfortable and held a commanding view of the alpine lake. On a whim he would find himself upon it writing letters to Arizona. He wrote about the raw, cold throw of the dice that moved him to the "Biggest Little City in the World."

On the rock Mitchell found a vision of his future while he quit his past. He quit football. He quit being a son and a brother. He smoked pot and worked at an A & W Restaurant, flipping burgers, biding his time by looking toward the day he would leave home. Then things would be better. Things would change. He would no longer be alone, and would suit up again to play the game he adored. He would quit the foggy hell that had become his parents' lives.

On the rock he fell in love with what would be—of the day when his life would rise above the wake of his family—he would never become anything like his parents—his angst was complete. He had cemented it to his feet and felt the pull of it as his legs hung over the edge of the rock.

The rock was home. The immovable impregnable rock was his floor, the three hundred and sixty degree views around the rock his window, the winter storms his ceiling, and the hope he found there his door. The time spent on the rock became the current of his life. On it his imagination was cultivated; he would consider things: his feet able to stand on their own, his hands able to make their way. He often found the light blue alpine sky above Lake Tahoe more comforting then the blankets he had long lain under in his home—stoking thought and daydream into words he knew would transform his world.

Yet another move was announced five short months later. His parents informed him that as soon as school was out, they would pack up everything into a U-Haul truck and move to the small northern Nevada community of Elko, at which time they would celebrate Christmas. On his rock high above the crystal clear water, Mitchell drew a deep breath and thought, *the bullshit continues—Bumfucky Egypt, here we come.*

The owner of the A&W in Reno knew the owner in Elko—a transfer was arranged. He went from flipping King burgers in Reno to flipping Papa burgers in Elko. He went from frozen nights in Reno to frigid nights in Elko; from the external hope of Lake Tahoe to the internal hope of what would be found in letters from his friends; the focus of his return from school each day.

Frigid was too mild a word to explain the cold, gray world of Elko. Ice was everywhere, old, dirty ice, the kind that was shoved once too often to the side of street or walkway by snow plow or howling wind. It was the town where a giant icicle fell from a third story balcony, piercing the leg of a passerby. Ada saw it when she was ordered, as a laboratory assistant at the local county hospital, to draw blood from the victim. She described the shaft of ice as sticking through the leg of the man like a compound bone fracture. Mitchell saw the icicle pierce his own existence, making each step in Elko laborious. The winter was long, and its grip on Elko would not break until the end of May.

Mitchell lived for his letters, both written and received. Presley and Dalton sent all manner of contraband and illicit humor to him; joints wrapped up in *Playboy* centerfolds, *Mad* magazines, self-portraits of their stoned mugs, and local sports write-ups came through the U.S. mail every day. Their descriptions of life on Oregon Avenue always made him smile. Mitchell was grateful.

The home in Elko would be the last home Mitchell would live in with his family. At too young an age he left. He took with him a final memory of his father, alone, under the midnight cast of a streetlight. There, his father's lit cigarette made a lonely arc from mouth to ash tray and back to mouth again, glowing red as the isolated and sad man inhaled another puff.

Of his mother, his last impression was of a woman angry beyond hope—her pathetic lot in life—to blame her every sad breath on Mitchell's father, damning what light there may have been in seeing something good in him. He said goodbye to a leaderless family beyond the help of a gunman or preacher, to what would have been his life's greatest teacher: that of sticking it out when it got tough. Instead he burned the bridge, taking the easy way out, postponing a lesson that would someday be learned the hard way.

The home in Elko was back to Arizona to finish high school, and played one more season of football with his friends. They graduated with several hundred dazed and confused 1976 bicentennial seniors. The fallout from the sixties and early seventies hung around many of them—unsure if trusting the establishment was the right thing to do.

They took a year off to figure out what their next moves would be, hanging out and having a good time on Oregon Avenue.

Decisions were made. College beckoned all of them. Presley would head south to Tucson and the University of Arizona, Dalton to Phoenix College, and Mitchell to Northern Arizona University in Flagstaff. The notion of a forest ranger fit him like the Hassayampa River on a hot alpine day.

Leaving for what they considered the adult life of college, the sobering thought of responsibility, as the antithesis of discarding time, hit them. They decided to throw themselves one last party. They did not know that "one last party" was really just the beginning of innumerable parties to come; that this one last party sent each boy into the life of men still drunk and stoned the next day.

College changed them. Trades were made, priorities reset, experiences had, and revelations unmasked, that would take each boy into manhood, far beyond their understanding. Social unrest and questioning authority would be replaced. Greed and self-service would contrast themselves in a favorable light over "live and let live." The expansion of mind, found in higher education, delivered them to the changing paradigms of previous generations, as the calamity and the beauty of living life, claimed them for its own design.

Chapter Twenty Nine

NOT wanting Sian to leave, Mitchell resumed the play of "That's The Way" and hoped to hear her voice again. Some moments passed. He heard Sian quietly speak his name.

"Mitchell?"

"Yes, Sian," he said.

"Why do you listen to songs over and over again?" she asked.

"I've done it all my life," he responded. "It is a meditation of sorts, and it's only done with certain songs. It's like pedaling a bike but for my ears. It gives me a sense of roots. I've had the stereo you hear for thirty years. The music it plays has a sound un-matched. I've grown accustomed to its quality, and together this stereo and the music heard from it have added immeasurable joy to my life. It's a view of the world for my ears. It's châteaubriand for the auditory nerves."

"Hmmm," Sian said, as she faced the woods, having no impulse but the peace that found her on Mitchell's porch. The trees swayed to the wind as it whistled through, mixed with the singing of guitar from the stereo.

With hands placed upon the front porch railing, baby fingers just inches apart, the two stood looking beyond the horizon. Collectively their eyes were set upon the distance of trees; their hearts set upon the space between their fingers; that gap filled with the love they shared for Red.

"Are the words written as the voice of a spirit speaking to a loved one still living?" Sian asked.

"They might be," Mitchell said. "I believe that, as it is with most everything, it's up to the beholder what things mean. For me it's the rhythm of the instruments being played in the song that captures my imagination and not necessarily the words, even though they prompt thoughts of sunlight and holding hands with the memory of love."

Mitchell closed his eyes, turning toward Sian, and without looking, picked her hand up from the railing. As the song repeated, Mitchell opened his eyes, took her other hand, and began to move to the rhythm. He smiled at Sian, encouraging her to join him—to dance with the gentle whistling wind around them. She obliged, and found the invitation to dance intoxicating. She let go of Mitchell and moved about the porch, eyes closed, with hands open to the breeze and to the music. Mitchell was stunned by her immediate meditation to the song and her body's interpretation of what she heard. *She dances just like Red.* Sian was mesmerizing. She put her hands over head and opened her fingers as if to create sounds in the breeze. He watched in wonder as her fingers fell through the air. She moved in time with the music, responding to it holistically, allowing the song to strum through her.

The composers must have intended the song to induce such responses. Its harmonious use of guitar, dulcimer, and tambourine had always, from his days as a boy along the Hassayampa, to his enchanted study of Sian's graceful interpretations before him, inspired Mitchell to contemplate his association to God. He was grateful to the songwriters for making his world a better place; feeling joy as he and Sian made "That's The Way," an unearthly experience—grateful for the lack of pain before him. *This* was God—*this* was the Holy Spirit—exiting off the Catholic altar—playing gentle air guitar with him and Red's daughter—abandoning all fear—breathing in the playful nature of the divine.

The song ended for the umpteenth time. Mitchell turned off the stereo. Sian stood motionless for a moment, understanding that Mitchell had been watching her, yet she felt oddly unencumbered by the thought.

He joined her again out on the front porch and bowed to her in gratitude for the dance. She curtsied to him in lighthearted acknowledgement. Together, arm in arm in a courtly gesture, the pair re-entered the home of their beloved.

As if in transition between musical notes, the peace presented itself to the desert. He listened.

He closed his eyes to feel the sensation of falling back, like slipping into a spiritual gap that cradled his hands and feet perfectly.

Illuminating his mind, the peace around him became visible through the lids of

his eyes, and the filter of oxygen-rich blood,
bending the reddish white glow from a warm
winter sun into an abstract of sincerity
unknown in his life before.

Chapter Thirty

THE early morning, high-altitude sun, blasted through the windows high above the classroom desks. Mitchell narrowed his eyes, letting them adjust to the brightness as he opened the large, heavy wooden door to go in.

Summer school at Northern Arizona University was underway. Mitchell was required to do well—as proof to the university's academic department that his sub-par effort throughout his high school career would not follow him to Flagstaff.

The room was sparsely populated; there were plenty of old wooden desks available. He moved toward the back of the classroom—which was of a time gone by—old in its architecture and amenities.

He kept his eyes to himself. He had left the party in Phoenix just hours before. His pals gave him a sendoff that included too much beer, pot, girls, and not enough sleep. Mitchell felt just a touch irresponsible for allowing his first day of college to begin with a stale buzz and no sleep.

Entering an aisle from the rear, he found a seat one over and one back from a woman with long blonde hair, who steadied a very odd item on her desk. He rubbed his eyes and looked hard, right into the blue eyes of a toddler, a girl, maybe one year old. She leaned over, camouflaging her own head of hair in her mother's, shielding her face from the unwanted attention Mitchell, and the entire class, gave to the unusual situation. The woman reached up, and instinctually patted the toddler's back.

While this exchange unfolded, a psychology professor walked into the room and wrote his name, class identification number, and date on the board. Mitchell watched him, registering his reaction when he turned to face his students and found the curious blonde-haired pair in the middle of his classroom.

"I couldn't find a sitter," the woman said without being asked. The professor's face turned red, revealing some private rumbling of emotion through his skin.

"Okay, but try to get it taken care of by Wednesday," he said.

"Sure, no problem," the woman said. "I'm new to the area and couldn't find the address of the sitter I spoke to yesterday. Sorry," she said, smiling at the professor, holding his gaze as he stared, confidently waiting for his reaction to her beauty.

Mitchell didn't notice the deeper exchange between the professor and the student. He was green when it came to the subtle innuendos between men and women. He had no idea how overwhelming, and treacherous female relationships could become. If he had, he would have taken a leery, sidelong glance at what was about to unfold before him.

The class identification number was PSY101—An Introduction to Psychology—a required course for forestry majors. Mitchell fancied himself as such. The idea of becoming a forest ranger sat well with him. He recalled treks up and down the Hassayampa River with the same friends that threw him the party just twelve hours earlier. He liked the snapshot of himself walking along country roads, smoking pot, and listening to a playful acoustic guitar as background to his notion. *Yes,* he thought, *Forestry would fit him like a glove.*

Mitchell was ten minutes into his daydream when he caught movement from the woman and her baby. She was reaching down for something in a big bag that occupied space next to her tanned legs. He took note of her thin arm and delicate fingers, which were suddenly covered by the long tresses of blonde hair that fell out of place from behind her.

He was stunned by the beauty in the cape of hair now draped across her chair. Every cell in his body responded to the sight. He looked up at the professor who had stopped in mid-sentence, and to other men in the room who had turned to watch. The professor stared at the sight of youth and innocence contrasted against the implications of a baby in her arms. While he did his best not to gawk, Mitchell's peripheral vision registered more movement from the pair.

This time, to Mitchell's disbelief, the woman extended her hand toward his desk. Without looking at him, she placed a Tootsie Roll on the corner. He peered slowly downward at the candy, and then around the room to find every eye watching.

The professor worked to regain his composure and control of the small class. Mitchell yawned, shaking his head to shed the funk that remained from the night before.

He eyed the candy, its wrapper, and where he would place the tip of his thumb to open it. He imagined placing the sweet chew in his mouth. He thought of the awkwardness of eating in a classroom, then remembered he was in college where the expectations of his younger student years no longer held. The Tootsie Roll would go a long way in dismantling the aftertaste of the previous night's party.

He looked at the woman's profile, now pointed in the general direction of the blackboard. Her delicate Scandinavian skin appeared to have enjoyed the morning sunlight, revealing the lightest blush on her forehead and cheeks. From his view of her lips and chin, Mitchell observed they would be easy to kiss.

Mitchell decided to accept the offer, and as he reached for the candy, the woman's hand reappeared from behind her flaxen drape, and snatched it back. Mitchell's hand was still moving when he realized it was no longer there. He looked up in time to see her lips curl into an enticing smile. She winked at her daughter as their foreheads leaned into one another, amused at their ability to so easily befuddle a fellow student.

Mitchell should have interpreted the placement of a sweet on his desk and its quick removal as a sign of things to come, but inexperience prevailed. He found the temptation placed and then removed fascinating.

A wild rush flowed through him. Looking around, he sensed every guy in the room was under the same feral charge. Gone was the thinness and funk of a mild hangover, as was the romantic notion of a forest ranger.

Regaining his poise, Mitchell listened as the professor introduced Pavlov's salivating dogs, not equating his own unwitting eagerness to succumb to unfamiliar instinct a perfect example for the professor's lesson. He looked up at the clock and realized only a dent was made in the class's scheduled time. He observed the changing position of sunlight in the room, and wondered what he would say to the playful woman when the class ended.

The hot Arizona sun roasted the morning away. Flagstaff, an alpine wonder for most of the year, was now the largest stand of dried bark and brown ponderosa pine needles in the world. The civil twilight began at 4:45 a.m. By the time psyche class was over the sun had been up for five hours, turning the cool morning into a bright, white day.

The first day of Psychology 101 finally ended. Mitchell left the old classroom, turning right for the nearest exit. To his dismay the blonde-haired woman turned left, and headed for an exit at the opposite end of the classroom's hallway.

Walking outside, he covered his eyes with a copy of the campus newspaper, noting a headline that warned of an increased risk of forest fires due to a lack of rain. The great stand of ponderosa pine that surrounded Flagstaff was suffering through one of the lightest winter precipitations on record, leaving the stand in a severe drought condition with the danger of fire extreme.

He watched the blonde walk out under the sun at the other end of the building. His disappointment continued. He had hoped for another offer of candy at the conclusion of the lecture on the reasons why dogs—and men—crave things. None came.

He looked away—to get his bearings and head back to his dorm room—needing to unpack and settle into a summer of study. He was curious to find out who his roommate was. Looking one more time in her direction, Mitchell noted the sun blasting its way into her hair. The mass of yellow made him squint. It was inspiring, as if it were the reason why flowers bloomed and butterflies floated, and he found that he could not resist the temptation to stare.

By now she was encircled by half the male student body of NAU, or so it seemed. The child in her arms discouraged none of them. She enjoyed the attention; like Brigitte Bardot walking down a street in an Italian seaside village.

Turning away, he focused his thoughts on which path to take back to his dorm—walking past her—giving up on the prospect of another Tootsie Roll.

"Hey Legs," she said to him.

He dismissed the comment as not being directed at him.

"Do you always wear shorts like that to class?" she asked, this time directly into his ear.

He looked at her with a mix of shyness and curiosity—his smile an answer to her question.

"I see," she continued, "care to walk me back to my apartment?" She pointed to a half circle of rock cottages that housed married students.

"Yeah," he stammered. "Sure, but I have to get back to Sechrist Hall to unpack before my next class . . ."

"That's right on the way," she said, interrupting his excuse with another offer of candy, as a conclusion to the flirting begun during class. Mitchell smiled and quickly took the candy from her, making sure not to fall prey again to her quick reflexes. She introduced herself as Chloe, and her daughter as Bae, who again dove for the concealment of her mother's hair.

As they walked toward her apartment, she gave a short history of her journey from Rapid City, South Dakota, and her rush to get out of town before her soon-to-be ex-husband found out she was leaving. Her story included her husband's discovery of her departure and his pursuit that ran from Rapid City, through the Black Hills, to the border of Wyoming. As Chloe told him of the chase, he pictured her hair waving in the wind as contrast to the hills behind her, all the while just beyond reach of the outstretched hands of the raving lunatic husband.

Chloe's introduction was done. They agreed to share another Tootsie Roll in psyche class. Mitchell said goodbye, tickling the top of Bae's hand with his index finger. Both Bae and her mom smiled at him—his fascination growing.

As he walked away, he heard her say, "Nice legs."

He shook his head in embarrassed delight while walking toward the eight story tower that was now his home. A minute or so passed when he turned back to get his bearings on exactly where Chloe lived, not realizing she was looking at him through her kitchen window.

His attraction to her was a 'first' for Mitchell. He had had girlfriends before, and had enjoyed intimate relationships with a handful of girls, but this was different. Her attention made him smolder inside. Her living alone brought up endless possibilities when and if the smoldering caught fire.

Mitchell made his way to the eighth floor and was relieved to see his window facing away from Cottage City toward a grave yard, and the San Francisco Peaks to the north. He had feared all he would do was look out the window toward Chloe's small rock home. Out the window, above the headstones, he saw a giant column of white smoke rising up from Mount Elden, east of town, and remembered the predictions of a dire forest fire season.

Chapter Thirty One

IN letters to his friends, Mitchell described the campus of Northern Arizona University. NAU was established in alpine ski country. Like most universities, its new expansions were built around the older lawns and malls bordered by buildings that displayed a romantic use of materials and design.

The trees were young and tall. The sky was blue and full of possibility. The summer sun shown down on the green lawns of the university, and Mitchell's red blood flowed through his veins as he stretched his days forward from a boy's life to a new man's world. He was young but a man nonetheless, and he enjoyed the rebirth of himself in this summer season.

Chloe and her daughter were not the only females to take note of Mitchell. His propensity for blondes flowed beyond the morning psyche class, out into the campus in general, and he found himself beside other girls with blonde hair, along the banks of Oak Creek and the canyon it cut south of Flagstaff. The girls were young, and like Mitchell, had found the freedom of college a conduit to capricious behavior—not all of it good—cutting class on a perfectly temperate Monday morning for Grasshopper Point north of Sedona, Arizona, happened often with the accompanying rebellious, youthful yawps echoing down Highway 89A.

Pot was the common chord between Mitchell and his summer girlfriends. Jalene in particular, liked to drive Mitchell to quiet spots along the canyon in her T-top blue Corvette. She would pull out her freshly rolled joints and show them to Mitchell. He would smile and together the two would get stoned, go for walks in the beautiful world of the ravine, and kiss.

Mitchell learned that he was not the typical pothead; he could study and earn high marks while stoned. Sharing his pot with girls and going for hikes in the geologic wonder that was Flagstaff abounded.

His summer progressed—as did his interest in Chloe. She was different than Jalene and the others. Chloe had a rich, experienced sense of the world that was new and exciting. He looked at Chloe as another one of his professors—teaching him many things, the most profound the art of having sex. The alluring siren was base and liked sex dirty, on the spot, and full of fantasies of every kind. Sex in cars, on tables, and in roadside rests were the experiences she gave, pulling from Mitchell sensations he did not know were possible.

The billow of smoke Mitchell saw on his first day of summer school, that became the Radio Fire on Mount Elden, was a symbol of their relationship. His passion burned out of control, leaving him exhausted and confused. Their relationship was strangely familiar to Mitchell, as if it had always been in his soul, as if it were an answer to a calling in a life previously lived. Chloe was already in his heart, in a way he could not explain. He had literally "fallen" in love, into a hole that would never fill, only level off for short periods of time. The birth of this love, revealing disconnected gaps in his life, gave Mitchell a keen sense of his own lack.

Yet this love for Chloe called for his understanding of humor, passion, and a spirited stretch toward excellence in his own efforts as a man. The two shared intellectual ideas that put his mind under new light and scrutiny. He entered into the delightful recognition of his own renaissance.

As the summer waned, change colored the landscape. Mitchell, Chloe, and Bae often took day trips to a place where nature logged an enchanted moment in her creation of the Coconino National Forest. Aptly named Hart Prairie, the yellow leaves, an azure ceiling, and white bark of the Aspen became the colors of the unofficial family they had become.

On these afternoons, John Denver's "I'd Rather be a Cowboy" and "Rocky Mountain High" found a perfect home in Hart Prairie, as if the songs had been written on the very spot Mitchell sat with the young woman and her daughter. The air, filtered by a rare stand of Bebb willows and aspen, was fragrant, at times icy, as fall weather could turn to winter storm in one heartbeat around the San Francisco Peaks.

At night, while a sitter watched Bae, Mitchell and Chloe would make their way to Granny's Closet, a restaurant and lounge near campus. On countless evenings the two would dance to songs that would become landmarks in Mitchell's life. Songs like "Wildfire" and "I Go Crazy," would stop his mind mid-track in the years to come, remembering his young heart in the embrace of the chaotic aura that was Chloe.

Winter did come. An ominous shadow followed him into the long, dark winter night; sorrow would be his consequence for taking Chloe into his inexperienced heart.

Chapter Thirty Two

MITCHELL moved in with Chloe, unofficially so. He kept his dorm room but was rarely there. Every waking and dreaming moment of his life was about Chloe and Bae. School had become unimportant. He had become a father of sorts and established a meaningful bond with the toddler.

Time alone was a thing of the past. He was either changing diapers or feeding Bae, chasing her mom around the bedroom, or was engaged in lively conversation about any topic. Chloe was serious about things that Mitchell never considered.

Gone were the nights hanging out with friends, as was smoking pot; Chloe would not have it around her daughter. Gone was his innocence about sex—depraved and base he had become. He no longer took it easy; Chloe burned her life at both ends of a candlestick and had now lit Mitchell's at both ends as well. He was absorbed into the world of another and was awestruck by the atmosphere she created in his life. He loved the incense she burned and the soft scented things that she wore. He was turned on by the way she enjoyed every material thing carnally. Everything made her have an orgasm, including Mitchell just looking at her. She was ablaze. Her ideas flowed molten in her blood, alive with a mind that questioned everything, including love. With Chloe, Mitchell was often left completely exhausted. Reckless in her pursuit of every desire—without regard for what or who got in her way—she thrust forward. This was Mitchell's life with her. These very things about Chloe not only watered his mind but burned his soul as well.

She broke his heart, often. Mitchell didn't understand why she would choose other men over him. Without the benefit of experience to help him navigate through her insatiable appetite for sex, he left her cottage apartment, and returned to the dorm room at Sechrist Hall.

He often thought back to the first day he saw her, surrounded by so many men, all interested in what her charms would give to them. When his trust was broken and his heart was on the mend, he would ask himself if throwing his hat into the ring was worth it. Just when the search for the answer would begin, he would see Chloe walking toward him with Bae in her arms and tears in her eyes. He would feel the soft things that remained new to him, and sense the world that she made for herself and her daughter. He would enter again into the turmoil of her world and find the things that remained precious to her.

His friends saw him change, too. Yet what they recognized in the way of change was not the same change Mitchell perceived, and this dichotomy brought on hard feelings between them. They saw Mitchell lose his focus on his goal of an education, abandoning it for Chloe's brand of love. Yet the experience of living his life with Chloe could never be explained, only lived from one moment to the next, as he saw her hair fall over his heart at dusk on the living room floor.

December had come. Chloe had painted a detailed portrait of her childhood home with a nut for a father who had embarrassed Chloe throughout her young life, by exploiting her youthful beauty to his adult male friends. He would make her parade herself in front of him and his friends scantily dressed, teasing her unmercifully about her skin, breasts, and hair. As Mitchell listened, he felt her shame in himself, aligning it with his own, in an attempt to understand her. He was drawn to the hurt in Chloe's past, and was connected to those times that reddened her face and scared her soul. Her pain became his.

This was the upset in his friends: Dalton and Presley saw Chloe for what she really was and often told Mitchell he was making a mistake. In her was the wretchedness and insatiability of the literary black widow; she was the woman whose beautiful and symmetrical web had ensnared their friend. Chloe saw in them their recognition of her, feigning Mitchell's warmth toward them, often complaining loudly that Dalton and Presley hated her for no apparent reason.

Not able to watch their friend "throw his life away," they stayed away, not visiting Mitchell in Flagstaff. Distances grew between them. It would be many years before they would see one another again.

Chloe often talked with longing of her time spent in San Diego, where Bae was born. "The holidays are beautiful there," she would often say to Mitchell.

"Why don't we go?" Mitchell said.

"You mean move to San Diego?" Chloe said with delight in her voice.

"No, not move, just visit," Mitchell explained.

"Oh, but you don't know what it's like to live in San Diego on the beach," Chloe said. "It is the most romantic place; the beaches are beautiful, and the restaurants are amazing."

Mitchell could see her keen interest in living there again. San Diego had been her home when her ex was stationed there as a sailor. Bae was born in the naval hospital.

Answering the spontaneity in her life and what simmered in the woman's veins, they headed west on Interstate Eight. With no money and no plans on how to make the move work, Chloe insisted they would find jobs and a place to live in no time, adding that they could live in the car if they had to.

The gypsy in Mitchell went for it. It took six weeks showering at the beach and sleeping in Balboa Park before they had enough money to move into an apartment in North Park, nowhere near the beach. They worked on making their Felton Street apartment a home. Chloe got a job at the Little America Westgate Hotel, in the Plaza Bar, as a cocktail waitress, and Mitchell as a waiter at the Sheraton Harbor Island Hotel, in the Portola Restaurant.

The makeshift family seemed happy to Mitchell. They enjoyed the beaches when they could and made Fat City, a restaurant near the wharf, the favorite place to eat on their days off. Underneath the contentment that Mitchell thought he saw in Chloe, however, was not contentment at all. The Plaza Bar, located off a side entrance into the hotel's main lobby, had a den-like feel to it, and in this lair, Chloe spun a different deceit each night she worked. Patrons and performers of the nearby Old Globe Theater found themselves mesmerized by Chloe's web of glittering blonde hair. Singers with great voices and millionaires with thick wallets were caught by Chloe, and under her beguiling spell, were devoured by her.

❧

Mitchell, Chloe, and Bae were enjoying lunch together at Fat City on a rare day off. While eating, a suited older man stopped at their table, alarming Mitchell by stooping over to have a hushed conversation with Chloe, engaging her in an all too intimate way.

The stranger stood too close. Chloe noticed Mitchell's face questioning who the suited man was. She ignored him. Her flirtatious responses and giggling told Mitchell everything he needed or wanted to know. Whether he was a doctor, a lawyer, an architect, or simply her boss at the Westgate Hotel, he, too, was alarmed by the presence of, what was to him, another man in Chloe's life. She was in her element however, enjoying the confrontational energy from two men, and privately hoped a fist-fight over her would ensue.

Both Mitchell and the suit looked at Bae, who knew that the scene in front of her was not a good one. She could see the trouble on Mitchell's face—who she considered now to be her father. She began to cry, which forced the suit to leave. Mitchell watched him exit, ordering the valet to fetch his Porsche, parked nearby.

Dark rage descended on Mitchell; his jealousy and wretched heartbreak spilled out when he knocked a glass of water off the table purposefully.

"Who is he," Mitchell demanded.

Chloe went for his exposed heart. "What? Does it bother you that he drive's a Porsche?" Chloe asked curtly, staring at him with disdain for what was to her a pitiful display of envy. She despised Mitchell for it. "Or is it because, unlike you, he's hung like a horse?"

The question drifted slowly through the air, floating above Mitchell like a storm cloud. Every patron in the restaurant heard the rant, turned toward Chloe, then to Mitchell, waiting for his response.

The storm came; lightning pierced him; thunderous humiliation smote Mitchell and he began to feel his naked truth sink in—a snake from Eden had pulled the fig leaf from him. He turned red with shame, drenching him to the bone.

It was true then, Mitchell thought. *I'm not hung like a horse; didn't I hear, as a child, my mother burst out such a statement at my father in one of their drunken late night battles; hadn't Chloe told me that she thought my penis was perfect for her; did Bae understand what her mother had blurted out?; am I not enough for her?; why can't I get that through my head?; how could she talk to me this way?; I love her; I need Chloe.*

As the torturous self-talk continued, he slid out of his chair, stood up, thought he heard Chloe spewing more obscenities in his general direction, and walked out of the restaurant's main hall, looking back once at Chloe—her countenance riddled with contempt.

He entered the men's bathroom, rushing into a stall, shutting the door as quickly as he could behind him. His breath was shallow, dizziness set in, compelling him to sit. His guts turned—hands shook—sweat filled the pores on his forehead.

He stood up slowly, still shaking, still feeling the rot of words take him through dark tunnels within. He unbelted his pants and let them fall to the floor. He slid his underwear slowly around his knees and in complete self-scorn he looked at his penis. He put his hand around it, squeezing it as hard as he could, hating it—hating the truth that was his life; he was not worth what he thought he was.

For a long period of time Mitchell was too mortified to move. Facing the restaurant patrons would be hard but seeing Chloe's face would be harder—she had enjoyed watching Mitchell succumb to his deep-seated, and until now, unrealized inadequacies.

Trapped in the bathroom stall, walled in by his disabled mind, breathing heavily, he felt the fracturing of abuse renew the paralyzing hold it had on him. With eyes vaguely focused on the stall door in front of him, Mitchell beheld a stick man coming toward him from the many indentations and lines of washed graffiti, saying clearly: *this is what you deserve—yes, this cold, harsh reality of your life—to your future goes her darkness —upon you, her words—in you, her scorn—to you, her belittlement— this is all your life is worth—to your fate, her unfaithfulness—to your dreams, her wickedness—it is all yours to own—take it—keep it—all of it, in your quiet, miserable heart and never, ever let it go.*

Crossly, into Mitchell's eyes, the stick man peered. Coming close enough for Mitchell to touch, it lunged forward, thrashing at Mitchell's face, then writhing into his skin. Into Mitchell's mind it went, coating his nerves, and lining his veins with self-loathing.

Snapping his head from side to side, Mitchell connected to the instinctual insulation found in an abused dog. And like a dog he started to heave. Over and over again his abdomen constricted then released. The urge to vomit rose up, overwhelming him—he faced the toilet, and released the horror of the stick man, and shame built upon more shame.

Time had passed. He had pulled up his pants, and fastened his belt, but sat back on the toilet seat—waiting—for what he was no longer sure. Without the grace of a decision about what he would do with Chloe, he rose from his position in the stall and headed out into the restaurant.

Chloe and Bae were gone, as were most of the patrons. The lunch rush had quieted down. He was relieved. He left the restaurant by foot, and headed toward the boardwalks around downtown San Diego's wharf.

Without notice of passersby, his hands in his pockets, Mitchell's mind began its drift away from any thought of the bathroom stall. The dismantling of his life as he lived it continued its form. Like any good dog he was already forgetting the vile of her words—thinking of their home—missing them—hoping they were there.

Chloe's devouring of Mitchell persisted. But like all who agree, knowingly or not, to live in such a state, hope for a better day remained. It was a hope born of the confusion Mitchell dealt with as Bae's father. A hope found in his empathetic understanding of Chloe's childhood, as one kicked dog might see another. Both wanted to be loved—even if, for Mitchell, that love came through the horrifying justifications that somehow Chloe's words and actions—no different than her breaking his bones, and pulling them through his skin—were forgivable.

He had arrived by bus to the apartment complex, and stood in the small garden walkway to his front door. She appeared, rushed toward him, tears flowing freely, in what was always, to Mitchell, a genuine display of remorse. She threw her arms around him, pleading for him to take her back, exclaiming how sorry she was.

He did.

Later, in bed, as he lie next to her, the words she repeated at the front door played over and over again. *She said she was sorry* echoed through him just before sleep would take him into a dreamless night—on a bed filled with her flowing hair, soft things, and compelling scents—in a small apartment on Felton Street.

Chapter Thirty Three

"I'VE been thinking about the bloody sock prints you found in your research at Sharlot Hall Museum, Sian," Mitchell said, as he sat down in her station at the Dinner Bell. Other patrons looked at him, alarmed that he would brazenly discuss evidence revealed during his trial.

Mitchell noticed Sian looking around the room to see who might have heard him say such a thing. "I'm sorry for speaking so plainly, Sian," he said. "I don't mean to embarrass you."

"It's not so much that, Mitchell, as it is something private between you and me," Sian said. "It's no ones business what we talk about, okay?" she said, gingerly.

"Of course, Sian, I get it," Mitchell said in an understanding tone.

When Sian had completed another breakfast rush, she walked over to Mitchell's table and sat down. By now, regulars at the Dinner Bell had grown accustomed to Sian's kindness to the man who had killed the killer; the loner who appeared from behind the steering wheel of an old, rusted, barely red, *F-100*.

"I like to maintain a private profile here," Sian said. "No one needs to know me as anything more than a plate of scrambled eggs and a cup of coffee."

"I understand," Mitchell said. "I've got no use for most people, Sian, save a childhood friend or two and now you."

Sian listened thoughtfully to Mitchell's words. "Why are you and I such recluses?" she asked.

"Sian, I know the world as a beautiful place," he said, "its people who tarnish it. I've got no time for politics, religion, gossip, and other such nonsense. I know what I know and need nothing now from humankind. I am more or less content, and I will always have my wife to thank for that."

Some of the customers overheard Mitchell refer to his wife. A minuscule percentage thought what he said was insightful; the rest shook their mystified heads, shunning him.

"I'm of the same mind," Sian said quietly. "I too have little use for people. I'm not able to trust or to make friends. Let's not talk here. I'm finished at two. If you are not doing anything today, why not meet me at the courthouse and we can talk more."

The request took Mitchell back to his youth, when he had met Lynn there. Quickly her address and old telephone number filed through his mind and while doing so he answered Sian with an absent-minded "okay."

Mitchell finished his meal and headed out into a bright, clement spring morning. The town was busy being itself minus the tourists, who for the most part, make Prescott a destination only on weekends. Facing the street, Mitchell turned right and walked slowly up a small hill to the corner where the Hotel Saint Michael stood. The courthouse square appeared larger than life across the street.

He stared at it. Townspeople reacted to his presence in the exact fashion found inside the Dinner Bell, with a lopsided mix of fear more than deference.

He remembered Lynn. She had long ago moved out to Chino Valley, searching for solace where she could find it. He recalled her saying hello to him at the conclusion of his trial, her eyes both happy and sad for him; happy that he was acquitted—sad that such a cruel twist of fate would bring them together again on the courthouse steps.

The light changed and Mitchell made his way to the courthouse lawns. He looked down the cement-lined walkways and tall trees renewed with fresh green leaves. He sat on a piece of grass on the back side of the courthouse, furthest away from the hustling and bustling corner of the Saint Michael, and leaned against an elm. The PJHS football field could easily be seen. He crossed his legs, closed his eyes, and let the childhood mechanism of unseen things blend into random themes—filtering out the leering population of Prescott.

Mitchell fell asleep; the breeze and bright sun were too much. His last thoughts were about digging his cleats into the banks of Granite Creek during football drills, charging up the side only to turn and run down again. Such thoughts turned to mild dreams of the four seasons as the elm took over the hidden parts of Mitchell's mind.

Some time had passed when he felt Sian's presence. She was leaning against the same tree, facing the courthouse. He opened his eyes, stretched his back, and was delighted to find his friend there with him.

"How'd the day go for you?" Mitchell asked.

"It went good," Sian said. "Your appearance is always good for breaking up the monotony of the shift."

"Oh, yeah?" Mitchell said sideways toward her.

"Yeah," she said. "You sure do give them something to talk about."

"Whatever you say, Sian," Mitchell said playfully.

"You do," Sian said convincingly. "Everyone is in awe of you, be it fear or admiration, including the thugs you chased away—the ones who tormented that old woman a while back. Zac is looking at us right now—the one who runs around in filthy socks," she said, nodding deliberately toward the steps.

Mitchell stared back at the group of boys. Two of them turned away, but Zac held Mitchell's gaze. Mitchell quickly yelled at them, wildly flailing his arms about. He made the first two bolt. Not Zac, who walked lazily down the courthouse stairs—dirty socks falling half way off his feet—then in the direction of his fleeing friends. This disregard for Mitchell unsettled him, and a warning sounded clearly within. He looked down at Sian—he now understood that Zac not only knew Mitchell and Sian but also knew that Mitchell and Sian were known to one another.

At that moment Zac turned sharply, gazing hard at Mitchell, and without taking his eyes off him, spit. His friends grabbed him by the arms saying, "Are you crazy, don't you remember what he did?" They hauled him off around the far end of the courthouse.

Mitchell flashed back, remembering the wickedness that overcame him. Just as quickly he let the flashes go, and turned back toward Sian—who had been studying him intently.

She took a deep breath when her eyes found Mitchell's in a relatively calm state. He returned to his spot leaning against the tree, looking at his childhood football field. Sian sat close to him. Taking his turn at a deep breath, Mitchell stated quietly "It's still here."

"I know," Sian said.

"I didn't kill it," Mitchell said. "It just travelled through that night to another home, now in that boy. We need to be diligent from here on out, or move," expressing his assessment of what was to him a serious threat to their safety. "I'm not going to let that evil take anything from me again."

The words Sian heard surprised her. He wanted to protect her, as if she were his family. She was thankful to him for everything that the statement meant and said quietly in return, "Thank you Mitchell."

Mitchell took another deep breath and another look around their surroundings, deciding they were safe for the time being. "Sian, its time you move out to the cabin and stay with me for awhile. Take the spare bedroom behind the kitchen—I cleaned it out—it's all ready for you."

Sian leaned her head against the elm in contemplation. "Let me think about it for a couple more days, okay, Mitchell?" she said.

"Fair enough," Mitchell said as he eyed each corner of the courthouse, looking for Zac's reappearance. "Don't wait too long, Sian," he said.

"I'm grateful," Sian said.

They got up together. Both stretched, putting their hands on the tall elm tree to steady themselves, then walked away: Sian toward her apartment above the record store, and Mitchell toward his old truck parked near the Dinner Bell. Waving goodbye, each walked a bit then simultaneously checked on each other's progress, smiling.

Mitchell perused the courthouse, looking for Zac. He found him sitting near the courthouse, deep in conversation with his pals, not noticing Mitchell strolling along Whiskey Row. Sian was no longer seen. Finding his truck, he noticed Thumb Butte throwing a long shadow over the town as the sun set behind it.

The tall Saguaro contrasted daylight and shadow across the Sea Man's face, making him keenly aware that the very simplest of life's moments were found between the changes of the day—where peace maintained its quiet domain.

Chapter Thirty Four

MITCHELL rested comfortably on his forearms, spread out on the living room floor, reading his favorite novel, *Atlas Shrugged*.

With Chloe at work on a rare morning shift at the Plaza and Bae down for a nap, Mitchell had gone out onto his apartment balcony on a perfect San Diego morning and smoked a joint. His old habit had returned, underground, however. Chloe remained adamant about its non-use around her daughter. Mitchell didn't care about Chloe's feelings regarding pot, and was not convinced on this morning that working as a waitress at the Plaza Bar was what she was currently doing.

When Chloe was not present, Mitchell worked on his self-assessment of being a functional pothead. He participated in his life: he worked hard as a waiter, he read much, and was good to Bae.

Good and stoned, Mitchell made his way back into the quiet apartment, grabbed the hardcover edition of the aforementioned book, and began reading more about the best within. Moments passed as great things were delivered at the hands of grand individuals in a story built upon the foundations of the great characteristics of life. Hard work and self-knowledge, as portrayed in the book, impressed Mitchell, and he fancied himself in possession of such characteristics.

Mitchell heard one of his favorite sounds high overhead; the drone of a small, single-engine airplane, and its light hum taking him back to the early morning summers as a child on Orange Drive. He continued to read as the great lives in the story brought the world to a standstill. He closed his eyes for a moment, letting the serenity and smell of a rare ocean breeze in North Park relax him further into the pot-induced high.

The airplane hum stopped suddenly. Mitchell took only a small note of it and kept reading. Ten seconds passed, maybe ten minutes; he couldn't be sure. Suddenly a fierce, ripping thud—a rattling roll so ferocious—a cracking resonance so foreign, besieged his body. Each window in the apartment exploded, first out, then into the apartment, creating a gale of marble-sized glass blowing past Mitchell's face. The concussion from the blast, still unrecognized in Mitchell's mind, threw him against the living room wall—the heavy book was drilled into the drywall above him. Distant indiscernible screams were heard through the now empty window frames. Much closer were horrifying cries for help. Mitchell remained motionless. The book fell from its notch in the wall above, hitting him in the head, forcing him out of the shock that had encased him.

The silence from Bae's room was deafening. Pushing himself up, he rushed into the toddler's room to find glass everywhere. He looked at the little girl, whose eyes were open but frozen in the mystery of what she just felt. There was no blood to be found on either. He thought; *how is this possible?*

They had survived something. He picked her up and went outside, careful not to step on shattered glass or walk into parts of the apartment complex that may have shaken loose in the explosion. They made it to the street, already filling with neighbors, all struggling to make sense of the blast.

An eyewitness related that he had seen a small single engine airplane crash into a passenger jet. Horrified, the witness watched both drop out of the sky, slamming into the neighborhood just two rows of rooftops over.

Dozens of ambulances converged on the area. Still high, the facts of what happened just moments before and only one hundred feet away brought Mitchell to his knees. There was no way for him to know as he stood hand in hand with Bae that one hundred and forty-four souls had lost their lives in an instant, leaving thousands more reaching beyond the terror of the fiery crash into their own shadowy understanding of mortality.

It was a catastrophic reference point, and Mitchell struggled to make the devastation personal. He knew that he had to try. One hundred and forty-four shredded bodies became the collective voice of what could have been. He looked up, following the pillar of smoke as it rose over North Park. With Bae now secured tightly in his arms, he envisioned souls, made from sticks, rising into the sky, repeating their last thoughts over and over. *Dad, I love you. Son, I love you. Please come back. Please don't go.* Mitchell saw lives leave their routines. There was work undone, now ascending upward with the smoke. There were words unsaid, now elevated beyond their usefulness. He closed his eyes and found one lone soul, its light resonating, asking Mitchell why he had to die. Mitchell shook his head and said out loud, "I don't know."

The lesson Mitchell took from these moments, while flashing lights and smoke and bewilderment brought Bae to tears, was that life can be over before it starts, especially if one doesn't take care to share what and who he was.

The aftermath of PSA Flight 182—the black swath cut through San Diego neighborhood by the exploding jet, lingered on. As did a collective dialogue between friends and neighbors about what the disaster meant to each of them. For Mitchell, there was a ritualistic evening drive-by on his way home from work. For months he would stare at the giant scar as it struggled to heal. *Life answers its own call regardless of what is hoped or feared,* he thought, *marching toward the unknown moments that were just ahead.*

For Chloe and Mitchell, the crash, and its column of smoke rising above San Diego, which mirrored the column of smoke out of Mount Elden's Radio Fire in Flagstaff—became the bookends of their relationship.

If Mitchell were to pick a point that marked the beginning of his adult life, it would be the PSA jet crash. He had witnessed both the calm, and calamity of life, on that September morning in North Park in 1978. Life was short. He decided then and there not to follow any predetermined outline. He would resist the coat and tie corporate world, by anti-establishing himself, ignoring icons that he was expected to embrace. He wanted the beach and the mountains as home with work that required running shoes rather than dress shoes—considering himself capable of eliminating ties to his parents' generational footsteps—choosing instead the observations of a full moon or a rising sun as indications of a life well lived.

Leaving Chloe and Bae, Mitchell moved to a small apartment in Pacific Beach—furthering his embrace of the marijuana culture—believing fully that smoking pot was a positive experience—an enlightened ritual—shared by many friends of like mind. He believed that because he remained physically, emotionally, and spiritually active, even though high, that smoking pot was an asset to his regard of himself. He liked the label "pothead."

The Portola Restaurant where he waited tables was a high-end eatery located on the harbor. Getting to work was by the kindness of his newly purchased, 1955 *Ford F-100*. Waiting on tables was anti-nine-to-five. He embraced the hours of five to ten, with social events following to bolster his night-owl life. Paradoxically, he adopted the higher ideals found in *Atlas Shrugged,* finding much pride in doing the very best he could as a waiter.

It was the evening social events that originally led Mitchell to the beach. The sound of the crashing surf and the beach culture became his new life, finding old world hippies and fourth-generation surfers as sounding boards for his thoughts and ideas.

God and religion were often discussed—anything organized was a negative. To Mitchell, God was an organization called the Catholic Church, which had holes in its logic, putting all that God stood for first—in a long line of hypocrisies Mitchell had suffered from his parents' lives.

The door of his Pacific Beach apartment opened to what Mitchell considered now to be God—a view of the sun setting into the Pacific Ocean. On his nights off Mitchell found himself sitting on his balcony, with a joint and a conversation, letting the deionized sea breeze blow over him, mesmerized by the sun setting into the ocean. Viewing the sunset was easy, and he wanted to get to know the sunset—where he found God—in every way he could.

The apartment was located on Santa Barbara Place. The darker recesses of his mind remained hostage to all things Chloe, but the beach helped. The boardwalk, bikinis, ocean-borne breezes, and the daily buzz all contributed to keep him out of dark places—the special ambiance of beach life was regarded as an exceptional way to live—and gratitude abounded.

His truck added to that special feeling of a bohemian lifestyle. He liked what the old *F-100* said about him to the rest of the world: *I could give a shit what you think of me.* He might as well put it on a sticker and paste it to the rusted bumper. He was only one of thousands who felt as he did. Life on the beach had nothing to do with pretension. You were what you were, and Mitchell devoured that notion, becoming the very essence of how he interacted with the world.

It was during this time of his life that Mitchell grew into his own regarding the fairer sex. He had become familiar with the subtle language of lust; Chloe had taught him well—and although Mitchell did have the likes of Chloe as a teacher, Mitchell would not become her. At heart were the makings of another kind of person; a man that he would not recognize for years to come—there—but hidden by columns of smoke that had risen often in his short life.

Chapter Thirty Five

"YOU'VE seen me a hundred times a day, Sian, out there in the world," Mitchell said, in answer to a question regarding who he was before he met her mom. The two sat on the front porch of Mitchell's cabin. "I was like a three-legged dog just trying to get through another day as everything ugly in human nature. I was a liar. I stole. I was unfaithful and self-serving and I limped through life because of it. I also looked for and found people just like me to bond with. I always took the easy way out and then burned that bridge after crossing it. I invested in the moment ahead and never anything beyond that."

"Don't you kinda live that way now?" Sian asked.

"Yes, but now I'm not hurting anyone in the process of living my life," Mitchell said.

"You must have hidden yourself away from the world before you met my mother," Sian said. "I surely can't see you being any other way than you are now."

"How's that, a tortured soul?" Mitchell laughed.

"No," said Sian. "You must have been you all along."

"Red said that time and again, Sian," Mitchell said. "I would tell her that if it were not for her love and God's grace I would have been long dead. She would respond by assuring me that her unconditional love had watered what rested dormant in my soul. I have always been me, just not loved without condition. As I look back at those I've loved, it has always been so. Each wanted to change me into their particular vision of me, and I'd let them. With Red, I was told that I was a good man just the way I was."

Mitchell thought for a while then said, "I wasn't always like that. I had times when I was younger that felt right, I knew who I was and had a warm affinity for myself, but those times were only had when I was alone. Whenever I was in a relationship, my heart would sour somehow and I'd let go of the warmth and the belief that I was okay."

Sian looked at him as if she were looking at herself and knew of those moments he described.

"What makes a heart go sour, Mitchell?" she asked. "We all start out with the same prospects, right? I mean at least we all start out with a clean slate."

"You know what sours a heart, Sian?" Mitchell said. "It's the cruelty, unintended or otherwise, from others that sets each and every one of us up for that rough journey to enlightenment. Some of us make it. Some don't.

"I've given this some thought, Sian," Mitchell said. "I look back at the breaks in my heart and now realize that had it not been for those pains, I would not be the person who stands before you right now. We all have a will to decide what to do with inequity. Will it empower us or embitter us? Do we forgive our unpaid sums or hang on to those very things that hold us back from living today? This world, on every level, reacts to our wake on a grand scale. As a child I may have suffered the abuse from family only reacting to a wake set in motion a thousand years ago. The trick is to stop the wake's ability to play out in my day to day life. That three-legged dog I mentioned earlier was the end product of such a wake. Your mom's wake changed that three-legged dog into a man worthy of her respect, and I hope to help her wake continue its course through the current of this expanding universe. One way I'd like to do this is to insist on your moving out to our cabin right away. She would have it no other way if she were still here. You belong under your mother's roof even if it is for a short while. I don't like you being in town by yourself now that Zac has seen us together."

"Okay, Mitchell," Sian said. "I'll come. When?"

"What are the terms of your lease?" Mitchell asked.

"Month to month," she said.

"Let's start packing; give your land lord notice," Mitchell said.

"He'll ask for thirty days," Sian said.

"I'll give him notice for the end of this month, you'll be moving out, and if he's got a beef, he can come and see me about it," Mitchell said. "I think he'll be okay with this."

"I think so, too, Mitchell," Sian said, feeling strange as the notion of someone looking out for her wellbeing trickled in.

She looked at Mitchell with kindness in her eyes.

"Your mother's wake," Mitchell stated.

"My mother's wake," Sian echoed.

❧❦

Your mother's love . . . a mother's love . . . your mother's love . . .
Mitchell felt his foot twitch. Suddenly it jerked up and kicked his
coffee table, startling him out of a sound sleep. Hemingway's *The Old
Man and The Sea* had fallen to the floor. The fire had died; the sun had
long set, and Mitchell heard said again the words—*your mother's love . . .
a mother's love . . . your mother's love.*

His mind was awash in thought. "Whose mother?" Mitchell
spoke out, as he looked at the cover of his paperback book.
"Hemingway's or the Old Man's?" he asked out loud, then at once
recalled the dream which shook his foot.

"Red and Sian," his said. "Red and Sian."

> *The Sea Man took note of how the
> winter sun had furthered the textures and
> contrasts of all living things. He was a part of
> something perfect and beautiful. He
> remembered her.*

Chapter Thirty Six

LIVING in Pacific Beach had its own brand of religion and ritual, set up by the cycle of sunshine and moonlight lapping over the tops of waves. This ritual helped to lighten Mitchell's load—his heart still reconciling the broken trust of the past. Standing alone on the boardwalk one evening, Mitchell understood what the waves provided for his and countless other lives. *The waves are making the world a better place,* he thought. *They are a reminder of what is and what isn't, and the breath I get to take in between.*

⋰⋱

At work on any Saturday night, Mitchell found himself engaged in lively conversation with people from all walks of life—but only after his guests were able to put either food or drink in their bellies.

Hungry people generally behaved badly. They had no patience when waiting for food. Seconds seem like hours in the expectation of the three-minute egg. Hungry people considered no one, least of all their waiter. "Bring me anything handy, now" they demanded, "anything that isn't tied down."

Despite this behavior, Mitchell took some pride in his ability to calm them, finding satisfaction in facilitating the diverse needs of each table, resulting in a nice percentage of the bill as his tip.

It was more than just money, though. It was about building relationships. After their stomachs were satisfied, most of Mitchell's guests were kind, generous in thought, and over time became "regulars" of his.

Waiting on tables gave Mitchell the highest degree of people skills. He became an expert at reading the subtle gestures of face and hand. They would bring every imaginable problem to the table, putting them on the edge of their service plates like chewing gum, fully expecting to pop them back into their mouths when done. If they did not let their problems dissipate by the end of the main course, Mitchell's sense of humor and heart for service insured that by desert, they would.

Saturday nights in the Portola saw many menu items prepared tableside. Mitchell delighted his guests by making culinary delights to their specific orders. He never said "no." If, in his high-end eatery, they requested hot dogs, corn, and baked beans, he got it for them. Teamwork and anticipation of problems were also demonstrated, rounding out his belief that if he were waiting on John Galt (*Atlas Shrugged*) that Galt would admire his skill as a waiter.

He did what he had to do on Saturday nights, to keep his guests happy when the kitchen sank; and sink it would. Full of egomaniacal chefs from foreign lands, great battles ensued, often ending in fist fights and pink slips, followed by sheepish grins and remorseful apologies from those very chefs the next day—made to the entire staff—with management standing by to intervene when the ego show re-ignited, and re-ignite it always did. He did what he had to do when entrees ordered were suddenly unavailable; when diners took hour-long phone calls away from their table; when unexpected persons showed up unannounced and uninvited for dinner; when in-house romances imploded on the restaurant floor, and in the face of any and all kind of mayhem and mishap.

Mitchell did all of this while high on whatever legendary homegrown weed was brought into the Portola by the connoisseurs on staff. There was a quiet, hidden corner of the restaurant that opened up to the harbor, providing a constant pull of ocean breeze through the dining room, lifting the telltale odor and smoke away, leaving no sign of what oddly, to Mitchell, remained an illegal activity.

The Portola had an ambiance unsurpassed in San Diego, save the Sky Room at the La Valencia Hotel in La Jolla. At the end of any dining experience, the giant bay windows, the yachts, the waters around the harbor, and the smells of the ocean blowing over Point Loma, all placed the guests of the Portola and Mitchell too, in a mood to take a deep relaxing breath, a great book, and a finer weed or wine with them into the rest of their Saturday night.

Regardless of how early or how late Mitchell went to bed on Saturday night, he would rise at dawn on Sunday morning for a walk down the boardwalk—to a cup of coffee and a Sunday paper. At dawn on Sunday all was still; even the waves seemed to keep their rolling to themselves. And in the winter, when the beach was left to its year-round residents, early Sunday morning provided a great sense of solace up and down the length of Pacific Beach.

Little by little, like the creation of a coast, Mitchell shaped the beach life around him. He found plenty of sand in his shoes—damp ocean air in his lungs—overcast mornings overhead—an open bedroom window that presented to him the sound of surf—and the caress of an ocean born breeze upon his skin—all night long. Asleep, his soul sensed the light of a full moon—over the ocean on a cloudless night—every night. He was welcomed by the coastal elements—blending into the ambiance of beach life—blurring the distance between his spirit, and the ancient cycle of white capped waves, endlessly reaching for higher ground.

One by one, as Mitchell walked down the boardwalk, residents of the beach would find their routine. Not all were light-hearted. Some had longing in their expressions, as if the ocean had taken something dear from them. Yet even those souls remained profoundly attached to the ocean and what its sun–moon cycle presented to them. Seagulls found their rite of petty picking and quarrelling—allowing discernment between what was living on the beach and what was just trying to survive. On Sunday morning, the residents—under an overcast of solitude and fog—found either warmth in it or loneliness beyond expression; the latter echoed in the sound of an empty beer can falling off the boardwalk wall—its resonance tunneling into Mitchell's memory—where it would remain, without his consent, forevermore.

The sun rose in the east, burning the fog off the boardwalk and beach, chasing it far into the west over the Pacific. This reminded him of scenes in his collection of literature where characters found their own reasons for living next to horizon-bound stretches of salt water and sand.

Like a fever, the sunlight would greet Mitchell, requiring the use of sunglasses and a long-sleeved shirt—common sense was an often-used tool on the beach. Like paying the rent, one had to do certain things to maintain a sense of well-being; the seafaring sun demanded it.

❧❧

High noon on Sunday was a time of rest for Mitchell, who found immense comfort on a hammock tied to separate ends of his upstairs patio.

Jazz played on his stereo. Distant voices of children lost in the delights of imagination lulled Mitchell into a nap, where sand castles and discoveries made just under the surface of ebbing tides, became precursors to what life and dreams are made of.

The afternoon marched on. Mitchell's thoughts were about dinner; a deli sandwich and a soda from the shop down the boardwalk were chosen. In bare feet he walked. He would stop to consider the sun, which was setting behind the same bank of clouds it pushed out that morning, appearing and disappearing between lines of mist, growing rich in color as it began its descent into the curve of the earth.

On the boardwalk he sat as a party of one, occupying the best table in the house. Facing the end of the day, he finished the last few bites of his sandwich, wadded its wrapper in his hand, placed it absent-mindedly in his shorts pocket, and stared with some intensity at the giant orange-red ball falling through the distant bands of slowly dissipating vapor.

Along with the colors of dusk, Mitchell heard the distant roll of a thousand kettledrums washing ashore. Soon haunting bagpipes and the delicate strum of a magically played lute pulled him into the ritual perception of colors changing hue, and into a meditation of time standing still. From orange to amber and from red to rust, the sun's rays transformed, followed by the empty light of the sun as it vanished into the grey Pacific Ocean.

The dusk deepened—it's light no longer able to cut through the horizon's massive prism. Out of that darkened cross blend of ocean and sky came a moment that always remained as a question for Mitchell. His spirit called the moment a blessing—his heart, a rendering of life's fickle moments—his mind; a phantom of what was hoped for in living. And his eyes—which remained objective when color was presented—beheld above the sun's exit, a brush of green light, which appeared—then disappeared, between heaven and earth.

Standing for some time, he looked about to see if others were similarly affected. None were. Was it a unique moment he shared with no other, save the creators of heavenly bodies and their associated elements of fire and water?

Returning to his apartment, he walked upstairs taking with him a notion of something grander than he building sand castles in dreams, and laying mysteries to many things below the surface of an ebbing tide.

⊰⊱

Sunlight kicked its way through the window over Mitchell's head as he slept in a wave-induced slumber. It was Monday morning, and the light made him blink even before he opened his eyes. Blindly reaching for the curtains to shade them, he gave up and used the sheet as cover until he could get his bearings. Sunshine at the break of day was unusual.

Disoriented, Mitchell slowly recalled the night before, having spent it on the cold sand, around a bonfire, in front of his apartment— a ritual after sun down for the neighbors in his complex. It was right where Mitchell wanted to be on his nights off—engaged in conversation, listening to music, and passing around what seemed to be an endless supply of joints. Every one contributed to the cornucopia of weed at the fire, most of it home grown, with roots in Humboldt County or Maui.

The pot culture had become something of a sophistication since the sixties. Laden with energy and focus, pot smoking was further defined by its users. Some believed that sharing joints around the bonfire was a new activity started by baby boomers.

Mitchell rebutted. "It's the reason why religions were and continue to be created. Even now, while we sit here, we're reaching out to one another at the altar of weed. We have found friendship, common ground, and acceptance of who we think we are to one another. I cherish this ritual. Each of us performs a task; gathering wood, building a fire, making music, and contributing to our conversations. This, my friends, is our religion."

With that the circle became very quiet. The guitar player stopped to take a drag on a joint, passed it to on, and began to strum Don McLean's "American Pie."

"I remember watching him sing that song on Johnny Carson," Mitchell mentioned to those who were listening. "I can still recite every word and recall where I was the first time I heard it. I was sitting on the front porch of a cabin in the woods; my friends brought the album up during one of their summer visits. It gave me hope and made sense out of what seemed to me, as a kid, a world a million miles away and completely out of control. It made me okay. It gave me a sense of direction by telling me where I had been."

The lyrics of the song meant different things to the neighbors; all with their own associations and memories attached to the song as it played then on their A.M. radios and now on the neighbor's guitar. The pot culture was wrapped up inside many of the song's references, all of which were open to interpretation, filtered by personal experience to the point that the song and what it meant to the songwriter were no longer recognizable. Yet the song remained a calling, like a church bell, for every young person to pick up the notion of change, of youthful determination to see a world different than what their parents unwittingly made.

McLean sang of love and its heartbreak. He sang about music and its spirit of hope. He wrote of teenaged desire—of what a dance could do to a boy's soul—of pushing society's conventions aside, describing the spirit of a girl who could now, through release, rise above those expectations. The song helped Mitchell acknowledge who he was in the collective reform of the sixties and its fallout during the seventies.

The final chorus ended in one quiet collective voice around the bonfire with each heart wondering about some moment in the future when his life, by some cruel twist of fate, might run dry.

Chapter Thirty Seven

THE days grew colder, and the coffee seemed hotter. Mitchell wrapped his grateful hands around the mug. The floor heater in his apartment creaked on; its metallic odor filled the room. The coffee and heater comforted him.

On the kitchen table stood a small collection of Christmas cards. The one from Chloe and Bae stood out among the rest. He reread the card, noting her impressive penmanship; ornate and open with an accuracy that *implied* discipline.

Her words portrayed loneliness and longing, yet it was her handwriting: it's style and accuracy, that haunted Mitchell, especially in this particular correspondence. Although just a few weeks older than Mitchell, Chloe's worldliness made her words seem unnatural. Mitchell reviewed her relationship with her father many times, and had often, in the past, allowed Chloe back into his arms because he believed she was the product of horrible physical and emotional abuse. He was truly akin to her in that regard.

He frequently wished the love he had for her could help her, but it had not. He knew she would never rise above her father's wickedness, which was now hers and Mitchell found that a sad thought to carry into his Christmas Eve.

Her feelings in the card described his own, which had always been her particular talent. By describing her wants and desires, her wishes and dreams, her trials and tribulations, she would pull Mitchell in, back into the arms of the past.

She played as smoke and mirrors, mesmerizing him. In truth they looked more like brother and sister than lovers, and as he read the letter again, a letter he could have written to her, he saw the spell of her words blend their two reflections in the mirror into one.

She wrote:

My dearest Mitchell,

As I sit here at my kitchen table, in my home and in my town, a thousand miles from you and your kitchen table, in your home and your town, where I know you sit close to a cup of coffee and that old noisy heater, I long for and miss your face and your grace and your hands.

My daughter misses you, too. She misses your love and your tummy as she often laid there for the comfort and security you gave to both of us.

I miss your passion and your laughter; both brought to me such relief from my own darker moments. I miss the way our hands fit together and what it meant to me to see my daughter's fingers rest on yours.

We are too perfect a fit it seems, my love; our spark too bright, our love too intense to touch, yet how beautiful it is to behold even now.

I wish you now and for all eternity the peace that I know you feel even as our love succumbs to the motions of a world we did not create, and for reasons that we do not understand.

There is one regret that I cannot seem to overcome. It is what your love would have meant to Bae. She could have used a father like you in her life much the way I could have used a father like you in mine. She misses you and finds her wings without the lift you have given to her since she was able to walk. It is sad for me to know that this regret of mine will soon become hers and that regret will be the bond that ties us to one another.

God Bless you. I wish you love this Christmas and always.

Chloe

Mitchell closed the letter. He wiped the tears from his eyes and tasted salt in his mouth. The moment was filled with the bittersweet that was his life with her. He was filled with heartbreak and the memory of intense physical pleasure. He reached over for a napkin to blow his nose, looking down at his feet, to the pair of shiny black *Red Wing* work shoes, reminding him of where he was headed for Christmas Eve. He stood up, grabbed the tools of his trade, and headed out of his apartment toward the Portola, where he would share the evening with perfect strangers.

He looked back once more at the kitchen table still feeling her pull at his heart, still longing for one more chance to see it through and to have her and her daughter at his side on Christmas Eve. He closed the front door and locked it, putting his forehead against it for a moment, a moment that was becoming easier to face as time went by, a moment when he could turn his back on the ebbing tide that was Chloe and Bae.

With a start, he unlocked his apartment door, walked to the kitchen table, picked up the card and letter, and threw it into the garbage can.

✤☙

Sympathy tips on Christmas Eve made such an evening worthwhile, Mitchell thought as he looked down at his feet, rolling them one way and then the other, stretching his muscles and tendons after a long night on the floor of the Portola.

He had one table left; a pilot and a stewardess alone together, thousands of miles from their homes. Mitchell observed no progress in their service cycle: each still had a mostly full snifter of *Frangelico*. The fingers that held each glass had moved closer together however, succumbing to loneliness and the hazelnut liqueur. Whatever else in the world that was happening in their lives and homes, Mitchell hoped that this last table would find comfort in each other's company on this night.

He turned back to his own company; Debbie—a fellow co-worker and friend—was closing the restaurant with Mitchell. They shared a joint and found a moment of rest as a parade of sailboats, dressed in holiday lights, moved effortlessly passed the Sheraton Harbor Island Hotel.

"Do alright tonight?" Mitchell asked.

"Yea, you?" she asked in return.

"Yea, sympathy tips, you know," he answered, noting a far-off look in her eyes. "Where are you?"

"I can't wait to get out of here," she said. "No one would close for me, and I've missed Christmas Eve with my folks."

"Do you have any open checks?" Mitchell asked.

"No, I'm just waiting to close the service bar; I can't until the last table leaves," she said, nodding to Mitchell's pilot and stewardess.

"Go home," Mitchell said. "If they have another drink, I'll get it from the lobby bar."

"Are you sure?" she asked.

"Of course, I'm sure. I got it covered; go home."

"Thank you so much," Debbie said, hugging Mitchell's neck. "But what are you doing tonight?"

"I have a date with that sidewalk and those holiday lights," he said, pointing to the walkway that lined the perimeter of Harbor Island. "I'm in the mood to just walk and think tonight," he said. Mitchell's life had come into its own and he took great comfort in recognizing this. It was good to be inside his own skin, liking who he was alone.

He finished the closing side work, feeling fine as he called the manager on duty to cash out and inspect the restaurant. As he stood in the lobby of the hotel ready to leave, he heard a violin play Cat Steven's "Into White," haunting his Christmas mood as he took in the festive decorations and lighting that abounded.

In his pickup he played a homemade cassette of his family's Christmas music. The New Christy Minstrels' version of "We Need a Little Christmas" brought up memories of Christmases past. Downtown San Diego's skyline illuminated the interior of his truck. He sparked a joint—a thank you from Debbie for closing the service bar—took a deep breath, and instantly felt the pleasant warmth of another high coming on.

ॐ◌◌

On the front porch, Mitchell took note of how the ocean wrapped itself around everything he could see. In a Mexican pullover, warm wool socks, and with a cup of coffee in hand, he realized, as the morning fog burned off overhead, that he almost slept through Christmas morning.

He looked up and down the boardwalk as Bob Dylan's "Desolation Row" played through a neighbor's bathroom window. The beach was absolutely vacant. Not one soul could be seen in any direction, and it struck him as odd.

Looking up, the winter sun bathed his face with gentle warmth, interrupted by the floating shadows of birds in flight. He shielded his eyes from the white light of the sun—feeling for an instant the stillness of breath in him. His spirit rose to meet the shadows moving in their origin, and found himself inside the moment of their creation—moving with the wind—hearing what could be heard when light becomes shadow.

From among the playful birds in flight, he turned back to look at his life—he saw the solitude—he felt the lone corners of his soul—knowing where they started and where they ended—holding the light of his world in a cup made with his own hands. Turning again toward the sun, he acknowledged the warmth—the here and now—on his skin—his breath moving through him; this, his moment in the sun; this, his day of dreaming on Christmas Day—coming to a temporary end in the realization that he was being watched.

Not self-conscious, but rather a touch annoyed that his space on Christmas Day would warrant a stare, he cocked his head to stare back.

He smiled in surprise to behold another source of light—the toothless grin of a baby in a rocker on the porch below him. Bundled up—almost beyond recognition—the joy in the baby's eyes broadened Mitchell's smile, affecting a giggle in the bundle below.

The infant's mother suddenly, seeking the source of her baby's countenance. She quietly waved to Mitchell and moved out of the way, allowing the exchange to continue.

Mitchell meditation resumed in the brown eyes of the new life—perceiving sunlight evolving from shadow—sanity from chaos—warmth as insulation from the precariousness of living, and found in this shared meditation with the baby what he had known before in his life, as hope. Life was full of mystery—full of unanswered pleas—full of paradox, confusion, and contrast. Yet there, in the infant eyes, was *the* example of renewal.

The child's eyes closed, sleeping within the care of a mother's love. Mitchell wished to remember the baby's message: *that in the light of the sun, he would find love, reason, and a chance to know joy and thunder, passion and grace, and the sweet surrender to warmth, from a winter sun, on a Christmas Day.*

ↂ

The message stayed with Mitchell for many days. From Christmas Day through New Year's, he would time and again see infants about, in stores, on the boardwalk, in TV commercials, and again in the baby on the porch below. Each time he was struck with a notion of something profound lying just underneath the obvious nature of the exchange. The baby said, *"In the light of the sun . . ."*

Mitchell pondered the words often and made a home for them in his daily routine.

In the *F-100* he drove the same back streets to work, staying well off the interstates and tourist's routes from Pacific Beach to Harbor Island and back. He would pass several neighborhood churches on the way, observing many different kinds of nativity scenes; some ridiculous with their plastic statues and lights.

There was one, however, that made him take a second look as he passed by. It was solemn and humble in its presentation of the birth of Jesus. From somewhere in his mind came a nudge to stop and look, taking ten minutes out for himself before the approaching shift would begin.

The nativity scene was to the left of the Catholic church's front door and as Mitchell moved toward it, the front door opened. An ancient woman came out holding a rosary in one hand and a white cloth in the other.

Unsure of the appropriateness of his presence, Mitchell moved to one side of the walkway and allowed the slow moving woman to pass by.

"Can I help you?" she asked very candidly.

"Well, I just stopped by to see the nativity scene," Mitchell responded.

She nodded her head and moved toward the spot where he stood. She stopped suddenly right in front of him, looked up and said very quietly and with distinction, "You've come here for the boy, haven't you?"

When she reached the sidewalk she looked back at Mitchell and said, "Be careful of what you look for; you just might find it." She turned toward the ocean, not looking back. To Mitchell, she did not have to; she was still looking right through him.

He turned away from the ancient woman but not her words. As he moved closer to the nativity scene, he studied each statue. Their faces were worn and ancient in their years of use except for the baby in the manger. The baby statue's face was in perfect condition while the rest of its body looked like its counterparts.

How odd, Mitchell thought to himself. He finished taking in the scene and again found his gaze set upon the baby's face. It was smiling,

173

almost a giggle, it seemed. Mitchell perceived warmth and comfort on a bed of hay; this observation opening the window to a recent memory from Christmas Day the week before.

Chills ran down the back of his neck as the blending of the baby's face below him one week earlier had become one with the statue's countenance before him. It was a face that enchanted him, with eyes that led him to many thoughts about kindness and generosity—a face that said, *"in the light of the Son, one would find love, reason, and a chance to know joy and thunder, passion and grace, and the sweet surrender to warmth, from a winter sun, on a Christmas Day"*

Stunned, he turned toward his truck. Down the street, the ancient woman was watching him. When he saw her, she smiled. He got in the truck and continued his drive to work, not sure of what to do with his thoughts that were, it seemed, being handed to him.

✎ℭ℞

Mitchell crouched down; stretching ankle joints and quadriceps while letting the cold, damp, San Diego Harbor air refresh his skin on the close of New Year's eve.

The third turn, which started two hours before midnight, was now officially toast. His patrons each had one hand on a flute of champagne and the other thumbing a freshly filled cup of coffee; a combination required by most of his diners to maintain a spirit of gaiety through the midnight hour.

As it was with the staff of the Portola; each had joined the celebration as he saw fit, combining various drugs with assorted libations. They had gathered in the aforementioned employee pot smoking lounge. Looking up, Mitchell noticed an unusually clear evening over San Diego Harbor, which revealed the lights of homes and streets running up and down the length of Point Loma. The meaning of their visibility on the eve of a New Year became the focus for banter, a short-lived moment as the Portola staff reminded one another of the mountain of work that remained to be done before they could call their New Year's Eve finished.

One by one they filed back into the front lines, working their stations and tables to the conclusion of the service cycle.

Mitchell remained behind. He wanted to view Point Loma and its lights reaching into the night sky. He had been putting this moment off all evening; a moment when he would consider the words that had come to him, by coincidence or design, concerning the notion of a deity, born as a savior of his soul.

All of it's hard for me to swallow, he thought to himself. *I can't believe that I was born a sinner, that I need to be forgiven as I live my life, that I am responsible for my fellow man and that the beautiful baby I saw on the porch below me is like the baby born on Christmas Day who ends up on a cross bleeding and dead as a sacrifice for my salvation. I don't buy it, not one iota of it.*

Bitter about having beliefs stuffed into his mind since birth, he got up and shook it off, wanting very much to get back into the spirit of the evening inside.

At that moment a star fell from the sky. In that very moment he sensed great mystical works unraveling in the vast universe. He wanted to make sense of the mystical cosmos and what, in truth, resided there.

The falling star faded and so did any answer for the mysteries of life. He turned his back on Point Loma and the universe beyond, opened the door to the wet stench of booze and cigar smoke that was now the Portola, finding in that atmosphere familiarity. He was at home here. Looking down the aisle at his three tables, their occupants were lost in a celebration that had spread beyond the borders of the booths themselves. As he walked purposefully toward them, Mitchell was greeted by drunks with hearts as big as the harbor itself. He was fortunate to have 'happy' drunks to wait on. He fell into the intoxicating wit of San Diegans who didn't care what was happening in the universe or beyond the moment before them.

∽CR

As a manner of routine, Mitchell stepped out on to the front porch on New Year's Day. With coffee in hand, he remembered he did not have to work due to the efforts of the evening before, and a sense of gratitude grew in him for the day off. The surf roared, and an urge to hear music accompanied his first thoughts on New Year's Day.

In celebration of a new year, Mitchell blasted his early Led Zeppelin albums, enjoying the blues influences found on "Babe, I'm Gonna Leave You," and "Dazed and Confused."

Eventually, New Year's Day would turn out like any other day for him, subject to the waves moving in and out of his consciousness. The winter sun's cast of shadows across the surf mesmerized him. By day's end, he was as a pea in a pod, happy not to be sharing it with anyone, finding glory in his all-time favorite Led Zeppelin song "Ramble On," feeling the release of its words and its music in the setting of the sun.

He fell asleep knowing certain things: that the surf would be there tomorrow; that the things he allowed to define his life; the boundary of his thought, the old truck, the modern stereo, and the most valuable of all, his life alone—would keep him set in his ways— secure in who he was to himself, and to the world around him.

Chapter Thirty Eight

SIAN stepped inside her mother's home. She carried a box of belongings up the stairs from the basement and found a place for it in the bedroom behind the kitchen. Mitchell pulled other items off his truck, turned toward his cabin and was suddenly taken by the loss of life found within. But Sian now moved about the four walls of his home, and Mitchell found that fact quite amazing. *Is this real,* he asked himself. *Is she real,* temporarily questioning the plausibility that Sian was nothing but a hope in his heart to have Red back.

At that moment Sian came bursting out, surprised to see Mitchell just standing there. "You okay?" Sian asked.

"Yeah, I'm okay," Mitchell said quietly.

"You sure you want me here?" Sian asked in a steady voice. "I would understand if you didn't. It's not too late to get my apartment back."

Snapping out of the trance, Mitchell quickly said "Not a chance," and headed up the stairs to the cabin's main floor.

Now it was Sian's turn to look at the cabin under the same spell that stopped Mitchell. She looked at what was lost, then found, and saw her life a bittersweet experience to date. She saw Mitchell glancing at her from the kitchen window. Smiling at one another, both wondered why they had found each other—why Red's death was the catalyst to their relationship. Mitchell left the answer to the question hanging off the kitchen window's sill, and walked away from Sian's view. He appeared at the basement door and took the items in Sian's hands, winked at her, then nodded toward the truck, indicating they should continue getting her things moved in.

Once settled in, Sian moved about the home, familiarizing herself with the locations of things like laundry detergent, towels, and the kitchen garbage. Mitchell let his peripheral vision take her in. His mind's eye stilled on an effort to comprehend what he had done; she was now a part of his home. Suddenly he was sharing the air in his home with another, yet not Red. There was the possibility of running into another body while rounding a corner, yet not Red's. There were manners and courtesies to observe, but not for his Red. He had not thought this through. Yet still, it seemed the right thing to do.

The phone rang unexpectedly, ending his trail of thought. He looked for Sian. Not seeing her, he picked up the phone and said, "Hello."

"Mitchell, this is Laurie. How are you doing?" Laurie asked.

He stumbled mentally for a moment. *This is Laurie?*, he thought. "Oh, Laurie . . . hey . . . I'm fine . . . how are you," he said as memories of his trial and his lawyer came flooding back.

"I'm okay, Mitchell," Laurie said. "I'm not used to guys turning me down, you know," referring to their one and only date at a restaurant in town many months ago. Mitchell remembered. He was not comfortable dating at the time. He still wasn't.

"I'm sorry about that," Mitchell said. "I've pretty much kept to myself." He thought about Sian and wondered whether he should tell Laurie about Red's daughter. He decided not to for the time being.

"So what do you do all day, Mitchell, out there in the woods by yourself?" Laurie asked playfully.

"Well, Laurie," Mitchell said. "I'm doing my routine. I get out under the sun and canopy of trees and walk the Hassayampa. I listen to music. I miss Red. Not much has changed since seeing you last."

"Would you care to have a visitor?" Laurie asked.

Mitchell thought about it, creating the telltale pause that answered Laurie's question. He was overwhelmed by having another person in his home, but a gut feeling spurred a surprising answer; "Yes, I would like a visitor, Laurie."

"Well, I'm not just any visitor Mitchell" she said again in her playful mood. "I was hoping you might like to see me."

Mitchell sighed, loud enough to be heard at the other end of the phone. "Of course *you*, Laurie," he said, flustered by her teasing.

"How about I come by tonight after work with some take-out, and we can eat out on your front porch," she suggested.

Mitchell looked about the open area of his cabin. Sian was nowhere to be found. *How will I explain Sian?* He asked himself. Needing to spend some time with someone other than just himself and Sian, he agreed to a six o'clock meeting with Laurie for dinner on his patio.

*He took a deep and quaking
breath—in an effort to will from his heart
concealed truths.*

*The Sea Man found his will no
match for the truth—a truth already evident—
one that accounts for an infinite and universal
love—one both scientific and spirit-filled—one
known in the sun's light or the moon's
shadow—one that will forevermore present
itself to those who allow it to be known.*

Chapter Thirty Nine

A weekend retreat and conference center, located south of Big Bear Lake, California, had offered Mitchell an interview for a summer job as a camp maintenance man. On his apartment balcony, watching the beach swell with *Zonies* (residents of Arizona), with their sunburned backs, crying children, and loud complaints about sand in places where it didn't belong, he accepted the invitation. Not that he was done with the blues of ocean and sky, but moving to higher ground between Memorial and Labor Days suddenly made sense to him.

Within the week Mitchell found himself headed toward Big Bear. Next to him on the bench seat was a container of food and a change of clothes. He grinded his way through the southland freeway system—exiting finally at the Redlands/Highway 38 off ramp on Interstate 10.

The truck needed a rest. He pulled off the highway outside of Redlands and was overwhelmed by the majesty of the hills. He checked the fluid levels; the ascent he was about to make required that he pack extra radiator water and oil.

He pulled out onto the aged highway, got up to speed, and realized that second gear would be the best use of his truck's slant six on this first trip up into the San Gorgonio Wilderness.

He passed farmland first. Old farmhouses, with hand carved canals and clotheslines as boundaries, dotted the view. Mitchell imagined generations of family growing old in them, and wondered if those families found fulfillment as workers of their land.

An increase in elevation into the San Bernardino National Forest brought growing isolation in the buildings found along Highway 38, which appeared to be as old as the earth they rested upon. The truck slowed to a crawl. In first gear, Mitchell was grateful he could ride the shoulder of the highway, allowing other motorists to keep up their momentum.

Inland empire smog disappeared, clearing the view for alpine tree and snow lines. Up and up the truck trudged, at last pulling alongside a large green mailbox with a hand-painted inscription: *de Benneville Pines, a Unitarian Universalist Camp and Conference Center*, in white, on its side. A right turn off the highway took him up Jenks Lake Road and the entrance into the retreat.

He stopped and got out of the old pickup truck, taking in the smells and shade of an old-growth forest of ancient cedar and oak. He opened the tailgate, sat down, and took several deep breaths of thin air filled with abundant scents of wild things. He was overwhelmed by the views of a bald peak to his right and a ridge of mountains hiding the shores of Big Bear Lake to his left. He heard nothing but the sound of air entering and leaving his body, and contemplated making the area his home.

"Welcome to de Benneville Pines," A voice said behind him, surprising Mitchell. "I'm Bud, and you must be Mitchell." Mitchell extended his hand in greeting. Bud admired Mitchell's truck, inquiring how it did coming up the hill. After some pleasantries, Mitchell offered Bud a ride up the remainder of the dirt drive.

After Mitchell backed his truck into a parking space, the two men took a long and difficult walk around the seventeen-acre retreat. Bud conducted a hands-on interview. He asked Mitchell how he would solve problems in particular situations, all of which were new to Mitchell, but involved some grasp of the use of tools and common sense. He was given tours of a camper cabin, the maintenance building—its wealth of history and tools, the sewer plant, and the back way into the lodge.

Mitchell was taken by its size, and by how much light its huge windows let into the interior. It was quiet and on this day, warmed by the sun's rays. At the front was an enormous stone fireplace stocked with wood on both sides. Behind the fireplace was a full service kitchen. Bud suggested that they sit and talk about salary and benefits.

What was offered would work for the summer months. Mitchell had never worked in a situation that included room and board. With the small monthly salary, Mitchell calculated that ends could be met. On the spot, Bud offered Mitchell the job, more on personality than experience, taking into consideration the value of a person who is easy to get along with in a communal living situation.

Mitchell walked out under the open sky, taking a deep breath and feeling quite enamored about the possibility of moving to the mountains from the beach. He stopped and looked around at what would be his new home and quietly smiled inside.

The wind was the first memory Mitchell took with him. On his way out he stopped again at the same spot he visited when going in. He turned off the engine, opened up the tailgate and sat, this time facing the massive wooded area that was de Benneville Pines. Sitting quietly, the tops of the trees whispered to him. Similar to the echo of waves, the delicate wind would crescendo, then recede, but do so in a cadence much slower than the surf.

The message was clear. It came via the branches on ancient trees high above him, fixed at certain angles, producing vibrations in the wind. It said: *Life is short when compared to how long we have stood at de Benneville, and how long the wind has made the sound of the surf in our reach for the heavens above. Behold all the human lives that have come and gone in our woods, with their worn stairways, door handles and footpaths. Old cabins that held generations of human families, built long after we began our own growing, now crumble, and their memories fade under the weight of our roots and branches.*

He heard, *Life is too fickle not to listen to time passing in the tops of trees. You have found a place to live that will allow you the chance to do so.*

⊷ᏰᏣ

The decision to move to the mountains was losing ground. The greener side of the wilderness that surrounded de Benneville Pines faded in contrast to the bright sun, blue waters, bikinis and routine on the beach. The trip back from de Benneville to Pacific Beach was filled with thought. A decision to decline Bud's offer was made. The trip home felt much shorter than the three hours that actually passed and he had the sublime feeling of providence confirming the decision to stay put. The sentiment imploded upon itself instantly when a dusty Chrysler Imperial with Arizona plates had taken not only his but his neighbor's parking space in a rabid attempt to secure time on the over-crowded beach.

A sign, Mitchell thought. *A sign that says I need to get out before the crowds of Roadrunners and Gila Monsters, with their crusty backs and spoiled children, consume me.*

He called Bud and accepted the position as maintenance man for four hundred dollars per month, with an allowance for room and board. *How am I going to live on four hundred dollars a month?* He asked himself. *And room and board, what does that mean exactly?*

He trusted his impulse, however, knowing it would work out. He gave notice to the landlord, who was happy to have Mitchell leave for the summer; he would make ten times the rent in the summer months. He was also just as happy to hear Mitchell would come back, taking possession of the apartment after the Zonies returned home. He gave notice to the Sheraton. They responded positively, offering his job back upon request.

Two weeks passed since giving notice of his intention to move. He suspended all of his utilities. He packed his clothes, albums, three small pieces of furniture, and his stereo, selling the rest to the landlord. All were loaded into the bed of the old pickup truck. A tarp and rope insured their place while journeying from one heaven to the next. He took one last look around at his apartment and his life. *A quiet one for sure,* he thought to himself. There were butterflies in his gut as a new horizon awaited him. A sense of adventure consumed him, and he could feel the grip of a new life at de Benneville calling him.

He thought of the historic explorers—of the great lands, seas, and skies they travelled to—not knowing what was beyond the tips of their fingers. He thought of the gypsy life—of never settling down into a routine of familiarity. He already missed the beach. James Taylor's "Sweet Baby James" played in his mind as background to the ambivalence of his soul, and its desire to serve two fates. It was the loneliest of places—the first steps of a decision—that took a man from his past, and into his future. He watched other roads not chosen fade away—roads that would visit him in decades to come, as reference points of what could have been.

∼ॐ೮ॲ

His truck idled behind an endless stream of red lights. His move to the mountains was underway. Slow and go, then gaining speed, he watched the road float under his feet—a hole in the floorboard allowed such a view.

He became entranced with the romantic notion of being a drifter. A childhood TV show, *Then Came Bronson,* was recalled, and he found himself answering the question of where he was headed the same way Michael Parks' character would; "Wherever I end up, I guess." Mitchell found himself in exactly those same shoes. He could go anywhere he wanted to go. He smiled. He shone a penlight on his face and looked in the rearview mirror. He was Jim Bronson, on any day of the week with nothing to do, nothing to tie him down. *This was something every man should feel in life,* he thought. He was ready to feel it as often as he could.

The truck pulled up to the Forest Service sign marking the right turn into de Benneville Pines. It was pitch black in the dead of night, and Mitchell was unsure about arriving at such an hour. He turned off the engine, got out of the truck, and was immediately greeted by a startling absence of light, forcing his other senses to pitch in.

Standing disoriented, Mitchell did a check of himself and his truck. He made a mental picture of his limbs and where he placed them. He felt for the truck, touching the cold steel doors and warm engine compartment. He reached for his penlight and turned it on.

Suddenly several pairs of eyes flashed—a family of raccoons—which vanished silently and quickly around him. At once, through the dark filter of memory, Mitchell saw a stick man looking at him and felt a chill crawl up his neck. He heard the sound of running water, and pictured himself at play as a boy in the waterhole. *A stick man,* he thought. *I remember.* Just as quickly the image disappeared. He let the memory go as the dark night covered and sealed the image away.

He shone the penlight on the ropes and tarp. Everything seemed to be in order save his own comfort. The night air was full of scent, rich in the flavors of spring, rich in life renewing. Anticipation of the dawn made him yawn. Sleep overcame Mitchell as his unsettledness turned to fatigue.

His night jitters stopped. His jaw relaxed. Opening an overly creaky steel truck door, he climbed in and lay down upon the bench seat. The smell of old leather and decaying steel comforted his thoughts. He rolled out his sleeping bag, put the pillow under his head, and folded the sleeping bag around his feet. He took a long, wide yawn, feeling the 6,800 feet in elevation for the first time since his last trip up two weeks earlier. The windows were cracked to let in the night, which was cold and clear. Mitchell gazed out the rear window and observed a carpet of stars cutting a giant swath of light across the sky. *The Milky Way,* he thought. Rich and deep, with the seamless boundaries of a blue-black universe surrounding it, Mitchell realized how significant the moment was alone in his sleeping bag, in his old Ford, in the wee hours with the wild unknown night as his sleeping companion.

He dreamt of a great tree growing beside a golden gate. Mitchell faced the great wooded soul. His heart longed for and loved the tree—this keeper of the gate—and he heard many words come through it. Mitchell heard the keeper say that what waited for him at de Benneville would open him up to many countless things that he had not considered before. The great soul said that what will come upon him would be endless thought and breathless beauty, walking beside great solitude and much hard work. He would discover in the ancient wilderness the exquisite voice of paradox—the language of nature. The keeper said Mitchell would take the hand of peace, and embrace the chaos and the cycles of living life.

The dream came to an end when Mitchell observed the golden gate open up to the entrance of the seventeen-acre wood known as de Benneville Pines.

Chapter Forty

MITCHELL paced about his home nervously, unsure of what to say about Sian to Laurie when she arrived. He did know it would be a shock.

He looked down to where his truck and Sian's car were parked side by side, and knew that would be the first thing to raise an eyebrow from his ex-attorney, who might now be his friend. He looked about his cabin and realized that Sian had moved very little of herself into it. *That's odd.* He found her sitting on the bed, reading the old man's journal.

"You okay?" Mitchell asked.

"I'm fine, Mitchell, how are you?"

"Good," he said. "Actually Sian, I do have something to tell you. An acquaintance is coming over for dinner—Laurie—she was my attorney. Maybe you remember her?"

Sian hesitated for a moment, surprised to learn that Mitchell had other relationships, having never seen him with anyone socially save at her mother's memorial service. "That's fine, Mitchell," Sian said. "I don't want you to worry about me."

"What will you do for dinner?" Mitchell asked, feeling again the awkwardness of having to consider another.

"If I get hungry, I'll run into town and get something. Don't worry."

"Okay." Mitchell turned around to wait for Laurie, who pulled up just as he walked out onto the front porch.

He noted that Laurie had not seen, or at least pretended not to notice, both vehicles.

She stepped out of her BMW. In one hand she carried a plastic bag containing their dinner. Mitchell noted the graceful balance of her tall, lean figure. Her long blonde hair was tossed about her shoulders.

"Hi," Laurie said.

"Hello," Mitchell responded, at which point Laurie smiled and nodded toward the side door, conveying her familiarity with the entrance to his cabin.

Mitchell greeted her at the top of the stairs with a light hug. Laurie responded with a kiss on his cheek and a bigger hug. He nervously thought of Sian.

"How are you, Mitchell," Laurie said tentatively.

"I'm doing alright, considering. How's business?"

"I'm busy, no doubt," she said. "Defending the public can be hectic and depressing, but for the most part I have a sense of pride in the job I do."

"Well, it's important that you feel that way about what you do for a living," Mitchell said.

"How are you maintaining?" Laurie asked.

"I don't need much to live," he said.

At once Mitchell saw first headlights—then taillights—move away from his cabin along his driveway. He was alarmed and saddened that Sian had left without saying anything.

Laurie didn't notice the lights or Mitchell's reaction. She was taken by Mitchell's simple existence. His rustic cabin walls were lightly decorated with watercolors of rock formations, worn bridges, and 19th century wagons. As contrast, on an opposing wall, Laurie found a collection of lighthouses and beach fronts done in pencil, and then was taken by what was, to her memory, a new collection of old photographs of Red—each in different styled frames—each placed next to one another in a collage in the corner of the kitchen. She moved closer to the photos and found each one to be unique. Some in black and white, some profiling her face, some playful in their presentation of her smile, all beautiful. Laurie stared. Gradually the pictures, courtroom testimony, and visits to Mitchell, incarcerated on the top floor of the Yavapai County Courthouse, came to the forefront of her thoughts. *How could someone like this end up the way she did*, Laurie wondered.

"I've not been able to answer that question," Mitchell said. Laurie was shocked to hear her silent question answered by him.

"How did you know what I was thinking?"

"When I look at those pictures, I ask the same silent question," Mitchell said. "It comes with the territory, or at least when a person stands in the corner of this kitchen facing them."

"You still miss her," she stated.

"I feel like I'm losing my mind some times, Laurie."

"I'm sure you will never stop missing her. How could you not?"

Mitchell set the table where they would sit. Laurie followed him out to the porch with their takeout. Mitchell looked at Sian's tire tracks, and wondered why Laurie had not asked about the car that had been parked there.

"It's a perfect evening," she said.

Mitchell focused on the silhouetted trees, noting the light blue arc on the horizon. He looked at Laurie, who smiled. She began to serve but he stopped her by placing his hand on the back of hers, saying, "Let me. It's the least I can do."

Looking at him, Laurie noticed lines around his eyes. His hair was longer than the last time she saw him, but the goatee and mustache were trimmed. She thought for a moment about his hand touching hers, trying not to remember what that hand was capable of. She noticed him humming softly and asked him about the melody.

"I'm not sure," he responded. He continued his humming, this time paying attention to it and recalled the Simon and Garfunkel song "America."

"Its "America," by Simon and Garfunkel, isn't it?" Laurie said, happy to have guessed it.

"Yes, you're right Laurie. I wasn't sure myself for a moment."

"I adore Simon and Garfunkel," she said.

Without hesitation, Mitchell went into the living room and put *Bookends* on his turntable, then returned to his spot, continuing to hum the chorus of the song. He was feeling a touch more comfortable and wanted music to communicate this. He was at the same time maintaining his distance from the statuesque Laurie, who sparkled, even under the light of a blue dusk. He remembered Laurie's comments on their first date many months ago when she told him that her father would have done the same thing. He remembered feeling a little flattered from the remark but still found its justification a mixed blessing.

"So, what's new in your life, Laurie?"

"Well, since seeing you last at The Rose, I've been living the life of a public defender. I'm inundated with work. There are a lot of

188

people in this county making poor choices and do not have the resources to pay for their consequences. I do the best I can, but at times it's not enough." Laurie hesitated for a moment. She appeared overwhelmed and sad all at once.

"What is it Laurie?"

"I feel like my soul has been absorbed into the culture of crime and punishment," she said. "I'm not sure who I am outside my office. I know what I am and who I am everyday at work, but I find just sitting here with you, or anywhere outside the office for that matter, unfamiliar. I don't know what I feel about things. I get the objectivity of my job but not the subjectivity of just being Laurie. Make sense?"

"Yeah, I get it, Laurie," Mitchell said. "I get so absorbed into the change my life took that I can't see anything else, yet even though I know this, I can't seem to break into the present."

"What exactly do you mean?" Laurie asked gingerly.

The next step in the conversation was to tell Laurie about Sian. At that moment Mitchell saw Sian's car pulling up the dirt driveway to the house. He looked anxiously at Laurie, asked to be excused, and bolted from the porch to the stairwell.

"Why did you leave without telling me where you are going?" Mitchell asked Sian, as she walked up the stairs.

Laurie watched the scene at the stairwell, observing Mitchell speak. She turned away, not wanting to meddle in what was obviously a private moment. She could still hear his voice, however, and grew concerned over the words he used. The next several seconds seemed like hours in Laurie's mind.

He came to know it. The winter's sunlight opened around him, contrasting the longing he was normally accustomed to, whispering . . .

Chapter Forty One

THE sun's rays cracked through the moisture that had built up on the windows inside the cab of the old truck. Mitchell yawned deeply, shaking his head as he exhaled. He pulled himself up by the steering wheel to see the sun rising through the old forest. *Not a cloud in the sky,* he noted. Hunger set in at the same moment the call of nature did. He guessed it was just past six a.m. beach time but was unsure of how the sun rose in the mountains. He looked up Jenks Lake Road and saw two girls popping out of the woods on one side, only to disappear on the other.

He popped the gas pedal twice in the usual ritual, turned the key, and listened as the slant six gave up what would sound, to a passerby, as its last breath before starting. Mitchell gave it some more gas and heard the engine oil itself up, coughing a couple of more times before getting its timing just right. A combination of butterflies and a sense of adventure built up in his gut as he put the truck into first gear. He rumbled forward through the property to the staff parking lot and got out.

"Are you Mitchell?" a voice said from inside a window of the staff cabin.

"Yea. Am I in the right place?"

"Yea," she said. "I'm to show you what rooms are available here in the staff cabin. Bud had to head down the hill for a couple of days. He left me in charge. C'mon up the stairs. I'll meet you at the front door."

She introduced herself as April. Mitchell shook her hand. This gesture, along with Mitchell's short hair, caused April's left eyebrow to lift, as her first impression set in. *A square, just what I need in my life, another up-tight square.* She led Mitchell into the main communal room of the cabin, then showed him two rooms at opposite ends of a long hallway. Mitchell was not taken by either—finding their untidiness unappealing.

"There's also a room up there but you have to climb the stairs on the far side," she said, pointing to the attic.

Mitchell walked outside, to the end of the porch, where the railing of a white staircase appeared. At the base he looked up. The hairs on the back of his neck stood up as he watched a white door, at the top of the stairs, open slowly—inviting him to come in. At the top, he beheld the morning sun blasting its way in, illuminating a small but secluded bedroom off the beaten path of the staff cabin. He knew immediately that the room would be his new home.

Mitchell turned around to view a world made of ancient things. Giant oaks and pines were lost in each other's shadows, as they played havoc in their designs on the horizon. In a long slow stare from the blue sky back to earth, Mitchell took in all that he could detail. A well-camouflaged platform came into focus—made of loosely fitted branches. It was shaped to fit a body in a lounging position—well hidden in the stand.

April popped her head around the corner and said, "Don't tell me you like *that* room."

Surprised by her remark, Mitchell said, "Yea, I do."

Again she raised her eyebrow, changing her assessment of him from a square to a loner.

"Well," April said, "it's all yours. Have you had breakfast yet?"

"No, not yet," he replied. "I would like to unpack first though."

"Suit yourself. Come and find me. I'll either be in the kitchen down there behind the lodge or at the office. I'll show you where the food is so you can eat, and then take you on my own tour of the camp."

"Sounds good, shouldn't take me long. I don't have much," he said, thinking about the walk-around he had made with Bud.

"None of us do. We pretty much show up here with the shirts on our backs," April replied.

April had waist-length brown hair and was pregnant. She wore no makeup and her attire matched that of the hippie chicks on the beach. When she turned to walk away Mitchell noted that from behind she didn't look pregnant. He wondered who the father was. He was impressed with the color and tone of her skin, the natural way she carried herself, and of the way she spoke matter-of-factly to him.

He stood for several more minutes looking at the view from his room. He could not have found a more perfect setting, moving from his view of the Pacific Ocean to a view of the ancient wilderness.

He began the process of unloading. He placed his stereo on a makeshift shelf suspended from the ceiling with rope. This serendipitous design prevented heavy feet and shutting doors from disturbing the turntable. He again got a feeling that the room was waiting for him. He found just enough space on a length of pipe to hang his clothes. He set up a makeshift desk for his books and journals, placing a candle and his father's radio near the head of his bed.

Breakfast was next. The loading-dock door led into a commercial-sized kitchen—large enough to feed two hundred hungry campers three meals a day.

Between two rows of island-style countertops and shelves—stocked full of kitchen pots and cutlery—stood yet another female: Jamie. She too had the hippie look; her hair, blonde as best as Mitchell could tell, was braided and tossed up around her head. A tie-dyed shirt and bell-bottoms rounded out the portrait. Mitchell introduced himself and again got the once-over. While doing so she pointed through the large rear kitchen window to the building at the foot of the parking lot and said "April went to the office. I'm Jamie, is there anything I can get you for breakfast?"

"I'm Mitchell," he said. "A bowl of cereal and a glass of milk sounds good to me."

"Let me show you where the dry goods and cold storage are located," Jamie said, turning toward Mitchell with a purpose and poise that he was not used to seeing in women his age. He followed Jamie into a huge storage room with every kind of dry good imaginable, all laid out in an organized manner. Anything in the way of food could be had by Mitchell if his order was given to her by Tuesday morning of each week, Jamie explained.

Next on the short tour was the huge cold storage refrigerator located off the loading dock. It contained every imaginable fruit and vegetable, including a meat cage at the back of the case—kept under lock and key. "It's to keep the wildlife out," she explained.

"Where are you from?" she asked.

Mitchell was pouring Cheerios into an over-sized bowl, feeling self-conscious. "San Diego, Pacific Beach to be exact, Arizona before that."

"I love Pacific Beach," Jamie said. "What street?"

"Santa Barbara Place."

Jamie looked puzzled. "It's a short street from Mission Boulevard to the boardwalk. I had a view of the ocean. It was nice."

"So why'd you leave?"

"The Zonies were coming."

"Wait, aren't you a Zonie?" she asked.

"Yes, but that's a secret." Mitchell smiled and they both laughed at the remark. "There's nothing wrong with being from Arizona, it's just that in Pacific Beach, during the summer, we make such asses of ourselves, thinking that we know what the summer sun will do to our skin, and that we know how to body surf as we lose our suits in the waves. I spent many a day watching my fellow Zonies crowd my routine. I jumped at the chance to replace a view of the ocean with a view of the woods."

"And a view of bikinis . . . with what?" Jamie asked lightheartedly.

Mitchell smiled, appreciating her sense of humor. Like anyone, he was happy to be engaged by self-effacing wit, and was grateful to Jamie for bringing a sense of ease to the breakfast table.

It was no table at all. He sat on a large stainless steel counter top, holding the bowl of cereal in his hands. His feet were swinging to and fro, bringing back a moment on the porch of his childhood cabin. Jamie began preparing again for an upcoming annual weekend of girl scouts.

Mitchell was thinking about the woods south of Prescott. Something was now full-circle in his life. The skills he used as a kid— to play in the woods—would come in handy here.

A large ruckus erupted in the lodge. The kitchen door swung open and three young men busted in. Demanding breakfast be served in absurd pirate fashion, they teased Jamie about waiting on them hand and foot as one shouted "Ahoy wench. Bring me a bagel and show me your tits."

Jamie flipped all three the finger and then pointed at Mitchell. One stepped forward, introduced himself as Colin and apologized for their bad manners. He put out his hand in greeting. Mitchell set his cereal down, grabbed Colin's hand and shook it. Farny came next, and Todd after that. They were all aware of his arrival. Mitchell was embarrassed at the attention as everyone sized up the new guy.

Mitchell was different than the other men. He was clean-shaven and had short hair. All three of the young men maintained the hippie look with long hair and beards. Mitchell had not expected the communal setting would include five hippies yet there they were.

"There's still one person left to meet, right?" Mitchell asked.

"Yea," Jamie said. "Her name is Monica. She and I do all the cooking for the camp—she should be down any minute."

Mitchell took a moment to take in the enormous kitchen. He realized it was the focal point for the communal living of de Benneville Pines. It was the meeting place where the day started and ended. The camp housed a mix of youthful exuberance with coming-of-age. Mitchell's first impressions of the group were of its free-thinking members—bringing to one another new ideas on a daily basis. The camp was the perfect Petri dish to test their liberal ideas against the contrast of conservative parents. The group was anti-establishment, and had surrounded themselves with notions of revolution, agreeing that they were there together to help each other without profit, or obligation, to one another—each was equal to the other.

When breakfast was finished, he walked out into the center of the lodge's main room where Bud had hired him. The thirty-foot-high apex of the lodge's A-frame construction minimized his presence. The fireplace was grand. While he walked toward it he could feel warmth emanating from a fire that raged the night before. The great room had large windows that ran the length of it on each side, with an arrangement of chapel-like glass rising to the zenith of the ceiling. He was mesmerized. His focus drifted beyond the tall glass into a wooded area beyond. He noticed movement deep in the woods. Wearing white, a woman appeared, her strawberry blonde hair flowing. *It must be Monica* Mitchell guessed. He watched her move down the path toward the lodge, her movements presenting a girlish yet spiritual grace. "Wow," he said.

"Agreed," said Jamie, who had come out to see what Mitchell was up to.

"Everyone, men, women, boys and girls alike, are all enchanted by her," Jamie said.

The comment was lost to another outburst from the gang in the kitchen, as they barreled their way into the lodge.

"What are you idiots staring at?" were the first words Mitchell heard from the beautiful Monica's mouth.

"Oh, great one, may I put my life down for you today," Colin said.

"Here, here," the other two added.

"Oh, brother," Jamie commented as she turned to go back to work in the kitchen.

Mitchell was surprised by Monica's candor.

"I'm Monica and these guys are assholes," she said, as her introduction. "It's nice to see a clean cut guy once in awhile rather than the heathens I'm forced to live with."

With that, Monica disappeared into the kitchen. A moment passed before Todd mockingly impersonated her remark to Mitchell, making for another boisterous laugh from the young men.

They ran from the lodge, heading up the same path from which Monica descended. Mitchell turned in the opposite direction. He walked out through the kitchen door and headed toward the office. As he approached he saw April standing outside the office with her face in her hands. She was obviously crying, and as Mitchell moved toward her, she looked up and turned toward the woods as if she wanted to be alone. Mitchell turned back toward the kitchen. He saw Jamie and Monica looking through the window at April with concern.

"What's going on?" Mitchell asked, shutting the kitchen door behind him.

"I think we should let April tell you if she wants to," Jamie said, wisely keeping a cardinal rule of successful communal living intact. "April said that a tour of the camp was in order for you this morning. If you're ready I can take you."

"I'm ready," Mitchell said, looking out the window toward the office, hoping that whatever April was feeling would soon pass.

They headed out—another walk-through of the camp had begun; this time without the dry business-like manner of the camp director, but with a long-standing member of the community of de Benneville Pines. Jamie was full of lore and personal experience regarding the birth of the camp, and of the lives that had shaped it.

She spoke of the people initially responsible for the creation of the camp—giving credit for the camp's unique feel to a play, written for the dedication of the camp in 1961, entitled *Farewell to Eden*. The play had three characters; Adam, Eve, and God. I sent de Benneville into orbit as a freethinking cornucopia of new age thought, attracting every kind of character that could be found in the sixties and seventies. Each had left their mark on the camp in unique ways and those marks were revisited in discussions of every kind over the years prior to Mitchell's arrival. Jamie shared with him that living at dB, as she called it, happened by way of the Cosmos. Each person that arrived at dB, for work or play, left with the camp's distinctive heritage as part of who they were.

Mitchell had suspected as much. His first night spent there—at the camp's entrance, and the dream he had—set him up for the camp's uniqueness. Three hours into his first full day, the camp's history and ambience confirmed his suspicions—it would offer him more than just a job, a meal, and a roof over his head.

≈≪

Mitchell was huffing quite laboriously as Jamie led him beyond the maintenance building, to a path that cut hard up the mountain behind the camp.

"Where are you taking me?" he said, losing his breath so quickly he had to ask Jamie to stop for a few minutes.

"To the well," she said. "To get a good feel for the physical workings of dB one must appreciate where the life force of this camp comes from. The water from the well is made of alpine snows that have filtered through the decomposing granite, flora, and fauna of the San Gorgonio Wilderness. It is crystal clear and tastes of high altitude rain. It's a tough hike for a flat-lander, so rest when you need to."

Difficult it was. He would come to know the path as the Forsee Creek Trail, arriving finally at an alpine marsh lush in vegetation. It sat high enough to provide a view of the Santa Ana River basin and the surrounding mountainsides.

Jamie had arrived several minutes before him, and sat meditatively on top of what appeared to be a woodpile. She sat tall— her eyes were closed—she had let the length of hair fall down around her. Mitchell was taken by how well she fit into the natural setting.

The alpine meadow was deep green with high grass and a multitude of flowers. Jamie's woodpile was the well itself. She unlocked a cover and opened it. Mitchell looked at what appeared at first to be an immense eye. He was pulled by notions of old, mystic things, and by the well's calm reflection of him.

"Reach down and drink from a well that has been watering man and beast for as long as the forest has been here," Jamie said. "And while you do this remember that the time you spend in these woods, drinking this water, is a gift from the gods and should not be taken lightly."

With that, Jamie left Mitchell to drink what he wanted, and to make his own way back. Today's trip to the well was enough for the new guy. "Lock up when you leave," she said.

Mitchell stayed at the well for a while, contemplating his new home and work place. He thought of his room, of the self-assured women, and the rambunctious young men—of the altitude, the abundance of food, and the quiet. His legs were warm from the hike. The water was complete refreshment.

Blazing light and rolling waves of scent lifted Mitchell's chin skyward. He took a deep breath, then stood up, feeling exhaustion overtake him. He had visions of a nap on a form-fitting platform near his room. The notion of a nap caught him off-guard. He moved here to work; to think of a nap on his first day surprised him. He reached for the sky and yawned deeply, trying to oxygenate his body. While doing so, he closed his eyes to the warmth of an alpine sun on his face.

A twig cracked, startling him out of his relaxed mood. Something large, white, and moving through the brush disturbed him greatly. He stood up, then froze, unsure of what to do next. The large white animal came out of the brush toward him. He was astonished by the size and color of what was obviously a dog. Sitting down on the well again, Mitchell maintained his slow movements, uncertain of what the dog would do next. He noticed that the mammoth-sized white

German shepherd had hardly taken note of him. He was looking around the area, glancing only once or twice in Mitchell's direction. Sitting in a patch of green grass, the dog turned its back to the stranger, and viewed the immediate surroundings.

"Hello," Mitchell said to the dog. He looked around at Mitchell, licked his chops, and turned back. Mitchell got up to begin his trek back to camp when, to his surprise, the dog jumped in front of him, and proceeded to lead Mitchell back to de Benneville Pines, stopping behind the maintenance building where Todd, Farny, and Colin were working.

"Blanco," the three yelled simultaneously. "You found the new guy! Good boy"

"I was just sitting on the well when he appeared from the surrounding bush," Mitchell said.

"The well!" Farny exclaimed, "What were you doing at the well?"

"Jamie . . ." Mitchell started to explain.

"We know—she has convictions about the camp and what it should be, not only for her, but for everyone who sets foot in it," Colin said.

"I think it's cool that Blanco decided to meet you there," Todd said. The others agreed in silence as they looked reverently at the dog.

Blanco meeting Mitchell at the well boded well for the new guy. It brought nods of approval from the young men, and soon everyone was impressed with the story, as it unfolded at dinner later that evening.

Blanco was a very old and much loved dog. Unlike his three-year-old side kick Honky, who was prone to puppyish antics, Blanco was reserved and stately, holding both his tail and his head high in a wise and mature fashion. Blanco was the soul of the camp. He was a hero to many, having found countless campers who had lost their way in the woods. He could be trusted to lead anyone where they told him they wanted to go even in the pitch dark of night. The fourteen-year-old Blanco was the cornerstone of the lore and legends of the camp. As dinner ended, Mitchell felt the large dog plant its self at his feet. He was a little uncomfortable with the attention the dog was giving him, knowing now that Blanco's affection brought the admiration of others.

When Mitchell got up and walked his plate to the dish room, Blanco followed him—out the side door—up the steep hike back to the staff cabin—to the stairs—and then finally to the white door and his bedroom—Blanco followed him. Such was Mitchell's first full day at de Benneville Pines.

∽ଚର

Time passed at de Benneville. Mitchell saw many things he had not seen before. The camp played host to a variety of groups from one weekend to the next: from Girl Scout troops to nudist organizations.

He met many of the camp's long-time supporters, developing relationships with them. Friday nights, at the start of each weekend, the staff would witness many harried and stressed campers, who carried with them the trials of their lives from down the hill. However, by Sunday morning, when they filed in for breakfast, calm appeared in their eyes. Mitchell understood their heavy spiritual investment into de Benneville; the camp seemed to save them from themselves.

Mitchell worked the routine of maintaining the camp, as summer moved into fall. He cut wood, thawed pipes, plowed snow, and worked on the different problems that arose in the physical plant that was de Benneville Pines—honing his practical problem solving skills. His experience grew. He welded pipes, participated in fire prevention projects, and walked the property with rangers in tree management programs. The work satisfied him. Pride, and a sense of well-being, followed him into each evening. The idea of four hundred dollars a month making him happy brought laughter from deep in his soul. He was content in knowing that his time, at last, was not traded for money. And although the salary put him well into the category of poverty, he wanted for nothing.

His hair began to grow. His beard had filled in. He spent the off-hours hiking the centuries-old trails in the wilderness, or swimming in the camp's large heated pool.

The mountains had a large hold on him. After six months of living and working at the camp, he slowly began to look the part, much to Monica's chagrin. He liked not shaving, and although he lived the life of a mountain man, a shower at the end of every day was a must.

On weekends, seven year-round employees, the director, and the kids who washed dishes in exchange for room and board, swelled the population of the camp to fifteen. Throw in Honky and Blanco, and on any Saturday night quite a party unfolded in the staff cabin. Pot and mushrooms were the catalysts that solidified the staff into a family of sorts. Peter Gabriel's song "San Jacinto," always pushed Mitchell into an orbit of thought and haunting calls from his past. High on mushrooms, he and Blanco would exit the party, out the back door, and head into the woods together. He would tell Blanco where he wanted to go, and while under the hallucinogenic flush of psilocybin, would follow Blanco's white tail, as it wagged to and fro—creating tails of its own.

On these walks with Blanco, he became familiar with the same stick man who had called on him in the past—it would walk with them while not revealing any clue of what or who it was. It was standoffish yet maintained a near-enough presence to illicit a one-way conversation from Mitchell to Blanco about its presence. Whether a full moon night or pitch dark, Mitchell could see it mulling around him. "Blanco, is it an angel or a devil?" He would ask his companion. Blanco would stop, look at Mitchell, and then move forward, giving Mitchell his answer; that it didn't matter who the stick man was—just that he and Mitchell kept moving. He would frequently think of the baby below him on the porch at his Pacific Beach apartment, and the vision of light found in the baby's eyes.

The music from the staff cabin followed them to whatever destination seemed right. Mitchell sat on the forest floor with Blanco, and flew over imaginary grounds—spiritual in temperament—understanding that the nature of the woods was what he made it. Communion between his life—and the life of the forest—with the great white German shepherd at his side—helped Mitchell find deeper meaning in his own existence.

❧

A flurry of activity ensued from noon to five p.m. every Sunday when the camp emptied—it was cleaned and restocked from head to toe. On these superb Sunday evenings, Jamie and Monica would make dinner for all the staff, and build a large fire in the Homet Lodge fire place. Hearty meals were delivered amid much banter about the odds and ends that traveled from the big cities, to lose themselves among the charms of dB. People-watching was a giant pastime among the staff. There existed the very best opportunity for a person to study human behavior in the campers—yet the campers were doing some study of their own.

Each weekend brought with it one pleasant intrigue after the next. When staffers entered the lodge at dinnertime, on the start of a weekend, male and female campers alike swooned at the sight of them. Residents of the camp were never lonely. Getting to know a staff person meant a free place to stay whenever that person wanted to come up. Visitors were always present. Romances formed. Love was in the air, as was heartbreak—more so for the female staff. Why this was Mitchell could only guess—men and boys were short-term, heat-of-the-moment types—women and girls hoped and dreamed of a dance that would last longer than one full moon.

Full moons came and went. Mitchell had found a groove in the mountains of South California. It was a groove that allowed only enough room in his bed for himself, and a dog at its feet. Uncluttered and uncomplicated were the gifts he offered the women who came into, and out of, his life as a maintenance man at de Benneville Pines.

He was unfettered, his wings untied, loosed from the debts of his parent's lives. He was healthy and strong and in tune with the mechanics of his life.

Chapter Forty Two

LAURIE looked again, back at Mitchell, who was walking toward a back room behind the kitchen. He was talking but she could not discern to whom. She thought Mitchell's behavior strange, but held what she saw unfolding in the kitchen under the light of compassion rather than judgment. She could tell he was still suffering.

She turned back toward the west and noted the dusk had gone, leaving the dark night in front of her. At that moment scenes from Mitchell's trial crossed her mind. She peered over the edge of the porch railing, down to where the events took place—pacing her way through his case files—recalling the first responders' description of Mitchell as being in a trance. *He was singing a song* she recalled. *What was the song?* She asked herself, straining to remember.

"I'm sorry for the interruption," Mitchell said, walking out onto the porch.

"It's okay," she said. "What's going on?"

"I've got something I want to share with you, Laurie." She looked at him with more of the same compassion she had felt moments before.

"I'm not sure why you have not asked yet about that car down there, or who has been coming and going since your arrival," Mitchell said. "I can only guess that it is your ability to read me, and that you'd give me the space I need until I'm ready to talk about it. Well, I'd like to tell you now."

"Okay Mitchell."

"Red's daughter, Sian, has come to live with me," Mitchell said matter-of-factly, through a blank expression."

"Oh," Laurie said. "Red's daughter you say?"

"Yes, that's her car," Mitchell said. "I met her one morning a while back when I was walking along the Hassayampa. She just showed up and started asking questions about her mom. She works at the Dinner Bell café in town and lives in an apartment above the record store on Montezuma. She did—until today. I asked her to live with me . . . to live in her mom's house . . . for the first time in her life." The lines around Mitchell's eyes deepened. "We've gotten to know one another pretty well—it's been rough for me—she's the spittin' image of Red."

"Her name is Sian," Laurie said, half as a statement and half as a question.

"Red told me about her a long time ago," Mitchell continued. "She was not sure if Sian was still alive because she was kid-knapped at birth by the child's father and Red could never find her again. Sian found her way to Prescott via the media, when she saw Red's photos in newspapers and on TV. I remember seeing her at both my trial and at Red's memorial."

Laurie listened to Mitchell intently. He went on to describe the many conversations he had with Sian—about a sock print made of blood—how it re-appears in coroner's reports found in Sharlot Hall Museum archives. Laurie's alarm, and curiosity, was piqued. *What archives.* More thoughts—pictures of evidence—slithered to the forefront of her mind. She immediately cast them aside as poison—a spell that previously took her months to break.

"Where did you go?" Mitchell asked Laurie.

Laurie realized she had stopped listening to Mitchell. "I'm sorry," she said. "There is just so much about that night that could haunt me, if I let it, as I'm sure it does to you."

"Not so much anymore, Laurie," Mitchell continued. "I've got Sian to talk to, and it seems to be helping me relax a little more."

Laurie looked painfully down toward the area where Mitchell said Sian's car was parked—then again back toward the rear of the kitchen. Some jealousy passed through her face, her eyes and cheeks revealing the heat of such an emotion.

"Are you sure it's such a good idea?" Laurie asked quietly. She watched Mitchell's expression as he answered.

"Yeah, I think it would do her good to at least have some of her mother about her for a while," Mitchell said. "Her first time in here was quite an emotional experience for her." Laurie heard Mitchell describe Sian's reaction to Red's things, and in particular, a throw that Sian buried her face in as she inhaled her mother's scent, for the first time in her life, crying herself to sleep in Mitchell's arms.

"This is another strange conversation, isn't it?" Mitchell asked.

"Yeah, you could say that," Laurie stated. "It is amazing how well you seem to be doing despite the appearance of Sian now in your life. I suppose I should be jealous of her, and I guess I am Mitchell."

"Laurie," Mitchell said. "I've not one romantic inclination for Sian. I could never entertain such thoughts. She's just a kid who could use her mother in whatever way she can get her."

"I know, you are a good man Mitchell. You are honorable, and I like being around you."

Mitchell looked into Laurie's eyes. "And I, you," Mitchell said.

The conversation turned to lighter things. If Sian where there she would have heard quiet laughter coming from the porch, as Laurie talked about her job, and the silly situations Prescott's citizenry got themselves into.

Sian had left again, quietly, into the night. This time, Mitchell had not noticed.

. . . white and still.

White and still, the Sea Man

thought.

Chapter Forty Three

APRIL'S baby had come. He was born in the residence end of the camp's maintenance building. The father had come back just in time to witness the birth of his son. April's love for her son's father was made of heartbreak. He hung around for a couple of days and left. The new baby, and his mother, turned to their de Benneville family for things a father, and husband, would normally give.

Alone in his room, as evening approached, Mitchell languished in memory of his own father—of the beer, cigarettes, and Ada's infidelity—that all worked to betray Sorber. The image of him, alone in the dark—a cigarette ember glowing red as it moved from ash tray, to mouth, and back again, haunted Mitchell.

Thoughts of his dad uprooted the peace he had enjoyed, for several months, as a resident of de Benneville. Dark clouds appeared out the small window of his room. Mitchell sighed deeply, exhaling a hope not to think of Chloe.

The turntable spun "San Jacinto." The room had turned noticeably damp. He sat on his bed while the red glow from the controls of his stereo penetrated him.

The night grew ominous. Using the remote, he played the song repeatedly. With his head on his pillow, a vision of Chloe, moving away from his outstretched hands, played out. Tears rolled over his face. He ached; sick inside, he wondered why she would not love him.

Another vision—this time of April's baby—passed through Mitchell. The boy was watching his father walk away from him.

He thought of Sorber as a boy, and the abandonment Sorber had suffered by his own father. Drowning in grief, Mitchell shuttered. He had no recourse but to let the damp despair cover him; he was what his grandfather had made him.

Closing his eyes hard, Mitchell saw a vision of hands holding a light above him—extending it to him. As he reached for the light, his tears faded. Gripping the hands that reached for his, Mitchell allowed himself to be pulled from the gulf, that was his father's past.

Sitting up, Mitchell turned off the stereo, and pulled the string that illuminated a light overhead. A small wall mirror revealed misery on his face and neck.

The vision, he thought. *Whose hands were reaching for me?* Impressions of God, and angels, came and went in his thoughts. A stick man was not considered.

"Knock, knock. Are you home?" It was April.

"Yea, what are you doing all the way over here?" Mitchell replied, reaching for the door, to let April and her son in. The staff cabin and the maintenance building—which had a family apartment attached to it—were at opposite ends of the camp. He was surprised to see April childless.

"I don't know, I felt like going for a walk. Jamie and Monica wanted to babysit so I decided to take a walk. It's a beautiful night. Have you been crying?" she asked, surprised by Mitchell's expression.

He looked at her gingerly. She kissed him gently on his forehead, knowing what it was that upset Mitchell. "You missing her tonight?" she asked.

"I was but I'm over it now," he said.

"I've got a great idea!" April exclaimed. "How about a night hike to the West Fork?"

Without any hesitation they both were out the door, and down the stairs, heading directly east.

"Take us to the West Fork Blanco," April said, as both she and Mitchell smiled at the German shepherd's willingness to lead them.

Twigs snapped under Mitchell's shoes. A lively conversation ensued, yet at the mercy of gasping breaths. All that he could see in the dark, dense forest, was the white silhouette of Blanco, who walked ahead, often stopping to wait for his followers to catch up.

The West Fork was a deep ravine carved out of the millenniums by water and ice moving through it. It took on the shape of a long, arching bread pan. In earlier hikes to the top, Mitchell found a huge ice shelf with a streamed carved cave tunneling through it. Upon closer examination, layer upon layer of snow was revealed— compressed through the seasons of time—forming a giant berg that reached back hundreds of feet. On those previous trips to the ice shelf, Blanco could hardly be seen, as his coat camouflaged him perfectly.

Mitchell spoke of those previous trips with April as they walked. Sights had become familiar to him, and he would look for confirmation from each landmark as he traveled from the staff cabin to the West Fork. His eyes adjusted. Ahead he could see the light from the moon rising over Snow Summit, northeast of where they walked. The moonlight allowed the old woods to come alive, while thoughts of nature's routine were spoken between the walking companions.

Blanco's confidence in the natural world gave each trek with him special meaning for those he walked with. If aware enough, Blanco's companions would be treated to many things that were rare in the world of human sensibility. April and Mitchell were treated to one such moment; Blanco stopped short, raised his head in the half moon light, and pointed his nose at the passing of a great horned owl—its wings spread in a soundless glide over the West Fork.

They sat down together on the edge of the ravine, next to a huge Jeffrey Pine, that cascaded thick short branches out over the fork. One such branch suspended a tire swing. April decided to do a night leap on the tire swing—Mitchell gasped at her childlike trust of the rope, and the tree it was tied to. She swung wide over the center of the ravine, putting fifty feet between her life and the stream below. She screamed with fear and delight. Rotating once above the ravine, she glided back to the side, making a perfect landing onto safe ground. She looked at Mitchell and shoved the tire swing toward him.

He shoved it back to her playfully, then asked her to lead him in a trick jump over the ravine. Timing was crucial in this stunt. Either party, missing their cue, meant Mitchell would land hard on the stream bed below. He gave the signal; she put the tire out over the ledge in perfect form. Mitchell landed on the top of the tire, thrusting the swing out over the crack in the Earth. At the swing's apex, Mitchell yelled as loud as he could, trying to shake the spell he had succumbed to prior to April's arrival.

His approach and landing were awkward, and required April's assistance to steady the swing while he dismounted. Both laughed wildly at the daring move.

They were warmed by the spirit of the moment, joining Blanco next to the tree, sitting shoulder to shoulder against it. Mitchell took note of April's scent, and how well it blended into the air of the surrounding night. Without pretense, she laid her arm over his, leaned her head against the tree—breathing deeply—through a smile that could be seen by the glow of filtered moon light. Her touch created a bridge from friendship to intimacy. Under the spell of the half moon, her arm became both background, and object of desire, as the light both covered, and exposed, the texture of her skin.

There were many magical moments at de Benneville, when physical and spiritual imaginings found a home in Mitchell's mind. This was one of them. He was in perfect harmony with every living thing. They laid their heads into the cracks of the giant Jeffery pine; its sap—the scent of vanilla—encircled them.

The subdued moonlight waxed another deep breath from both. The deep inhale, through their noses, was followed by a purifying and relaxing exhale, out of their mouths. With each passing breath, April and Mitchell fell further into the vibration of the ancient tree. Their spirits were welcomed by it, as if embraced by a mother. The tree gave Mitchell many thoughts—the sun's rays—the cloud's cover of rain—the moon's tide of gravity—its stationary hold upon the moving Earth. These were the things that the tree loved. The vibrations from the tree prompted considerations of faith, of confidence in existence. The tree understood how simple, yet how beautiful, even one day was. It knew only sweet in its life, and did not comprehend bitterness, envy, or possession, or the dark experiences humanity had brought upon itself. Mitchell understood that the Garden remained a part of all living things, save man.

They continued their communion with the Jeffrey Pine, and understood the unimaginable wonder of Eden—its perfection making a momentary claim on both of them. When the message came through, April wrapped her fingers around Mitchell's. Without opening his eyes, he tightened his fingers around hers, acknowledging their shared meditation. Their deep breathing continued as the meditation moved with the slow ascent of the half moon. It moved through the thick of the forest, and in time, disappeared behind the upper elevations of the West Fork, marking the end of the golden silence, shared by a tree, a dog, and two humans.

Mitchell stood up, released April's hand, and stretched, breaking the serene connection he shared with her. She opened her eyes, looked up at him, smiled, and said "that was wonderful, why did you get up?"

"I was thinking that it was time to get back to camp. Blanco seems restless, and I am ready to stretch my legs a bit," he said. "How about a fire and something to eat?" he asked.

"I am starving," April said with enthusiasm. "I made a seven layer veggie loaf, and the thought of it is making my stomach growl."

"Okay, you get the food, and I'll make a fire," he said. "Blanco, back to camp!"

Fifteen minutes later they met on the sofa. With no light save the glow of a fire, illuminating the expanse of Homet Lodge, the two sat quietly together, shoulder to shoulder—in peace—and in the warmth of the Eden that followed them home—a blessing from the Jeffrey pine.

After dinner, they pushed the dishes to one end of the large coffee table, put their feet up on it, and leaned them against one another. The Garden of Eden came up in conversation. The fire moved between the silhouettes of their fingers, as they held each other's hand. Time passed intimately. As the fire dimmed, passions rose, and warmth remained until dawn, which stirred the great hall to life again.

With the dawn came the happy voices of April's baby and her sitters, whose smiles greeted the well-fed and loved faces, of Mitchell and April. The young men erupted into the lodge in their customary banter, oblivious to the scene in front of the fire place. They barreled into the kitchen, ravenous for food. Everyone joined them. April's baby cooed, providing a toothless smile to the beginning of another day at de Benneville Pines.

⋘⋙

Days grew short. Storms blew in. Maintenance of the camp took on the seasonal changes. Mitchell became proficient at plowing snow—at times having to do so all night long.

On one such occasion the sun rose on a well-plowed, winter wonderland. Snow banks were stacked six feet high throughout the camp. The morning sky was perfectly blue—the snow flawless in its symmetric assault on the camp and surrounding wilderness.

Needing to sleep, Mitchell proceeded up his white stairs, and saw the morning sun shine brightly into his room. Thick covers and a soft pillow waited. The day went on without him.

Mitchell awoke at midday to the gentle tune "The Last Thing on My Mind." He was hungry, but the song made him stay a little longer in bed. He listened to the words—they prompted thoughts of his father—of things that should have been said but were not. The long silence between them only made their situation worse. The song's lyrics provided motivation to perhaps make a connection before it was too late.

Tired but willing, he donned the clothes he wore in his all night effort to keep the camp open, walking back down to the lodge for some lunch. April gave him a note to call home—that it was urgent to do so.

He took a tranquil walk down to the camp office to make the call. The reflection of sunlight on the snow, casting a billion different points of light toward him, and reminiscent of a moonless midnight sky, made him think again of his father. In a whisper he recited Neil Diamond's song while he walked. The urgency of the call from his mother passed his thoughts while he sang.

"Hello," he said to Ada.

"The son-of-a-bitch is finally gone," his mother said to him, spewing forth the venom that had always been Ada's litany about Sorber.

Mitchell had waited a long time to hear those words. They meant his father's suffering was over. His handless life had now become the responsibility of angels, and God, who could surely give back to him what living, had taken away.

"There is a memorial planned for him and I want you to be here if you can make it," she said. "Everyone, including your father's half brother, is going to come."

"I'll be there. When did he die?"

"Last night," is all she said. "He took his last breath at 2:30 a.m."

Quiet passed. He realized he had been up plowing snow when his father passed away.

Saying goodbye, he put the handset back into its cradle, walked out into the white, blue, snowbound wilderness, looked up at the sky, and felt intense relief. He had waited a long time for such news. Heart attacks, drinking, smoking, bad diet, but mostly a lack of self worth, finally brought an end to his father's days, mercifully so. April was there to hug him, as he headed back to his room to pack for the trip. He told her about the memorial, and that he would return to dB soon.

Mitchell looked at his father's radio, turned it on, and heard only static. He imagined him as a baby, becoming a boy, then a sailor, husband, father, and now, a citizen of the universe.

There was never much said in the years they lived together as father and son. If he could have said goodbye, there would have been few words spoken, with the silence between them carrying the burden of truth. Even now he still did not know what to say to his father.

What Mitchell did not comprehend, was that his understanding of Sorber was the product of heavy propaganda—perpetrated upon him—and his siblings—by Ada. Sorber was nothing like the man Mitchell knew. Living would someday reveal the truth.

He threw a small travel pack over his shoulder, and headed out to his pickup. He paused at the base of the white stairs, and looked back at the entrance to his room. He felt different now, as the son of a departed father, becoming the root of a fruitless family tree. He was tugged by a responsibility not to repeat, what he understood to be, his father's mistakes.

The truck radio played Neil Diamond's song for a second time on the day his father died—leaving its final thoughts hanging in the air—as he drove off the camp. He waved to his de Benneville family, looked with longing into April's eyes when he passed, as both heard the lyrics extol effort—through love—to change unkind acts toward the ones they loved.

❧◖◗

Winter on the floor of the Sonoran Desert registered tropical to Mitchell. He left the icy de Benneville Pines behind, and found the popular sun-belt climate a reprieve from the cold bright mountain days.

He looked on incredulously, arriving at yet another place of residence for his parents. The bright yellow apartment building, west of Park Central Mall in Phoenix, put Mitchell in a sour mood. He watched its front door fly open—the entirety of what remained of his family—including never before seen nieces and nephews, gathered around the old truck to meet him

One by one his brother, and sisters, filed out of the yellow box. His sour mood was met with looks of exasperation. Mitchell's long-haired, mountain-man exterior surprised them—a beard, flannel shirt, worn blue jeans, and boots. His eyes were hidden behind a pair of flight sunglasses—the perceptions of his family hidden behind a smile, and a wave "hello."

Upon entry into the apartment, awkwardness turned into several rounds of the peculiar laughter that flowed at Mitchell's family gatherings. He closed his eyes as the past crept in around him. Nothing had changed except for the stage on which the past would creep. The same suffocating lock filled the air.

He stepped back outside, into the bright light of the Sonoran winter sun, and took a deep breath, exhaling the cigarette smoke that consumed every house his parents ever lived in.

Phoenix had changed. It was no longer the destination of asthmatics. It developed a cough of its own. Towns in the Valley of the Sun that were once separated by agriculture, now blended into one another. Downtown Phoenix had been cursed with its first brown cloud.

Cigarette smoke, brown clouds, creepy vibes from the past, or de Benneville Pines? Mitchell thought, sarcastically. Forcing himself to go back inside, he was met at the door by Julie. "You got a minute?" she asked.

"Yea, what's up?"

"I found dad's ashes in the kitchen garbage can."

Mitchell shook his head and asked "Where are they now?"

"In my purse, in a plastic bag. I can't imagine what is going through her mind right now."

The shock of Julie finding their father's ashes in a garbage can led Mitchell to say; "I was relieved. How odd is it that I've been waiting most of my life for him to die. Where did such a notion come from?"

212

"I've been waiting too," Julie said. "Its like I gave up on him a long time ago. So did mom. She has told me for years that he was dying . . . that she was hoping he would die."

"That's it," Mitchell said. "Mom instilled in me that dad would be better off dead. That's kinda sick, isn't it?"

"It is. There's a dark secret that makes up the mud in this family, and even though I've been away for years, it remains a mystery to me."

Mitchell looked hard at his sister. He, too, could not see the truth. Julie thought for a moment, and then asked "How would you like to scatter Dad's ashes on Squaw Peak with me?"

The idea resonated with him; he wanted to do something noble for a man who had led such an unfortunate life.

At that moment Brent appeared at the front door, looking at Mitchell. It was an uncomfortable moment; both brothers had grown—Brent as a soldier—Mitchell as a man—who suspected he was worth more than beatings he suffered at the hands of the brother who stood before him.

"Mitchell," Brent said.

Mitchell met Brent's eyes.

"You, and our sisters, did not deserve the rough and unwarranted treatment I gave you," Brent said. "I'm sorry."

Mitchell knew that somewhere inside him, his brother's words were welcomed. Slowly, Mitchell raised his hand, taking Brent's, shaking it. All that he could say was, "Okay Brent," followed by another uncomfortable moment—a hug.

"How about coming with us—we are going to Squaw Peak to scatter Dad's ashes," Mitchell said.

Brent looked pallid. "I've got something to tell both of you," he said.

The two brothers and their sister walked together toward the apartment complex parking lot. Julie and Brent looked dubiously at Mitchell's truck, as they walked around it.

"And you drive this, why?" Julie asked.

"Cuz it's paid for," Mitchell said, looking sideways at his sister.

They drove north on Central toward Glendale Avenue. The route took them by the family's old stomping grounds. It was a somber experience. No one bothered to look up Orange Drive. On Glendale Avenue, Brent spoke:

"I went to see Dad the day before he died," Brent said. "I hung around and talked to him for quite awhile. When I left around 7 p.m., he was not on his death bed. He was sitting upright, in a chair next to the bed, with no IV. He stated to me that he was in for a check up. Now he's dead. I believe Mom did it."

Julie and Mitchell stared ahead in disbelief. Not because they couldn't believe what they heard, but because it made perfect sense; Sorber's life would end in such a way—and at the hands of such a person as Ada. She spent her existence meticulously dismantling Sorber's life, who had mistaken Ada's control for love—seeking her sanction in the same way he sought his father's. Ada could have easily exercised her craft on as many hospital employees as necessary, to orchestrate the deed.

"It is odd that he was cremated so quickly," Julie said. "Within hours of his passing, he was already in a plastic bag."

"Why?" Mitchell asked. "Why would she do such a thing?"

"The life insurance," Brent said. "Dad had a hundred thousand dollar policy. She was tired of being poor, and being married to a drunk. But he sobered up. He was sad and lonely. He felt worthless, being raised by a father—then married to a wife—who were both ashamed of him."

Brent continued; "There was a heavy set nurse who couldn't look at me when I went in to see Dad the next day, only to learn he had passed away. She had something to do with it; I know it in my bones. Mom had complete control of Dad's chart, and medications. No one at that hospital crosses her."

They arrived at Squaw Peak Park. They got out, and began a quiet and laborious hike to the summit. Sorber's children were trying to reconcile his life, but they could not make sense of it.

At the summit, Brent spoke; "To our father—a World War II sailor, who served his country in its great time of need." Mitchell looked quizzically at Brent, never considering his father as someone to uphold, and to be proud of. Their thoughts were carried with the breeze, mixed with ashes that spoke more than their father ever did.

214

The image of his father's ashes in a garbage can shamed him. Irreconcilable anger layered itself between memories of a stick man and its silence. Mitchell had had enough.

He said goodbye as all eyes watched him climb into his truck—its door slamming hard. Through his long hair and beard, he gazed upon the sum of what his family had become—which on any given day—could fit behind the hatchback of a Yugo—sacks of secrets—charging over the next fiery bridge. Looking at the yellow door of the apartment left him sick. And bitter. He turned the wheel of the truck hard, and pulled away, from the last family gathering he would ever know.

Interstate 10 appeared to bloom before Mitchell. Life's possibilities moved further away from secrets, and closer to what was ahead—as the road moved him further away from chaos, and closer to what he knew was his. What resided east, in Phoenix, in the form of family and tradition, bitterness had tilled. What was found west, in de Benneville, would be tradition on Mitchell's terms. It would be one day's worth, then two, and so on, as the days of his life unfolded without the aid—or ash—of a leaderless family. He made Highway 38, as it left Redlands, his own—rising up into the ancient stands of oak and cedar—their roots now his, by his occupancy among them. Amid the landmarks of his de Benneville home and family, he realized that possession of his life could only go back as far as the sunrise. He held the ritual of getting high, as his tradition. He let go of any sense of family, holding firm to his childhood impression that stated; what he could not see did not exist—like his past—locking away events that still held sway over his destiny.

This was a mistake. The idea of being free of unseen attachments was flawed, and in some subtle undertone of his understanding—in how he wanted to live his life—he knew it. There was a price to pay for disconnecting from his past, but he could not place it. He put that price on a back burner, with no heat. He removed himself from the residue of his father's life, and the hopelessness in his mother's disturbed mind.

He would hear his mother cry on the phone in the decades to come. She would call him from her own early morning lightless despair. Loneliness had been found in her waning days, as she beheld the terror of none but her own footprints, left behind her.

Before Mitchell was laid this familiar fate; he would not look back at what he left behind, cutting off not only the source of his lone heart, but the remedy of it as well. He would make the loneliness of his parent's lives, his own, unwittingly so; as it is with all children of handless parents—whose own childhoods spoke the repeated evil chants of their ancestors.

In the intense blue of the day with the tops of ancient trees pointing the way, Mitchell turned in a circle with his hands outstretched, unencumbered of gypsy ash. The seconds before him were of only him, of what only his senses could touch. He turned without the filters of any life lived before, without the paradoxical light found in archetype models; examples of living that would have left him at least aware, then enabled, in the dark blue of midnight.

✌ℭ℞

The winter nights froze the sleeping things that were stored for another day. Space heaters kept their warmth, and left the occupants of any room on the camp to fend for themselves.

Under the security of many blankets, and the comfort of skin touching skin, Mitchell shared his bed with the women of de Benneville Pines. Obligation, and rigidity of relationships, based on things that lasted longer than the next snow, held no quarter in the young lover-friends, who did battle with the cold by generating their own special brand of uncommitted heat.

Woodstoves were utilized during the short days—and long nights—under the cyrstaline canopies of snow, leafless branch, and stardust. The wrong kind of stoking put out heat that would toast skin at ten feet. Lightly toasted was better, where a bare back to the stove at three feet would take the heat into a bed, remotely located in another room.

Hot-tubbing, as the Milky Way looked on over the tops of alpine peaks, was another way everyone, who lived at de Benneville, passed the cold nights. Heated by a giant wood furnace, the hot tub was a legendary meeting ground for countless thousands of southland residents. On any given weekend, one could expect a long wait for a turn in the alpine tub. It was during the week, when the residents were alone, that it would become a very unique space. It was the "living end," as Sorber used to say.

Next to the camp's large pool, the hot tub was the starting gun for every kind of human union. Its elements of water from the well above the camp, and its heat, generated by the fallen generations of oak and pine, took it's occupants into love's reach of the eternal. Infatuations rose. Conversations soared. Answers to the problems of the world were obvious. At the end of the evening, choices were made in bonding, like molecules in the expanding universe. The cold, but steamy walks, back to more private surroundings, were followed by the sun's realities, suggesting that the clarity of the moment, found the night before, was not enough to change one's perception of the sunrise.

And so the life of a winter's day for campers, and residents, went on. The mornings served up activities and work respectively; meetings, workshops, and crafts for campers: thawing pipes, hauling wood, and preparing meals for residents—all while looking into the eyes of strangers—who were lovers the night before.

Mitchell's life had become the playfulness found in a particular Robert Frost poem. He could do worse than being a maintenance man at a camp and conference center—which, in some ways, fulfilled a once-held desire to be a forest ranger. He certainly could not do better than life as it presented itself—from one season to the next—among the trees and the loves of de Benneville Pines. It was a blessed existence—unfettered amongst the old growth wood. He learned the importance of doing in life what he loved to do. He was free to sleep unencumbered by worries, stress, rush hour traffic, office politics, and three different women—who were all willing to share him with one another. He was a man of the mountains—loved for who he was. Harmony had, at last, defined his life.

Chapter Forty Four

APRIL'S eyes caught his, as she stood in the threshold of the office door; Mitchell knew she had upsetting news. She was visibly distressed. From the back of the lodge he began a long walk toward her, trying to guess what the news could be. A subtle change of energy grew larger, as the distance between April and Mitchell, grew shorter.

The message was from Chloe. He looked at April, and she him, confused at how Chloe would know where to contact Mitchell. *Ada,* he thought, incredulously.

He wadded the message in his hand, then shoved it in the front pocket of his jeans, breathing deeply, wanting to quell the rush of adrenalin gushing through him. Chloe's name pricked him. It stung him much the way a line of cocaine stung an addict, who was sinking into a physiological and spiritual quagmire.

She wanted to join him at de Benneville. He thought back to the Plaza Bar, some seasons ago, when he could not find Chloe. She was upstairs in the Westgate Hotel, with one of her corporate lovers. The bartender, bellhop, and front desk clerk knew it. They looked at him pitifully, as he waited for her to come downstairs, thinking of her in a room, above his head, fucking another man. He staggered, both physically and emotionally, at the memories.

April could see him struggling with the cold hard realities of heart break. She wrapped her arm around his neck, whispering the truths of angels into his ears:

"You can say 'no'," April said compassionately. "Your love for her can remain a part of your past. I know that none of us here want to lose you to your pain," she pleaded, "and I know that this extension of your life should fall under the grace of lessons learned."

Mitchell looked at April. She wore the face of life's truths in her kind and generous advice. Allowing Chloe back into his life, would end bitterly, again. It would not only be his heart that would break but Bae's as well.

He got up from April's side, putting her chin in his hand, and said he needed to be alone. April stood up and hugged him, knowing what being "alone" meant.

Departing her embrace, he headed back up the hill to the staff cabin. In his backpack he put forty eight hours worth of supplies, then walked back downstairs to say goodbye to his friends, informing them of his intention to hike to the summit of San Gorgonio Peak. He would be back in a couple of days.

Jamie and Monica begged him not to go. "It's dangerous to hike Greyback in the dead of winter."

He would go anyway. There was nothing Mitchell needed more—before agreeing to let Chloe return—than swaths of stars at eleven thousand feet in elevation. There, he hoped to understand the unimaginable pleasure—and burn—found at the talented tips of Chloe's fingers.

He walked the long stretch of open field that was the camp's parking lot, and headed toward Jenks Lake Road. He heard barking behind him. It was Blanco, who would make the hike too. His six companions waved goodbye. Turning back in the direction of the road, he and Blanco navigated a small stand of wood in time to hitch a ride from an old man, who was also making his way to the San Gorgonio Wilderness, for reasons of his own.

Mitchell put Blanco, and his backpack, into the truck bed, and himself in the cab. "Where you headed," the old man asked, in a rich, and oddly familiar western drawl. Mitchell took note that the old man immediately began to hum a familiar melody, before and after he sang the lyrics; . . . *Carmen and the Devil* . . .

"The summit," Mitchell said, as he listened further to the song the driver hummed. "'The Weight,' by The Band, right?"

This got a sidelong stare, then a smile, from the driver, again striking a sense of familiarity in Mitchell. The driver looked ahead on the road. He put his truck into gear and resumed his humming, driving toward the wilderness boundary.

"Why do you look so familiar to me?" Mitchell asked.

"I don't know, maybe it's because you see what you want to see," the old man said.

Mitchell looked ahead. *Maybe in a movie, maybe somebody I've waited on, maybe a camper on a weekend retreat at de Benneville*, he thought. *Somewhere I've seen this guy before.*

Mitchell found the Poopout Hill trailhead, and without hesitation, began the ascent into higher elevations. He stopped often to view the slow appearance of Big Bear Lake, gauging his progress on the trail by the lake's increasing presence over Snow Summit. He stopped often to catch his breath; Poopout Hill was aptly named. Daylight waned, but Mitchell did not stop.

He knew not what to do. His desire for Chloe was an addiction. He knew if he touched her he would pay for the pleasure she would give him. Yet the desire to do so was overwhelming—he was often tempted during his hike to turn around, and run off the face of the mountain—to where ever she might be—to hold her again in his arms—to feel the un-earthly passions—to smell the mystic scent in the tresses of her hair—to hold the vessel of her soul, that was half of his own.

He voiced things to Blanco that he was surprised to hear himself say: "She is my spirit's sister. I lose myself in her reflection. I only say what she would say, and feel what she feels. I hear what she hears. I can't find my own hands and feet when she sits next to me, and living my life becomes an extension of living hers. That's what is wrong with how I love her."

Blanco continued his cadence with Mitchell. The hours grew as did the night, and their presence in the wilderness passed deeper into the ages of time, which stood still among the trees, springs, and meadows. Chloe stayed with him. He could not let go of the spell she cast upon his life.

Atop the summit, he stared out over the curve of the Earth; stars appeared below him in all directions. His spirit reached out to those stars, wanting to touch the lips and the smile of a woman who held Eros in the palm of her hand. He stood with his white friend, among the blue-black world of midnight, on the summit of San Gorgonio. He slowly re-laced the puppet strings of her love, around that which he had become.

With the frozen elements all around him, he hiked off the summit, toward the moment when he would wrap his arms around Chloe again. The downhill midnight hike, with Blanco as his guide, went on through the night. Blanco was perfect in his delivery of the Poopout trail head. As the sun came up over the icy wilderness, a new day dawned on many old hurts, that still found no release, only an old friend, in the face of who he loved.

❧❦

The old man had set up camp near the Poopout trailhead, where he had dropped Mitchell off the day before. He greeted the man and his dog when they rounded the bend, giving Mitchell a cup of hot chocolate, and Blanco the rest of his bacon and egg omelet. He looked knowingly at the pair, finding exhaustion on both faces.

"Did you make it to the top," he asked.

"We did."

"Did you figure things out," the old man asked perceptively.

There was a pause in Mitchell. He solved nothing on the summit, and struggled to answer the old man's question. Mitchell suddenly realized that whatever was decided on the summit, it was not he who had made up his mind.

"One thing's for sure," the old man said. "There's always a price to pay."

"Even when following one's heart?" Mitchell asked.

"Blindly?"

"If need be," Mitchell said.

"The dual-edged sword in the flesh," the old man said kindly, pointing toward Mitchell, and then turning back to the tasks at hand.

Mitchell thanked the old man for the hot chocolate. He and Blanco turned toward the road, and resumed their trek back home. He stopped, turned, and looked at the old man once more—the familiar feeling that he knew him came and went—and waved goodbye, hearing the old man hum ". . . *Carmen and the Devil* . . .," as he departed

❧❦

Tears welled up in Chloe's eyes. There was a smile on the tornado, as she walked up the hill, across the camp parking lot, toward Mitchell. He smiled in return.

He looked at the women of de Benneville. A sudden, sour change of energy encircled all of them. He no longer saw the wonderful chemistry of his de Benneville family. Blanco instinctively growled, uncharacteristically so. The tornado, with her hair and rich self-confidence, walked directly toward Mitchell, leaving no room for the life he shared with April, Jamie, and Monica—blowing clean any sign of love between them.

She was in his arms. *How strange to feel her here again.* He looked down at her neck and shoulders—his arms now lost in the net of her hair. She pulled away from him—just enough to put her breath between them. He looked at her lips and they kissed.

Mitchell whirled. *How odd that I feel nothing but her. I feel no sense of my own time. I have no idea where I am standing. It is only her that I know.*

He looked around to see everyone, one by one, depart, returning to work in different parts of the camp, save one. April, who was now joined by Blanco, was looking just above the couple. Mitchell thought, *what does she see?*

April walked over to where Chloe and Mitchell stood. In her eyes Mitchell saw what she was looking at. It was a refection of his de Benneville spirit leaving the camp. With a tear in her eye, April embraced Chloe in a welcoming gesture. Mitchell picked up Bae, and tossed her into the air. She was reserved, understandably so. Mitchell would give Bae all the time she needed to get used to him being in her life again.

In her life, Mitchell repeated to himself. He repeated it again, while he looked at Chloe. He pictured himself walking through the front door of Chloe's life, leaving his own behind. The vision continued; after closing the door—he noted suddenly that there were no other doors or windows *in her life*—only her impulses—her electrical charges—only her visions and desires. He had only been with her for five minutes, and was already lost in the web of her intoxicating hair—losing his sense of self—losing the recently understood wisdom, of who he was.

April brought him back for a moment when she hugged him, saying she was happy for him. As April hugged Mitchell, he looked at Chloe, and saw the nervous, jealous closing of her eyes, as she looked away. Mitchell cut the hug short, instantly regretting doing so; he had denied his heart for April. She sensed the life of her friend, and who he was to her, slip away. She turned to go, Blanco too. Mitchell looked at the departing woman and dog, watching them become something else all together. They would be the road not chosen, an unanswered longing that would remain with him forever.

✥

Mitchell, Chloe, Bae, and the history that cemented them together, changed everything about de Benneville Pines, and not for the better. Their history came with obligation, jealousy, lasciviousness, and loss, replacing the good-natured, grace-filled community of youthful cheerfulness.

Chloe's old form returned. Instead of suits, she now devoured men in hiking boots with unshaven faces. Women too. She had become very popular at the hot tub, and Mitchell again watched as her infidelities became legend in the southland.

Her web encased him. Not able to breath, he would run from his upstairs room into the wilderness, trying to escape the cutting of his heart by the clawing and pinching Chloe. April often found Mitchell hidden on the camouflaged platform he discovered on his first day at dB, lost in despair.

At last, and with the gut-wrenching news that Chloe had had an abortion, Mitchell gave up. He would again lose his home—to save Bae from another, in what was already, an endless series of debilitating moves.

✥

Plans were made with his childhood buddies. They were to come up to de Benneville and get him. His destination was Phoenix by way of the Prescott National Forest. Standing in the back of Homet Lodge, on the delivery deck of the kitchen, Mitchell heard a rumbling coming from Jenks Lake Road, and saw a trail of dust flying up into the air. It was Dalton and Presley—boys who had become men—yet still possessing grins and laughs that took Mitchell home to their childhood lives.

Chloe watched bitterly through a distant window, her countenance revealing the resignation of consequence—a resignation that would mean nothing to her as soon as Mitchell was gone.

It was time for Mitchell to say goodbye to his friends. Sadness grew immeasurably as he walked toward the men and women who had loved him—for him. He took all of them into his arms, whispering to April that he would never forget her.

When the hugs were done, he asked everyone to follow him into the lodge. Grabbing a tall ladder, Mitchell tied a large crystal prism to the top steel beam. It swayed gently in the air, casting giant rainbows about the room. He asked everyone present to remember him, whenever the crystal gave them the sunlight in its parts—its rainbow of colors the love he held for each.

They walked back outside—Mitchell's childhood friends waited in the car. He looked back once more, toward the window where Chloe had stood, and saw only Bae. Tears were streaming down her face. Mitchell could see that she was crying. There was nothing he could do but break the bridge that had become their impermanent relationship. Turning from her was as cold a moment that Mitchell had ever experienced in his young life.

Blanco sat away from the group, staring at Mitchell. Looking into the dog's eyes, Mitchell unwittingly beheld the full and complete acceptance of who he was. He slowly ambled over to the great, white German shepherd, sank to his knees, and buried his nose and lips between Blanco's eyes, kissing the dog—in a great quaking of love from his heart for the animal. He said goodbye to the great friendship that had defined Mitchell from the first day.

He took one last deep breath of de Benneville air, got into the car, looked at Dalton and Presley, and simply said "Okay." He knew that what he beheld before him, the passing of trees, roads, and landmarks of de Benneville—would never be seen again. They were landmarks of his life, of what he was made of, and he was proud to have created such a life for himself.

Two items helped Mitchell let go; the first was "Cowboy Song," a tune by Thin Lizzy—playing at full volume. Heard back at the lodge, the song made each of his camp friends smile. The other was two grams of cocaine. It rested on a mirror. They pulled over, cutting out a line for him to snort. He did. His first.

The song, the goodbye, and the wonderful high of cocaine, speed-walking through his brain, was all Mitchell needed to release himself from the world, found in the car's side view mirror.

Dalton put the cocaine in a small container, put the car in drive, and stepped hard on the gas. They rumbled upon Highway 38, turned left toward Angelus Oaks, then Redlands, then Interstate 10, and then to points east of the inland empire.

No one could stop talking. Mitchell rode a wave of song and mental dance. Life was full of promise. The alpine air was gone—the frost in his heart melting the moment cocaine entered his nostrils. The subtle communications between three great friends were back, and the week ahead unplanned.

"Well, Beetle," Dalton said, "which way do we go?"

"Prescott," Mitchell said. "It's nonstop partying there during the Fourth."

In unison they sang with Thin Lizzy. "Cowboy Song" had the insides of unattached males written into the beat and lyrics. They understood how they could run free with herds of buffalo.

"Great idea," Dalton said to him. "Look on the map, and tell me how to get there."

"Well, pal," Mitchell said, "I already know. I've been looking at a few maps since this little rendezvous was set in motion. You take the 10, to the 60, to the 71, to the 89, and you don't fucking look back. How's that for directions!" Mitchell said emphatically.

Dalton and Presley looked at him with appreciation for still having the gusto, and the 'go-for-broke' attitude, that came alive when they played football, and swam in waterholes together.

The rest of the *Jailbreak* album, by Thin Lizzy, was meeting Mitchell's spiritual needs, taking the words, and music, as his own private anthem to a new life.

There was something to be said for having friends like these, Mitchell thought. He looked at the profiles of the men he had known for more than half his life. They gave him roots. They were there for him before, as childhood friends, providing a roof over his head when his teenaged years grew chaotic in his own house—and now, as a ride east away from, for the last time, the confounding confusion of love—as an addiction.

The antithesis of such a relationship sat in the seat of the El Camino. His old friends fit his boyish heart like a glove. There was a deeply rooted camaraderie between the men that left nothing confused. It was simple, clean, and void of the drifting emotional debris that was Chloe. They knew what the road ahead would bring, and what applying the gas toward that end, would mean.

Chapter Forty Five

LAURIE faced her office window. Through the old panes of glass she could see Cortez Street, and the shops that lined it. She sat in a giant leather swivel chair; her head tilted to one side, resting upon her hand; her contemplation finally forming an imprint of knuckles into her cheeks. A tear tilted on the edge of her eye closest to her hand, and she felt it fall there. Using her other hand, she wiped it away, and found as she did so, her aggravation overcame her.

The tear was due in part to Mitchell's behavior during their dinner date some evenings earlier, and by her inability to understand the affinity she felt for him, which remained in her quiet moments, alone in her office or home. Performing mundane tasks, she found herself staring into the bottom of a kitchen garbage can or in the mirror as she brushed her teeth, thinking about the old fool. *He's a coot,* she would think, as she wiped toothpaste from her lips, taking note of the way her lips moved as she brushed them with her fingers, wondering how the old coot's lips would feel if she kissed him.

And too, on this morning, the tear represented her sadness in response to a new piece of the puzzle, one that disturbed her significantly. This, on top of all that she had already considered regarding Mitchell, which included the insanity of his actions before, and during his trial, when she acted as his public defender. *What about that old greasy truck, Laurie?* She asked herself. *He's a loner. He endeavors not to see me, I do all of the calling, and exert effort to journey out to that damn cabin, and spend time with him, and all he can talk about is Sian.* "Who the fuck is Sian?" She heard herself ask out loud, and was surprised by the tone of complete frustration found there.

A part of Laurie wanted to ask other questions. The public defender in her wanted to hear them coming clearly from her mouth as a point of reference. The question blurted out moments earlier had an answer that presented a brutal reality she did not want to face, one that carried with it implications that would crumble many a hope in her for Mitchell.

Her largest worry was how she would talk to Mitchell about Sian. How was she going to refer to Sian as an object of Mitchell's mental, and spiritual anguish—a phantom of Mitchell's longing—a ghost? She imagined his reaction to her claim on his sanity. She imagined his realization that her attack upon Sian's legitimacy no different than any other attack. She was anxious that Mitchell might loose what grip he had on reality, but she wanted to help him. She, moving against her own expectations, loved him.

Using her connections, she uncovered the mystery of what happened to Red's daughter, assembling a collection of police and coroner's reports that put an end to Sian many long years ago. It was unreal for Laurie to find Red's name mentioned in the reports. She noted frustration written between the lines of the investigating officer—who had lost track of Red when they finally caught up with Sian's murderer. Laurie had rubbed her eyes in disbelief—in shock—as she looked closer at the report—to the name of the person in the report who had taken baby Sian's life—it was a name that was known to her.

She sat down again on her leather chair, turned and faced Cortez Street—and the shops that lined it. She was subdued by the comings and goings of townspeople—whose lives—for the most part—were left untouched by tragedy. Laurie, whose heart was caught in the tragic crack that had become Mitchell's life, saw her own life become less like the townspeople she watched through her office windows—and, through association—more like her clients—who were singled out as the thrashers of horrifying times. *He did not ask for this,* Laurie thought. *He did what his heart told him, and that is why he gets my sympathy—and empathic heart.*

"White and still," *he said out loud to himself, allowing the syllables and their inflections to become something more than a spoken thought in a painful and ordinary world.*

Chapter Forty Six

YOUNG men often feel invincible. It is a combination of energy and inexperience that consumes that portion of time considered by so many as being wasted. *It* is a thrilling ride—outlined by events, places, things, and people—that transform those young men—through critical decisions that are made—into who and what they will be for the remainder of their lives.

᠕᠊᠊᠊᠊᠍᠊

Mitchell, Dalton, and Presley sat about the east facing steps of the Prescott County Courthouse—in just such a period of their lives. Their long drive from dB was complete. They were feeling the clean, mile-high air engulf their travel-weary senses. As in their younger days, each found their own story blending into their current surroundings.

Idle thoughts came and went. Glancing left of where he sat, Mitchell studied the shiny black finish of iron work surrounding a fountain where, in the movie *Billy Jack*, Billy threw a bad guy. He looked at the store front that was once Dent's Ice Cream Parlor, where he met Lynn after football practice. Chloe took center stage, forcing bitterness and anger to gush threw him.

Mitchell leaned back, in an effort to remove the anger from his thoughts, bending his head up to take in the courthouse in a backward, and upside down perspective. He followed a long, neoclassical, granite column from the base to its tip. He noticed, in the shadow of the spire, the shape of a young woman standing behind a pane of glass. She was tall, business-like, and staring back at him with a somewhat disagreeable look upon her face. When he straightened out his neck, and head, to get a normal view, she was gone.

Other thoughts took shape—under the spell of people-watching. The park-like atmosphere of the grounds was being enjoyed by all. It was revealed to Mitchell, upon closer study, that a general apathy accompanied the countenances of the people parade, as it floated by. He looked at the back of his friends' heads— two shapes as familiar as any other thing is his life. Craning his head again, toward the pane of glass above him, he searched for the suit seen moments earlier.

At once, the pragmatic lyrics from "Time," Pink Floyd's haunting melody about English melancholy, strummed its way into Mitchell's people-watching perceptions. The song, always enjoyed by Mitchell under the influence of marijuana—as an accompaniment to being stoned, suddenly became something else all together. The memory of a blue arcing sky—with whirling hands in a carefree spin—yielded to visions of an approaching storm. The lyrical euphoria of the song instantly became a joyless staging of life to come, where a new and awful sense of foreboding creased his brow. He looked up again at the pane of glass. It remained a colorless reflection of the granite column next to it, and was representative of his future days, when ignoring the start of his society's expectations for young men his age, passed as a cold vision of his future, and of life in general.

Suddenly, he *was* considering his future. His mood turned sour. Hanging around Prescott for the weekend lost its appeal. He asked his friends if they would not mind skipping the Fourth celebrations and head back to Phoenix early. They asked why. He told them about the sense of foreboding he felt—that he was missing the start of the very race described in "Time." As he spoke, another glance up at the colorless window produced a surprising re-appearance of the young woman. Mitchell looked gravely at her, and then asked "Can we go?"

⋞જ

The *Ford F-100* had left an oil smudge at several different restaurant parking lots over the coming years. The restaurants, opening in and around Mesa, Arizona, were indicative of the housing boom–bust cycle that roared through the southwest time and again. Like eyes in hurricanes, pockets of prosperity led to business development, mostly by giant corporations that spun everything from air-conditioners to spaghetti. Mitchell was there each time one of those giant corporations planted itself in the hospitality game—depositing himself on the ground floor of restaurant openings—riding the wave of curiosity and popularity—which was enjoyed by everyone from busboys to the boards of such corporations. Their profits meant a full station for Mitchell, as he continued on in his life as a waiter.

He needed corporate restaurant openings to live. The oil smudge on freshly-rolled and painted parking lots served as a reminder of that need. He enjoyed the movie houses, and other amenities of city life, but he did not become a part of the greed represented by economic boom–bust cycles.

He lived life as a man removed from common prospect, but not from the mistakes and challenges that defined this period of his life. From both outside his family of origin, as well as within, Mitchell lived with seen, and unseen influences. He got to know Bob Dylan and Tom Robbins. He began a lifelong habit of writing in a journal format and liked who he was when he wrote. He continued his use of pot as a way of life, and was confident he was not following his parent's footsteps.

But it wasn't *the* rising and falling prices of the criminal housing industry that eventually got to him. Nor the viewing of the space shuttle Challenger—exploding through the air—time and time again—on every TV screen across America. It was not the 'crumbling at heart,' over an American justice system—that allowed the maniacal OJ Simpson off the hook—for what any child could see he had done. It wasn't the death of professional sports—which best represented the greed of the last quarter of twentieth century American society, that got to Mitchell, nor the personal computer, or the advent of AIDS. It wasn't the ignoring of a world suffering at the hands of so many brutal and evil men, or the abortions he was, and was not, a part of. It wasn't his relationships, and the endless betrayals he suffered. It wasn't the flattening of the world—brought on by the laying of oceanic fiber optic cable, or the wreck of the Exxon Valdez, or the death of protestors in Tiananmen Square. It wasn't the endless passenger jet crashes, terrorists attacks, cigarette deaths, or automobile fatalities. It wasn't the number of unsolved murders in the country, or the selling of the electoral process. It wasn't the death of his father, newly discovered as a murder; the truth revealed in a hand-written suicide note from Ada—scribed just before the one hundred and twenty sleeping pills she took—took her. It was not the memories of loss in leaving Central High School's football program, or the endless parade of U-Haul trucks floundering down highways, that often froze him in a momentary gaze—as if an old man—caught in the bitter glare of a cold fire—in the dead of night. No, none of these memories, or events, got to Mitchell, as he lived his life, working as a waiter in Mesa, Arizona.

What got him was the *cocaine*.

࠷ୠ

In a dream, he made his way to the edge of Lake Tahoe, where small waves lapped over one another, rippling the starlight at his feet. He looked up the mountain side, to the silhouette of Mount Rose Highway rolling over the crest, and to the outline of his rock high above him. Mitchell saw the shadow of his younger years standing tall upon it. The song "Landslide," sadly set the scene before him. He looked dearly at the boy. He thought he saw the spirit of an unborn child rise above the boy on the rock, into the star-filled heaven above. He noted the boy's broad shoulders and hair, shimmering in the alpine night sky. Staring at what was embodied within, Mitchell saw the boy fall from the rock head first, and without resistance, out of his mind's eye, saying goodbye to an anchor of hope, and an arc to love, that was dreamed of, and written about, a long, long time ago.

Chapter Forty Seven

MITCHELL had fallen over, stumbling head first, out of control, toward the embankment on the side of his girlfriend's apartment. His arms rolled beneath him, ending on his back. He coughed wildly, as tall Eucalyptus trees, illuminated by yellow streetlights, spun heavily. He closed his eyes to stave off vomiting on himself, as his sense of balance whipped in circles through his head. He was unable to catch his breath—his mind reeled at the growing dread he might suffocate. At last on his side, he tried to move his hand toward his face, to rid his skin of the embedded grass that had been lodged there. Grasping for air—as if he were drowning—he finally passed out.

Hours later, after regaining consciousness, he was slow to recall how he had gotten into the position he was. His shoulders and forearms were numb, and his shirt was wet and reeking of vomit. His forehead burned like a hot coal—fierce with pain. While he sat up, he checked himself for blood, then saw one of his shoes propped against the block fence that surrounded his girlfriend's apartment patio.

What happened? He asked himself. *Where am I* . . . Before he could finish the thought, he remembered—he had become an expert at colliding head-on with total, horrifying recall—finding himself in this same condition countless times before. Remorse gushed in him with the same regularity as the pounding surf. But this time something far worse than remorse, something evil, had landed firm upon him; it was desperation. This time, intense, crushing despair had tunneled into him. It was a hole that gouged at him deeper and wider, and made him consider, vividly so, that he might be better off dead.

"Oh God, what have I done," he cried out loud, though only he could hear.

With anger that shook his body, he sat up. Mitchell put his head in his sticky hands and began to rub his temples. Bits and pieces of a fight he had with his girlfriend were coming back into focus. He remembered now that she had locked him out of her apartment, and that he had tried to climb a gate to get back in, but fell backward to the ground, stumbling, and then passing out right were he sat.

He thought: *what a despicable existence. I feel such anger and numbing remorse. I want to change but can't seem to muster the gumption to do it. Why am*

I here again? What happened to my life? Why have I become everything that I said I would not? Why have I landed on the same slippery slope to hell as my parents?

The manageable, pot smoking addiction had progressed to an unmanageable cocaine addiction; now known to Mitchell as the *wrecking ball*; its alternating highs crashed back and forth, through his life, destroying everything in its path.

⊷ఁ∅ఆ

Self-determination is a gift handed down from father to son. A father gives a son, through action and kind word, a road map of how to be a man.

At age thirty six, Mitchell found himself lost. His hands held a map of self-determination, but it was drawn by countless lost cartographers in Mitchell's generational line, with the latest additions made by his handless father, and sociopathic mother. Mitchell's map was not legible. Fate had delivered his father to loneliness and despair—un-loved by his mother, murdered by his wife, and unknown to his kids. By his mid-thirties, it was evident to Mitchell that his father's leaderless life was now becoming his own.

The morning sun beat on him, forcing him to get up from the side of his now ex-girlfriend's apartment, find his car, and go home. Suffering from the worst hang over he had ever known, he sat alone on his small kitchen table, silence his companion; self-loathing his skin.

He stared blankly into the space before him, gaining a fragile sense of time. He wanted to fall asleep, but was unable to close his eyes. He became aware of a distant outline moving toward him, as he stared at the quiet, kitchen walls around him. The outline was now clearer; it was a road that split in two. Each was lined with straw and moved into unseen horizons. Slowly the straw-lined road, its two forks acting as legs, stood up before Mitchell, taking on the shape of a stick man. Its expression was cross, as it floated in the air in front of him. Mitchell stared at the stick man's leering, down-turned eyes, questioning what it wanted.

It is not what I want he heard the stick man's voice say. *It is what you want* the voice continued.

"What are you talking about?" Mitchell asked out loud.

Experience, the voice said, yet without any movement of expression on the stick man's face. Mitchell looked further into the apparition's angry eyes.

"Why do you keep coming back?" Mitchell demanded, his voice shaking.

Experience, a voice said again.

"I have seen you before," Mitchell said.

Never, as you do now, the voice said.

Two things happened simultaneously, before and behind Mitchell. First, a beautiful, sunshine yellow light appeared to his rear, throwing his silhouette upon the kitchen wall opposite of where he sat. Second, as the light grew in intensity, the stick man cowered, turning away from the heavenly light, and then vanishing into Mitchell's shadowed outline.

The light, filling the room, passed through everything, making the kitchen table, chairs, appliances, walls, and roof of the kitchen, transparent. Abruptly, a further outline appeared on the wall opposite Mitchell. This new source of vividness, which now passed through him, filled his silhouette with shining circles of interwoven radiance. A divinely feminine figure took shape upon the wall, her hair filled with the colors of auburn and ginger, enclosed around a finely set pair of shoulders. The source of light extended her hands forward, and over Mitchell, and as she did so, her delicate arms turned to white, feathered wings.

Her movements illuminated shapes on the transparent kitchen table, causing Mitchell to think of tools. A hammer and an anvil moved through the vision before him.

"What is this stuff?" Mitchell asked.

It is experience, replied the angelic voice behind him.

Startled, and unsure of where the response came from—either from inside his head or heard with his ears—Mitchell said to himself that *experience is not a shape that I can pick up, and put in my hands.*

You are wrong, the voice said. *Experience is exactly what you put in your hands.*

"Who is this?" Mitchell demanded.

I am your heart, the voice said, *and you are my eternal hope.*

"Dad?" Mitchell asked.

No, the voice said. *I am the voice of all life, and I am here to give you a map out of the hell you have chosen to put yourself into.*

"Are you God?" Mitchell asked.

I am the answer, the voice replied.

"How is it that I am hearing you now, when so many times before I begged for something or someone to show me the way?" Mitchell asked.

You know the answer to that question, and if you keep asking such uninspired ones, you will lose your newly found skill of hearing me now, the voice replied, impatient with the game Mitchell was about to commence.

"You're right, I'm prone to blame my lot on anything," Mitchell replied.

You are now able to hear me, because in you, a notion has passed that you may need help in living your life, the voice said. *You have stumbled upon a paradox that is difficult for most to comprehend; it is the paradox that states: a weakness recognized becomes strength.*

"You're referring to my inability, despite all will and design, to stop using cocaine, right?" Mitchell asked.

And you are referring to the very tip of the ice berg," the voice replied. *Your drug habit is but the visible part of your life gone to hell. Your drug addiction is what has grown out of what was planted long ago. I am here because you stated that you have lost the knowledge, and the skill, to become your life's intention. In truth, you have never possessed such knowledge. You asked, 'why have I landed in the same seat to hell as my parents,' remember?* The voice asked Mitchell.

"Yes, I remember that moment, but I had asked that question countless times before, why was this time different?" Mitchell asked.

Because you had made a choice, the voice replied. *Because you asked why, and how, and where—and now you have an opportunity for a new inheritance—the stuff these tools are made of. This experience tells you to look to them, to engage them, to trust them, and to have faith that they will deliver you from the road to hell you talk about.*

Mitchell looked at the tools of experience. Not knowing what they were, he picked them up one at a time, and looked at each to see if there was any idea in his head how to use them.

At that thought the voice replied to Mitchell; *the instructions on how to use these tools are not in your head; they are in your heart.*

Mitchell sat at the edge of his seat. The illuminating light of the angel began to fade. He was in the last stages of coming down; his body was recovering from twenty four straight hours of cocaine use. His eyes began to glaze over—his heart to beat slower. The nervous sweating ceased, and a shower followed by sleep was next.

He was already letting go of the angelic message. Stress was leaving his body, as was the resolve to do something about the state of his life. Crumbling back into the seat, his back muscles caved into exhaustion. Sprawling his legs out under the table, he put his head and neck on the back of the chair.

He focused on a point in the ceiling above him, noting no heavenly light and no stick man, and began warming up to the familiar notion that there was nothing really wrong with him. All he needed was a shower, something to eat, and a nap. When he awoke, he would get right back into the routine of his life.

He wondered if his girlfriend would accept the usual round of apologies. A blind hope began to creep back in; the same hope he always had at this point in the cycle of his use—he could stop—he could fix the financial strain—he would remember the promise of who he once was . . . full of talent and ideas . . . full of hope for the future . . . full of what made life worth living.

Oddly, the memory of angelic light snapped him out of the usual forsaking of terms—agreed to during the coming down–grinding hang-over phase—that always followed a coke binge. The discussion twenty minutes earlier returned. He recalled the tools. The voice suggested that one of those tools was courage.

The notion of courage had nothing to do with the self-delusion he had just set in place. Courage had nothing to do with getting back into his routine, fixing his budget, and going on like he had not just spent the last twenty four hours tunneling through a cocaine bender.

So what he thought. *What I have done this past twenty four hours means nothing. I can get back on track . . . back on track . . .* the thought

trailed over itself like water over the edge of a cliff. *Back on track* . . .
back on track . . . *back on track.*

He sat up in shock, as the tool of courage became undeniably
present in front of him. For a moment it reminded Mitchell of a
sunrise. He stared at it, and thought it was an admirable thing to
behold. Closing his eyes to rub them, he shook his head, then stopped
moving. With his eyes closed, he stared at the memory of the tool, as it
burned through the neural cells of his retinas. It would not fade away.
Opening his eyes, dismay dug through his mind; the tool of courage
had remained present before him.

"I don't need courage," he demanded out loud. "I can fix this
without the help of any amount of courage." His anger rose in protest
of what was now obvious to him. He stared in disbelief that it would
not go away. He knew that picking up the tool meant changing the
course of his life; that the plans he just made to get back on track
would be tossed out. Shock grew within him. Not only would the
"back-on-track" plan be tossed out, but many others as well:
justification and deceit, which he used as stilts, moving precariously
through every day, would be kicked out from under him.

As he continued his stare, the tool of courage rose into the air.
It was vibrant, lucid; its color made Mitchell's eyes water. In his
disbelief, the tool moved ever so slowly toward his heart.

He grew desperate. The paradigms of a drug addict began to
fight for their presence in Mitchell. He breathed heavily. His heart rate
grew, and he began again to sweat profusely—as if he were using. He
cussed out loud as the tool touched his chest, and sank inside his skin.
He threw his fists down hard on the table, screaming at his life, and
the pathetic moment before him. A stick man flashed its sneering glare
at Mitchell, then disappeared again. He stood up, still screaming, and
kicked the table over, lashing his hands about the room, knocking
small pictures and gadgets off the walls and counters of the kitchen.
He stopped suddenly and looked down at his chest. His throat burned.
He swallowed painfully. Courage had entered his body.

A decision had been made—one without regard to his own
selfish ways—a path had opened up; it was the dawning light which
still sank inward. It was clear to Mitchell this was being done to him—
not by him. Grace was still unrecognizable by Mitchell.

He reached over and put the kitchen table upright. He sat back down on the chair, putting his head to rest on the edge of the table. He cried.

The tears came from deep within. They fell off his nose, and mixed with the mucus running from it. His eyes were red and parched, from the emotional release of giving in—of giving up—of letting drugs finally take their toll on him. He could no longer handle his life as an addict. He had, by the grace of an angel, been given the courage to understand this. As this self-realization became something in his quaking body, he fell off the chair, again on his side, in a home he shared with no one, and fell asleep.

Chapter Forty Eight

A short time had passed since Laurie's thoughts about Mitchell had filled her work day, and of the discovery of evidence that would help him understand the phantom of Sian. It was early, and there was another busy day at court ahead for her. She looked over at the thin file containing press and police reports about Sian's death, and wondered again how she would break the news to this man—for whom she had come to care for.

A voice came over the intercom cynically stating that a man named Mitchell, who refused to give his last name, was on line one for her. There was no need for Mitchell to make an effort at anonymity, but he did not know, or care, that everyone in the courthouse already knew him, especially in the public defenders office.

"Mitchell!" Laure stated with surprise.

"Hello Laurie," Mitchell said.

"What's going on," she said, not as a question, but in an effort to keep a conversational tone.

"I was wondering, would you like to take a short road trip with me?" he asked.

"A road trip," Laurie repeated. "That's different."

"I want to drive down to Sierra Vista, in Southern Arizona, actually just south of there, to a Catholic church—'Our Lady of the Sierras.'

"Well, I guess that's something we could do, but it sounds like more than a day's trip, there and back again," Laurie said.

"You're probably right, but we could keep it open, and take it as it comes," Mitchell said.

Laurie thought for a moment. *His life is so different than mine. He can just roll when he wants.* "I'd have to plan a little ahead to make something like that work," she said. "Are you flexible on when you'd like to go?" she asked.

"Of course Laurie," Mitchell said, realizing Laurie had responsibilities to her career. "Would a weekend work better for you?" he asked.

"I've got vacation time coming," she said. "I can take a couple of days off during the week too."

"Yes, I was thinking week days would be better," he said.

"So Mitchell, what's so important about this church south of Sierra Vista?" she asked playfully.

"How about I tell you on our way down," he said.

Laurie thought the trip would be a good time to approach the subject of Sian. "Okay Mitchell," she said. "Let me get myself organized, and I'll get back with you on a date. Does that work for you?"

"Very much so," Mitchell said. "I'll wait for your call."

With that, each hung up the phone, and processed the moments after such a call—moments that stated they were entering into a further phase of their relationship—a phase that called for the tilling of some boundaries—and the setting aside of certain fears—that kept the world at a ten foot pole's length. Both were in wonder of such a threshold; of who stood there on the other side.

Mitchell pulled up in front of a restored Victorian home, which sat up the hill on Union Street, a short, steep hike from the courthouse, and Laurie's office window. It was in pristine condition. Mitchell looked out his truck window at Laurie's home, and was awed by the setting in front of him. Laurie had a life separate from the law, and the events that brought them together.

He was anxious to get going, and arrived thirty minutes sooner than was scheduled. He got out, walked the familiar four or five steps around to the back of his truck, opened the tail gate, and sat down upon it. He looked down the street, slowly lifting his eyes, to gaze upon the balcony suite of the Hassayampa Inn. He took a deep breath, surprised that Laurie's home had a bird's eye view of it. Great sadness engulfed him. He closed his eyes, remembering himself, and Red, enjoying their honeymoon, in the rich atmosphere of the hotel. He remembered holding her hand on their slow walks, and long talks, among the hotel's charms. He remembered her loving him; her believing in him. The sadness turned to tears that fell to the surface of Union Street.

He sat on the tailgate for sometime, looking on, heartbroken, at the balcony. The white door and windows had held his precious wife within. He travelled back in time, and was consumed by the memory of their love-making, of her soft, fragrant, firm, skin—of those moments when her body became his. He stayed there, letting all of his senses take her memory in. He had found heaven on earth again, while passersby beheld upon his face a tear soaked smile.

From inside her bedroom window, Laurie saw a man captivated by thought—oblivious to his surroundings. From the back and to the side, Laurie, too, beheld Mitchell's posture, and found in its form the broken life that was his to bear. Yet within the form of his profile he seemed to be happy. She noted his legs swaying back and forth, his muscular arms stretching the rolled up sleeves of his tee shirt; one of only two, she had ever seen on him. There was a moment of astonishment, as she took in his shoulder length hair, spotted blonde and grey, as it contrasted against the rusted color of his red truck. *Look at him*, she thought, in an all too familiar tone, agreeing—with the walls of her restored Victorian bedroom—that this man would never agree to a resurfacing. He was what he was, and cared not for the judgments of the rest of the world. If she moved forward with a relationship with him, it would be on his terms; there would be no changing him.

She bent over, and lifted the window that she had stared out of for some time. "Hello Mitchell," she said. "How long have you been here?"

Mitchell did not respond immediately. He heard Laurie's words but could not leave his memories of the balcony suite. Reluctantly, he gestured a "hello," then said simply, "Not long. Are you ready to hit the road?"

Laurie was. In two clicks, Mitchell was behind the wheel, about to put the truck in reverse, when he looked over at Laurie. He shook his head slowly at the prospect of heading south with this woman—who had become his friend, and acknowledged the passing of yet another fork in the road—that allowed both passengers a certain grace—for him to leave his memories alone, and spend time with a friend; for her to leave her professional life behind—at least for the time being—and let her heartfelt fondness grow.

"White and still," *spoken, became a message that stirred, then flurried about the Sea Man.*

Chapter Forty Nine

NEIL Young's "The Old Laughing Lady," was heard on a clock radio. Mitchell heard the song in a different light now; it was now about a drunk falling on a curb; a drunk that was no longer able to discern his legs, from his feet.

The song had had warm memories—he remembered listening to it as he, and his friends, walked the length of a country road, harmlessly high on pot, feeling joy in the day that they were living— those remarkable days as a child playing along the Hassayampa River. His memories then were too unlike the setting now before him.

The reasons for becoming a cocaine addict were numerous, and would be examined in the days and weeks to come. But on this day, with his life stripped of everything that kept the drug use in place, he was overcome by what had gone wrong in his life.

Mitchell looked out a small window, on a cold December day. *It was cold yesterday, too,* he thought, as he reviewed the steps he took to check himself into a drug rehabilitation center. *But why during Christmas?* He asked himself.

Lonely beyond description, he remembered a stroll he took one Sunday morning, along the Pacific Beach boardwalk, many years earlier, when hearing the hollow clink of an empty beer can—falling off the boardwalk wall—had found a home in his psyche.

A nurse had instructed him to pick out a plaster object—one that reflected an emotion or memory—and paint it. It would be used in the next group session as a reference for his life—to be shared with his fellow recovering addicts. With a deep breath through his mouth— his nose still too stuffed up from sniffing cocaine—he rummaged through what was available to paint.

Mitchell held up a thin object with two facades. He wrapped his hand around the symbolism of such an object, and then proceeded to paint each side with a different color scheme. He began with 350 East Orange Drive, remembering the colors of the walls and trim.

Turning it over, he found a thought or two about the future: he did not trust it, or himself—he had been dry for only 48 hours, and found the notion of a "future" quite absurd. Yet he continued to look at the colors he chose. He painted the window panes yellow—for understanding—that would illuminate his new life; the stone walkway was painted with the colors of an arching rainbow—representing the straight and narrow path of sobriety; the front door was already white, and he left it that way—imagining a glass door handle, fitted inside his outstretched hand, and himself with the ability to turn the handle—open the door—and walk through.

He shared these thoughts in group two hours later, and found his hopes no different than any one else. All hoped for a future minus the insanity of drug use—all hoped to be loved, and to be able to take a sense of dignity with them to bed at night.

✺☾☙

There were several different kinds of group therapy sessions. Mitchell's favorite was the room with the giant sponge bats and targets. In there, Mitchell got to beat the living shit out of the foul and petty memories of his past. He put faces on the targets, letting out years of repression, as he wailed at their transgressions. Flashing now and again on a stick man, Mitchell had long ago accepted its presence in his mind, as one accepts the names of colors, or the notes on a musical scale.

Anger was the largest part of Mitchell's cycle of drug abuse. Shame another. What became clear to him, however, was that the drug habit was truly just the tip of the iceberg. It represented only what could be seen, of what went wrong in Mitchell's life.

In rehab he un-raveled long held emotional patterns—most of them constructed during his childhood—about who he was. He came to the conclusion that, over time, those constructs—which were put into effect at 350 East Orange—had become the foundation of deep-seated shame. There, he found many reasons why he became an addict: his parent's losing battle to alcohol—his grandfather's as well—Brent's physical and emotional abuse. An exception however, always followed each reason—"but . . . ," kept coming out of his mouth—each reason was missing the mark.

Lagging behind one afternoon, while the group session thinned out to go to lunch, Mitchell quietly said to himself that "I longed to be loved."

"Do you feel then, that in this leaderless, loveless home, for which you grew up, you were not loved," his therapist whispered quietly, in response, overhearing his subdued realization.

"I long to be loved," he replied. "I know I'm no different than so many others out there in the real world, who only knew selfishness in their 'family of origin,' as you call them. But that's it in a nut shell, I longed, and long, to be loved. In my relationships to date, and I mean all of them, love, family, friendships, etcetera, I have always acted quite selfishly. It's all I've known."

"It," his therapist responded, "the *'longing to be loved'* part, has also delivered to your addiction, a set of very damaging devices; the need for approval for one, and a lifetime of shortcuts and short-term thinking, that have left you empty as a person, and very dry as a man."

"Dry?" Mitchell asked.

"Vacant," his therapist said. "There is not much in you to give. Longing to be loved, and actually being loved unconditionally—which is what most of us hope to find in this world—are two parts of a puzzle rarely ever solved. That's where a higher power might serve you Mitchell. That's where unconditional love might be found."

"Your drug of choice carried a dual-edged sword, giving you relief from your loneliness at the start of a binge, but also, in the end, the remorse and self-damnation that your life, to this point, demanded was yours to feel," he said. "There in lies the treachery of cocaine, and any mind–soul altering chemicals."

⊷ℭℜ

A Native American, and Mitchell, were the only patients left in rehab from Christmas Eve to New Year's Day. The New Year would see a heavy intake of desperate souls, who would begin their unique journeys, inside the four walls of rehab.

The light of Christmas morning made its way quietly into Mitchell's room. He opened an eye, and found the empty room white and still. He let the quiet pastels into his focus. His physiological life was now days removed from the chaos of active addiction. Closing his eye, gratitude grew for being sober on this morning.

Although he was alone, it was okay. He was not swirling around the dead-end of cocaine abuse—covering tracks, or lying, or hiding, or ashamed—he wasn't blacked-out on some part of the desert he lived in, or making deals with the cosmos, or constantly blowing his irritated nose. He wasn't what he was—just days earlier.

He allowed himself to become part of an emerging paradigm—found within the framework of the workshops in which he participated. The challenge was the realignment of associations and interpretations—of the people, places, and events—of his past. He could re-script his subjective past—making it a useful reference for what he was, and who he could become. Why he had lived his life the way he did, up until the point of entering the program, was open for interpretation—and that interpretation would be more useful—if he were to introduce the element of a higher power, into it.

Opening both eyes, Mitchell took note that more of the Christmas daylight had joined him in his room, illuminating not only colors, but elevating temperatures, sounds, and smells as well.

Framed, and hanging next to the entrance of his dorm room, was the poem; *As the Ruin Falls,* by C. S. Lewis. He read it again for the umpteenth time since his arrival:

All this is flashy rhetoric about loving you.

I never had a selfless thought since I was born.

I am mercenary and self-seeking through and through:

I want God, you, all friends, merely to serve my turn.

> *Peace, re-assurance, pleasure, are the goals I seek,*

> *I cannot crawl one inch outside my proper skin:*

> *I talk of love —a scholar's parrot may talk Greek—*

> *But, self-imprisoned, always end where I begin.*

Only that now you have taught me (but how late) my lack.

I see the chasm. And everything you are was making

My heart into a bridge by which I might get back

From exile, and grow man. And now that bridge is breaking.

> *For this I bless you as the ruin falls. The pains*

> *You give me are more precious than all other gains.*

Mitchell had trouble connecting to the words. He was reluctant to—they were slippery slopes—known as self-realizations, that were to be read between the lines of the poem. His gut said to get there, but the addict in him, begged him not to.

He sat up in his bed, turned, and leaned against the wall, took a deep breath, and read the poem out loud again.

In the corner of his peripheral vision, Mitchell saw his head and shoulders appear in a mirror above the room's sink. It was a mirror made not of glass, but of polished stainless steel, and his reflection was less than sharp.

As he read, he noted his lips moving; *All this is flashy rhetoric about loving you.*

The sensation that he had read the first line to himself, overwhelmed him. He was suddenly stricken with intense sadness: *I never had a selfless thought since I was born.*

Tears welled: *I am mercenary and self-seeking through and through:*

I want God, you, all friends, merely to serve my turn. Sobbing, as the slip on the slope claimed him, he laid his head upon the hospital pillow, finding in the Lewis poem, perception not known before. He read the poem again and again, finding in it the very essence of the meaning of forgiveness. The full light of Christmas Day made his room—and its lack of Christmas cheer—very apparent.

As the Ruin Falls smote him deeply, and tears rolled freely while the pains of many years of abuse left his anguishing heart. It was a re-birth to Mitchell. In it's clawing out of the abyss, his heart shuttered in its transformation. Demons departed, chains broke, and the deepest parts of him began the process of wiping the slate clean. He looked forward to feeling nothing—save the touch of a higher power—moving within.

Walking out into the vacant nurse's station, he found the rehab's front door locked, and cold to the touch. He bent over, to peer out the bottom half of the door's glass, and noticed the corridor to other wings of the hospital lifeless. The community room was silent, the TV was off, and the moment seemed to Mitchell, to be as bare a moment as he had ever lived.

Looking down at his feet—which were in thick socks to keep warm—still felt ice cold. The chrome paneling, and the indoor–

outdoor carpeting, was the smell of his holiday. There was no place to go, nothing to see, no one to talk to, and at that thought Mitchell knelt down. He put his hands behind him, and allowed the frozen floor to burrow into his fingers. Leaning back, he laid his head gently on the floor. Prone and staring up, Mitchell thought that there might be snow falling from the ceiling.

Closing his eyes, the snow alighted on his forehead. He rolled a full, and delicious cashew, around in his mouth. A painted picture of a cabin in the woods came to mind, with snow covering its roof, and large Christmas lights and reflectors glowing on a tree. Tagging his friends in a card game of War, he brought to his lips the taste of lime sherbet punch—and eggnog—sharing the small portions of each with his sisters. He took a joint from his friends, and took a big hit off the marijuana cigarette, laughing warmly with them—as they got high again during that first Christmas in the cabin of his youth.

Opening his eyes, the snow stopped, the cashew lost its flavor, and the picture painted began to fade. The idea grew that smoking that particular joint—on that particular Christmas day with his friends—was the beginning of a long, winding, strange, yet common road, that led to the very moment—pressing cold and hard—on the back of his head.

He became aware of his position. On his back, in an isolated drug wing, cold, hungry, lonely, and quite weary of his lot, he was embarrassed by the end result, of a hit he took with his friends—innocently so—long ago.

He stood up—somewhat emotionally scattered—having realized the moment his drug addiction began—wondering what he would do for the rest of the day—now that the self-knowledge of his addiction's origin—became his only present on Christmas Day.

Walking back into his room, he picked up the poem, and read it one more time, understanding in his bones the words: *But self-imprisoned, always end where I begin.*

≈∞≈

The remaining days in rehab were spent considering Mitchell's notions of God. Being asked to relate to a higher power put a barrier between Mitchell, and his successful indoctrination into the twelve step program. Higher powers lurked behind green, glass, church doors—or dark, pulled curtains—as residents of gold chalices, and wearers of creepy garb—with robes made of rope—of chants in languages little understood—of confusing paradigms, where a soul could commit the same set of sins, over and over again one week, then be given a reprieve, to start them again the next; and worst of all, the stretch of any imagination, that accepts as kindness, the pain and anguishing torture, and death, of a good man—the best man—as the key to entering heaven.

I don't understand why he had to die that way for me, Mitchell stated to himself, as he waddled his way back to his room after another group therapy session. *Christmas was just two days ago, why couldn't the church have built an altar with a baby, in a basket, instead of a cross of brutality and agony?* he asked again, not comprehending his religion's take on the task of getting the flock to heaven.

The words resurfaced from his past: *In the light of the Son, you will always find a love, and a reason, and a chance, to be filled with joy and thunder, passion and grace, and the sweet surrender to warmth from a winter sun on a Christmas Day.* Mitchell wanted to believe in God, and to make God a personal part of his mind and heart. He remembered the baby under his Pacific Beach apartment, and the nativity scene he visited on the way to work many years earlier. *Had a higher power been there all along?*

Soon the repetitive chanting, at the end of therapy sessions, and at day's end, began to take hold; the *Lord's Prayer* in particular, was somewhat successful in pulling new understanding from the skeptical Mitchell.

And in the church of his youth, when in idle memory, he would visit, the first word that began to roll out from behind the ghostly robes and curtains was 'lost,' soon followed shortly after by the word 'found.' At some moment during the remainder of his stay at rehab, he admitted to himself, that there might be something there, for him to build on, that concerned itself with the meaning of the word *grace.*

Chapter Fifty

PASSING through the steppes east of Prescott, still annoyed that traffic delays were now a part of this stretch of road, Mitchell looked past the town of Prescott Valley—to Mingus Mountain—to those days when he traversed the mountain highway—where he found endless memories of the woman he still loved.

He looked over at Laurie, who stared out the passenger side window of the *F-100*. "What are you thinking about?"

"I'm watching the horizon," she said. "It's nice to be out on the road."

The road . . . this road, Mitchell thought. "I've been on this stretch of road all my life. I remember seeing only herds of antelope out here, and my screwed up family, in a U-Haul, traveling in the opposite direction, toward Prescott, hoping that a change in latitude would change their fortunes."

"Did it?" she asked.

"It changed mine," Mitchell said. "I met the woods, the Hassayampa River, the waterhole, and a spirit in me that I didn't know I had."

"Did I know you lived in Prescott as a child?" Laurie asked.

"I don't know if we've ever talked about it."

"When, how long?"

"1971, I believe—for two years" Mitchell said. "We moved to Ponderosa Park."

Laurie realized that Mitchell's night of horror happened just a short distance from where he lived as a boy. "No, I *didn't* know that you had lived south of town before."

"Yep," said Mitchell.

Laurie wanted to ask Mitchell why Sian wasn't with them, but was unsure if pursuing the conversation any further was wise. Laurie changed the subject; "So Mitchell, what the heck is so important about this destination of ours today?"

"Our Lady of the Sierras, is a Catholic church, built on the side of a hill south of Sierra Vista," Mitchell said. "On the premise, is a shrine dedicated to unborn children."

Laurie's face turned pale. Mitchell observed her countenance—and pause—in responding to him, and saw on her face a secret, that was not her intention for him to know.

Miles passed by in silence. "Do you want me to turn around?" Mitchell asked. "We can pick another destination . . . another time."

"Mitchell, why are you going to such a place?" she asked.

"To remember my unborn child," Mitchell said. "I had no idea it would strike you the way it did. I didn't mean to be insensitive to you."

Laurie sighed. "It happened years ago. I was young. I've thought about it less as time has passed, but it still troubles me. I'm amazed that I'm still sitting here, in this truck, going to this place," she said, not quite understanding what it was that prevented her from demanding to Mitchell, to turn around, and take her home.

"What about you? When did . . . who had an abortion?"

"Someone I once loved—she told me after the fact." Mitchell said. "I guess who it was, that had the abortion, doesn't matter for me today, just the spirit of the unborn child. I want to say to him, or her, that 'you are loved.' I guess it's been decades now."

"Why do you feel the need to do such a thing now?"

"Grieving still, the loss of my Red, other things have come to light, that I never grieved the loss of before."

"Would you like to tell me what those things are?"

Mitchell looked down the road—viewing in memory—where he had been in his life. Bob Dylan's "Knockin' On Heaven's Door," played loudly in his mind.

"I am what I am, because of these key moments in my life, Laurie," Mitchell said. "Some are not finished. This is one of them. It's time to remember the potential of this unborn child, to accept the passing of his, or her, unlived laughter and tears—and to ask him or her, to forgive my not seeing, the decision to abort . . . coming. Red told me once that I should do this—so I'm doing it.

Religion, right or wrong aside, it comes down to a decision I let pass without any protest, which ended the passing of breath, next to the beating of a heart. It has stained me—as a person playing God. It was wrong to accept it as normal.

It was also my chance to be a father. Who knows what would have become of us—the baby, and I. When I think about it, it's always in the 'father and son' theme. Perhaps I feel that the life in the woman was a boy." Odd, random thoughts about fatherhood moved from one side of Mitchell's mind to the other, floating away into the horizon in front of him.

"For me, the thought of a baby in my life was the antithesis of where I saw my life going," Laurie said. "I realize now that it was my fear of that responsibility that kept me from going through with the pregnancy, and I'm left with a quiet despair, that sinks into my heart, from out of nowhere, when I think of the life that was in me."

Mitchell let the road take the phrase—*from out of nowhere*—with it. Looking past their conversation, to forks in the road of his life, he recalled how often those forks chilled him, just before falling asleep at night.

⊰ଔ

Mitchell and Laurie were chugging south of Sierra Vista on SR-92. They had talked of many things. Mitchell entertained Laurie with his many tales of mis-spent youth; tales that trailed off one side of I-17, or the other.

"I can hardly believe you are still alive," Laurie said.

"God's grace . . . speaking of . . . look!"

Mitchell pointed to a huge cross, built on the side of a hill in the Huachuca Mountains, that could be seen for miles in many directions. Next to the cross, and standing about half as tall, was a Madonna, and in front of both structures: a small chapel.

The pair turned off the highway, and rumbled up the winding road, to the sanctuary, finding a place to park in a small lot at the foot of the property. The creaky metal doors of the old truck opened up. Legs were stretched, and yawns were exchanged. The air was clear. Elevated above the valley floor, Mitchell could see for miles, and watched the curve of the earth extend forever—well into Mexico. He turned, looked up, and eyed the top of the cross. He stared beyond the apex, into the crystal clear blue hyaline, toward his childhood understanding of where Heaven was. He thought of his spirit as a boy, and of the spirit of the child he wanted to honor, at the foot of the giant cross, on this day.

They hiked up steep pathways to the chapel, through the Stations of the Cross that were built along the way. Mitchell located the small shrine, erected near the entrance of the chapel. He passed through a miniature gate, and found a small box that contained the names of other unborn lives. Laurie remained outside the gate, but watched Mitchell closely, as he made his attempt to reconcile this part of his past. He pulled from his shirt pocket a piece of paper. Opening it up, he revealed to Laurie the name he would christen the memory of his aborted child; *Landslide*.

He opened the box, and inserted the small piece of paper. As his did so, the sound of a heavy chain, being pulled through large hooks on a golden gate, rattled in his mind. He looked up at Laurie with a questioning look, put his hands to his temples, and began to rub them, as if he were in pain. Over and over again, the sound of the chain ripped through him. Mitchell did not know that it was the sound of a cold, calculating decision—followed by a reverberation—an accounting—made by the Universe, when one life—and a *way* of life— is chosen over another.

The rattling in his mind subsided. Staring at the box, he remembered the day Landslide had left, escorted by angels from above. He thought of Sian; whose life was left to the witless hands of her father—a destiny quite unfair when Mitchell set it on a scale.

He spoke: "Landslide—a child with none but the Hand of God to hold onto. A child—who fell from above—from Heaven— into fear, confusion, and ultimately—selfishness." He thought of the boy he once was, and of the brutality he had become accustomed to. "I wish Sian were here."

Laurie looked at her friend. Sadness abounded. She thought of the talk she must have with him about Sian, and held her hand out across the small gate, touching his. Mitchell saw in her eyes what he felt in his heart. "Life is tough. We rip and spit our way through, to what end? My Red knows, but look at the door she had to walk through to get there. I'm not sure about life, Laurie; the level of cruelty is absurd."

Mitchell said nothing else. Laurie kept her distance verbally, giving him the space she knew he needed. He put his hand down on the small box, and left it there for a moment while he said one more goodbye to Landslide, feeling a tear fall quickly down his cheek. He looked out on the valley below them, and followed a line of shadow, up toward the sky, and the sun, which now sat behind the seventy-five foot cross, silhouetting its intersect. The shadow of the cross flowed across Mitchell's face, forcing an intimate reaction to the light and shadow found there.

This is life, Mitchell thought. *It is the play between light and dark, between good and evil, and the moments that give those opposing forces their meaning.* Mitchell took Laurie's hand, walked through the small gate, and slowly descended the path back to the old truck, in silence.

"White and still," *spoken, rolled into moments that pounded the Sea Man's heart.*

Chapter Fifty One

Mitchell flung a backpack over his shoulder. He leaned to one side—so the backpack would not slide off, and signed documents, formally excusing him as a patient in a drug rehab center.

He walked out, into a cold Sunday morning, in a brand new year. On Jan 2nd, he was twenty two days clean and sober. The cold, crisp winter air invigorated him, as he walked out to where he had parked the truck twenty three days earlier. He stopped cold looking at it. Memories flooded back of his chaotic life, and how often he sat in the driver's seat of his truck, to get his dope, holding close everything a drug addict embraced while using.

A sickening gut feeling rippled through him when he opened the door of his truck; appearing before him were the icons of what he hoped was his old life: a piece of paper with a dealer's number scratched on it, a straw, a spoon used to push cocaine through a wire strainer—all protruding out from underneath the bench seat. He heard blood rush through his ears when he caught sight of the white powder lodged on the back of the spoon. He picked it up slowly, reeling with a sense of looming disaster. His heart rate skyrocketed as one by one, his triggers to use, kicked in.

As he sat down beside the truck, pending doom rose, clouding his resolve not to lick the back of the spoon. Overwhelmed, he despaired at his willingness to throw twenty two days, and tens of thousands of dollars in treatment, down the drain—all in one weak consideration to lick the back of a spoon—for stale cocaine.

Pathetically, he realized he would not make it out of the parking lot of the hospital. He reached over his shoulder, found the handle of the spoon, then licked it—losing all hope of ever changing his existence as a drug addict.

It tasted like metal, immediately numbing his tongue. The physiological reactions all fell into place: first was the need for a bowel movement, immediately followed by paranoia, then cottonmouth. *This is fun*, Mitchell thought to himself, in his best self-loathing—another step in the use cycle. When the self-loathing played itself out, loneliness set in, and Mitchell began to wrestle with his life-long wish for a *normal* life.

In the next heartbeat he grew wildly angry—insanity whipped through him, as he yelled at the top of his lungs, striking the back of his head against the truck. He stood up, throwing the spoon in the air as hard as he could, desperately wanting to throw his worthless, addicted soul with it.

Realizing that it was not—and would never be—that simple, resolve and acceptance of his plight put him behind the steering wheel of his truck. He turned it over. The sounds of the engine and radio station took him further away from the security of rehab—where he was safe from himself. He pulled out of the hospital parking lot, headed toward the next phase of cocaine recovery.

∂∽

Checking into the halfway house was a simple process; they were ready for him. Recognizing some of the faces that were with him in rehab early on, he settled in, and called a general manager he knew at a local Olive Garden, who offered him a position in his restaurant over the phone.

He informed the halfway house management of his intention to work while living there, and gave to them his training schedule for the upcoming week. In return they gave him a cup to pee in, and said he would be expected to provide urine each evening for as long as he resided there.

The day wore on; evening descended upon his new residence. In the communal living room, on a coffee table, rested a disheveled Sunday newspaper; Mitchell opened it up to the movie section. Looking at the communal living room clock, he planned his first evening away from rehab around an AA meeting, and then a start time for a movie called *Tombstone*. *Appropriately titled,* Mitchell thought.

∂∽

His first day of training as a waiter at the Olive Garden was brutal. He had lost his waiter legs. His feet ached. His uniform, at day's end, was filthy; stained from ten hours of slinging sauces, dressings, and pink lemonade, in the general direction of the ravenous dining public.

After a brief review of his first day of training with the general manager, he walked out into a cold January night. His breath froze in billows around his face. He looked up and down a deserted thoroughfare, and felt loneliness encircle his senses. Lining the broad sloping parking lots of the massive mall, were twenty other chain restaurants, lined up like castle battlements. Located at the main entrance to the mall itself, was the same dollar theater Mitchell visited the night before. His plan, as told to the halfway house management, was to see *Tombstone* again, after the completion of his first training shift.

He approached his truck, struggling with cocaine triggers. Reciting a prayer about understanding courage and acceptance—a prayer that was becoming a minute-by-minute ritual to reach beyond what his life had become—he made his way slowly through the giant mall parking lot, toward the deserted dollar theater.

Isolation crept in. Looking through the windshield, he saw a fellow waitress with red hair drive by. He waved, but she did not wave back. He watched the red tail lights of her car disappear around a darkened mall wing.

With popcorn and soda in hand, and in complete solitude, as not one other soul occupied a seat, the movie began. Previews came first, and then a famous Hollywood voice provided the opening narration for the start of *Tombstone*.

Mitchell again, as he was the night before, immediately lost in the cinematography. Big and expansive in its portrayal of the southwest, and true to the delicate beauty only a desert rat could appreciate, he was instantly at home in the motions and sounds, of the moving picture before him.

The ensemble of actors worked their craft with great skill. Of all the finely tuned aspects of the story, the one that stood above the rest was the way Wyatt and Doc treated one another. With great respect, the characters continually honored each other's lives through acts of courage, kindness, generosity and humility; characteristics that Mitchell longed for. As he watched the story progress, he became keenly aware of just how plain and un-eventful, the call of his life, had been; an antithesis of the story unfolding on the big screen.

As the final scene played out, when Doc told Wyatt, on his deathbed, that *there is no normal life, only life, and to get out and live it,* Mitchell sat stunned, at what he had missed, in the abyss of addiction and fear. Tears rolled. Embarrassed, he checked to see if he was still alone. He was.

The tops of trees—answering the wind—fell into memory as the credits rolled by. His feet, cooled by the recall of water falling over them, caused his mind to reach back in time for moments under the golden sun of his youth. The Hassayampa was calling him back, asking him to remember who he was as a child of the forest, and who he knew as his friends. *Dalton had helped me,* he thought. *Presley had encouraged me and would not let me give up.* He did know this kind of love, as a boy in a world made for boys. It was the Hassayampa River, and it's falling from a spring, over granite and sand, that had held him above his leaderless life. *I have lived the life of the men in the movie, yet I was only a child. I knew the love that Doc and Wyatt had for one another.*

Mitchell missed his friends. He had lost them as a cocaine addict. Dalton and Presley had to turn away as Mitchell's behavior put their own lives in harm's way. *I would like to see them again,* Mitchell thought.

He had the remaining week of training ahead at the Olive Garden. This he knew, and was not looking forward to the tough shifts. What he did not know, at this moment, was that he would visit the same theater, at the same time, to watch the same movie, eight more times, on eight consecutive evenings, as he reached desperately to make the final scene in *Tombstone,* something he would know again in his life.

Chapter Fifty Two

RED was a different kind of woman, a kind unknown to Mitchell previously in his life. She was the same woman in the car who refrained from waving to him on his first night of training. He would not learn until later that she could not wave back to him, fearing her husband's verbal reprisals for doing so.

Red required Mitchell to demonstrate a degree of respect and manners toward her. She reminded him of descriptions in nineteenth century literature, where a woman would be treated with dignity and politeness, or any further opportunity to engage her would end.

Though not her name, he called her 'Red,' for two reasons: the first because it made her smile, the second because of her long, thick, curly, scarlet tresses.

It was not only her hair however, that possessed him while he worked. It was her nose as well. It mesmerized him. *It's as perfect and as delicate a nose, that divine evolution ever created*, he thought. Often, as they stood side by side at the salad station—piling trough sized bowls with lettuce and assorted garnishes—Mitchell would stare at her profile. She sensed it, and dismissed his attention by flicking a piece of carrot or olive in his general direction, before heading back into the chaos of a lunch or dinner rush at the Olive Garden.

Not a button nose, he thought in silence after she walked away. *It lacks any noticeable characteristic save a presence on her face that comforts me*—he measured internally and intently, while he worked—*like an Adirondack chair*—rushing through long double shifts—*where I could rest my forehead, as I kiss her subtle chin*—slinging soup, house dressing, and breadsticks.

He had learned early-on, that his new friend would not tolerate suggestions considered inappropriate to her married status, however unhappily that status might have been. His eyes could not hide his thoughts though, often forcing Red to look away, as her skin tones reddened, revealing shades of emotion in her that startled him—leaving him breathless—as he looked at the back of her cascading pony tail.

He admired her. He enjoyed her outspoken demand to be treated with old-world respect and looked forward to opportunities to do so. He soon found out that a 'please,' and a 'thank you,' went a long way in securing assistance out on the floor, on a busy Friday night.

No one had ever out-worked Mitchell in a dining establishment, yet there Red was, a woman no less, working circles around his highly tuned skills, and ego, as a waiter. Before long though, it began to make him smile. He enjoyed the challenge to step up his game. In their developing friendship, they also became rivals for contests, and the size of tips, bantering with one another constantly about who was best.

Enchantment grew for this unhappily married woman, and her ability to frame ideas, that ran contrary to popular opinion, eloquently describing her thoughts on many things. From her Scottish head of hair, to her hard working feet, Red was a beautiful woman. Her lightly freckled, faultless skin, her first-chair, flute playing lips, and her deep brown eyes went to bed with Mitchell, every night. He possessed a rich anticipation for her. Red's figure pulled on memories of his younger days, passing through the Markgraf Pharmacy, stealing views of large breasts and tiny waists, on fantasy fold-outs. It was never something that was actually tangible in front of him, talking to him, challenging him, and teasing him, as she did when they worked together.

He exerted effort not to stare at her figure because she asked him not to. He did not acknowledge her figure because the rest of the world did it every day, all day long. He wanted to be different. He wanted to be her friend, in the truest sense of the word, holding close to him the value of that friendship—the same way it was portrayed in *Tombstone*—to honor her request of friendship, while she moved through the difficult end of her long marriage to her husband.

This would serve another purpose for Mitchell; it was suggested by his AA sponsor not to engage in an intimate relationship for at least a year. It made sense to Mitchell. The Step Four inventory confirmed what his hospital stay suggested; his understanding of love was skewed, and that any attempt to engage another, under such an umbrella, would be disastrous.

There was one thing Mitchell knew; he did not want to lose himself in Red. He believed that remaining her friend was the best thing he could do for both of them. His efforts at sobriety required it. He stood at arm's length, as Red untied, from the life she made with her abusive and bitter preacher–husband, the girl–woman she once knew.

Eight months went by. There was thirty two weeks of enlightened banter and wit, as the friends adopted characters in the Tom Robbins novel, *Still Life with Woodpecker*. Red became Princess Leigh Cheri, and Mitchell, the Pecker himself. Red didn't know the book existed; Mitchell would not have survived himself without it. The book's magic had become their own language, as Red opposed what she termed 'common,' in the book's finer points—a discourse that Mitchell loved—believing not that someone with red hair would refuse to embrace the genius that was the author. On this day too, their banter played on in the server isle:

"It will be a cold day in hell before I give the *choice* to any husband of mine, not to make love to me," she whispered. The point seemed mute to Mitchell, as his jaw dropped, breaking his own rule, by allowing his gaze to wonder over the hills and dales, of the most incredible figure he had ever witnessed.

Blushing from the exchange, each turned and walked in opposite directions, out of the server isle. They worked on opposing sides of the restaurant, and the sexual tension created by the exchange, bubbled a batch of cream in the kitchen, turning it into the most exquisite Alfredo Sauce the Olive Garden had ever produced.

Mitchell stopped for a moment, gathering himself before stepping out into his station to serve his guests. He closed his eyes, overcome by the physiological pinprick that starts when two people inadvertently, yet passionately, connect through metaphysical thoughts of physical love. The shock of it rushed through him, forcing him to draw deep breaths, which still had not prevented the sensation that he was flying. He acknowledged these moments as the ones that made his entire life right. *Grace*, *hope*, all of the great words that elevate existence above anything petty and mundane, flashed through his mind, falling straight down into his heart, causing it to completely flush each measure of blood, straight into his cheeks and ears.

She likes me, he thought. *I need to get my act together.* Standing tall, he rounded the corner, into the subdued lighting of the restaurant.

Walking up to one of his tables, long time regulars of his, he placed yet another basket of breadsticks next to the extra Alfredo sauce, ordered to dip breadsticks into. Looking up at Mitchell, his regulars smiled at him, and then said: "What has gotten into you?"

Mitchell—now in his element—doing what he loved to do best—when facilitating elevated dining experiences—became very animated, and very eloquent in his delivery of the source, and reason, for his scarlet ears, calling Red over, and introducing her—saying simply; "have you met Red?"

Red knew most of Mitchell's regulars, often vying for their attentions in hopes of stealing them from him. It often worked, prompting more banter in the dining room, over who was a better server. It was turning out to be a great night at the Olive Garden.

Mitchell and Red were the 'closers' of their shifts—they were responsible for the quality of side work done by fellow servers. They worked double shifts, from the start of lunch straight through to the close of the restaurant. During this phase of closing down the restaurant each night, the closers found themselves absorbed in long talks about any number of topics. Their discussions helped to pass the time. Sitting quietly at the end of a very long day, waiting for the manager to inspect their work as closers, Red brought out to Mitchell, a nightcap of a relaxing tea, and black coffee for herself.

Sitting across from one another, after the midnight bell had rung, they slipped their fingers closer to one another. Mitchell was wordless, save an almost inaudible request to ask her out—to a matinee of *The Lion King*. After eight months, and expecting to hear again, that she was not ready, Red looked at him, smiled, and said, "okay."

Still no manager had appeared to check them out for the night.

"I want to tell you something that I have not allowed myself to think or talk about in a long time," Red said. "I had a daughter. She was taken from me in infancy by her father. We were not married. He came into my apartment one night while I was at work, and kidnapped her, and the baby sitter, at gun point, killing the sitter, and tossing her body on the side of the road. The police never found my baby. The only clue the killer left behind was a bloody sock print on the ground, next to the babysitter's body. I don't know if she still lives or died years ago. I named her Sian. It means 'God's greatest gift.' A tear fell forward from the emotion Red displayed to Mitchell. He wrapped his hand around hers in friendship. Red responded in kind.

"I just wanted you to know this," Red said, as she stared over Mitchell's shoulder—her mind wandering into her past.

"What are you thinking about right now," Mitchell asked.

"I've never been able to let go of the memory of the bloody sock print," Red said. "It has haunted me for years."

Mitchell tried to picture the scene that Red described in an effort to make it real for himself. "Thank you for telling me. I'm so sorry for you. After all these years to see you still hurting so much . . ." He was not sure what to say.

"Thank you."

"I have something to tell you too," Mitchell said. "I got a woman pregnant once, long ago—she chose not to have the baby. I don't think of it often, but somehow, right now, it feels heavy in my heart. They suggested in rehab to make amends. How do I make amends for an abortion? Who do I tell I'm sorry to?"

"Maybe you could go to a church—maybe say a prayer—tell the life you loved him . . . or her," Red said. "Have you ever thought about what the baby was . . . a boy . . . or a girl?"

Mitchell looked forlornly into Red's sad, brown eyes. In his expression she saw a mystery—almost as if Mitchell did not know what he felt about it. She watched him shake his head in a gentle, quiet fashion, communicating to her that he did not have a premonition about the sex of the baby.

"Mitchell, I'm not able to have anymore children." There was another, long, sad pause. "Sian's father . . . he kicked me once in the stomach . . . he was angry that I had retained an attorney to get full custody of Sian. He barged into my apartment one night, drunk, and kicked me so hard that I started to hemorrhage. I had to have a hysterectomy. It was soon after . . . that Sian was stolen from me."

The realization that cruelty had played its hard hand in their lives—hung between them—like a pendulum swaying to and fro. In that silence, the friends stood up together, put the coffee cups in the dish station, said goodnight to the manager, and headed out into a hot summer night.

ɛᴐɕᴑ

Trying to breath in August, in the Valley of the Sun, was like sipping hot tea in a sauna. The monsoons had blown in, humidity was very high, and the temperature higher. Sweat formed on the brows of all who were not tied down to an air conditioner, including Red and Mitchell, as they walked out of the theater to his truck.

The Lion King was delightful—a perfect first date movie, Mitchell thought, voicing such as they sat down on the bench seat of the truck. Two hours earlier, they had walked into the cold, dark theater, sitting much too close to the wide screen. Red suggested they sit away from the crowd, so that any one who might know them, would have less chance of seeing the two of them together. Red was now divorced, yet was beside herself with the presence of her friend, sitting next to her under the umbrella of a 'date.'

They found their seats just as the previews began to play, and hunkered down in them for neck support, then leaned in, toward one another, keenly aware of their close proximity.

I'm lucky, he thought, recognizing he was part of a budding romance that unfolded as in days gone by, thoughtfully written one line at a time, with quill feather and inkwell. The dignity of their friendship prevailed over the anticipation of physical proximity. He gave Red credit for their relationship's 'old world' feel. The pair had chaperoned themselves, allowing many parts of their lives to be known first, even before a kiss.

As he sat next to Red, the notions of coming home crossed his mind. He wasn't comfortable with such thoughts. It was too soon to think that way. He respected her deeply. Waiting to kiss had allowed their relationship to become other things. He knew her and her him. *In that knowledge was found the willingness to see through tough times,* he thought. Because they had waited nearly nine months to touch one another, they had become friends while under the shade of falling in love.

The summer heat always led Mitchell's thoughts to water, and he suggested next that they head out to the Salt River to soak their feet in its cool waters. She agreed. They headed north over Usury Pass, which held a commanding view of the winding river and the surrounding geography.

Mitchell pulled over to look at the view. They got out of the truck and began to walk together under the enormous Sonoran sun. Mitchell was accustomed to not touching Red, and entertained no thought of holding her hand or waist. He could not help reeling for a moment at the sight of her body warming up to the heat of the day. The outline of her figure burned in him. She was the cartoon character *Blondie*—come to life. Her figure roared in his loins. The sight of it had inspired many a dream for Mitchell, yet he remained respectful in her presence; something he believed had built trust in Red.

Mitchell stopped to watch Red walk in front of him. The sun's rays slid off of her shimmering red hair. Long and full of curl, her hair flowed past her delicate shoulders, that were partially exposed in a blouse, contrasting her fair skin perfectly. She was stunning to behold. His throat tightened, and his mouth dried out, making the possibility of a plausible kiss impossible on his part.

"What is wrong with you," she asked him, knowing already from the look in his eyes.

"I'm speechless, Red," Mitchell said. "I've only seen you in magazines and comic strips, never in person, and yes I know who you are, and I am glad you are my friend, but my God, Red, right now I feel like if I don't turn around, I'm going to make a royal fool of myself."

She approached him, looking right into his eyes as she took his hand. He looked down upon her, taking in her small, divine presence. Through the shade cast by his head, leaning toward hers, she moved her lips toward his. In his memory, there was never such a profound awareness of a woman near him. She kissed him. His knees buckled under the intensity of her touching him. He shuddered in release as he put his hands around her waist, touching finger to finger and thumb to thumb, as his hands encircled her body, holding his friend's life.

The kiss continued through the seconds, which turned into minutes, under the eternal sunlight, each tasting the sweet salt of life in the other—he inhaled her skin intensely—she opened her eyes to behold the texture of his skin. He wrapped her in his arms, lifting her off the Sonoran Desert floor—her breasts filled his chest, as his breathing heaved with passion unknown in his life.

They were feeling the weeks and months of their friendship change from reserved dignity to a stampede of blood flushing through them.

It was true, Mitchell thought. "Waiting to kiss you has given me a gift I've never known. I feel the very sweetest of desires. I'm flying.

I'm so happy and so high, I feel as if I could kiss you until I die." Red put her lips on his again. Again the whirl of loins—in a march to blessed ecstasy—began. He again embraced her, as though she was a part of his own body. She felt for the first time his excitement grow for her. She pushed her thigh in toward him.

Mitchell could not comprehend his feelings—never waiting for any woman—never making a sexual union special. It had always been hurried, and typically male. Now, before him was the most stunning, most beautiful woman—in the flesh—turning a kiss with him into a spiritual experience—one that transcended who he had been in his life—into what he would eventually become; the hope of love, in the kiss of a woman—for whom he held in the highest regard.

With a deep breath, Mitchell asked her if she was ready to leave. She said "okay," and together they walked back to the truck, unaware that the minutes they spent in each other's arms had turned into hours.

Suddenly his friend had stepped inside his heart. He could feel her there. There was a change in his chest, and when she stirred, he could feel her radiance making a home inside of him.

It was a dizzying experience. He stopped the truck and parked it often, so that he could use both of his hands to help himself to her mouth again, taking an hour to travel a ten minute stretch of road.

He did not want to say good night, but knew that she was reluctant to invite him into her apartment. She knew that it implied things that she did not want to answer to just yet. They kissed one more time, at her door, and then said goodnight.

Having left Red at her door moments before, Mitchell suddenly grew very hungry at exactly the same instant he spied his favorite late-night burrito place. He pulled in, drove around to access the drive through, and was blind-sided by another sight; his old cocaine dealer, a man he had not seen in almost nine months.

The dealer recognized him, and honked. A shock wave of desire for the drug instantly overheated Mitchell, flushing out the spell of warmth, cast by Red just moments before.

He stopped his truck while a fight ensued in him; he had been warned about moments like this, and knew the dealer was carrying—

Mitchell could smell it on him. The slow progress, of weeks and months of sobriety, came crashing down upon him. He was weak with desire for cocaine, and worked the mechanism of the Serenity Prayer to no avail. The colors of his AA chips; the twenty four-hour, the thirty day, the sixty, ninety, six month, and the yet to be received nine month, all flashed before him. As did his new, precious, sober life. The old life had one overpowering and wicked moment of gratification— pure in its decadence, which freed him from himself, in a rush of undeniable brilliance, followed by a mad, hopeless chase for more of that same brilliance.

He looked in the rear view mirror, and could see the complex where Red lived. Thought of her scent, and her lips, and the day he just spent in heaven with her, moved gently through him. In the mirror he saw his eyes darting back and forth, from the hand-waving dealer to Red's apartment.

In AA meetings, other addicts talked often about finding something to believe in, that was larger then one's own life. Mitchell had never crossed the bridge to a higher power, and was now desperate as he stood alone before the insanity of his addiction. The meetings also impressed upon him the importance of not using another life as that power, as people, places, and things could not sustain an addict from his addiction.

Mitchell had no other choice. What he held in the mirror was a day unlike any other—filled with the hopes and faith of another. What was before him in the parking lot was a hell he had yet to experience; an end to his life.

At that thought Mitchell saw his head hit a casket. In a vision of his memorial, he saw one person; it was Red. She was heartbroken. She, like he, had fallen in love the day they kissed forever. She, unlike he, believed in him. Mitchell looked at Red through the top of his casket, and watched her place two items on the coffin, that shook him to his soul, making him kick and beat the inside of the box in despair: a pen, laced to a leather-bound journal. The vision had ended as quickly as it had begun.

Wiping the tears from his eyes, Mitchell viewed something quite remarkable unfolding. As he regained his bearings, he saw the dealer's car rolling away from his view, and rolling toward him was one of Mesa's finest.

"Everything all right here?" the cop asked, as he stopped next to Mitchell's truck, shining a light directly at his face.

With obvious relief in his voice, Mitchell's said "yea, yes, everything is all right."

"You sure?" the cop said, observing the emotional state Mitchell was in.

"Yea, I'm sure," he said

"Do you know the guy driving that car," the cop asked, pointing to the dealer as he drove away.

"I used to. I haven't seen him in almost nine months."

"Good," the cop said. "Take care." He rolled up his window, and headed after the dealer's car.

Mitchell was stunned. *What just happened? What just stepped in front of my pending doom?* He recalled his vision when the hunger for the cocaine kicked in—of his death, Red's love, and of a pen and a journal.

He continued his analysis of the situation, noting the appearance of a cop, at the precise moment of his despair, realizing he would not have said no to his addiction. He thought of the cop—*he knew who was in the car!*

Mitchell could not shake the events. *How could the universe unfold like that,* he asked himself? *Nothing ever got in the way of my cocaine use. When I wanted it I got it, always, and now, it is being denied me. How strange this is, and how wonderful!*

Was it Red? He asked the night sky. Looking up, he wondered about a higher power, and wanted to consider the idea of divine intervention. Whatever it was, Mitchell felt blessed—as if luck were on his side.

Hunger came back to him full steam. He ordered two of his favorite burritos, and headed home to his studio apartment, to telephone his friend—who now liked to kiss him—to tell her what happened.

හⓈ৯

Suddenly, there was Doc Holiday stating to Wyatt Earp that there was no *'normal'* life; there is only life, and to get on with living it. Mitchell stated to himself; *by all means sir.*

Doc's last breaths in the movie appeared in Mitchell's mind. Doc looked down at his bare feet, and said, "that's funny." He was astonished by the way his day, and his life, was about to end.

໕ঔ৯

He parked his car, grabbed his burritos, and headed into his small apartment cocaine free. Thoughts raced through his mind, about the many ritualistic motions, he was not suffering from in his addiction to cocaine, simply because something intervened.

But what? He wondered.

Puzzled, he sat down on his used sofa, in front of his used TV, and called Red on his used telephone to say hello. Although the day's mood was temporarily crushed under the weight of his ever-present habit, he desired to recall the entire day with Red, on the phone, in spite of what unfolded on the parking lot, less than one hour earlier.

He heard the dial tone and called her home.

"Hello," Red said.

"Hi."

Red yawned while she said, "What's up?"

"Saying good night to you, again, and to tell you how wonderful today was for me," he said. "I have never spent the entire day, in the heat of the day, kissing while completely oblivious to time or temperature. One minute we're walking in the desert, and the next you're moving toward me . . . to kiss me," he said, playfully reluctant to state it.

"So that's the way our first kiss is going to be remembered." she stated coyly.

"Well, yes, I think so," he said. "You did walk up to me and kiss me, which floors me . . . I had all but given up . . . or not given up, but completely put it out of my mind, for the most part."

"You are a real schmoozer aren't you," Red said. "I better watch myself with you."

Mitchell laughed. She made him feel good inside.

"I speak the truth," he said.

She yawned again. He felt her settle into his heart, putting her forehead into his neck, even on the phone. Mitchell was enchanted. He was giddy, and although physical exhaustion had settled in, the delight in her voice kept his mind fully awake.

"Red," Mitchell said, "I need to tell you something."

"Something happened to you tonight after you left," Red said, adding to Mitchell's awe of the events that unfolded after leaving her. Before he could respond she said quietly, "I prayed for you."

Mitchell almost dropped the phone. He put his burrito down and turned off the TV. He asked; "You did what?"

"I had a feeling something was wrong, and I prayed for you," Red said again, worried that she might be misunderstood.

"*Oh . . . ,*" he responded.

Quiet moments on the phone passed.

"It worked," he said hesitantly, into the electronic silence.

With reserve she said "I'm glad."

"It was the strangest thing," he continued, encouraged by her sincere tone. "I saw my old dealer. I got nervous. I knew he had it, and just as I was about to drive over to where he was parked, a cop appeared, making a deal impossible. The cop drove over, put his light in my face, and asked me if I was okay. He made it sound like he knew who, and what, was in the other car. Red, nothing has ever gotten in the way of me and my cocaine before, and I must tell you, while all this was going down, I had a vision of my death, with you, standing over my casket, placing a pen and a journal on top of it. What do think that means?"

Now it was Red's turn to be amazed. "I can't believe you had a vision like that," she said, as she looked at the top of her dresser, where a pen and a journal were wrapped, as gifts to be given to Mitchell, after his nine month anniversary meeting with Alcoholics Anonymous.

There was silence between them, the kind that echoed the mysteries of life, making conceivable, considerations of divine intervention for Mitchell, and growing faith for Red. They listened to the quiet on the telephone line between them. It was love growing in the revelations of a late night phone conversation. As both said goodnight one more time, the passing of the handset to the hook on the phone, found both under the spell of life turning.

The burrito and TV both became stale compared to the continuing revelation that was Red. After their conversation, he had lost his appetite, in a good way. He was just too amazed to eat.

Beyond tired, and beyond any experience he had known, he fell into a deep, deep sleep, as deep as any he had in several years. He had no dreams. There was nothing unsettled. Nothing was sensed but the cosmic hum of a universe expanding.

හ⁓ා

The lighting in Red's home was soft and feminine. Mitchell liked being under its spell. Red had delicate things, and old pieces of furniture about her apartment, things that made him feel like he was in the kind of home he had always looked for—even as a boy—yet had never known. Red's home was filtered with a yielding, womanly ambience, centered in principle and temperament.

They sat and talked at her tiny kitchen table, about the AA meeting earlier that day. He had received his nine month chip. Mitchell's expressed his gratitude to Red, for her thoughtful gifts, in the form of a pen and a journal.

The candle light took Mitchell's eyes on a tour of Red's face and hair, illuminating her skin, and creating stills of what the moment might look like in a photograph.

He asked her if he could set up a camera he saw sitting on the kitchen counter, and photograph her while they talked. She hesitated at first. She was last in line when it came to believing his sentiments about her beauty. She knew that she was attractive, but only acknowledged the fact with an acceptable degree of sincere humility, knowing through experience, that beauty carried with it both joy and pain.

He tried to make her feel as comfortable as he could. He put the camera on a tiny tripod that was fixed to the underside of it. He looked at her through the mechanical prism inside the camera, focusing in on the texture of her skin, and her bright clear eyes.

Through the lens finder he saw the profile of her face, graced by the candle light. She brushed the mane of her red hair back on both sides of her face. It fell back behind her shoulders, supple and bare. He asked her to lift her perfect chin ever so slightly, into the ambiance of her home. When she did, Mitchell flipped the shutter, taking the first of many photos.

Without using a flash, he took several more photos, as Red played along with his gentle suggestions. There was one frame left on the roll of film. He paused for a moment to consider one more way to put her beauty in a photograph. Hinting with his fingers to tilt her head low, she closed her eyes, and then opened them slowly. At that moment the shutter clicked; her eyes piercing his vision, and the film's chemical inlay, exposing both to a moment inside her soul.

He closed his eyes for a moment, remembering the still of the picture he had just taken of her. In that split second Mitchell recorded what Red held dearly in her own heart. In that split second, he saw her secrets, her cherished parts, her hurts, and her pleasures. As the image changed in opposing colors, and moved away from, and then closer to his own conscience, he slowly opened his own eyes to hers, and beheld a decision she had made to take Mitchell into her life, completely.

He took a deep breath and stood up. He knew what he saw on her face, though he had never seen it communicated with such dignity and passion. He set the camera aside. Extending his hand to hers, he gently lifted her up off the chair, and into his arms. Their lips fell together. He whirled with desire. She breathed him in and out again, making him feral with passion that rode the back of a caged and wild animal. They caught themselves for a moment, realizing that if they did not slow down, what they were about to do, would be over before it even started. Bending down far enough to put his arms under her legs, he picked Red up and gently kissed her lips. She put her arms around his neck, and with a tender gesture, pointed toward her bedroom.

Mitchell put his knees into Red's futon, noting the comfort of the giant cotton bed. With Red still in his arms, he slowly bent over, resting Red gently on to her back. She let go of his neck, keeping her hands near his face. Her gaze into him remained. Mitchell wandered all over Red, using all of his senses to mark the moments with her. They sat up together, facing one another. Red slid her hands down the front of Mitchell's chest, running her fingers over him. He shuddered. Her hands found the bottom of his shirt, and lifted it over his head. He sat bare-chested. She maintained her lock on his eyes. She leaned into Mitchell, and began to kiss him, first on his lips, then his neck. Red placed her hands on his shoulders, and kissed the muscles rising out of his chest.

Mitchell moaned lustfully. He fell backward on the bed, away from where Red sat. She looked down to see Mitchell's desire rise.

She looked at him, smiling at his anticipation of her next moves. She was a half second behind each of his impulses—delaying his gratification with purpose. Shutter after shutter spilled out from his physical experience. It was her smile, and her staring into his eyes, as she loved him, that transfixed and centered his senses toward her person. Rhythmical movements, illuminated by candle light, filled the walls of her bedroom. Mitchell committed her dancing wall shadows, moving on and around his own, to memory and into the experience of being loved by her.

He was transformed. He felt like a wild horse running through grass and wind. They became as one, galloping in perfect time over the expanse of her bed, both giving no pause for rest. Shoulder to shoulder, hip to hip, mouth to mouth, breath to breath, their hearts physically beat into one unified pounding of her cotton-filled futon, made of once blooming, busting, blossoming bolls, spilling out over the earth, as far as the horizon would allow.

She was patient with him. She was masterful in her use of fingertips and voice, transmitting much of her own desire into him—through the warmth and scent of her breathing, giving him cues to her next wish, where senses furthered both, into the spiritual touching, and rendering of emotion, that was physical love. It was her wish that became his desire. It was his desire that became her wish.

For Mitchell and Red, the sympathetic and hypnotic transference between her body and his soul resonated into the night as the pull of a bow across cello strings. Echoing and full, their bodies laid side by side, next to the shadow-making candle light, and in their exhaustion, discovered the full intention of love.

This realization floored Mitchell, as he looked at the nude and beautiful Red. They looked at one another and said in unison, "I love you." They kissed frantically as passions rose in the light of the love becoming something far more than friendship, yet even now, their friendship remained the lace between their fingers. Each spoke the words again and while doing so, Red lifted herself up and over Mitchell, her passion waxing, as their bodies joined again in physical love. Red leaned forward in exhaustion. She rolled off of him, lying on her back to rest. Mitchell held her hand, letting her do so.

Moments passed. Together they spoke again the words that became their physical manifestation.

"I love you," Red said.

"I love you, Red," Mitchell said

Half asleep, half awake, Mitchell rolled onto his side, facing away from Red, reflecting on her words regarding a man and a woman, and what made love between them. She moved into him, pushing her front side into his back; her chest into his shoulder blades, her knees into the cup of his knees. In a uniform movement she put her arm through his while he clutched her hand. In this way they travelled into their own hearts, finding for the first time, perhaps ever, a place of safety and joy.

Chapter Fifty Three

THE truck's tires, winding on the concrete of I-17, became the meditation both Mitchell and Laurie experienced on their way back from the church on the hill, south of Sierra Vista. The somberness of the events there, quieted Laurie's plan to discuss her findings about Sian's death, until now. She looked ahead on the interstate, watching Bumble Bee Hill approach. She looked east as they passed over the Agua Fria River, her eyes tracing the water's flow, as it descended in elevation from the mesas above.

"I've got something I've wanted to talk to you about for some time, Mitchell, and I can't seem to find the right time to do it," she said. "I'm afraid what I have to say will upset you, and I don't want to do that."

Mitchell looked with concern at Laurie. He took a deep breath and asked, "What's going on?"

"You've been mentioning Sian recently," Laurie said.

Mitchell's look of concern grew less apparent. "What about her?"

"I don't know how to say this to you, Mitchell, but recently I've been watching you talk to someone named Sian . . . but there was no one there," Laurie said. "You told me that Sian was Red's daughter, and that Red never found out what happened to Sian after her father kidnapped her, and killed the babysitter. I did some checking . . . and I found out some disturbing news, Mitchell."

Laurie was making a great effort not to use words that portrayed a crazy person, because she didn't feel Mitchell was crazy, just suffering under the wickedness of a fateful night.

"I asked a state official, a friend of mine, to look into the case of Red's missing daughter," Laurie said. "Within a short time, a New Jersey coroner's report was laying on my desk describing how Sian had died."

Mitchell stared at the road ahead, gunning the old truck in second gear up Bumble Bee Hill. The cruelty described in the coroner's report re-opened the newly healed wounds in Mitchell's mind.

A guttural moan from Mitchell echoed the sound of the slant-six engine, gutting out the climb up Bumble Bee; Mitchell had mercilessly floored the gas pedal.

Grabbing the steering wheel forcefully with both hands, he was apparently determined not to loose any speed; the old truck trudged up the steep hill. His knuckles turned white.

Laurie looked with grave concern at his face; the color had drained from his lips and eyes. She had made a mistake. There was no way she could have known, that he would loose himself in the madness of more cruelty, perpetrated onto the life of his Red, whether Red knew about it or not.

The truck's engine began to overheat, and steam started flowing out of the engine compartment. The whine and vibration of the engine had changed, alarming Laurie even further, as she realized Mitchell was oblivious to the truck engine's strain.

"Mitchell, do you think you should pull over?" Laurie asked. Mitchell did not respond. He was lost in a dark world, where evil reigned over the soft comforts that a husband and wife give one another, and of those things a baby cries for. She noted Mitchell was lost, his eyes gazing out the windshield, to points beyond the pane of glass. She remembered seeing this expression before; during his trial.

How could I have thought this would come out any differently? Laurie thought. She regretted saying anything. She thought she was helping him. Nothing was worth watching him suffer again. "I'm sorry Mitchell," Laure said. "I didn't know it would hurt you like this, I was trying to help."

At last he pulled the truck off the road above Bumble Bee Hill, where the interstate leveled off. Mitchell suddenly looked less agitated. He was assessing the overheated truck engine, and how best to get the truck cooled off. He got out and opened up the engine compartment, now coated with rusted radiator water. He left the hood as is, then walked passed Laurie to the back of the truck. He opened up the tailgate and sat down upon it.

Laurie was not happy with the situation. She suddenly felt like she was somewhere she did not want to be, confined in an unreliable truck next to a man who suffers from madness. She got out of the truck, and looked back toward Mitchell, whose head and shoulders

276

were now silhouetted by the sun setting behind him. She walked gingerly toward the tailgate, and joined him.

"I'm sorry I scared you," Mitchell said.

"I'm sorry I said anything about Sian," Laurie said.

He thought about Laurie's words concerning Sian. *She says I'm talking to no one,* Mitchell thought. "You don't see Sian?"

"Well, no, Mitchell, I don't see anyone," she said. "I didn't see anyone the night I brought over Chinese, yet you were very active in a conversation with someone named Sian."

Mitchell started to think back to the first time he saw her on the Hassayampa. *Could she be a figment of my imagination?* He thought. "It was odd how she started walking toward me in the water on the Hassayampa," Mitchell said.

"You first saw Sian on the river?" Laurie asked.

"Yes," Mitchell said. "It was on the river, and she walked toward me and asked if I was crazy. But I feel like I've seen her before. I was watching her work as a waitress at the Dinner Bell. She was hard working . . . and beautiful. She talked to guests about me even though I'd not met her before. Did I dream this?"

"Mitchell," Laurie stated, "I'm not one to judge anything about what's going on with you. I know what you've been through. If this thing with Sian is real enough to you then that's okay with me. Maybe you dreamt up this person, but it would be hard for me to visualize someone I've never met before."

"She's the spittin' image of her mother, only younger," Mitchell said. "When we met on the river, when we talked about who we were, and when I hugged her, I felt as if I was hugging my beloved. I had to fight off my deepest desires. It was as if she were a younger Red."

When Mitchell made his last statement, a great epiphany lifted him off the tailgate of the truck, and he shook with emotion, staring straight into Laurie's eyes, tears flowing, he said "she's a younger Red. Not Sian, but Red, a younger Red, the Red I never knew."

Laurie stared back at Mitchell. She looked passed him into the sunset, now in full bloom across the horizon, now afraid that sharing with him the fate of Sian, had made Mitchell's continued imaginings, with the phantom that was Red, worse. She made a choice to not reveal anymore of what she knew about his night of great sorrow.

"White and still," *spoken, moved to the forefront of the Sea Man's thoughts, as the three words presented further notions of forgiveness and acceptance in his life.*

Chapter Fifty Four

HE was thinking about how a house becomes a home when Red touched his face, wiping away a drop of sweat that had settled there.

"Is it the will of a woman that makes a man stay with her?" he asked Red quietly, his voice reflecting the soft, compressed candlelight fluttering through the room.

"Is it the heart of a woman that makes a house a home?" He asked again, not really as a question for Red, but for the universe, as he compared the rich intimacy of the moments he had spent with Red, to previous relationships.

"I am thinking back to earlier experiences," he said. "I remember how difficult it was for me to feel both trust and longing. They were void of the wonderful intimacy I share with you. I am so grateful to you."

"D you mean," Red asked, "that you like the way I make love to you, and that you can trust me?"

He looked at her, a bit stunned by her question.

"Yes," he responded. "It is both, and you do this with such a profound sense of compassion and empathy, as if you are inside of me, and know exactly what to do, to both please and calm me. How do you know me so well, even on our very first time together?"

"It is because I want nothing more than for you to want me, and for you to love me. I want to please you, and answer your every wish—this is how I gave to you my whole heart. Men and women, it seems to me, have forgotten that intimacy—for a man—is about answering a call from the wild, while intimacy—for a woman—is about answering a call to the hearth, and to the home. When these two opposing forces are honored, I think the secret—of making love stay—has opened up to them."

Mitchell smiled at her playful reference from the Tom Robbins novel. Resting beside her, taking note of her physical presence—how even after just making love to her—the vision of her was already generating another avalanche of hunger for her. "When you said 'answering a call from the wild for a man,' what are you referring to?" he asked her.

"You know exactly what I am referring to," she said coyly. "I am talking about the insane want I have seen in your eyes for the last several months. If I want you, to continue to love me, I must answer that want that you innately carry inside, and on the other end, if you want me to continue to love you, you must honor my heart, by being faithful to me."

"Did I not see want in your eyes, too?" Mitchell asked.

"My desire for you has come only because you have been true in your heart to me. This has given me a sense of security, and when I feel secure—when I feel loved—I become very enamored sexually," Red said, rather modestly.

"I have never met a woman quite like you," Mitchell said. "I have known women who behaved like men, with regards to lust, having sex casually, and not caring about the outcome, and I have also known women who cannot feel aroused at all, even with all the monogamy in the world surrounding them. You are better than both those situations, and I find it remarkable that someone as beautiful as you, can be an angel in the light of day, and an enchantress by the light of a candle at night."

A glow came from their collective skin. Red was chilled, as the beads of sweat on her back began to cool. Mitchell took the flannel sheet that was pushed to the side, and carefully wrapped it around her. From head to toe, he tucked it in and under every part of her, save her face. He looked down at her, and marveled at the feeling of falling in love. He would hold tightly to her uniqueness, blessed that she chose him to give her love to.

⚬⚬⚬

The couple could not open their eyes. They were held together by a mysterious force neither could name. They had been up far too late, and both needed to get up and get ready, for another long day at The Olive Garden.

Mitchell marveled at Red's modesty. After sleeping with her all night long in the nude, she would get out of bed, but not until she wrapped a sheet around her figure.

"You know, Red," he said, "you don't have to be so modest."

Entering the bath, she gave him a mischievous grin, then only a glimpse of herself when she dropped the sheet, just as she was closing the bathroom door. In less than one second, his heart rate rose and his jaw fell, to Red's immense pleasure.

On their way to work, Red asked Mitchell a question he was not expecting, and would not have considered to ask:

"How about, on our next day off, we go for lunch at the Lunt Avenue Marble Club down on Central and Camelback, and while we are there, you can show me where you used to live?"

"350 East Orange Drive?" he said surprised.

"I'd like to see this house where you spent part of your childhood."

"I'm not sure I want to go back, something about that house has never sat well with me."

"What do you mean?"

"I remember much about my childhood, and the days that unfolded there, but I feel like I have forgotten much as well.

Red, I have told you everything I can remember about my life, but there is one thing I have not shared with you, simply because, until this moment, I had not thought of it. There are things about it that still, to this day, are kept secret from me. They are events or thoughts that I cannot recollect, that I believe have shaped much of who I have become. I have only a nagging feeling—sometimes I feel in the middle of my back—that reminds me something terrible happened there."

"We don't have to go if you don't want to," Red said.

"There is so much to show you besides the house. I remember many things that I hold dear there, especially of my friends, and the things we did together. You know, I considered my childhood buddies, my family."

With that, they found themselves parked behind The Olive Garden. They looked at one another—took deep breathes in an effort to brace themselves for another long day as a waiter and a waitress—and hand-in-hand, walked toward another day of service, camaraderie, and human absurdity, within the four walls of the restaurant.

ꙮ

Dreams had a powerful presence in Mitchell's sleep as the sober life-style had nothing, save Red's love, to medicate the deeper recesses of his past.

After the long day, and after the romance of the evening gave way to a hot shower and a long bath, the two were side by side in Red's bed. Sleep had overcome both, and they followed each other's eyes into a much needed slumber.

An hour had passed when Mitchell woke Red with urgent heavy breathing. She watched him for a moment, listening for meaning in his desperate and half-spoken words.

"Wake up," she said while shuffling his shoulder. He continued a fight of some kind in his sleep. "Honey, wake up, you're dreaming, wake up."

Mitchell heard her from a distance and began to fight his way out of the nightmare. He woke to find Red's hands on him asking "what's wrong, what were you dreaming about?"

Catching his breath, looking around the room to get his bearings, he said, "you and I were young, and we were at the house on Orange Drive, on the driveway where a gate was. I was looking over the fence to find the source of a vicious sound. I was struggling to get a look over the fence, and when I did, I could hear the source of the sound but I could not see it; it was the strangest thing to look toward the horrible noise, but not see what was making it."

"It's the suggestion to go and look at the home, isn't it?" Red said sadly.

"I don't know, honey, I always get such a lost feeling seeing that place," he said. "I need to get to the bottom of something; I just don't know what."

He turned over onto his back, with Red right next to him. Through her thin tee shirt and tiny sleeping shorts, he felt her reassuring presence. As her beating heart set itself up against his, he felt the warmth of her home, and the things in it, become gifts to him. The soft feminine light illuminated not only the physical woman Red was, but the nurturer, confidant, friend, and messenger of grace she portrayed, to every whirling part of Mitchell.

A sense of security filled him. He closed his eyes; a picture of an old man came into thought. He was sitting in a chair, looking out a window, at the curve of the Earth. Mitchell could not discern if the window was in a cabin, or a castle, realizing it was not the window itself, but the view the old man held, that brought to Mitchell a sense of quiet. As Mitchell's conscience fell into the warmth of Red's embrace, he saw the figure of a stick man standing on the edge of the old man's view. *It is walking toward me,* was his last thought.

ဆာၺ

The drive north on Central Avenue in Phoenix brought Mitchell's past closer. Central Avenue, its architecture as landmarks, sent lucid memories across his minds eye. He could see roots. Whether they were living or dead were of no consequence.

Memory Lane was a warm experience for Mitchell, as he pointed to moments in his life: Central High School and a coach that he had respected there—the Grand Canal—Saint Francis Church and the church's school he attended when he was young—then the Markgraf Pharmacy, and Uptown Plaza.

From the access behind Uptown Plaza, and the delivery doors to the old El Rancho Market, Mitchell found himself on the curb of Medlock Drive. He allowed his foot to sink over the side of the unique rounded curb, and remembered countless moments as a child, with all of his senses mounted one half foot above it.

Red saw his face change from one of enchantment to loss, as he looked toward Orange Drive. On the long, slow-looping street, sat a home that held too many moments of his life that were no longer his.

But there too were funny memories, like the time Mitchell rode into the back of a parked car, and the many 'secret' paths and hiding places among the neighborhood's many oleander stands. The comments continued about how a child lived when he and Red were young, versus the over-protected and paranoid parenting of today's child.

He pointed out to Red the tree he climbed as a child, to carve his initials, and self portrait of a stick man in it. Upon closer examination, he saw that the branch had been pruned. This struck Mitchell harshly.

The pair got out of the truck and leaned against it. He was lost in the muddle of his past. He stared at the house, and spoke of changes in its appearance. Shrubs were gone. Colors had changed. The rock design around the front door entrance remained. The front living room window was also the same, and he told her about the Christmas tree decorations, and a fake cardboard fire place that was erected each year. These thoughts of Christmas lead to the descriptions of lime sherbet punch, and cabbage heads covered with bite-sized morsels of meats and cheeses, in the center of the Christmas Eve table.

He could still see the entrance to the oleanders where he and his friends hid and played in. He thought of the goodbye to Dalton and Presley, as his father and brother loaded the U-haul.

They travelled to Oregon Avenue and spent several minutes between the two homes his boyhood friends grew up in. The homes mesmerized Mitchell; his friends' parents were still there, spending over a half century in each. The stability found in each home was a reference of what life could have been for him. 502 and 503 East Oregon were the addresses found on countless letters between him and his friends; letters that he remained the custodian of. They were proof of his existence as a kid, as were the two homes he stood in front of. They were his homes even though in both, only distant pictures remained on hallway walls or scrapbooks.

Red was holding his hand when Dalton and Presley's parents came out to greet them—an unofficial family reunion—where smiles and warm memories rode piggy-back on Mitchell's own longing for a home he could call his own. Both sets of parents had unofficially adopted him, unbeknownst to Mitchell, when he was a boy. Neighbors talk. The occupants of 502 and 503 East Oregon knew what had befallen the children of 350 East Orange Drive.

Both Otis and Evan shook Mitchell's hand, and gave his Red the once over. Mitchell could see the admiration in both, and found it absorbing. The mothers greeted Red. The neighbors could see that Mitchell had changed, as any parent could. A burden had been lifted. They could tell he was no longer an active drug user, and could see the difference Red had made in his life.

He leeched the praise out of each moment. From a boy, to an upside down man, to standing on his own two feet, the parents of his boyhood friends were happy to see Mitchell had found find his way home again, even if the homes he spent most of his young life in, were no longer open to him as they once were.

They said their goodbyes. Hugs were exchanged. Mitchell opened the door of the truck for Red. As he walked around to the other side he was given thumbs-up signs by both fathers. Mitchell was proud. Getting in, he leaned over and kissed the woman whose love was grounding him.

This would not be the last trip through his old neighborhood for Red, as it would happen countless times to come. Mitchell was climbing to the tops of a Birch tree, toward heaven, where the branches would set him down on the ground lightly, to do it all over again. In his words, Robert Frost gave Mitchell a picture of what his life had become, finally. He thanked Red for planting a birch tree in the middle of the mud, making solid a place where his life could rise and fall with grace.

Heading east on the US60 toward home, with Red close to his side, he presented to her a notion that simply appeared on the horizon, with the Superstition Mountains; he asked her if she would live with him.

Her answer was spoken as easily as colors finding a rainbow. Her answer calmed him. It made him inhale and exhale in a way that endeared him further into her heart. Love was becoming a paradise to Mitchell. It fenced itself around what was known by him as a boy in the woods with his friends; by what was taught to her as a young girl on the Jersey Shore. It was becoming its own and real intention. She said 'yes,' to his request—to the possibilities—to the sound of her bare feet in his life. She said 'yes,' to his rising in her life each day and to her falling in his arms every night. She made their love a verb by placing her hand on his, and whispering into his ear, that she wanted to love him for the rest of her life—that she wanted to make his bed—both getting into and out of it—every day. She said she wanted to make his breakfast, and his dinner, and kiss him in their home, wherever that might be. She wanted to make his address hers, and to give him the things he found on Oregon Avenue. She wanted to be his longing for a home because she knew she could love him, to the gates of heaven and forevermore.

※

One by one Mitchell watched the clouds roll over the walls of the canyon—first one . . . then three . . . then ten. Before he knew it a thousand puff clouds, white on the edges, grey in the middle and laden with rain, appeared and disappeared, as they traversed the canyon below them.

The silence of the sky, first blue, then white and grey, then blue again, slowed Mitchell's mind. The Adirondack chair, with his legs spread out in front of him, placed his face toward the sun when it shone. His head was tilted back enough to keep one eye on his journal, and the other on the sky above.

He was in the middle of a patch of thick green grass, lined by an old wooden fence made of Mother Nature's past—of whatever was handy when the post holes were dug. To the right of his position, as he faced north in the chair, was one road of his life—Highway 89A—a road with many connections to Mitchell's past. To the left of him was a long stretch of housing known locally for its proximity to Slide Rock State Park—Slide Rock Lodge, and its rustic but cozy rooms, were located just a half mile south of the millenniums-old play ground. The idea was to take a long, slow, lazy walk to the water, and its play among the Toroweap and Coconino Sandstones of Oak Creek Canyon. But an Adirondack chair changed Mitchell's mind about the walk—the sight of the chair was too much for him to resist. It was newly painted and sat alone, smack dab in the middle of lush thick grass, complete with shade, and a table to rest a tall glass of lemonade.

Sitting down into its form, putting everything within reach of his hands, Mitchell took a deep, meaningful breath of the canyon's air, laden with its unique scent. It seemed to Mitchell that the fragrance of the canyon was rising up from its floor like the smell of sweet tea brewing in a teapot—warmed by the sun's rays reflecting off the canyons and crevices of the Mogollon Rim—for which it was a part of. The scent of the canyon was one of the foundations of his life, giving him short, but endearing roots that ran contrary to the unfulfilled legacy of his family. Oak Creek Canyon, and a camp ground called Banjo Bill, made up his very earliest memories of being alive, and a member of a family.

Highways 89, and 89A, stretched the length of his life. On both sides of the road, his life had stopped to regroup or refresh, to camp or to breathe, to love or be alone. He was in the mood to sit next to it, with his journal, and write about the sensual and delightful ways Red brought life to him.

Resting his head on the chair, Mitchell let the canyon become a part of the writing. He was in the moment. He looked down at the white pages, empty of thought, and put to paper these words to his beloved:

There were two hands that met here, in heaven on earth.

In these hands were cradled two hearts and at the feet and pleasance of pink sandstone and blue sky, the care of these hearts were delivered.

In witness and hope of the water and the trees, love was promised in the verbs of patience, compassion, gratitude and humility.

And in the setting of the sun, and sealed in a star filled night, two lovers yet two friends, became more together than what they were alone. The sunrise made it so.

In union, the two have become greater than one.

Let Heaven on Earth follow them home.

Let pink sandstone and blue sky cradle that moment in memory.

Let movements of hands care for the hearts they now hold.

Let patience and humility be the virtues that bind them.

And may the hope of water and trees, and the brightness of the sun and the stars, carry them through their lives.

He re-read the words endlessly. His love for Red was in them. He rewrote it on a fine sheet of antique paper. Having done so, he looked for his beloved, remembering she had kissed him goodbye— she was going to go for the walk to Slide Rock without him.

As he made his way out to 89A, he saw her heading back toward the lodge—the vision of her putting a lump in his throat. She was iconic. Every dream of love, every wish in fantasy, and every hope when his was alone, had come together in her physical and spiritual presence. They smiled at one another, and on 89A Mitchell presented to her his words. They made her cry. Her tears flowed through him. Hand-in-hand the two walked back to the warmth of the lodge room, and a fire in the fire place. The afternoon rains had begun, bringing alive every living thing in the canyon and every fantasy Mitchell had for his cherished Red.

ॐ

Less than a quarter-mile walk south of the lodge, nested west of the highway, was a little known and little used hiking trail called Sterling Pass. In the ascent, Mitchell looked constantly at the backside of his beloved. Not that he minded the view, it was just that he was never able to stay with her on the assault to the top of the trail. After Red's backside disappeared into the thick Ponderosa Pine and Douglas Fir, Mitchell slowed his pace a little, to allow more absorption of the colors, textures, and smells, observing the narrow sandstone canyon grow in its remoteness to civilization.

He was glad to know that he could do the hike, not necessarily with ease, but with confidence. No longer addicted, his health had completed a one hundred and eighty degree turn.

Mitchell stopped. The wind rumbled up from points far below him. It lifted his hair off of his head, blowing his clothing up, filling his tee-shirt with pockets of air. The exchange of cool air for warm sweat was invigorating. He looked up to see the branches and leaves of every tree and bush extending up toward the sky, reaching for the blue heaven above. Taking deep breaths, the peace of the canyon—its scents and breezes—moved about him.

Mitchell saw his beloved sitting on the saddle up ahead. She too, had found her own notions of the remote world that surrounded her.

There was peace between them.

With playfulness in her voice, she asked Mitchell where he had been. Raising an eyebrow, and grinning to ward off the teasing that often accompanied her victories, both on restaurant floors and hiking trails, he said; "I was going to ask you the same question, cuz you weren't here ten minutes ago when I was."

"You lie, you fry!" Red said, walking over to tickle him.

"Okay, I admit it, you beat me up here again."

"That's right Arizona, I beat you up here again," Red said, leaning into his face to kiss him.

"That's right New Jersey, you beat me up here again, and now its time to give you your prize," Mitchell said laughing, while Red scrambled away from him.

Mitchell still needed to catch his breath. He sat down to relax. She had picked up a stick, and sat down next to him. They leaned into one another, enjoying the quiet that had followed them up to the hidden saddle.

He looked at Red with tenderness and tremendous desire—an odd combination that he had grown accustomed to. They kissed, succumbing to the remoteness that was theirs to share, intimately so. The couple became another in a long line of lovers, in the history of man, to share Sterling Pass as their own private worship, in the passionate reflexes of Mother Nature.

ꕥ

The sun cast long shadows over Oak Creek Canyon. The fragrant canyon air mixed with the sounds of water over rock from the creek. The roar of cars and trucks flying by the trailhead below cued them to their proximity to the trail's end. Making one last leap onto the side of the highway, they turned left, and walked the short distance back to Slide Rock Lodge. Both were hungry and excited about the thought of another meal at the Heartline Café.

They headed back toward town, sitting side-by-side in Mitchell's truck, taking the six mile drive from the lodge to the edge of town slowly, making sure to never take the canyon for granted.

ꕥ

Marriage in the past tense was talked about often. It had been and remained a topic of conversation, first as friends, then as lovers. In Red's view, marriage remained special. She believed in the institution of marriage and who she was as a wife. Mitchell was not convinced he would be a good husband. He still heard the voices of the past. They haunted him still, yet less so, as more time spent with Red convinced him otherwise.

Sitting down at their favorite table, facing the setting Sedona sun, Mitchell could see the eyes, skin, and hair of Red reflecting what he already knew was a part of her heart. She was made of the perennial things that stood the test of time. Before him Mitchell could see that the setting sun favored her as he did. He could tell the sun loved to find her facing its offering of light and warmth. She closed her eyes and put her face directly toward the light, as it disappeared behind Mingus Mountain.

Mitchell closed his eyes, taking a snap shot of the moment. Opening them again, he found Red looking at him with ease, with the serenity of the breezes that made their way over the saddles of hidden hikes, to sacred places, where love is borne and set free.

A notion fell into his heart that he wanted to marry her. This thought stunned him. Up until the moment at hand, he loved her without expectation. He looked at her curiously, enough so to turn their waitress away as she approached their table, observing an exchange that required privacy.

"What's the matter with you," Red asked Mitchell.

"I can't say at the moment, I am just a little stunned at how much I love you," Mitchell said.

"Well it must be quite a profound thought," she said.

"Yes, it is, it is," he said smiling at her, and then at the waitress, indicating that it was okay to make her way into the service cycle of their table.

"Are you going to share it with me?"

"Not yet my love, not yet."

Red did know though, what he was thinking about, and marveled at her own openness to the idea of marrying Mitchell.

Chapter Fifty Five

AFTER some time had passed—after bills and rents were paid—and as one season changed into another, Mitchell, while at work one afternoon, handed Red a card that stated; "I'm taking you to California. Please pack for a stretch of beach, of sleeping in, of sunsets, of soaking up the sun's rays—and one another. I love you so much. Will you come?"

She leaped into his arms, put hers around his neck, and her legs around his waist. "I take it this means yes?" Mitchell tried to say, through her kissing him in front of fellow employees and guests alike. Mitchell was overwhelmed by her public display of affection. "Oohs," and "ahhs," were heard from all points in the restaurant. The next morning, they were headed west on Interstate 8, driving toward a coastal community that had intrigued Mitchell since his days as a resident of the beach: the San Diego neighborhood of La Jolla.

There he would find his reservation waiting in a hotel he had only admired from a distance; The La Valencia Hotel, which had long induced in Mitchell a strong sense of déjà vu, and left him transcending emotions of love, mystery, and longing. Since the idea of marriage had opened its veil to him, the hotel's large pink presence in Mitchell's memory banks had occupied his day-to-day doings, helping him to realize finally, that it was Red he was to enter into it, for the first time.

They were taken in by the hotel's large lobby, where each piece of furniture, each window, and each door greeted them invitingly, letting the hotel's charms into their collective conscience. Yes, Mitchell had been there before—perhaps in dreams—or visions of his life in his earlier years—or in his hopes—or finally, by way of the love Red had given him. The space created by The La Valencia Hotel was already familiar to them, and Red was glad that Mitchell had waited to enter the hotel for the first time, with her by his side.

They checked into a room that had a view of the Pacific Ocean framed by French doors that led to a patio elevated high above La Jolla Cove. The bellman left. They stood facing the ocean, and the moment before them. "Can I take you to dinner?" Mitchell asked Red.

"I would love it, where should we go?" she asked.

"I have made a reservation for the Sky Room," Mitchell said, which raised an eyebrow of playful suspicion on Red's part.

"Okay," Red said shyly, knowing something was up, enjoying the amplified level of romance that was revealed carefully before her.

"I will meet you downstairs in the lobby," he said kissing the top of her head, knowing that doing so would leave him with a feeling of standing tall before her. *She has always made me feel like I am better than I really am,* he thought, as he turned to go out of the room.

Mitchell made his way to the far west end of the lobby. He viewed the horizon through a huge pain of glass that framed the setting sun each evening. The ocean had taken on a rich, granite-blue color, as the sun hung low over its horizon.

He reached into his pocket, for the umpteenth time, to check for the ring he had bought, and in his breast pocket for the poem he had written for her. The day dressed itself up in the dusk, trying on, and discarding color and texture. He was mesmerized by what was to unfold upstairs, in the Sky Room—the hotel's fine dining establishment. He saw himself on the other side of the evening, as a man engaged to a woman, who placed him above her, in a love that was born of the sun, and all of its light, changing that which previously was predetermined—the destiny of his own life.

He wanted to marry her—to make her his wife. In her life he had become what she knew he was—those precious gifts—of who he was born to be—to be loved and liked—to be admired for his qualities and sense of humor—to be held in high regard and respected for the sake of respect. He was once lost to the assessments of others, but had been found by Red as worthy of loving, just as he was, and for that fact alone he adored his every unfolding moment with her.

He reviewed the poem one more time, finding in its incompleteness and frailty, the courage to be who he was to her, and to know in his heart of hearts that she did love him, and would be true to him.

He read:

This is your heart. Behind your smile she rests. Holding in her own, the white and wonder found there.

This is your heart. In your eyes I see her. She takes in the color of your world, and the admiration of all around you.

This is your heart. In your hands I embrace her. She is cradled by the delicacy and unimaginable softness that I have touched there.

This is your heart. In your laughter I hear her, finding delight between her intuitive whispers as ageless, timeless counsel.

This is your heart. In your imagination I sense her everywhere. In song, or in the telling of a moment, she unfolds her wings of beauty for all, yet she is unto her own, complete in her angelic being.

This is your heart. In your song I rejoice to her. She is the voice of Heaven, given to all who will listen.

This is your heart. In your name I call her. Bordered by traced lines of air, a murmur leaves my lips, with utmost confidence that she will hear me.

This is your heart. In your arms I desire her. I, who have been loved like no other, am amazed by her determination to love and to fulfill me.

This is your heart. In time and space I look for her. Among the light and pleasance of canyon walls, I recall and miss her. For always the road back to her will be longer than the road away. I cannot live without her.

This is your heart. In fate, she has been forwarded to me. She is Venus' extension, and I quake at the question; 'why me?' While the wheels of the world turn, she sits in companionship next to me. I thank the gods.

This is your heart. Forever held in favor under the sun and stars, and through all of heaven's creations, she is held in the highest regard, as the most tender and lovely of all things.

This is your heart. A statement without end. A voice without falter. A tree that stands for all time. A blessing that becomes a foundation. I am yours, . . . will you marry me?

A tear falling for Red turned the final rays of the sun into a starburst. It was everything he could do not to let his feet leave the ground. He returned the prose to his breast pocket. Red had appeared behind him. He heard her say, "hello you."

Mitchell turned around to see her dressed in white, her tanned skin glowing underneath. She had become the sun setting, as every man and woman in the lobby looked at her with admiration or envy.

Mitchell put his hands around her tiny waist, and kissed her with a vision of the ocean—opening up its wet world to the sun's hopes and dreams—passing before him.

They turned together toward the elevator that would take them up three floors to the Sky Room restaurant. A table had been reserved for them, in the corner of the small room that sat high above the foundation of the hotel. It was not ready, so the Maître d', Fernando, led the couple out to a perch, where they watched the dusk chase the daydreams of beachcombers, in the cove below.

Sitting down at their special table, they turned their evening over to the maître d', and his care of their night. Mitchell did not tell Fernando of his plans, but the flawless and timeless waiter suspected that something special between them, would unfold on this night.

Fernando was admiring Red's beauty in a very respectful way. Mitchell could see the growing affinity the waiter had for his beloved, and he let that become a part of the evening. Red's special concerns for her meal were discussed in detail, and Mitchell enjoyed the attention Fernando gave to her.

As the courses of the meal came and went, and the ambiance of the room played its hand in the mood of the moment, Mitchell reached into his breast pocket, and handed to Red the words that contained his hope—to hear the word that would allow his imagination of the future to soar—to hear the word that would allow possibility—and the notions of living well—reign.

She took the antique page, which reminded her of an earlier poem, and with earnestness, began to read. Each stanza of what he hoped was a song to her, brought emotions forth from her eyes. Each word rolled into the next, and Mitchell watched with much hope that his words would bank themselves, on the tip of her tongue, as one word that would define the rest of his days.

He could tell that she was about half way through. Fernando had summoned the attention of others in the room to watch, as she put into her heart, the words that Mitchell gave to her. He reached into his pocket, and pulled out the small box that contained a ring of engagement.

Time stood quietly beside their table. Red's hand began to shake, and her lip to quiver. Mitchell put the small box on her dinner plate. She looked at him, and without opening the box, offered to him the word that held the universe within it. She smiled at her love, and said quietly, "yes."

There was a great joy in the small dining room. A couple sitting nearby was celebrating their fiftieth wedding anniversary. Tears flowed from the elder couple's eyes, as they remembered their own beginnings. An impromptu toast to Red and Mitchell unfolded. The bride of fifty years asked if she could read the proposal of marriage, and after doing so, handed it to her husband to read. She walked over, and hugged both of them.

The Sky Room was full of life, and each person present felt the living of their lives ebb and flow before them. The room was the cradle of a love endless in its origins and forms. It was elevated by love to the physical manifestation of its own namesake, where the giving and the accepting of a request at one table, and the promise and the delivery of the same request at another, had now become a memory in the halls of time.

Fernando brought the newly engaged couple's dinners. He gave to Red his kitchen's creation for her; a large plate of California's freshest vegetables, steamed to perfection, surrounding two huge, perfectly rounded Yukon Gold potatoes. A moment of hysteria erupted between Red, Mitchell, and their waiter, as the large Yukon Gold potatoes mirrored Red's breasts, wrapped tightly inside her white halter top, providing a well-timed moment of comic relief to the rich sincerity that had defined the evening.

The elder couple stood up to leave, for the remainder of their evening celebration. Red stood up to hug the wife, and Mitchell shook the hand of the husband, and they watched as the doors to the elevator close on the couple who had kept the promises they made to one another fifty years earlier.

It was time to say goodnight to Fernando. He facilitated a perfect evening for everyone present, and became a hero of sorts to Mitchell as a member of the hospitality industry, acting out the very epitome and example of what service can mean to the lives he touched.

As the elevator doors closed on Red and Mitchell, they looked at the room and then at the Maître d', waving goodbye, with gratitude in their eyes for his care and thoughtfulness.

The La Jolla evening was large inside the lobby of the hotel, and the newly engaged couple found options waiting for them at any turn. First up: a moment or two in the Whaling Bar, from whence most of Mitchell's déjà vu originated—it was the bar that put the strings of another time and place at the fingertips of his expression, at the same time remaining a mystery, and source of inspiration in his writing.

After the visit, they walked toward the entrance to the hotel, and found themselves humming the different tunes that could be heard out on Prospect Street, as the nightlife of the small and quaint town center could be seen in every window.

They looked at one another, acknowledging the changing seasons of their love. Mitchell looked back to the doors of the hotel, making a mental note of what they meant to him—in an effort to remember more detail when future déjà vu would surface.

Together they turned to the night ahead. Red looked down at her finger, which held an antique silver ring and a ruby at its center, now a symbol of love from her fiancé, and smiled. Hand-in-hand, with one foot in front of the other, they embraced the passion-filled night ahead.

Chapter Fifty Six

WITH extra water, kept in storage on the bed of the old truck, Mitchell replaced what had spilled out of the radiator when he and Laurie ascended Bumble Bee Hill. The couple returned to the cab of the truck that had been allowed to air-out when they conversed on the tailgate. The full darkness of night was before them, as both faces were illuminated by two, small, incandescent lamps found in the truck's dash board. They approached Prescott proper late in the evening. The courthouse square was lit; activity along Whiskey Row brimmed with locals and tourists alike. Mitchell veered left up the hill, toward Laurie's house, watching the Hassayampa Inn move through his peripheral vision. Quiet followed them home. The revelation from Laurie about Sian's death dampened the trip. From Sunset Point north, not much was shared between them.

"Not an easy road trip Laurie, and I'm sorry for my part in it," Mitchell said.

"I'm the bearer of bad news, Mitchell," Laurie said. "It's poor timing on my part, and I'm sorry for saying anything. Believe me, I regret it now."

They sat in Mitchell's truck in front of her home, under a street lamp, reminiscent of the light on Oregon Avenue in Mitchell's youth. She longed for an alternate mood between them. She wanted to touch his hand. She had envisioned an intimate relationship with him, but with more hard news lingering between them, she took a deep breath, and reluctantly said; "there's more." Mitchell looked at her incredulously. "The man who kidnapped Sian, and killed her, was also her father. He escaped from prison." Laurie then took a deep breath, then paused her breathing for one moment, unsure if she should go on. "He is the same man who killed Red."

Mitchell's life stopped. He stopped any physical movements, any feeling, any breathing. His memory of the face of this man, this face of evil, came to the forefront of his mind. It was a face of horror, of terror, of wickedness, and hate, hanging onto the apex of a pendulum's swing into hell. Mitchell's body shook back to life, breathing again, yet still unable to fathom the notion that the same hand took both mother and daughter.

They sat in Mitchell's truck for a long time in silence. Finally, Laurie asked "Would you like to come in for some tea?"

"I would Laurie," Mitchell said. "I don't feel much like going home right now. Your news . . . has stunned me. I feel so sad."

Laurie watched him get out of the truck. He looked burdened. His face and body reflected the heartbreaking weight he carried in him. Crossing the threshold of his friend's house for the first time, he was taken for a moment out of his pain by the ornate beauty of it. The interior matched the exterior of the home perfectly, and the consistent Victorian splendor helped to temporarily lighten Mitchell's load.

"Why don't you have a seat somewhere in there," Laurie said, pointing to a perfectly appointed sitting room, with a fire place as the room's focus for furniture and other decorations. The home was immaculate; Mitchell felt oddly out of place. He dismissed these initial judgments, blaming exhaustion as the filter for his senses. He found a comfortable high-backed chair, and sunk into it, closing his eyes, trying to breathe deeply the serenity around him.

Moment's passed. *The same man,* he thought. *How strange. How evil.* His mind wondered. A theme song floated through his thoughts from the television show M*A*S*H. Suddenly present were the melody's lyrics, and in his mind he sung three words over and over again; *suicide is painless . . . suicide is painless . . .*

"Here you go Mitchell," Laurie said, handing him a cup of tea. "Where are you," she asked gingerly.

"Do you remember the theme song from the 1970's TV show M*A*S*H?" he asked.

"Sort of," she responded. "I remember my parents really liked that show."

"It was always on in my house," Mitchell said. "The melody had such a nice 'Sunday afternoon,' feel to it, but the lyrics are quite shocking in comparison."

"What lyrics," Laurie stated. "There are no lyrics that I remember."

"That's from the show, but the M*A*S*H movie, which inspired the television show, has these lyrics that start like this: 'Suicide is painless . . .'" Mitchell sung it half-heartedly.

"That's where you were just now in your head?" Laurie asked.

"Yeah, that's it, right there, singing those three words, over and over again in my head."

"Why?"

"I wonder about life sometimes, Laurie," Mitchell said. "It gets overwhelming. It has a slow but steady way of stacking things up, like a garbage dump cracking, spewing up in front of me, and the next thing I know, I've got my nose stuck in one of its cracks, and the crack stinks.

How is it possible that this same man killed both Red and Sian, twenty five years apart?" Mitchell asked. "How does someone get away with something like that?"

"He didn't Mitchell," Laurie said.

"But to hear that he was someone Red knew, for God's sake Laurie, Red knew him!" Mitchell exclaimed, without reservation. He started to cry. "She knew him; she knew the son-of-a-bitch. The terror and horror she endured, is beyond my ability to cope. I feel like I'm going to go insane right now."

"Mitchell don't," Laurie said, putting her hand on his. "Try to put it back in the file you keep these things in." She stood up before him, and then knelt down, right in front of him, putting her arms around his neck, allowing him to rest his head on her shoulder. He let the tears flow without sound, as Red's pain passed through him. Mitchell put his arms around Laurie, and held her. They stayed there for some time when Laurie stirred. She got up, put some pillows on the floor in front of the fire place, and started a fire. She reclined on the rug in front of the fire, and invited Mitchell to do the same. He joined her by resting on his back, looking up at the ceiling, still lost in the news of the day.

"Suicide is painless." Mitchell sang.

"How does the rest of the song go?"

"No clue," Mitchell said. "I never got passed those three words, they shocked me. It's like singing "Over the Rainbow," but with lyrics about horror and terror."

"Would you like to listen to some music?" Laurie asked, wanting to lift the mood he was in.

"Yes, that's a fine idea," he said.

"What's your pleasure," she asked.

"Surprise me," he said.

Mitchell stared at the ceiling, feeling time pass without pause, when he noticed Laurie return to floor next to him. "Gordon and I go way back," Mitchell said. "Song for a Winter's Night," took him back to Flagstaff, to the subdued lighting of another life. He thought of sharing with Laurie that period in his life, and the similarities in appearance between her and the girl he met in college, but let the quiet and ambiance of the song remain the focus.

Laurie sat up next to Mitchell, took a deep breath, and said, "Mitchell, there's one more thing I'd like to tell you now, about the similarities between Sian's death and Red's." She looked at him as he stared at the ceiling, moving his eyes slowly toward her. "There was a bloody sock print found next to Sian's tiny body. She was strangled; she was less than a year old."

Mitchell's memory flashed back to the moment on the table, at the end of a long shift at the Olive Garden, when Red spoke of such a print. He took a deep breath, and then sat up next to Laurie. He looked at the fire. The flames caught his thoughts, and found there a vision of who Sian could have been, and how she could very well be the spirit of who he had been talking to all these past months. "Laurie, I've been talking to her—a grown up version of her—or a younger version of Red, the one I never knew. This person I talk to, for whom I laugh and cry with, is real to me. If you cannot see her, it simply means that she is a spirit, and is helping me through the madness I have suffered. I've got some news to tell you too; this sock print you mention is found in several murders that have spanned the decades right here in Prescott. Red or Sian, or collectively, their spirit compelled me to enter the Sharlot Hall Museum, and look for coroner's reports detailing the same piece of evidence. It's like she, or they, are trying to warn me, to keep vigilant with this, and to watch for this kind of evil to show itself again. Laurie, I've seen it in Zac's eyes, when he was harassing that old lady at the courthouse square. He's got it in for me. I feel his vile hate for me, and I can sense deeply the same evil I encountered the night Red was killed. I feel like this evil lives on somehow, and its mark is this bloody sock print, the sight of which haunts me. This punk never wears shoes."

Laurie and Mitchell both reclined again on the pillows next to the fire place. Mitchell noticed peripherally that she was fading. She yawned and turned slightly toward the fire. Mitchell made the matching movements, and gently put his arm over her arm and shoulder. She accepted his touch quietly and gratefully, letting those emotions follow her into a deep slumber.

Mitchell remained awake, looking closely at her hair, and listening to her breath. He was solemn as the reality of his behavior began to sink in. *She must think I'm crazy,* he thought, *but I guess I don't care, what I've got with Red's spirit, via her daughter or her, I cherish and will never relinquish* . . . With that thought, Mitchell followed his own thoughts into a deep well of sleep, the dark of night becoming one with his soul.

❧

In the darkness of sleep, a startling dream forced Mitchell to sit up. The dream was more a memory of a walk he and Red had taken back to the Hassayampa Inn after dinner during their honeymoon. A grey figure was sitting on a bench in the shadows of downtown Prescott's street lights. He stood and came up behind the couple. Mitchell turned around and chased the figure off. Now Mitchell remembered—the man was not wearing any shoes.

> *White and still was the love he had known from the heart of his wife, giving flight to thoughts of God and his request that a free will would choose goodness, following in His dying child's example on the world's ever-growing cross.*

Chapter Fifty Seven

RED and Mitchell wanted their wedding day to have its own heart. They did not want elaborate or large. They wanted things around them of their own design, and not the latest trend. They recognized the courage present in each to face one another, and not their pasts, as they planned their wedding day.

Red, at heart, was a delicate creature, blessed with the bane of a woman whose talents and looks were often envied, rather than enjoyed. In the days leading up to their ceremony, Mitchell saw her delicate ways come to life. The tender design in the wedding cake she created resembled a garden of color, and would become the centerpiece of the wedding dinner, prepared under her tutelage, representing recipes of the many places where she and Mitchell had shared their love.

Red sang a song for Mitchell during their ceremony that reflected her deep spiritual commitment to him. Mitchell's tears, as he listened to her angelic voice, gave Red what her heart needed from him.

Joel, their minister, a regular diner at the Olive Garden, gave to them their passage into lawful matrimony. In hope the two turned to one another, and to the bread and wine of their ceremony. They gave to one another something more than the simple bands of gold on their fingers. They gave to one another a home for their hearts, and a floor of honesty to walk upon. They made for each other windows of faith, and doors of grace between them. In recognition of their time with one another, a ceiling was placed above their reach into space, giving their love an earthly dimension, pressed by the weight of their own bodies, against all that had come before, and of all that would come after the ceremony at hand.

At the ceremony's end, their hearts were contained in a house of love, with all of its parts making it a home for Red and Mitchell. Toasts were given, bread was broken, wine was shared from one hand to the next, and the well wishes sent the married couple on their way to their first night together as Red's husband, and as Mitchell's wife.

Longing since childhood to step inside a world long past, when love was measured not by what a man said but by what he did, Mitchell checked Red into the honeymoon suite at the Hassayampa

Inn in downtown Prescott. Lifting her across the threshold, the newlyweds kissed each other, making the room their own, as the spirits of past loves, both broken and renewed, watched on in admiration.

The heat and passion of their first night as husband and wife fulfilled the long-held wishes of Mitchell, making him a husband loved without inhibition or labor. Red was his dynamic, healthy, fit, enduring lover, in the white role of a wife. Mitchell answered her prayer of a husband filled with desire and passion for her, making her body and her soul his by wanton desire. He panted. Her skin showed the color of friction and beaded sweat. She needed to catch her breath. He needed her breath in him.

Their first night together was lived out with rigorous determination, taking the Eden within, from the spiritual to the physical, finding the glorious, sweet, Apple of Knowing, laced between their arms and legs, fingers and lips, with vivid visions of their skins melding together in love's bed. This, after so much time living together—this, after many a night spent with each other's fears, with one another's hopes, and of knowing who they were as they held hands in the middle of a deep, restoring sleep, in the middle of Mother Nature's blessed darkness; their honeymoon night.

Their rite-filled union was now complete. Their physical love had manifested into promises fulfilled; made so by a love borne in the Halls of Man—its meaning akin to that of all great literary love. In their union they had filled the intentions of a spirit becoming a soul-bound body. They loved one another, and knew it would continue so for the remainder of all their days.

Morning came. Hunger did too. They decided to occupy a table at the Peacock Restaurant in the Hassayampa Inn. They chose a deuce in the restaurant located in the middle of an arched window, which had previously held one hundred years of a husband's hopes and a wife's dreams. They sat and faced one another, awash in the notions of what marriage was. Red ordered love, Mitchell time, and together their world had found harmony. The promise of Eden had been delivered to their breakfast table.

Chapter Fifty Eight

RED leaned into the window of the Peacock Restaurant, to secure a better view of what was taking place at the Courthouse Square in downtown Prescott. Mitchell watched her delicate nose touch the pane of antique glass, separating the quiet ambiance of the room, from the chugs and squeaks of vehicles crawling up, or sliding down, the steep hill outside their window. Across the street from the table sat the entrance to the Elks Theater. Mitchell saw himself standing there as a boy, paying his fare to watch the movie, *Bless the Beasts and the Children*, its title track made famous by the voice of Karen Carpenter. The movie was filmed in and around Prescott, and Mitchell remembered the thrill of seeing landmarks he knew on the big screen.

"Are you seeing the younger you?" Red asked, knowing her husband.

"Yes," Mitchell said. "Do you remember the song 'Bless the Beasts and the Children'?"

"Yes, I do."

"Did you know that is the name of a movie that was filmed here when I lived here?" Mitchell asked.

"I adore that song," Red said. "I didn't know it was made for a movie. What was it about?"

"It was about the plight of a group of misfits working to save the slaughter of a herd of buffalo," Mitchell said. "I liked it as a kid because I identified with the misfits." Mitchell remembered the realizations of poverty in the cupboards of his youthful home south of town. That notion held sway for only a moment as the joy of living in that home came to the forefront of his mind.

"Living here was not only about being a misfit though, honey," Mitchell said.

"I know, you have described the life and wonder of a boy taken in by the woods. I love that part of you so much."

Mitchell smiled.

"Look," Red said. "There's an arts and crafts fair going on at the Courthouse. Wanna go?"

"I'd love it," Mitchell said.

⊰⊱

The morning light was bright. Spring was in full-bloom with summer trying to make a dent in Prescott's mile high elevation. The square was full of vendors and items of every kind, past and present. The couple separated some what, as different interests pulled them toward different booths. Mitchell found an old Matchbox car, a military transport, with a small swivel gun on top and the engine mounted on the front. It whirled Mitchell back in time, as he had once owned an identical Matchbox car as a boy. He bought it.

Red found fabrics and lace, and was engaged in a conversation with a vendor about what could be made. Mitchell kept vigil upon her, knowing at all times where she was located, in proximity to the sun reflecting off her mane of red hair. He was an observant husband. His boundaries around he and his wife were clear, in every respect, and he was grateful to God to know what was welcomed in the circle of their love, and what was not.

As thoughts of protecting his wife arched through his mind, his eyes fell upon a long, bright, knife with a handle beautifully stained in dark reds and greens. The leather scabbard was ornate with the design of an eagle in flight, skillfully etched into it. He stared at it for some time, not knowing why the sudden urge to possess it ran through him. He turned to see Red in conversation with a vendor, who sold antique dolls. He looked back at the knife, then looked up at the seller—a man who watched Mitchell closely.

"It looks new," Mitchell said to the vendor.

"I make them," he said.

"It's beautifully done."

"Thank you."

"How much do you want for it?"

The knife-maker stated a price, and without pause Mitchell purchased the long blade, and placed it hidden behind him, declining the offer of a bag to put it in. Mitchell turned away from the craftsman, hearing him state: "it's just been sharpened."

Mitchell strolled down the sidewalk toward Red. He loved old wooden boxes, and looked constantly for anything that would resemble his first—the one with a secret combination of sliding panels, revealing a hidden chamber within. A very well maintained oak box full of silver caught Mitchell's eye. He opened it up and counted the pieces. All were there. All matched. They were in good condition—the box in particular. He closed the lid with an approving nod to himself, and moved on. Mitchell and Red met up between vendors. He told her that she should go check out a box of silver in the next booth over.

A moment later, Mitchell heard Red gasp, and saw her put her hand to her mouth. She was looking at the silver. It was bought and became a part of their honeymoon. The set was an exact match to the same silver Red's dad bought for her mom on their honeymoon decades earlier. It gave Red the chills, and Mitchell an accounting of serendipity. With lace, an old Matchbox car, a set of one hundred-year-old silver, and an oddly placed knife, the newlyweds walked up the steep grade of Gurley Street back to their hotel for a morning nap. The honeymoon suite's windows were opened wide, the door to the patio as well, which contained a view of a perfectly appointed Victorian home nestled high on a hill south of the Inn. The mile high air breezed gently through the curtains of the room, creating a motion of time moving slowly through their honeymoon weekend. A generous notion of sleep emanated from the walls of the old room, built one hundred years earlier. They leaned into one another, their noses touching, their breath becoming one with the breezes and movements of sunlight through the transparent drapes.

The morning nap on their honeymoon weekend was a natural extension of what transpired the night before; they had worked hard as husband and wife, on their wedding night, erasing vague memories in both about relationships past.

❧

Mitchell rolled to his side, carefully placing Red's hand upon her hip, in an effort not to disturb her. He stretched. It was good to squeeze the resting blood from his muscles.

Standing up quietly, he walked out onto the patio, and took in the high noon Prescott sun. Yawning, he shook his head loose from the grip of the nap. He looked over the side of the balcony at a busy weekend day in Prescott. With the sun's brightness squinting his eyes, Mitchell suddenly wanted to visit his childhood playground—the waterhole. The Hassayampa River would feel invigorating on his bare feet.

"Mitchell?" Red said through the sheet of their bed.

"Yes."

"What do you want to do today?"

It was uncanny how a thought entered Mitchell's mind, and a question about that thought would come from Red.

"Can you guess?"

"You want to go to the waterhole today, don't you?"

"I do."

It only took about forty five minutes to get beside the blue granite and clear water of the Hassayampa River. Red had rolled up her pant legs, and was walking slowly south down the river, past the waterhole. Mitchell produced a camera, taking pictures of Red, as she moved away from him, into the sunlight. He pulled out his journal, and began moving his pen over the pages. There was something being said among the trees and the breezes that Mitchell wanted to record— it was admiration, growing among the elements of nature, for his new wife, and through an effort to press ink into an empty white page, Mitchell wrote these words:

> *The sun is perfect. My breath is deep—purifying the moments just lived for the anticipation of what will come. You move away from me, toward the light of the day ahead, and I see in complete delight, what the backlit sun says about its outline of you.*

> *The falling shadows from the trees above you, remark to the cosmos their luck in finding a moment on your red hair—a moment now mine to possess as a photograph.*

> *I hear the water of this river remind me—it was its design among hard and cold things that put this time at hand—this moment of love united—at my feet, long ago. As a boy these very waters told me I would find you someday, and there you are, your feet now among what the Hassayampa claims as its own.*

> *I have heard many things call me in my life—none clearer than the voice of your heart. Like this river—that knows what it is, I too will be measured by my self knowledge. I know this in my bones, and I willingly accept and embrace this life as a man—as your husband. Your love for me has made this so.*

These rocks, that held me as a boy, now hold me as a man, and as your husband, I will remain firm as granite in what that means. I will be true, and steadfast in belief in what you are, and through your love, what I have become—just as the water gives what it will—to the pull of what lays further down stream.

I thank you for marrying me, Red. The boy who once played here does too. I remember him well. Having you stand here among these rocks, gives renewed meaning to my life—further reason why I came to these waters so long ago. I thank you for loving that boy in me, for understanding him, for making sense of him, for helping him to come home to your hearth, and your heart.

I love you Red,

Mitchell

James Taylor's, *Highway Song,* closed Mitchell's eyes to the surrounding water and rocks. He closed his journal, looking forward to the moment when he could transcribe his words upon a page that would please the heart of his wife.

Time passed. One minute. One hour. Mitchell was not sure. He heard a couple of gasps coming from Red's direction and when he opened his eyes he found his wife chancing a dip in the water hole, without one stitch of clothing upon her body. When she stepped out of her comfort zone, she would drive Mitchell wild, doing so now in the waterhole of his youth. He tore off his own clothes as he ran toward her. He made a boyish jump into the waterhole. She covered her face from the onslaught of water, and before she knew it, she was in her husband's hungry arms, being lifted above his grateful heart. His vision of his beautiful wife, her breasts wet and cold left both the boy and man in him grateful.

Mitchell lowered Red slowly down upon him. He let her breasts find there way across his face. As she re-entered the water her legs spread open and wrapped around her husband's body. At that moment she found him. To Mitchell's astonishment, he was making love to his wife. He could not contain himself—the moment overwhelmed him. She smiled, knowing he was at the cusp—his first in the Hassayampa River.

It was the smile. Mitchell rolled his head back, letting the blue heavens hear his joy. He frolicked wildly around the waterhole, taking his wife with him, and in the next instant, Red too, had been ushered over the threshold, joining her husband in panting, joyful ecstasy.

Completely spent, they stood up on one of the granite steps, where Mitchell steadied his wife, onto the warmth of the rock surrounding the waterhole. Mitchell climbed out too, and sprawled himself across the rocks. He caught his breath, then asked the trees, and Red, if that was all they were going to do on their honeymoon: eat, sleep, and make love.

Red asked what else a wife was for. Mitchell responded by asking what else a husband could do but honor his wife for even asking the question. There were more smiles. There was more sunlight, more wind in the trees, and a lazy advance of time on a perfect afternoon.

☙

The newlyweds took the 'back way' up to the FR 63. Mitchell described to Red, probably for the umpteenth time, how his childhood buddy Presley, had discovered the shorter, yet steeper access to the waterhole.

"How long do you think the waterhole has been there?" Red asked.

"Well, I am guessing centuries, if not millenniums," Mitchell said. "I know our 'discovery' as children put us in a long line of humanity that has claimed it as 'their' spot."

As soon as Mitchell stated this, he and Red saw a family, wrapped up in bathing suits and beach towels, headed for the same spot where they had just made love.

"Boy," Red stated. "Aren't we the timely pair?"

"It has always been this way at the waterhole," Mitchell said. "It has always been just me, my friends, my sisters, and now you, at the waterhole. I've never shared it with anyone else."

They continued their lazy hike along the Hassayampa, to a point where the confluence of Groom Creek joined the river. At that instant, Red saw a 'for sale' sign nailed to a tree that faced FR 63. Both were curious about what was 'for sale.'

It was a rustic, but well maintained, A-frame cabin that stood in a clearing of land. It was a newer structure that appeared to have some amenities in it that were not found in cabins decades earlier, like a satellite dish for starters.

An old man came out of the cabin, and looked at the pair.

"Where's your car?" he asked quickly.

"We left it at one of the entrances to the waterhole," Red offered.

"You from around here?" the old man asked.

"Well, sort of," Mitchell responded. "I spent some time in these woods as a kid."

"Whereabouts?" the old man asked.

"Ponderosa Park."

"I see, I see," the old man said. "Looking to come back are ya? It's got everything you need. Lots of peaks. Lots of valleys. But there is always a price to pay, isn't there young fella," the old man said, looking right into Mitchell's eyes.

Mitchell felt an odd bell ring in the back of his mind but he could not quite put his finger on it.

"Yea," Mitchell said with earnest. "But there are some things that will always remain worth the price," Mitchell said as his eyes moved from the old man to the pitch of the A-frame cabin.

"Can we afford this place?" Mitchell asked the old man.

"You might, you might," the old man said. "I am not really lookin' for the right price, as much as the right people, to turn this place over to."

Mitchell eyed the old man again. His mannerisms and tone of voice were resonating in a long buried memory bank somewhere in Mitchell's mind. He had seen him before.

"What are you asking for your home sir?" Red asked.

"I'm askin' a price that's not easily paid by dollars alone, young one," he said, looking at Red with a rainbow of admiration. "I'm lookin' to have the right people take this home."

"You keep mentioning the 'right people'," Mitchell said. "What kind of people are the 'right people'?"

"I'm lookin' for people who got a good feelin' for the place," the old man said, as he arched his hand and arm out, referencing the cabin and the forest.

"How would we show that to you?" Mitchell asked.

"Don't know, it'd just be shown, and I'd just see it," the old man said.

Mitchell and Red turned to go. They waved goodbye to the old man, appreciating his kinship for where he lived. Mitchell told Red about his sense that he'd seen the man before, he just could not put his finger on where.

"Perhaps you waited on him."

"Perhaps."

For both, the notion of buying the A-frame, and living in the woods where Mitchell spent part of his youth, spun cogs of thought. They pictured themselves standing on the porch of the A-frame, as its owners, letting the breezes move through their hair, and the shade give them rest on a lazy afternoon. Both needed to be careful of their powers of visualization. Time and again it had brought them many things, both good and bad.

"I don't know, Red," Mitchell said. "I hear Frost and Clemens calling my name right now. I hear the boy in me wanting to live in that cabin more than he wants to do anything else. I would adore it. There are four seasons up here. We are close enough to the metropolis that is now Prescott to still enjoy the benefits of living in or near a city. We could get transfers from the Olive Garden in Mesa, to the one here."

"And we could use the trust my father left me to buy it," Red said.

"What trust?" Mitchell asked, surprisingly.

"My father left me money a very long time ago, when he died, I've never accessed it," Red said. "There's not much in it, but it is probably enough to buy the old man's place. We just have to show him that he would be selling it to the right people, but how?"

Red thought for a moment, and then suggested: "why not write him a letter, describing your own kinship for the area."

Lacking confidence in anyone else reading his thoughts but Red, Mitchell shook his head, and said "maybe," then added, "you have a trust?"

"It's all I have left of my father. I've just been waiting for the right reason to spend it. I think this is the right reason."

Mitchell smiled at her, stunned at the realization that he had married a woman with a trust, albeit however small she may have thought it was.

ଫ୬

Presently, Mitchell and Red were in the old truck headed back to the Hassayampa Inn. Saturday night was upon them, and a dinner reservation at Murphy's awaited the night ahead.

Quiet was the melody that played as they drove. It was the ability of Red to sit next to Mitchell in peace, with or without words, which endeared this wife to her husband. Red was at ease with herself. Constant stimulation was not needed, and Mitchell appreciated this quality in his wife. There was no call for anything else. Such moments gave Mitchell the distinct impression of a re-occurring piano theme playing between them.

ଛଢ

Mitchell let the day catch up to him. Red was cold and put a blanket around her shoulders, leaning against her husband on the sofa.

The sun was setting. Silence continued its cadence. Mitchell closed his eyes, feeling at home with Red. He put his arm around her, appreciating her fit under him, and his head back on the sofa, welcoming the hushed sincerity of their relationship. The setting sun, filtered by the old building, was allowed access to their room via other things, like the passing of cars, or windows on other structures, and by the memories of days gone by, as the boy in Mitchell remembered the sun setting on his bare feet.

The quiet between the two lovers grew into the opening of a spring. Mitchell watched the water rise silently up, out of the earth, to fall forward as its life under the sun began. A piano played again—this time the music rose up from the open window's of the hotel's lobby; the notes played were accompanied by lyrics, and Mitchell recognized Joni Mitchell's "Two Grey Rooms." The composition, as newlyweds basked in the ambience of the their room, complimented the mood

312

with perfection. The notes of the song took both Red and Mitchell into the black, beautiful, universe expanding.

Time moved through him. The pastels of a second-hand sunset continued to change, first brighter pink, then softer purple. Mitchell knew, at that moment, what the spring knew; it was simply lucky to have its moment in the grand scheme of time. It was as if this very quiet time and space was where creation took place. It was all things to him. It was gratitude and forgiveness. It was courage and generosity. It was all these things combined to create a great love between the couple.

He looked up to see the purple pastels give way to the rich blue arc above the earth's horizon—a goodbye to the day. He recalled it. He thought of his wife's nude body in the water of his youth, and of making love to her among those rocks and trees. He thought of the A-frame cabin, the old man and the déjà vu, and what that meant. He thought of the capacity of his own human heart to assemble meaning around action and idea, and his ability to do so having its origins along the Hassayampa River itself.

The Circle of Life; he was a part of it, as the evening blue assembled itself inside their hotel room.

"Hey Red, are you hungry?" Mitchell whispered to his wife.

"I am," she said, through a yawn. "What is this, two naps today?" she asked Mitchell.

"It was a perfect day Red," Mitchell said. "A day I will long remember."

Red kissed his cheek and headed into the small, rustic bathroom to get ready for dinner at Murphy's. Mitchell walked outside and noted the dramatic temperature change, after the sun left its mark on the day.

Opening his suitcase, Mitchell spied the outline of the knife purchased earlier in the day. He had never considered owning such a thing before, but knew that it was due to his newly-understood responsibility to protect his wife. Carrying the weapon tingled him in instinctual and spiritual ways, feeling obligated on these levels, to be prepared to intervene if she ever needed him to.

The problem was that he had not told her yet that he bought it. It was her history—her pain. He was afraid the knife would bring that back somehow. He decided he would tell her, just not on this night, slipping the hunting knife behind him, between his belt and pants, then turned and waited for his wife to appear in the bathroom door.

"You better wear your coat, Red," Mitchell said. "I'd like to walk to the restaurant tonight, if you are up for it."

"Of course," Red said.

༈

Evening in downtown Prescott had charm. It was well lit, and the hundred-year-old structures welcomed what color and shadow the street lamps offered. It was a comfortable down hill walk from the hotel to the eatery.

The meal passed almost unnoticed. Mitchell and Red were still awash in the magic of their day together. Paying their bill, they re-entered the night, and began the long slow, uphill walk back to the hotel.

Ahead on Cortez Street Mitchell spotted a lone figure sitting on one of the many benches that lined both sides of the street. The man was wearing a baseball cap, pulled low over his head. His hands were in his pockets.

Mitchell took a mental note of the man, and switched places with Red, putting himself between her and any possible danger. Red had not noticed the figure on the bench; she was absorbed into the magnificence of the courthouse lighting.

They walked passed the man, and Mitchell did not like what he sensed about the shadowy shape. He quickened their pace, then heard the man get up off the bench, and fall in line behind them.

At once Mitchell spun around to face the man while at the same time putting Red behind him. He assumed a guarded stance, and asked the stranger what he thought he was doing walking so close behind him.

"Take it easy," the stranger said. "I don't want anything from you that's worth fighting for."

"Back off, right now," Mitchell exclaimed, as his anger rose in defiance of memories and regrets of past transgressions.

"You talk big pal," the stranger said while he produced a wooden stick from his coat sleeve. "Now just give me your wallet, and no one will get hurt."

"No, you fucking asshole, you get nothing from me," Mitchell said.

"You're brave," the mugger said, putting the club back over his head, to swing it down on Mitchell.

Blinded by anger, and the audacity of their attacker, Mitchell reached behind, and grabbed the newly purchased knife in one hand, and the man's attacking arm in the other, letting out a banner of cuss words that could be heard up and down Cortez Street, stunning the mugger with his veracity and quickness. The man stumbled away, running for an alley across the street.

Red was on their cell phone, talking to a 911 operator when she yelled "Mitchell, don't!"

Mitchell stopped himself from winging the long hunting knife at the back of the fleeing assailant.

He stood shaking. Sweat broke through his skin. His breath beat wildly with his heart. Finally, he whispered out loud that "I passed the test."

Red did not hear him, she was trying to describe the assailant to the police but found she could not; she had not seen him.

Within a matter of a minute, a Prescott policeman was at the scene, calming both Red and Mitchell down, while removing the formidable blade from Mitchell's shaking hand.

The cop noted no blood on it, or the couple.

"You probably should have given him your wallet, that would have been the safe way to go, mister," the cop said.

"Is that what you would have done?" Mitchell asked the cop.

"No, it isn't," the cop said. "But it's what we are supposed to tell victims of muggings. You run the risk of injury or death by confronting a mugger."

"I think I would rather die than let some scum bag take anything from me, especially my dignity," Mitchell said.

The cop looked him in the eye, and silently agreed with him. He took their statements and gave them a ride back to the hotel.

"Sorry this happened to you," the cop said. "It's pretty rare."

"Thanks," Mitchell said.

The couple walked quietly up to their room. Upon entrance, Red said, "thank you for protecting me. I don't think I know what I would have done, had you not. I need my husband to defend me, and you did it, and I love you so much for being that man."

Mitchell was stunned by her reaction to what he did.

"I didn't know you had a knife," Red said.

"I'm sorry I didn't tell you about it sooner," Mitchell said. "I got it today at the craft fair, and it was an afterthought to take it with us tonight. I'm glad I followed through on the hunch."

They held each other. Tears came. They kissed each other, stilling their anxiety over the attempted mugging. The piano melody, heard earlier in the evening, was heard again echoing up the old hotel's red brick walls.

☙❧

Mitchell awoke at 4 a.m. The television was on, as was a lamp near the bed. His eyes looked around the room. He heard Red breathing and hesitated to move, not wanting to disturb her sleep. Upon the lamp stand rested his journal. As he looked at the leather-bound covers and the white pages between, he wondered what would be written there. He marveled at his wife's belief in him. *What would be written, in the time to come,* he thought. He closed his eyes, and resumed the slumber of a honeymoon night, thanking God for the many gifts that he had been given the day before—including the ability to protect his wife.

☙❧

Mitchell and Red were back in their routines at the Olive Garden. Hard work reigned. Life rotated on an axis of faith and gratitude. They believed that what went out into the world would return. They had seen this notion in action in the service cycle at the restaurant, where hard work was rewarded on the spot in a tip, or weekly in the schedules and stations they were assigned.

Time passed. Red brought up the subject of the letter to the old man. She had begun the process of seeing herself live there. A letter from her husband to the old man would most likely make it so. Mitchell wanted it too. Living close to the Hassayampa River, a body of water that was now iconic to both, gained momentum, as Red cleared the use of her trust to buy the cabin through her trustee, who was glad Red was finally going to use it.

This was the biggest change in them. They had begun the incredible work of defining who they were. Their refined reflections had begun to materialize in the mirror.

His writings detailed a spiritual connection, outlined largely by observing Red. She, still possessed of an 'old world' belief about so many things, helped Mitchell grasp the meaning of faith. Like his AA meetings, there was no dogma, or blind ritual in Red's faith—no spooky ghost inside a gold chalice—just belief in the natural working of God in her life.

To thine own self be true, was the knowledge AA brought to Mitchell, the addict. To know who he was—away from the addictions and abuse—was the secret Red had brought to him.

Hanging his head and arm out the window on their way home from another day at the Olive Garden, blowing the restaurant stink and drama off of him, Mitchell had decided that it was time to write the old man the letter.

"I'm going to see what can be written to the old man about his cabin." Mitchell said.

"Thank you," she said. "I was hoping the inspiration would come."

He wrote;

Dear Sir,

You have a perfect home, on a perfect stretch of land, and our time standing on it has traveled back with us to the Valley and our busy, productive lives. Your home remains the topic of our conversations. Both Red and I have attached ourselves to our unique visions of what life would be like for us there.

The Hassayampa River holds many priceless and unique memories for me. As I told you, I lived in Ponderosa Park. I went to Prescott Junior High School, where I played football. My biggest associations, however, are the memories of the river itself.

As a child it held one adventure after the next, from below the Oro Flame mine to the source of the river's water itself, I have tracked its movements. In summer, fall, winter, and spring I knew what the water had to offer, and although this experience lasted only two years, it remains as one of the premiere times of my life. I often see my time there as a boy in Robert Frost poetry, and Mark Twain prose.

I met you once before. I believe it was you that sat at the trailhead of Poopout Hill, below San Gorgonio Peak, decades ago. You asked me if I had found any answers as I stood on the summit of Grayback. I told you that I did, that I should follow my heart. I have, and it has taken me to you again. Do you remember that morning?

Life unfolded on the Hassayampa in a unique way for me as a boy. I want to return to such a life as a man. Red feels the same way about the home she could make for us there. Red is unique, much more so than what one sees initially. She comes from another place in time, and is possessed of 'old world' traits that have become lost in this maddening world. I am the product of that kindness and generosity. We were married recently, in fact we were on our honeymoon the day we met you on your porch. We are truly devoted to one another, and have found peace in life through our love.

We ask you to let us be the ones to live there.

Sincerely,

Mitchell and Red

Mitchell gave the letter to Red. She was pleased with it, and asked if she could mail it. As they drove out of the apartment complex, on their way to another long, hard day at The Olive Garden, Red held the letter to her heart, and then kissed it before placing it in the mailbox.

Chapter Fifty Nine

WEEKS had passed. Summer was on, in the Valley of the Sun. Electric bills went through the roof as did dining public tempers. Coming into The Olive Garden, kept cold by massive air conditioning units on its roof, the dining public relieved stress with food and beverage. Soda and water were always delivered by Red and Mitchell on-the-fly, as their stations filled up with grateful regulars.

Not all who passed through their stations were of the grateful group mentioned above. There were plenty of angry, shallow, seedy, creepy, and desperate diners as well; three sisters in particular—spoiled, and cranky, they were each in a large hurry to let the envy of Red surface. With lots of expensive jewelry, apparel, and accessories on display, they still held sour dispositions toward one another, to the world in general, and unfortunately, to Red in particular. During one lunch shift they let their expensive nails crawl, scraping the top of the table, as Red approached them for a drink order. They could not stand the sight of her.

When Red left to get their drinks, Mitchell, who was working in his station next to Red's, overheard the worst of the comments: "who does she think she is, looking at us that way," and "where did she get the money to get all that done to her." Mitchell enjoyed setting the record straight, explaining to the exasperated trio that what they saw in Red was simply Red, and that her discipline, in diet and exercise, made her look the way she looked. He added that he knew this because she was his wife, doing so with a warning tone in his voice to back off, and treat their waitress with respect. They did, and oddly, they became Red's regulars after that, wanting to know how Red did what she did, to stay youthful.

Men were a different story. All Mitchell ever did, when the situation escalated, was to simply take over the service of the table—but only on Red's request. That was message enough.

It was ironic for Red and Mitchell to know that it was the blue-collar man or woman that left the most appreciative tips. The white collars and the wealthy were more often the cheap skates; exceptions to every rule existed however. One known millionaire always left a less than ten percent tip, with dimes, nickels and pennies, in an odd effort to put his server in their proper place on society's totem pole. Red and Mitchell felt sorry for the man.

It took all kinds. There were many moments that were the exact opposite of the penny-pinching millionaire. In fact, Mitchell had a Friday night regular, a working Joe from one of the Apache Attack Helicopter industries, who would, on a consistent basis, leave Mitchell a $100.00 tip on a $100.00 tab, simply because Joe admired Mitchell's work ethic.

Often enough, shifts would end with their acknowledgement that perhaps it would be a good time to get out of the business.

But stay they would, liking the second shift—having their mornings together—their weekends that started on Monday—and enjoying the good rapport with the management—who would play a key role in a transfer to the Prescott Olive Garden, if one was needed.

ॐ

An envelope had arrived in the mail. The hand-written address was shaky. With no return address, Red still knew who it was from; the old man in Prescott. She hurriedly returned to the truck and handed it to Mitchell.

"I think it's from Prescott," Red said.

Mitchell leaned into Red, tired from the day, and opened the letter with her. All it said was; "It's yours if you still want it."

They were stunned. Not able to contain themselves, they hopped out of the truck, running in circles around it, hooting and hollering, waving their arms in the air in a wondrous celebration of having their dream of owning the A-frame, come full circle. In their last lap around the truck, Red leaped into Mitchell's arms, and they joyfully kissed.

Calming back down, Mitchell let Red get into the truck from his side, pushed her playfully to the middle of the bench seat—her spot since their date watching *The Lion King*—and together they stared out the windshield of the truck.

"We both feel a calling in our hearts about this move," Red said. "I feel like we belong there, and that we can forge out a good life together."

Mitchell sat quietly with her words. They drove through the apartment parking lot to find their parking space occupied by another car.

"It's a sign," Red said, mimicking a phrase they picked up from a beloved Nora Ephron screenplay.

They found an un-covered open space about a half a football field from their assigned space. Mitchell was tempted to run a key along the length of the offending car. Resentment built big-time, but he was able to let it go by the end of his hot shower.

They met on the sofa for some downtime and a deep breath.

"I want this," Red said.

"So do I," Mitchell responded. "I'd like to ride up there tomorrow and shake the old man's hand on this, and tell him that we will buy the cabin."

"Do you realize that it was the words you wrote to him that has made our wish come true?"

He nodded his head in half-hearted agreement, "I suppose so."

"Let's leave first thing," Red said.

"Sounds great, Red."

ॐ

I-17 was under foot—again. Mitchell had long lost count of the number of times he had traveled the length of the highway from Phoenix to Cortez Junction, Oak Creek Canyon, or Flagstaff. It was Mitchell's highway. And now he drove north again, along with his wife, to put palm to palm on a deal for the old man to sell his cabin to them.

A local bank assisted in the transfer of funds from Red's trust to the old man's account, who said, as they departed; "it looks like you found what your were looking for." Mitchell nodded his head, remembering the old man saying those same words to him long ago.

The keys to the place would be left at a local title company office, where Red and Mitchell would sign ownership documents. The deal was done. They owned the A-frame cabin.

ॐ

The routine of moving, one that both knew very well, was underway. Transfers to the Olive Garden in Prescott were completed.

Red and Mitchell looked forward to observing the change of seasons through the windows of their new home, which allowed ample light from both the front, and rear, of the structure—its apex sitting high above the ground. The living quarters sat above the two car garage and basement that ran under the length of the main floor. The stairs from the basement rose as a divider between the spacious kitchen, in the rear of the main floor, and the living room at the front. The living room's windows rose thirty feet from the floor. The view out of the cabin was dramatic. Upstairs, above the kitchen, was a loft that held the master bedroom and bath. It utilized the same set of windows as the living room below, which was in full view of anyone standing on the edge of the loft above.

They spent the days ahead assembling their possessions in the cabin. There was much discussion between the two regarding the placement of the Bang & Olufson, a thing that still occupied an odd place in Mitchell's heart. Red would plant well-timed humor, the kind laced with a deeper truth, which asked the question "if it came down to just me or the stereo, which would you choose?" Mitchell would respond with a well placed moment of hesitation, which sent a sofa pillow toward Mitchell's head, as a playful response in retaliation.

The stereo found a permanent spot on the left wall of the living room, and as the couple sat together on their disheveled sofa, Mitchell let his neck and head crane backward. The summit of the ceiling appeared high above him. A thought occurred to him as to how he and Red would clean the corners of their tall ceiling; a very tall sliding ladder of some sort would have to be purchased. He remembered using such a ladder at de Benneville Pines.

"Red," Mitchell said softly, not wanting to startle his wife from her rest. "de Benneville Pines had a roof and window just like this. We should get one of the double-decker ladders, and the first time up, I would like to hang a prism! Wait till you see the rainbows it will toss about the room!"

Red was observing Mitchell's delight in finding again, some moment in his life that, through the designs of others, was lost. Red had seen Mitchell re-capture much of his life and Mitchell knew that it was through Red's love that his life, all of it, began to make sense. Mitchell spent some time in conversation with Red, as to why she did not possess a sense of loss over material possessions, or places where she once lived, but rather, the gathering of formidable notions that enabled her—notions that gave her emotional and spiritual strength. Red would always find her way back to her father, and who he was to her as a child.

℘℘

Mitchell went outside on the front porch, sat in an Adirondack chair the old man had left behind, picked up his journal, and penned the following thank you to his Red:

> *It is in the soft twilight of the morning winter sun, and in the awakening of our new home, through the routine of opening windows and doors to let the forest in, that I see who you really are to me, and to the world.*

> *I have already put on my walking shorts and shoes, and tested the climate outside. All of my hiking gear is ready to go, but first, and before I go, there is a cup of coffee, a prayer, and the daily funnies, with you.*

> *For that moment we put the day down, and in each other's hands we hold our morning prayer. You thank God for me, and my eyebrow rises and falls at the sincerity of your petition, and at my unworthiness of it. I too, thank God for all of your gifts. I see them day in and day out, and from any perspective, I see you in everything I do.*

> *As we end our morning prayer, and ready our bodies for the morning motion of exercise, I reach for the cup of coffee, and my eyes fall on the morning comics in the newspaper.*

> *And there in the lively squares, from even livelier minds, come all of the qualities I hold so dear in you: you are a Family Circus—Baby Blues—Blondie, kind of woman—wife—babe to me.*

> *And now, in time together as husband and wife, and in time eternal as everything else, I remain blown away by your soft, morning face, and your hard, midnight body.*

> *You have determined my happiness for me, my love, and I thank you for every minute of it.*

He stood up, after transcribing the words, and asked her to accompany him to an old oak tree at the northern edge of their property, where earlier in the week Mitchell had cut a mark of his love for her into the trunk. It said, "Mitchell and Red forever."

They walked to the oak, stood under its branches, and upon the falling leaves of another season of growth and change. Red stared at the words inscribed into the oak and smiled. She picked up a leaf and rubbed the colors of the season into the palm of her hand, recalling the falling leaves of Manasquan, New Jersey. A tear rolled off her face, and onto the leaf, as she remembered her youth, longing for one more Thanksgiving dinner around her father's table.

Mitchell took his thumb and wiped the trail of longing from her cheek, kissed her, and gave her his words of love and gratitude. They sat together under the oak. She read what Mitchell wrote to her and cried some more. Mitchell knew how much he was loved by this woman. She was from another time and place, and he believed she came to him to save him from himself.

Red inhaled deeply. She looked out across their property, glad they had found a place in the universe to call their own. Sitting between Mitchell's legs, feeling his arms around her soul, she was sitting on the spot where she wanted to stay for time eternal. She stated to Mitchell that she wanted to rest here, under the care of an oak, and his mark, if he were ever asked to bury her first. Mitchell returned the same request, finding now a root he could call his own.

৪০৬

Two years had passed under the spell of a life in the woods. Notions about earning a living outside of the restaurant industry became the topic of discussion on a daily basis, asking how they could become their own bosses. Red offered the idea of a graphic design and print business. Before long the walls of the basement garage began to fill with items from the print trade. They advertised in a local monthly publication, stated what their purpose was in the market place, and before they knew it, the business had taken on a life of its own. They left The Olive Garden.

Yet the better life was not necessarily measured by dollars. What the business did for both Mitchell and Red was give them time. They had gone from working more than full time each week to working a third of the hours required in the restaurant industry. Red found more time to sing. Mitchell found he was spending more time on the banks of the Hassayampa River, filling the pages of journals.

Much work had been done to the garage below the house, converting it into a year-round comfortable room, full of light and decked with the tools of the graphic design and print trade. The conversion work in the garage took Mitchell back into a corner of the room away from the garage doors. He was prepping the area for an application of insulation when something moved at the touch of his hand. With a flash light, he looked it into the gap between the floor joists, moving cobwebs and debris from around the object. Dust preceded the movement of the object from parallel to perpendicular in front of Mitchell's face, floating to the floor in a slow-motion cloud. Mitchell took a deep breath and blew directly at the cover of an old book.

It was leather-bound. Carved on the front was the design of an eagle in flight. Mitchell sat down on a chair, and removed the dirt and grime from both the front and back of the book.

"Red, check this out," Mitchell called to his wife upstairs.

She stuck her head over the guard railing and asked "What is it?"

"I am not sure," Mitchell said. "It's a book of some sort; I found it under the kitchen floor."

Red went downstairs and sat next to Mitchell.

"Look at this," he said. "It is full of writing, easily two hundred pages. And the cover has an eagle on it, like the knife."

"Do you think it belonged to the old man?" Red asked.

"I can't tell," Mitchell said. "There are a lot of quotation marks, as if this is the recording of a dialogue. I also can't tell whether the conversation is fictional or not. Here, listen to this if you have a minute."

Mitchell recited the initial text of the book to Red, who listened intently t   o the prose:

> *What rose and fell from the Sea*
> *Man's heart took on the rhythm of the wind*
> *blowing about him—the tides of the sea were*
> *remembered, and he saw how the rushing of*
> *time receded, leaving bare the rock and brine*
> *below. He looked down, feeling the breeze*
> *encircle his ankles, and noticed a peculiar*
> *sight—the ground under him was strewn with*
> *hundreds of multi-colored seashells, and at once*

*he beheld the desert before him as the ocean he
once knew—and loved.*

*He recalled his endless discussions
with God about effort that ran parallel to
currents of energy running through His
expanding universe. It was God's hands that
steadied him, as he willed effort toward his
"blessed horizon."*

*He remembered his anger toward God,
bitter about the loss of his wife, resenting what
could have been . . .*

Mitchell snapped the book shut—dust scattered. He felt the hair on his neck rise. Red stared at the floor below her.

"It sounds as if you could have written those words, Mitchell," Red said.

"It does," Mitchell said. "This is very strange."

Mitchell fell into a contemplative mood. Red had cookies in the oven, and left Mitchell to resume her baking. She too was contemplative, and was negotiating the curve of serendipity in her heart. *How odd,* she thought, as she turned cookie sheets around in the oven, *that such a book would be found in this house, and that it contains such language and meaning.*

Mitchell ran upstairs, grabbed a hot fresh peanut butter cookie, and told Red that he was taking a walk along the Hassayampa, to read more about the Sea Man.

Red gave Mitchell a hug, one laced with some concern over what Mitchell was about to read. Her faith that the book was meant to be found by Mitchell remained the focus of what was in her heart, and she let her husband go, off to the country roads that led to the many points that Mitchell called his own.

On the Hassayampa, Mitchell opened the book again:

*"What of it!" the Sea Man
exclaimed, looking at the Current of the
Expanding Universe.*

God answered "Seizing this moment
requires an effort more distinct than simply
looking at this Current. The idea of testing its
flow comes first, yet what is beyond the curiosity
you have?"

"How in the hell am I supposed to
know?" the Sea Man shot back sharply.
"Where am I to go? What am I to do?."

"Infinite numbers have gone before
you," God said in return. "You are not the
first, nor will you be the last. And your life,
although seemingly insignificant in your
perception of it, can profoundly change the
course of all who cross in the wake of the choice
you make right now.."

"I can't worry about everyone else
right now," the Sea Man said. "I am called to
reach for my blessed horizon. I don't see yet
how that will be accomplished without her."

"It is already begun," God said.
"You see the Current. Soon you shall hear,
smell, feel, and breathe it. Your life awaits
you."

Mitchell closed the book hard again—more dust spread out,
falling downstream with the river. As he watched the dust settle, he
noticed his toes dangling just above the current of the Hassayampa
River below him. Between his toes the water ran, and in it he saw the
very picture the old book was painting.

Mitchell looked up to the tops of the Ponderosa Pine. He
listened to the wind make its way from tree top to tree top. Mitchell
was learning of a certain grace found in his own ability to create his
life. Looking back over the recent seasons of change, both he and Red
saw many things. They had become self-employed and were thriving.
The elements of the forest, simple and pure, became a part of who
they were. The love they shared was akin to the roots of a wide oak—
Red, the earth found surrounding its roots—giving Mitchell a place to

call his own. He could feel the love in his heart burrow deeply into the soil that was Red's heart.

Mitchell returned his study of the water below his feet. Work for the day was done. He was content to be living his life this way.

Chapter Sixty

I *feel good about my life,* Mitchell thought, one morning, as he walked along the banks of the Hassayampa. Things were in place. Order and routine, like bookends on the day, were the things Mitchell wished for in his life. Yet on this morning, as Mitchell walked a length of the river, a longing within took hold in his heart.

The old book referred to a 'blessed horizon,' and how it could only be reached by continued effort. Effort to what end? He thought, as he watched his shoes pass over the stones and grass beneath him. He pondered the growing sensation in him that perhaps life is never fully lived, even as the last breath is taken.

The air was particularly refreshing on this morning—filled with the fragrance of rebirth. As Mitchell walked the banks of the Hassayampa, toward Wolf Creek, he felt a yearning grow in him for something he could aspire to. His routine had served him well, yet there seemed something more, than just the peace of watching time stand still in each waking moment. The word 'adventure,' made him take a deeper breath.

Mitchell thought of his life as a boy on the Hassayampa, of how he lived out the minutes of a boy's life, leaving each day exhausted, but filled with what he now understood to be grace.

His walking along the river continued, and he thought of how he missed the starting gun as a career man. Haunting lyrics from the Pink Floyd song, *Time,* passed through his minds eye. There was regret there. He remembered his wish to be a forest ranger, and how quickly he abandoned that goal for the sake of another.

This regret did not last however—the choice to move to San Diego brought him the beach, and eventually de Benneville Pines, which furthered him into his life among the trees and blue sky. He thought of the ocean and its surf—a sound that could be heard in the tops of trees—and how he would not have known these things if he had pursued a traditional career.

He would have never met Red, or known himself as he does. He did have a career as a forest ranger of sorts—his daily navigation of river banks kept water and rock at his feet.

The momentary regret was not the overwhelming feeling of futility. It was nothing like those moments when, coming off of cocaine and alcohol, he believed he would have been better off dead. No, it was not like that. It was like the wonder of remembering a fork in the road—of what might have been. It was a shallow feeling, lacking any tangible bite, just the question, and the mystery, of the many roads a life can take.

The adventure in question then, was not the missed career. Perhaps it was his continued efforts to beat the odds of his DNA tree, where heart disease, alcoholism, and madness ended the lives of his forbearers. He worked at being fit and eating right, on a daily basis, and saw his life under a much different light than that of his father and mother. Not repeating the bad habits he was raised with was certainly an admirable thing to have accomplished, and if that was his adventure, his blessed horizon, then he could sit with that.

Yet being fit and eating right took up only a small part of the day. *Again, the search for adventure,* he thought. *It seems to be the key to successful living.* The Dave Mason song, "Can't Stop Worrying, Can't Stop Loving," said it all. The song was playing in Mitchell's head—it was a creation, by the hands of a life that knew its intention. *Fulfilling intention—is that what adventure is?*

Mitchell sat at the confluence of Wolf Creek into the Hassayampa. He reviewed the day's meditation, and his walk to the current spot under the forested sun. He went back to the thoughts of himself as a boy, in the very woods before him. He went to thoughts of his father, sitting alone, illuminated by a street lamp, and smoking.

Between these thoughts Mitchell found himself. The grace of a boy was in one hand, and the emptiness of his father's life, was in the other.

Under the perfect sunlight, Mitchell opened up the old book, and read the following entry:

> *On the edge of the Current sat an*
> *object colorless and shapeless. In the effort of*
> *comprehending it, the Sea Man was taken*
> *back to a memory of his father—a difficult*
> *one. The bitterness toward his father, as a*
> *youth, was remembered, yet his compassion for*
> *his father had grown with the passing of time.*

The Sea Man saw life unfold in bitter ways for many people and saw now, that given what his father had to work with, that he had done well with his life, when the final tally had been taken.

All these things he knew as he stared at the shapeless object on the shore of God's current. At last, the Sea Man asked God what he saw there.

God said: "It is a soul."

"But why do I see it, and why does it enchant me so?" the Sea Man asked.

"The soul belongs to your father," God said.

As the Sea Man beheld his father, he tried to make sense of his emotions—for what appeared to be a lost soul, trapped on the edge of its potential.

The Sea Man asked God: "Does the search for our Blessed Horizon cease after death?"

"Your movement through my universe will never stop, and after this life, your free will shall hold sway in the next. Heaven, hell, and all points in between, are but a creation of your free will, and the choices you make."

"What then God, has my father chosen by sitting on the edge of his potential, in this new life of his?" the Sea Man asked.

"He is not sitting on the edge of his potential, but waits for you, on the edge of yours," God replied.

"Why does he wait for me?" the Sea Man asked. He saw God make a gesture toward the edge of the Current, inviting the Sea Man to ask the soul himself.

As the Sea Man made his way over to the edge of his potential, his heart turned ominous. "Why do I fear this place?"

"Because I am still a part of you." The voice was that of his father. "All of the things you left behind, when you began your life as a man, are still a part of who you are, including me."

God said: "Let the past serve you today. You are, through free will, capable of re-arranging and re-aligning your past, to suit the paradigms used in living in the Current. Once the shift has been made, a shift from the past controlling you, to you controlling the past, your life becomes your own."

There is value in seeing yourself when you sat on the edge. It gives your soul the opportunity to contrast your living today, with your living in the past.

Take it as a template for yourself, and others who cross in your wake, to behold what the Current has already had to bear. Learn from it."

The Sea Man did so. He took his father's memory with him, and waved goodbye, as his momentum carried him away again—his life unfolding in the Current of the Expanding Universe.

Mitchell thought the story in the old book odd. Something about it did not sit right, but what that was, he could not name. He listened to the waters fall forward, in their movements to whatever end was naturally theirs to embrace. He looked downstream, and saw an image of his father motionless above the water's current. He looked upstream to see an image of himself as a boy, kicking the water in a playful fashion, and sitting in the middle of both, he understood that he was part of a story that was not yet finished.

Mitchell stood up with the old book in his hands, and began a somewhat solemn walk back to his home. His was ill at ease. His walk along the river lifted his spirits however; the familiarity of his surroundings put his heart to rest.

As he walked, he remembered thoughts from earlier in the day, one being the importance of showing his wife he loved her. It was not enough to rest on the efforts of days gone by. Each day was a renewed call to be romantic, and appreciative of whom Red was. Cards, flowers, surprises, and his words on fine paper, needed to happen often. Red's devotion was apparent everyday, in her efforts to make love and cook for him. He wanted to reciprocate. Marriage did not mean the end of romance. A lack of effort did. He walked over to the edge of their property, and picked wildflowers. He put them together in a bunch, and presented the simple gesture of his love for her. It made her smile. It gave her a sense of security. It was effortless, yet meant so much. He would remember always what romance, on a minute by minute basis, would mean to Red.

Chapter Sixty One

AT once, a shining light—a glow emanating from a place beyond Mitchell's grasp—a back light falling from the ceiling of Laurie's Victorian sitting room—filled the radiant image of the mother–daughter he knew as both Red and Sian.

She reached down and pulled Mitchell's face into her enlightened hands and held him dearly. She moved forward, toward Mitchell, kissing him, giving to Mitchell a steady force for which to lean against, while realizations from the past came forward to haunt him.

He looked at his beloved Red. Tears spilled out. "Why you Red, why you, with all of the wickedness there is in the world, why take you? I don't understand a God who takes the goodness in the world, and turns it into a horror. Why you?"

Red smiled at him, her countenance telling him that she knew of no horror, and of no wickedness. Her message continued on, as it always had, that living is a goodness that cannot be compared to the evil that will always reign over the heart of man. She knew no pain, only her love of him.

Gently, she released his face, gesturing for him to still his mind, and take from her the white light—the white love—surrounding her being.

Mitchell closed his eyes, resuming his slumber, forgetting, for the moment, his nightmare about the mugger.

Mitchell awoke before Laurie. He walked over to her collection of music, lined up alphabetically on shelves, and was drawn to the cover of a CD that was partially pulled out from the rest. "The Best of Glenn Miller," was printed on the spine. Gently, he glided the CD into the player. Lowering the volume to just a whisper, he scrolled down to the seventh track, and let the melody take him back in time, to his father's youth. "Moonlight Serenade," filled Mitchell with wonder about his father. The music stirred Laurie from her slumber. She sat up and smiled at Mitchell, cocking her head sideways, questioning his choice of songs.

"It makes me think of my dad," Mitchell said. "The song takes me into his youthful heart, and I believe that when he heard it, he knew who he was. Life took that knowledge away from him, but I do remember seeing him, cigarette in one hand and a beer in the other, confident in whom he was when he listened to this song. You know Laurie, after we had fallen asleep, Red visited me. I just wanted to let you know that."

"What happened?"

Mitchell looked at Laurie, at her eyes, and held some admiration for her willingness to believe that he actually did have a conversation with a spirit. "I had a nightmare, about the mugger, who killed Red," he said. "I dreamt that he, on that night walking back from Murphy's, on our honeymoon, was not wearing shoes. It startled me. She steadied me, and kissed me, telling me, as she always has, that there is no wickedness in her world. I accept that she is spirit, and not flesh and blood. I told her how I remained amazed by her healing touch and wise counsel. She smiled at me, Laurie, and as I looked at her, right here, her face and hair became a part of this room. She is still the air that I breathe."

Laurie put her hand on Mitchell's shoulder, and said: "this is a natural part of letting go Mitchell. It comes and goes with time. What I am amazed at this morning, is the revelation of bloody sock prints in previous coroner's reports that we talked about last night. It chills me to the bone. I'm headed over to the museum this morning to substantiate for myself these observations . . . from Sian . . . or Red."

Mitchell proceeded to tell Laure precisely where to look in the microfilm files at the Sharlot Hall Museum. Laurie cocked an eyebrow at his confidence in her finding the same evidence as he.

"It's there," he said, as an afterthought. He was concerned about how the evil sock print may yet play a further role in his life.

Mitchell's brow furrowed. "What's wrong Mitchell?"

"I feel in my gut . . . the sock print will continue its presence in my life. It's an ominous sense of dread in me, similar to what I felt walking home from the Hassayampa that night."

Laurie imagined being there with Mitchell when the madness consumed him. She was worried for him, yet he seemed to be moving through the revelations, and emotional–spiritual events in his life with some level of common-sense and maturity attached to them. "What about this sense of dread?" Laurie asked. "Is there anything specific that you can name?"

Mitchell thought for a moment. There were specific thoughts attached to the sense of dread. "It's Zac at the courthouse," Mitchell said. "He is evil. I can feel it when I see him, and he has noticed me. He's the same kid that was torturing an old lady at the courthouse a few months back. He knows who I am."

"Everyone knows you," Laurie said, interrupting Mitchell's chain of thought.

"Nevertheless," Mitchell said, accepting the assessment as inconsequential. "As I speak of this, I am convinced that my battle with this evil is not done. I must be diligent in observation and in the use of intuition. My gut tells me this Zac has the same evil in him, and I've got to anticipate his moves."

"I'm not sure which boy you are talking about, but I can find out who he is, and if there are any records on him." Laurie said.

The sun shown through Laurie's Victorian home—light that was filtered by leaded, stained glass windows. Laurie observed Mitchell's mind travel away from her, out the front door to his private life and thoughts. Almost absentmindedly he turned to her to say goodbye, and was called back to the present by Laurie's proximity to him. She wanted to hug him. She put her fingers to his face, moved the grayish blonde morning hair off his brow, and kissed him there. He looked at her as she did so, astonished by her presence in his life, on a morning filled with concern for their safety. He was thankful for her kiss—that she would care for him. They pulled away from one another. He smiled gingerly at her. He took her hand in his, and squeezed it gently, then placed it on her heart. At the door he looked back and said, "thank you." She smiled, and then watched him move out into the morning sun.

All this in a moment shared with the winter sun, a symbol of the love God gave to the souls of His Expanding Universe; the birth of love billions of years ago.

Chapter Sixty Two

MITCHELL built a fire in the fireplace; a simple iron casting set into the wall with a large, knotted cut of Ponderosa pine secured over it as a mantel. The sofa sat facing the corner of the living room toward the fireplace—the tall windows allowing the cycles of peace to enter at will.

He and Red sat quietly. Music played softly. The flames in the fire place had transcended all activity in the couple's collective heart. They were present in their evening together. A great blue arc of dusk hung as backdrop to the view of the forest beyond the windows. Their bodies were at rest; their hands idle upon one another.

"On my walk today, I had some peculiar thoughts about my youth and my father, brought on by something I read in the old book," Mitchell said.

"Tell me about them," Red said, happy to listen.

"Well, in the old book, the Sea Man saw the soul of his father, sitting on the edge of a Current," Mitchell said, explaining the unusual words and phrases that seemed to be the basis of the story. He had decided that the word 'Current' was the Sea Man's reference for life, and the 'Expanding Universe' was life's potential.

"Upstream from where I was sitting, as I watched the water flow toward me, I saw some memories of myself as a boy, playing with Dalton and Presley. It was nice remembering who I was. When I looked downstream, toward the afternoon sun, I started to think about my father. My memories of him are scattered. I remember the fights he would lose to my mom; her anger was much greater than his will to fight back, especially after a day of drinking beer. I remember him at night—and I know I'm repeating myself with these thoughts, but I feel like describing the scene again." Red just smiled, and encouraged him to continue. "He sat in the dark of his room, the street lamp silhouetting his presence. I saw the orange glow of a cigarette ember arcing toward his lip from the ash tray, flashing bright for a half second, and then make a return trip back to the ash tray. He looked at me, and said nothing, not even a 'goodnight.' This memory, more than any other, haunts me Red. Why was his life reduced to this? What happened to his will to live?"

"Even for the ten short years that I knew my father, he had made such an impact on me," Red said. "It was the way he treated my mother that I remember so well. He showed his love, never raising his voice to her, honoring her, as the mother of his children, and as his wife and homemaker. He showed me how to love."

"Your father was the leader in your life," Mitchell said. "My father was unable to lead. Today on the river, now that I am thinking about it, the thoughts I have had about this subject remain true. My friends raised me, the Hassayampa, and the challenges and comfort it gave, raised me. These woods were, for a short period of my life, my father."

Red looked at her husband. His unremitting effort to reconcile his leaderless life continued.

"The other thing that is upsetting to me, as I read the old book, was that the Sea Man stopped in the current, and talked to the soul of his father, and was told by God and his father that whether he liked the idea or not, his father was a part of who he was. I know I don't like the idea of my father, who gave up, who may have been murdered by my mother, being a part of who I am."

"Your father's addictions became yours," Red said softly. "Your mother's infidelity became yours too. As our parent's children, we have no choice but to live with their actions. They shaped us."

Mitchell stared at the fire. His eyes wandered to the end table next to the sofa. On it was a drawing, made by Red. It was a picture of forgiveness in the parable of the prodigal son.

"Do you think that there could also be a prodigal father?" Mitchell asked. "Do you think that the teachings of life could ask a son to embrace a father, who was once dead, but has come back to life somehow, to ask his son for forgiveness, to be a leader, as a father should be for a son?"

"A Prodigal Father," Red stated. "Like a man returning to his life, to amend what could be amended, but done so only by the grace and love of his son. It is a beautiful thought."

"I remember one very crucial moment in my life," Mitchell said. "It was on a cold and windy fall afternoon in Reno, when my family moved there, chasing some kind of financial stability. I loved playing football, as I've told you, probably too often. I played on a great team, playing varsity ball as a sophomore. Well, in Reno, in the preseason practice drills, as a junior, I was sent down to junior varsity. I took it wrong, and quit playing the game I loved to play. My father did not make me get back out on to the field, and tough it out. I knew that I would eventually, after a couple of weeks, have made my way back to varsity, but I quit instead. I needed a leader in my life, at that moment, to blaze a trail of discipline and effort; someone to make me face my pain and fears, and work through it. Instead, my dad, through his alcoholic heart, let me quit, as did my mother, who had tried to commit suicide the same week. I needed my dad to lead me through it, to kick my ass, to grab me by the collar, and wing me back into the game. I became a different boy that day. I became self-absorbed and distant from my family, and was then just months away from leaving them for good. It was the moment when I assimilated my parent's lives, rather than rising above them. This is hard to remember Red. It is hard because so many bad things came with me the day I quit football. I lost my identity, my escape, and my camaraderie with a team. I needed my dad, through the living of his own life, to show me how to work through humiliation and frustration, and to not give up. He was not the man to show me that. Perhaps he had been at one time, but Ada put an end to him. He had quit his own life. And now this thought of a prodigal father, returning to his son, as once dead but now living again, is a bit hard to swallow."

Red wiped a tear from Mitchell's eye. "Do you think it is about forgiveness?" Red asked.

"No, I don't. Today on the Hassayampa, as I sat in the middle of memories of myself as a boy upstream, and memories of my father downstream, it felt more like a reckoning—a balancing—like I was the scale of justice for my life. Forgiveness feels like the easy way out, yet that is exactly what the prodigal son parable is about."

Quiet returned. Life was rich in their hearts—full of paradox and symbolism—full of love for who they had become. Their hands slipped into one another—their hearts followed the lacing of their fingers. The firelight brought the bridge of Red's nose into view, as Mitchell brought his wife closer to him.

"Maybe there is a way for the son to bring the father home?" Red said.

"But it should not be that way," Mitchell said. "A son is not supposed to be a leader in his father's life. Too many things get twisted. How is a son supposed to give his father riches? How does a son reconcile his father's mislead life?"

"I'm not sure . . . ," Red said.

Mitchell nodded, but it would not rest easily. It felt like water flowing upstream—a reversal in the natural order of things.

The fire was dying. Flames had turned to glowing embers, urging the couple to bed. They stirred. Almost blindly through the dark, they climbed upstairs to the bedroom. Red ran a hot bath while Mitchell climbed into their tall bed, stretching his legs this way and that, as the cool, soft, flannel sheets swaddled his body. The sound of water splashing down around Red's legs lulled Mitchell into a half sleep. He unconsciously found the texture of their bedroom walls and rafters resonating in a song that had channeled its way from around Red, as her tub filled. "Cortez The Killer," with its lingering electric guitar, sighed in his tired breath.

Moments later Mitchell felt his wife's skin emanated the water's warmth. She found her spot next to him, offering her body for his pleasure. He placed his nose between her breasts, and inhaled deeply, again and again, feeling the home she had made for him. He slowly wrapped his arms around her, holding each part of her body in his heart. She moved her long red hair away from her face, cupped her hands around his, and kissed him on his mouth.

Mitchell opened his eyes to see Red's skin close enough to loose focus. He saw their shadows together behind her, on their bedroom wall and ceiling, as they slanted toward the apex of the A-frame. He noted through the filter of her earthly hair, and her peach-scented breath that their shadows were as extensions of a spirit world—as outlines of gods—as players of poems and prayers. Through heated exchange their shadows followed the vastness of a swirling universe ever-increasing. Mitchell saw all of these things cast upon the wall of their bedroom loft. Their shadows could be seen through the trees of the forest, in the eyes of the wild, from the orbiting planets and stars, through the crash and calamity of the past, through the outward and hopeful reach of their own future. He saw their shadows move into one another, two hearts making music not heard before, making time bend to the love between; finding in the smooth sketch of motion all that love could muster—a cosmic hope burning at the tips of outstretched fingers, as the flush and feather of colors blending, binding, into one expectant aspiration. At that moment Mitchell told Red that he and his shadow were blessed. That upon the bedroom walls and ceiling laid bare all that he knew as a soul with a body, walking upon the blue earth. He told her through his responsive caress—through his eagerness. She heard him through her trusting empathy—through the heartbreak of her life—through her mending of their souls—through her eternally youthful eyes and crowning crimson brows—through her grasping at the night ahead.

The heat of their ecstasy warmed the rafters. Through all that passionate hearts desire, through the falling beads of sweat, through the chill of after-breath, through all of what Red and Mitchell found, their shadows now knew, too.

Day after day, as year followed year, Mitchell knew his wife this way. Red was eternal in her honor of him; just a man, just simple instinct; an ancient gravitational yearning he floated upon, yet a pull she fully and completely comprehended and orchestrated through him.

Day after day, year followed by year, her disciplined love found him, its way shadowed upon wall, its light radiated upon ceiling, silhouettes seen by the entirety of a wild forested world, by all of a spirited world, by all of a good world. Their bodies' senses mixing in, as if clouds on a breezy day.

Their shadows, from the ceiling above them, sang to their loving union:

> *Pleasure, purpose—hearts vibrating.*
>
> *Ear, scent—clothes unwrapping.*
>
> *Light, sweat—pores reflecting.*
>
> *Understanding, possession—joy consuming.*
>
> *Breath, peach—union blooming.*
>
> *Wild, raw—time a blessing.*
>
> *Providence, rapture—sleep uniting.*

Through touch, sight, sound, taste, smell, experience, and dream, the couple was perfect in their physical union. Their marriage transcended, orbiting around the spiritual, to the physical, to the spiritual, and back again. Theirs was a journey—theirs a vow—beyond their true understanding but not beyond their perfect sense of one another.

The shadows sang again:

> *Theirs a dance, in the falling of water.*
>
> *Theirs a dance, in the burning by fire.*
>
> *Theirs a dance, in the tilling of earth.*
>
> *Theirs a dance, among the trees as wind.*

Their dance, as simple, yet as true as each part of nature; a dance ending each day as it began—connected through the natural senses of an inspired and spiritual universe, where joy and benevolence sparked as significant among the elements of nature.

Cathedrals could not contain their gratitude.

⁊⊙⳾

Work was done early. By late morning, Mitchell was already sitting out on the front patio, resting. He was looking at their business ad in a local trade publication, and thought it better to delete their address. *A phone number is all that is needed initially.* He looked at their picture, finding himself quite the mug next to his wife.

He walked in and put the magazine on the end table, and went downstairs to perform monthly maintenance operations on machines that made up the contents of a graphic design and printing studio.

Next he walked the property line. He took visual notes of the different prints left in the ground, looking specifically for bear tracks, as the local game and fish office issued a statement that noted a rise in the Black Bear population.

Then something odd caught his attention; it was an imprint of a soft soled shoe of some sort that was not there the week before. It moved off into the direction of their cabin. Mitchell casually thought of the various reasons why such a print would be there, but let it go as a vanishing afterthought.

⳾⊙⳽

Preparation for his daily hike was underway. In his back pack went his journal, the old book, a snack or two, and the knife. Water was never packed. The river was his way of answering thirst, submersing his head and gulping the ice cold mountain water. He kissed his wife, as if he was headed off to work, but play awaited the man child, out among the sapphire sky and timeless light and shadow of sun between the pines.

He walked across FR 63 and down the bank to the edge of the river. There was nothing to be looked for while he stood there. There was no need to reach beyond the moment. The woods offered Mitchell its grace presently. Breathing it in, tilting his head back, he put his face to the sun, hearing the simple sound of time passing, mixed with terse notes of survival, emanating from every point around him. It was his sense of smell however, that took him deep into the fearless places he had stepped as a boy. The ascending canopies of the forest each contributed to the moment's unique smell, from the forest floor, to what rotated over the cold sides of every mountain around him. It was the scent of his rolling, romping, valiant time in these woods as a lad that melted his heart on this day. Between the sun and himself, Mitchell let a tear roll out upon his face.

Joy for those two simple years became the template for what was right to feel as a man. He was now, in every sense of the word, a passionate man—a joyous boy within. He loved loving his wife. He loved loving the woods and his home. To know this was a deep rewarding breath all its own.

He set the back pack beside his feet, and pulled out the old book, focused his vision upon the pages, and read:

> *Nagging thoughts often surfaced in the Sea Man that drained his movements in the Current. Such thoughts played over and over again, rolling with him through his day. Inequity was the theme, and they pulled him hard, disrupting his daily efforts to move toward his blessed horizon.*
>
> *Time helped, and the petty memories diminished. Prayer helped too, and he would find the motion of his hands and feet again in the deepest parts of God's Current, where grace prevailed.*
>
> *Such grace showed the Sea Man that memories could be redefined—that life was a subjective experience.*

*Presently, before the Sea Man, moved
the Hand of Time. The hand held a letter from
his father. With a postmark on the envelope
from a half century earlier, he took the letter
and opened it. A simple note, in his father's
hand, appeared. Half of the note had faded. A
closer look revealed that the original intent of
the note was altered. It stated simply: "God
helps those . . ." Time had erased the note's
intention. Grace had brought another
interpretation.*

*With a prayer answered, the Sea
Man moved back into the Current, his mind
awash in the grace of God's love, and found
himself repeating over and over again the phrase
"God helps those . . . God helps those . . ."*

*He stated to no one in particular that
"there is a right, belonging to every soul, to see
its life on a higher path—a good path—one
that pushes the Current forward."*

*The day's efforts were at an end. The
Sea Man found shelter, pondered the day's
lesson, and saw in his heart the beauty of choice;
where a heart could say to itself or the world,
that at sunset, a dawning of the abundance of
life had risen, and that in this colorful,
spirituous world, the beginning, middle, and end
to a life, and the interpretations that are
attached to it, are what he decides them to be.*

Are what he decides them to be, Mitchell repeated to himself. As
the day moved on, Mitchell decided that everything around him was as
it should be.

What of the past? Mitchell wrote in his journal. *Can it really be
whatever I decide it to be?*

He looked down at the water at his feet. He thought of the
phrase, "water under the bridge," and regret for the past, as the drain
of hope for the future. He looked upstream, then down, then wrote:
What represented the future or the past on the river?

Mitchell looked at the word 'Current,' and how often it was repeated in the old man's story. Again he found the view of water beneath him. From its start in a spring near Mount Davis to some point downstream when it re-entered the ground, the river's flow of water was simply there.

What of living? Mitchell asked the flow at his feet, not expecting an answer. *There is a spring called birth, and a point when the ash of a life returns to the ground,* Mitchell continued in his thoughts on paper, *and what lies between is this body of water's line of life. The time that arcs over its movement on the ground is but a witness to the course of energy that rises at one point, and falls at another.*

This kind of living, the kind of living that the water exhibits in its reach for the inevitable, is full of acceptance of whatever the day brings. It is void of material things, void of animosity, and greed. There is a complete lack of fear and doubt. This water, the Hassayampa, knows what it is to the world, and will keep its knowledge of itself regardless of what rearranging its living brings. That's the secret. That's what leadership in a young life brings. An awareness that does not change, as the course of living changes.

Water is water, regardless of rock, stick, or bend, in its flowing from origin to end. That's what a father brings to a son . . .

Mitchell disengaged from the meditative thoughts, and put down his journal. He thought of his age. He remembered stating to Red recently that it was not his parents who raised him but his friends. It was not his own father who led him into manhood, but Red, who had finally showed Mitchell what it was to be a man. Mitchell was sad. He was sad for his father's misspent life. He wished that he would have seen his father in the stands at his football games, or beside him in those key moments that eventually shaped him. He wished his father would have raised his family with the firm but fair hand of discipline. He missed him, looking for some great sign, similar to what the Sea Man received from his father.

There were none.

Mitchell sighed. He wrote, *why do I keep looking for my father?*

Frustrated, he turned back toward his home, wanting to put an end to his need to reconcile his father's life, within his own. There seemed to be no way to make such a thing happen, and his efforts to do so diminished his own time as a man and husband.

He shuffled his feet. He thought of the pioneers on the river who staked their lives on the discovery of gold and silver, and what kind of fathers would compel their sons to live in such a fashion. He thought of the Yavapai Indians, and what kind of men and fathers they were as worshipers of the sun.

Suddenly, Mitchell turned back toward the river. He had walked away too soon from his afternoon hike, almost as if he had given up, or quit, and such a thought was unbearable.

He returned to the river's edge, opened his journal, and with pen in hand, he grappled with a mystery. He wrote:

I look upstream and remember myself, and my friends, at play in the water of the Hassayampa, fatherless as we did so.

I look downstream to see an image of my father floating on the bank. I behold him. He appears to be unaware of his surroundings. He does not see me.

Without warning, appearing at my side is the spirit of my youth. We behold our father. My boyhood spirit says:

"You are not going to call his name are you?"

"So you see him as well," I reply.

"Yes, I see him now. I didn't see him when I played with my friends on this river long ago."

"Are you upset?"

"I don't understand why he was not at my football games, or why he did not protect me from Brent," young Mitchell said. "Why did we have to live that way?"

"I don't have an answer for you," I say, looking down at him with tenderness. "I am still at a loss. There are many clichés that write-off tragedy, without much regard for the reasons why. It is as if life wants us to make whatever burden is present, our own, and that the universe expects it; as if the soul of the life should and will have it."

Young Mitchell looked on with me at the spirit of our father, himself too youthful, too innocent to follow my words regarding hardship and inequity.

The Prodigal Father. There seems to be more of those in the world than there are prodigal sons. I remember the drawing on the end table. I see the river continue its flow. On the bank I see my father's soul resting there.

The backlit Hassayampa courses through the Bradshaws.

I wish to bring him home. I wish to make my father, once dead, present again in my memory, and in my day-to-day. I call to him. He turns slowly in the direction of where I stand, smiles, and begins to move toward me over the Hassayampa. His blonde hair and ageless skin return, reflecting my own youthful photos. Soon I stand between both; my father and myself as a boy, and we became as one; a father, a son, and a spirit.

Mitchell put his hand behind his head and rubbed his neck and shoulders. The thought of acceptance and forgiveness, the intimate exchange that is seen in the painting of the prodigal son, was the very key of release that Mitchell needed to paradoxically separate, then spiritually bind, his blood to his father.

He opened up the old book again, reading the last paragraph of the story he had read earlier in the day. . . .

. . . are what he decides them to be . . .

. . . was read again. He had found a comfortable spot among the granite and pine needles to comprehend his own words. He was overwhelmed by his father and the life he led. Addictions, and need for approval, were long generational battles, fought and lost repeatedly. Could Mitchell change this?

We were chips off the same block, my father and I, Mitchell wrote. *Who am I to deny him love for being the same kind of man I had become? Who am I to withhold my blessing for a man who had not the good fortune to find the kind of love that saves, that believes, that grows, that rocks a disbelieving soul?*

A sudden, strange anxiety moved Mitchell to think of Red. Through the peripheral blending of light and shadow, Mitchell saw the shape of a stick man come and go. He hoped Red was okay, having been gone quite a long time on today's hike.

Mitchell looked downstream. *The Prodigal Father.* He stood up, taking with him, into the light of a late afternoon sun, the memory of his youth. There, together with who he once was, Mitchell looked into the eyes of his father, and walked to him.

Mitchell looked at him for some time. A great rush of emotion rose up from Mitchell's gut, and from this deep trembling came words that Mitchell did not know were his to say:

"I thank you, Father, for this river and for these memories," he said, alluding to himself as a young boy. "This river, where it comes from, and where it goes from here, up from a spring and through waterholes and slot canyons that filled my young life, and that remain such a deep part of the romance I feel, are mine because your journey brought me here as a young boy. I have life long friends, who remain a part of my life, and had become so, because you were living yours. I have known other places, like Lake Tahoe, and the rock I sat upon as a teenaged boy, learning to cope with the mistakes and eventual lessons that your examples brought me. In ways, I am the answer to many questions you asked in your days, as a man on this blue Earth. Your folly became my hope, as I fought and clawed my way out of our lot in life. I know you Father, because I have lived your life. I traveled to that point in every boy's life, where the mistakes and missteps of his father are seen, where each has a moment to choose what will become of their own. While I looked over the edge, into the darkness of your life, light was the design that looked back at me. I see now that it is not my lot to accept and forgive you, but your lot to accept and absolve your own life. My love for you could help you, if you let it. My embrace, as I wrap my arms around your shoulders, is a sign that you are real to me again. My tears, as I feel the frailty of your life in my arms, are your reminder of how much one life can affect another. My joy, that you have found your way home to my heart, will remain with me now, as I offer the memory of you, to what peace can be found by doing so. Dad, I have missed you so. I am a man now. When you died I was not yet twenty. I am no longer bedeviled by the mystery of our dark legacy of addiction. I have found, by some great luck, true love. I am living the kind of life that starts in my heart each day, and ends by a fire and a love beyond measure. I am practicing a great faith in what my life can mean, beyond what little expectation was placed upon it. I accept that you could not lead me into this life, as you had already lost your own way. I feel that forgiveness is yours; you have already paid dearly for the mistakes you made as my father."

Mitchell stopped talking. He had nothing more to say. He saw himself hugging his father, bringing him home, back into his life and into his heart. He saw the weight of those years, being lifted from the cosmos.

The Prodigal Father. The three words hung in the air. A tear appeared as Mitchell saw his father playing next to the river with his son, a boy starving for leadership in his young life. *As it should be,* Mitchell thought, taking in the vision of what could have been, unfolding before him.

The sun was hanging very low above the hills to the west. Mitchell wanted to head home, and share with Red how a broken relationship, between a father and son, could mend, in a decision to make his father's life, what he wanted it to be.

Chapter Sixty Three

MITCHELL shuffled his feet under the park bench, one that faced the courthouse on the southeast corner lawn. He waited to see Laurie make her way down the long granite stairway, and move briskly toward him, still finding it odd that she would take an interest in him—the town nut.

"Hello," she said with reserve.

"Hi, are you all right?"

"Yes . . . I'm having lunch with you," was Laurie's automatic reply. "That makes me happy."

"Soggy peanut butter and jelly sandwiches, and a thermos of coffee, have sparked your joy today," Mitchell stated.

"You Mitchell, you've sparked me. Thanks for meeting out here. I really needed to get out of that office—the drama with my staff sometimes—it's enough to, well, I know you are not interested in that."

Mitchell nodded in agreement. He said nothing in return, making Laurie a tad self-conscience, as she stood in front him.

"I've got some more difficult news." Laurie sat down on the bench, next to Mitchell, and opened a file containing information about Zac, and copies of the coroner's reports Mitchell had mentioned.

"This is something strange here," Laurie said, handing to Mitchell documents copied from the Sharlot Hall Museum. "Bloody sock prints appear every ten years or so throughout the twentieth century, like you said, ending with your trial Mitchell. How you knew this is still odd to me, but there is one other thing," Laurie said, almost unable to let the words come out of her mouth. "Sian and Zac . . . were . . . are . . . were related—they're first cousins."

At once Laurie could see Mitchell's defense mechanism kick in. He appeared to be aloof, pretending not to hear her. It was the same face he exhibited in his trial, and in the truck, as they charged up Bumble Bee Hill.

Mitchell casually looked over the documents. He looked above the file, and let his eyes travel toward the changing leaves filtering the sky above them. Fall was blooming around the courthouse—it was stunning to behold. He looked at the leaves that had already fallen to the ground, and took a deep breath. His mind began to reel, as he calculated the odds of Sian sharing Zac's blood.

✦❧

Mitchell's body had stiffened.

He saw unformed, powder-colored shapes—spirits—rushing around and around, high above an alter, rising up, further and further, into an ancient cathedral, its tall walls lined with conquistadors, swords, cobwebs, and the pocked faces of the spiritually dead. Moving quicker, the spirits took on the shapes of sticks, and branches, and the stems of fallen leaves. They formed an upside down funnel, whipping about in increasing velocity, colliding with the cathedral's stained glass ceiling. The sound was deafening, and as Laurie looked on, Mitchell silently moved his hands over his ears.

The spinning sticks had turned to ash, which floated down upon the alter, like snow alighting on a virgin forest. From that snow, the shimmering, angelic presence of Red came forward, and said, very softly—very quietly; *the boy—you've come here for the boy.*

❧✦

Slowly Mitchell's focus returned to the file in his hands, and to Laurie, sitting next to him.

"Ash to ash," Mitchell said quietly toward Laurie. She nervously pulled out the sandwiches, and set them on paper towels.

"They get one season Laurie. Three months to get what they can out of the sun, wind, and rain," he said, handing her a leaf that had fallen near him. "I think it's too easy to take time for granted. I want to count my blessings again, and find peace in my day. I want to lessen the burdens of the past. I still live with visions I've had since childhood. I see a stick man. I find it when I'm alone at night, or when danger is present, as if it was a messenger of foreboding."

Laurie looked at Mitchell with kindness, as he continued. "I've seen it around me all my life. It would stare at me with cross eyes, when my older brother was about to go on an abusive binge."

"What do you mean by 'stick man'?" Laurie asked.

"Like the shapes we draw on paper, with thin arms and legs, and a face made out of straw, and it haunts me, yet 'haunting' is not the word I'm looking for, because it has come to me when I was not in danger as well. I remember one night it appeared at the waterhole, on a moonless night, with the Milky Way so bright it cast a shadow of me on the ground."

"Why have you not mentioned this before?"

"I'm already crazy enough as it is," he stated. "I've not seen it in sometime, not since that night. But right now, it's staring at me from that direction." Mitchell pointed to the courthouse steps, where Zac stood.

This angered Mitchell, who rose to his feet, and began to walk toward the boy. To Mitchell's alarm, Zac got up, and started walking toward him. Laurie, surprised by the sudden change in Mitchell's behavior, called her office, and asked her staff to meet her out on the southeast lawn.

Mitchell and Zac walked to within a yard of one another and stopped, starring into each other's eyes. As Laurie and a number of her staff approached, they overheard Mitchell state: "I know who you are, and what you carry inside that ugly heart of yours. I've seen you before, and I've torn the heart you possess to shreds. I will do the same to you if you don't stop taunting me."

He stared hard into Zac's eyes, seeing in them his own rage. Mitchell knew him, not only now, as a relation of Sian's, but deeper . . . somehow he knew the boy. Yes, there was a memory of him.

Mitchell broke his gaze, and looked around the courthouse square. It was not Zac that he knew, but realized it was the boy's isolation, the emptiness, the lack of connection to . . . what . . . Mitchell struggled for a word, or concept, or memory. He was lost in thought, and did not acknowledge the stares he received from everyone. But the memory came: it was the words he had written in his journal, on the eve of Red's murder.

Who am I to deny him love for being the same kind of man I had become? Who am I to withhold my blessing for a man who had not the good fortune to find the kind of love that saves, that believes, that grows, that rocks a disbelieving soul?

Suddenly, as he took in the textures and colors of the courthouse square in the full glory of a fall season, he found the word he was looking for—the memory—delivered to him through his vision of Red—through the ash—just moments before—prompting him, to *help the boy.*

The word, the memory, was:

Father.

Mitchell looked again into Zac's eyes. He felt the years of lack: in the form of discipline, in the form of time, in the form of advice, and felt compelled to ask him a question that had fallen from the sky—from the color of fall leaves—from the past, the present, and a future not yet considered:

"Where are your goddamn shoes?"

> *All this in a moment taken by the heart of a man who had not taken such moments before: A man who had not known love—in light. A man who had not known love—in shadow. A man who had not known love—in the moments in-between.*

Chapter Sixty Four

MITCHELL walked up to FR 63 rather than traverse the banks of the Hassayampa in the dark. The night sky was putting the day to bed. He loved the exchange of shade, as the color blue traveled the length of its own parts. Step by step, the night moved with Mitchell, down the ancient dirt road. The night shadows of many things moved with him. The color gray filtered his senses, changing the three-dimensional world of the forest into a hushed subdue.

He stopped to take it in, inhaling the night air deeply. Unsettled in his lungs, he coughed upon exhale. The lines of the trees—the branches, bark, and leaves—appeared subtly to Mitchell, as sharp down-turned angles, taking on the faces of many ill-tempered stick men.

Mitchell remembered his fear of the woods as a boy. His first adventures and campouts at night in the forest came with the faces and sounds of the beatings he endured, before he lived in Ponderosa Park. He remembered learning how to tolerate the vision of a stick man. He thought of the new memories of his father, and how he had faced many things without him.

Mitchell tripped, uncharacteristically so, on a small piece of granite wedged into the ground. He stumbled forward but caught himself by extending his arms and hands to the ground, breaking his fall. His back pack fell forward however, over his head. The hunting knife fell out of the bag, landing flat and hard, on his right hand.

This is strange, he thought. Unexpectedly so, he was unfocused and unable to get his bearings emotionally, physically, and most importantly—especially for Mitchell in the woods at night—spiritually. He looked about his immediate surroundings, and found angry stick men everywhere.

What's going on? Why so many?

He gathered up his belongings, arranging the books again in the back pack, but decided to unsheathe, and hold the knife.

Why the knife?

Moving slowly down the road toward his home, he kept a vigil on the apparent foreboding that had made its way into his psyche. He took deep breaths, asking the woods out loud, "What gives?"

Nothing, just the continued sense of dread emanating from his surroundings. The hilt of the knife in his hand was now warm and wet with sweat. His intense grip made his fingers ache. As he made his way around the bend, and the long walk up the drive to his home, he immediately sensed something was wrong.

"Why no lights?" he asked out loud. The A-frame, through thickets of pine and brush, was dark and silent, save one soft night stand light from the loft. His breath was shallow. His legs quickened their pace, as unthinkable scenes raced through his mind. They were of Red. He was suddenly afraid for Red.

Bear? A snake? She would not go to town without me. Why is the house dark?

He approached the front of the home, his breath continuing a rapid cadence of trepidation, determined to find out why the home appeared lifeless. Mitchell stopped. Through the tall windows of the cabin, through the dark interior, through a disbelieving mind and eyes, thick with angry stick men everywhere, Mitchell saw the head of a man, move as a shadow across the ceiling of the loft. The soft light went dark.

He quietly dropped his backpack to the ground, and walked to the side of his home. His limbs turned to ice—his breathing intensified—his mind raced. He needed to calm down. The side door to the basement was open—he went through it slowly, wondering if he had left it ajar. Finding his way to the stairs that led up to the first floor, Mitchell heard them creak for the first time. He stopped and listened to the dark. He stepped on the side of each stair in an effort to minimize the creaking, when a great need to rush up them erupted in him.

From deep within, a growling, howling scream burst forth from him. His legs dug hard into the steps, first on the stairs leading to the main floor, then on the stairs leading to the loft. He looked up and saw an intruder leap from the loft, his feet landing on the sofa below. For an instant, Mitchell, knife in hand, was torn. He wanted to destroy the intruder in blind rage, but Red's precious face appeared in his trembling mind. He made his way up the remainder of the stairs slowly, unsure if any more of the enemy remained.

His head peered above the floor. He saw the top of the bed and Red's feet, toes up, spread apart, and motionless. This sight rippled through his gut. He felt, and then fought off, an urge to vomit. At the same time, the front door that led out to the porch slammed open, and as Mitchell turned back toward the sound, he saw the intruder take another leap off the porch, to the ground below. He howled—breaking or spraining some part of his body.

Mitchell turned his head slowly back to the bed he shared with his beloved. "What's wrong Red?" he asked softly, his voice quaking, his thoughts pulsing through his brain, his blood pounding behind his eyes, filtering the darkened loft in crimson shades. He walked to the side of the bed, knife still in hand. In the dark, he was unable to make out exactly what was happening to his wife. He noticed her silence first. She was motionless. As the shades of crimson dissipated, as the darkness revealed slowly the outline of Red's body, he saw that her face was turned away from him. He wiped sweat away from his brow with his free hand, and while doing so noticed her hair had been pushed across her face in a peculiar way. He looked for the bedside lamp, which had been knocked off the night stand. When he bent over to pick it up, his cheek brushed against her hand. It was wet and cold. In these long and sad moments, he felt the moistness from her hand, evaporate on his skin, leaving him in a grip of madness and tears. The evaporating coolness crumbled him, and he fell fully prone to the floor beside their bed. Moments passed again in utter horror. He cautiously turned on the lamp, then slowly turned his eyes up, toward her hand.

The silence he heard in his own head, when he gazed upon her lifeless hand, was foreign to him. He slowly lifted himself up into a kneeling position, and saw his wife had been brutally attacked. He knew she was gone; the silence emanating from her bloody body pierced him. He gazed upon each part of her, each intimate place that he had kissed or touched. He shook his head, disbelieving the scene in front of him. It wasn't adding up. He stood up, and accepted the momentary notion that this was not Red.

It's not her, he said in his mind. *It's not her.*

Moments passed. Long breathless moments passed. He stood there, his knife now melted into his hand. His eyes squinted toward the body on the bed. He tried to focus—to find out who it was.

Who is it? He asked himself. *Who is it?*

At once his mind, his heart, his breathing, all stopped. He fell back, toward the floor, landing on his lower back, knocked off his feet, by the notion that it was Red. It was his Red.

On the floor, looking up at the ceiling, Mitchell came to some kind of momentary accounting of the scene before him.

Her ordeal was over. She was free now of the unimaginable horror she had suffered, as he walked the Hassayampa just hours before.

Quietly he sat up, knife still in hand. The silence continued its quiet presence as he beheld her. Tears began to pour out of his eyes, mixing with sweat on his cheeks. His hands shook. He could utter no word. He picked up the phone to dial the police. It was dead. Holding the handset, he looked over again at his wife; her pants and underwear were gone. Blood was smeared on her thighs. Her blouse had been ripped open exposing her breasts. They had been slashed. He could not tell the extent of the mutilation, but his mind was flashing over the bed, focusing, and then rejecting, the horror Red endured by her attacker.

He gently put his hand to her face, moving the hair that had been pushed out of place. From a hole in hell, where demons clawed for him, and for his wife, Mitchell screamed out loud the denial of what was before him. He screamed for a reversal, for a refusal to accept the scene before him, at a volume that he could not maintain, his voice lost to the strain of the shattering wails. "No!" he wailed again, as his vocal chords gave in to his emotional horror, of his bloody wife, gone to the evil in the world.

Silence in the home was heard again. He looked up to see the tall windows baring nothing from the outside world. He remembered the stick men on his walk home, and their angry, still, stares. He took a deep breath, and for the first time in his life, he could smell human blood, Red's blood, as it dried against what warmth remained in her.

The silence in his mind was broken by cramping in the hand that still held the knife, then again, as he heard a moan coming from the front of the home. Mitchell stood up, and walked quietly to the edge of the loft, then leaned gently against the guard rail, and peered out the tall thirty foot windows. His mind was still. He heard blood gushing through his ears yet was feeling nothing. He now knew Red was dead. Yet he felt nothing.

He turned toward the stairs, walked down to the main floor, then slowly out to the front porch. There he saw through the darkness what the stick men were now looking at; the femur of the killer, breaking upon impact, had ripped through his skin and pants. It appeared to Mitchell that the killer kept coming into, and out of, consciousness.

He walked back inside, knife still in hand, and then downstairs, through the basement, and out the side door. He walked over to the man lying on the ground, and without hesitation or thought, kicked the end of the femur bone, then pushed on it with his shoe. With great effort Mitchell finally heard the bone release—he had forced the femur out of the hip socket. The killer wailed. Mitchell leaned over and looked at his face. He saw the man screaming but heard only the silence of his wife's life within. He looked long and hard at the face of the man who had taken his beloved.

Mitchell's tears had stopped but sweat was now rolling down his face, falling onto the face of Red's killer. They washed away spots of grime, making white skin appear where dirt once was. Mitchell threw his large knife off to his side, out of the reach of the killer, and then grabbed the killer's ears, pulling his face closer to his own. A small memory forced its way to the front of Mitchell's mind:

I have seen this face before.

It was the face of the man who had tried to mug them year's earlier, as they walked back to the Hassayampa Inn from Murphy's, on their first full day as man and wife.

He remembered the moment he did not let go of the very knife now on the ground near him. Red had stopped him from throwing his knife into the back of the man, this man, as he ran in terror years earlier. Red had pleaded for his life, and tonight he took hers.

He remembered the desire to take Red's picture and their address out of the ad in the monthly circular, and stumbled at the thought that this bastard found Red through the ad.

Mitchell dropped the man's head to the ground. The killer opened his eyes and tried to move, but his injury immobilized him. Mitchell stared at him blankly, as fate and the years between the two moments Mitchell had spent with this man, were now connected by cruelty beyond measure.

358

He took a deep breath. Again without thinking, Mitchell put his hand around the end of the killer's femur, as it stuck through the muscle, skin, and fabric of his pants.

This is your reckoning, take it, take it, voices said. Releasing the bone, Mitchell looked up from the killer to find the stick men looking directly at him.

In unison they said again, *this is your reckoning!*

And again, *take it!*

And again, *take your reckoning!*

He looked down at the killer's femur. He grabbed it again. It was warm and slippery to the touch, and he could not get a good grip on it. Mitchell stood up and took his shirt off, put it in his hands, then wrapped both around the end of the broken femur bone. At once, with the same grip he used to hold a baseball bat as a boy, in the very woods he now stood in, he began to twist and yank the heavy bone back and forth, in an effort to remove it from the killer's leg. Mitchell began to feel the killer's blood on his hands, arms, and face, as he continued to twist and yank. He reached out, grabbed his hunting knife from the ground, and began to cut away muscle tissue and tendons. The killer, now awake, comprehended the horror of his life being shredded from him. He began desperately to hit Mitchell in the face, squirming like a chicken about to be beheaded, screaming for mercy, screaming to the spirituous woods, and to Mitchell's stick men, who watched from deep within the night, to no avail. Mitchell passed the blade across the killer's arms, slicing muscle and tendon, disabling the demon from swinging at him any longer.

With both hands again on the bone, Mitchell stood up and began to yank as hard as he could to pull the killer's bone from his body. The killer looked up at Mitchell in lost and hopeless terror. Mitchell took note of the killer's eyes succumbing to the torture.

He had dragged the killer demon twenty feet. Finally the bone slipped from the killer's body, causing Mitchell to stumble back into the brush, femur in hand. A branch stabbed him in the back side, cutting him. Mitchell took no note of it.

Blood was now everywhere, pools of it on the ground reflected both the black of night, and the black of heart that once beat in the killer. He was dead, tortured to death at the hands of a husband, still not feeling anything in his heart about the mutilation and murder of his wife. He looked about and watched without feeling each and every stick man turn and walk into the night. Mitchell stood up, bone still in hand, and walked back into his home. He walked up stairs into the kitchen, and picked up the cell phone, turned on all the outdoor lighting, and walked back downstairs. He grabbed a folding chair, and sat out under the bright lights, about twenty feet from the killer's body. He dialed 911. In the other hand remained the killer's femur, now fixed by dried blood and other bodily fluids.

"911 Operator, what is your emergency?"

"My wife is gone," Mitchell said. "I just killed the man who did it."

There was a pause.

"What is your location sir," she said without emotion.

"I'm about two miles south of Ponderosa Park, on FR 63," he said.

"Are you armed?"

"No," Mitchell said. "My knife is over there lying next to the bastard."

"Please stay on the line for one moment," the operator said.

Mitchell remained on the line but was slipping further into shock. In morbid curiosity, he smelled the bone he held in his hand, which made him vomit instantly.

"Are you still there?" the operator asked.

Coughing, Mitchell yelled wildly "yeah!"

"Two Yavapai County sheriff's deputies will be there shortly," the operator said. "You are required to stand and face the officers when they arrive, with your hands in the air. Do you understand?"

"Yes, I will stand and face the officers, and put my hands in the air when they arrive," Mitchell said robotically.

"Please hold," the operator said.

Still moments passed. He looked around at the evening. There was a sense of paradox in him. He noted that something of great significance had changed in him, yet the woods remained unchanged.

From the darkness, now unseen, the stick men whispered *you took it, your reckoning, you took it.*

He turned his attention away from their chant. Mitchell did not think of Red. Her bloodied and lifeless body had not yet become a part of any memory or feeling. He remained dead to any other sensory inputs, except for the chanting stick men inside the silence around him. That, his senses did feel. It was a personal sensation hearing time stand still, and space become something that is past rather than present. It was the intimate association of shock claiming the mechanics of his body.

At once, the silence was broken by visuals of light and silhouette. Flashing blue, red, and white lights broke through the brush and pine, and as the headlights of two police cars approached, Mitchell stood and faced them, hands in the air. He felt like he was going to pass out.

"What in God's name is he holding in his hand," one deputy said to another, over the police band.

"I don't know," the other deputy said, "but he was told to discard any weapons."

Switching to the loud speaker, the second deputy told Mitchell to cast whatever he was holding in his hands aside, and hit the ground. At that moment both deputies saw the gruesome display of a dead body across the open area from where they were parked. They also saw, as Mitchell tried to release it, the bone sticking to his hand. It fell to the ground in an odd arc in front of him. Mitchell kicked the bone toward the deputies' cars, and then fell to the ground, as he was told to do.

The deputies got out cautiously, looking in all directions for any further threats.

"There is no one else here," Mitchell mumbled.

"Dispatch," one of the officers said on his hand held radio. "We need the captain out here right away. There's something not right here . . . I am not quite sure what we should do."

"Like what officer, what do you see?" dispatch asked.

"Like I said dispatch," the deputy replied. "I'm not sure what it is I am looking at."

"I can tell you if you would like. That dead bastard over there killed my wife, and I just had the pleasure of torturing him to death," Mitchell stated as a matter of fact. "He broke his leg when he jumped from that balcony. His femur poked through his pants, and I took it upon myself to remove it. That's what that is," he said, pointing to the bone on the ground.

The deputies exchanged looks of horror at how the man died. They looked at Mitchell, and wondered how he could remain so calm.

"My wife's body is on the bed upstairs," Mitchell continued, sounding as if he were drunk. "I didn't touch anything except for moving a lamp back onto the night stand. I moved her hair; I couldn't make out her face. When you see her, you will understand, that what lies here before you, is the natural conclusion to what lies upstairs."

Cautiously moving toward Mitchell, the officers removed hand cuffs while holding their revolvers on him. "You are under arrest," one deputy stated while the other subdued Mitchell, cuffing him. His rights were read.

"Did you know that the reading of the Miranda Rights came from a case right here in Arizona," Mitchell said.

"I would advise you to say nothing further," the deputy cuffing him said, and set him back down upon the folding chair.

They remained outside with Mitchell, standing behind him in guard over him, waiting for not only the captain, but the Arizona Department of Public Safety (DPS) evidence collection team, as well.

While waiting, they took note of a set of words—a poem or lyrics they guessed—that were being repeated over and over again by Mitchell, as he stared off into the woods. The deputies could not have guessed it was a song that Mitchell was reciting, and that he was reciting the words to childhood phantoms. Mitchell's rumblings were incoherent to the deputies.

Mitchell's reciting of the song to the hiding stick men began to repeat, is if he had fallen into a trance:

> *You know we hadn't been back at home two hours*
> *We heard a hawk cry out in the night*
> *And you know that's a signal from young Billy who's our sentry*
> *Saying something here ain't exactly right, oh . . .*

The captain and the DPS unit were now upon the scene in front of Mitchell's home, looking at the bone and the blood, and the strangely bent dead body, at the other end of the clearing.

We quick grabbed some of our hardware
Stumbled out of our home

The DPS unit made quick work of what was before them, identifying the femur and its owner, and in their collection of photographic and sample evidence.

"What's going on in your home?" the captain asked Mitchell.

Mitchell responded:

Two minutes flat we had found her
An Indian girl all alone

"The 911 operator informed me that you said your wife was murdered, and that you killed her attacker, is this correct?" the captain continued in his questioning of Mitchell.

Mitchell responded:

And Eli said let's take her back to the cabin
I said you don't know she might be the law, yeah

"Are you injured?" the captain continued, showing Mitchell some compassion, as he now realized that Mitchell was in a state of shock.

Mitchell answered:

He said smiling kind of nasty, it ain't too damn likely
She'll beat me to the draw, oh no

"Get the paramedics out here right now," the captain said, giving up on questioning Mitchell. "I need one deputy and one DPS out here, and everyone else upstairs with me. Let's see what the hell happened here tonight."

As we were walking back through the darkness
I heard the Duke, he's our dynamiter, say

The captain stood and listened for a moment to the words Mitchell recited.

He said what's your name sweet little Indian girl
She said Raven, and she looked away

Deciding that the words were just random thoughts of a man in shock, he turned and followed the men and women upstairs to the sight of a body, that was once a woman, and a wife, of the man downstairs reciting words none present recognized.

Now Eli he's our fastest gunner
He's kind of mean and young, from the South

While evidence was collected that night, Mitchell plunged into abysses and darkness only cruelty beyond measure delivers. Except for the initial call to the 911 operator, he could no longer discuss what had transpired that night. He was unable to. He had lost all sense of time and direction, all sense of color and sound, and at present would not know the back of his hand if it hit him. He had lost his mind and found only the world described in the song "Cowboy Movie," as a place to hang whatever was left of his sanity.

He said Fat Albert you're getting kind of old and weird now
You'd better get your 12 gauge shotgun right out and I did oh you know I did

It was the trip up the stairs to the loft that helped the law enforcement of Yavapai County put together the holes that Mitchell had created by succumbing to shock, unable to produce a timeline of events.

Now Eli and the Duke they got down to it
They each wanted that Indian girl for their own

Red had been tortured by her assailant. There were rope burns on her wrists and ankles. At what point she was freed from the lengths of rope scattered around the bed, would be up to the DPS team to determine. There were knife cuts across her breasts and vagina. Blood was everywhere . . . on the bed and floor as fingerprints, and in haunting and horrifying photographs, and testimony as red and crusting sock prints.

When they finally got around to asking her
You know she said she'd come to take young Billy home, oh no, no, no

Because the captain felt that Mitchell was a threat to his own safety, he was taken to a secured hospital room at the Yavapai County Hospital in Prescott for observation.

Chapter Sixty Five

MITCHELL had been charged with murder. He had found the killer alive, but immobilized, and proceeded to end his life in vengeful payment for Red. This was the basis for the charge, according to the Yavapai County Prosecutor.

Mitchell remained withdrawn—inside his skin, which was a familiar place to him—as if underwater at the bottom of a swimming pool—looking up at the blue sky—safe from harm. He had not thought of Red or her killer. His existence was veiled; his senses covered by the boyhood machinery of experience, when brutality reigned in a wildly dysfunctional family.

He was moved from the hospital to the County Courthouse jail. When he stepped out of the transport van he looked to his right, and saw the steps he sat on as a boy, waiting for love to find him—in the form a girl with jet black hair. He remembered the judge who watched him kiss her on the cheek, and realized that although he had seen the courthouse most of his life, spending many a day on its steps, he had never set foot inside. *How odd*, he had thought.

He ate little. He saw no one. He was still officially "under observation."

He did not dream or notice the sun or moon; their light and shadow not recognized. He did not think of her hearth or her lyrical voice. Silence now her song, stillness now her life. The horror had not come with him. He left the smell of blood, the sound of twisting bone and tearing tendon, and the cries for mercy—her cries—as her last breaths tried to make their way to him, to the banks of the Hassayampa, from inside the cabin with the thirty foot windows.

More songs. More lyrics of forgotten tunes that helped Mitchell partially gather the present around him; the past was obliterated the night he killed the killer.

I thought I met a man
Who said he knew a man
Who knew what was going on

I was mistaken

Only another stranger
That I knew

Revenge had burned bright in him. Justice found its own end. Both were now known to his muscles but that was where memory ended. He had unwittingly succumbed to that part of his own life, long put away as irreconcilable. That rage had found release.

And I thought I had found a light
To guide me through
My night and all this darkness

I was mistaken
Only reflections of a shadow
That I saw

It was the balance of right and wrong. It was his mother killing his father—his broken heart—his brother's fists. It was loosing his beloved—her shinning walk of faith—her knowledge of Eden, her heart, mending his. It had become something else all together—his reckoning.

And I thought I'd seen someone
Who seemed at last
To know the truth

I was mistaken
Only a child laughing
In the sun

Dalton and Presley had stood out of sight and listened with the captain as Mitchell recited the words to the muted darkness around him.

Whispering, Presley said, "yes, I've heard them before, it's been a million years, but I've heard those words before."

"What do they mean?" the captain asked.

"Mitchell loves his music," Presley said. "They're lyrics, probably helping him cope."

"Well, I'm glad you guys are here."

They walked out to the front of the observation cell together. Mitchell looked up and saw his friends appear.

"Hello, Dalton," Mitchell said. "Hello, Presley. What're you doing here?"

Presley looked at Mitchell with compassion and shock. Mitchell was changed. The image of him behind bars, locked up as a murderer, did not equate to any sense Presley possessed. The years as friends, from boyhood, to the air and iron now between them, collided ferociously.

"What the fuck . . ." Presley said under his breath.

"What did you do?" Dalton asked unexpectedly, rushing the cage, grasping the iron bars in anxious fear, unable to find the compassion innate in Presley for their friend. Observing Mitchell incarcerated, in a windowless cell, his odd serenity, his quiet voice, now pushed Dalton backward, against the observation room wall, his palms grasping the cold hard brick behind him, powerless to see his old friend as he once did. Dalton let fate close in. He let go of his accepting nature, succumbing, as a surprised Presley and an unfazed Mitchell looked on, to the public outcry, and media fury over blood and revenge, jailing Dalton's mind under a heavy iron grate all its own.

"Why didn't you let him live?" Fear grew within. "Why torture him to death?" Images came into, and out of, Dalton's mind. "What's wrong with you?" Looking deep into Mitchell's expressionless stare, he filled in the answers to his apprehensive questions, finding the blood and the public hysteria, too much to live with. Anger surfaced. Presley put a hand to Dalton's shoulder, silently imploring him to remember why they were there. Dalton knocked Presley's arm away in a quick, harsh fashion, his eyes flashing the dark fear boiling within, refusing to accept the situation at hand.

"You're crazy Mitchell. You didn't have to do it. Now they're going to fry you, or lock you up for the rest of your life."

Dalton stared on; incredulous at what looked back at him.

Presley looked at Mitchell for a moment, recalling the details that fanned shock and conjecture over the gruesome ordeal. Presley too let fear step in. It sparked intensely then faded an instant later. He turned back to Dalton, asking; "What the hell are you doing?"

Dalton returned his stare. Sweat broke across his brow, and his hands began to tremble. "I'm not staying here, not with him, look at him, Presley, look at his hands, his eyes, he's not a sane man, he's gone, and he can't be trusted, ever again . . ."

"Shut up, Dalton. Get the fuck out of here if you can't take it, and leave him the fuck alone. You're just like the rest of this fucked up world. Leave then, and don't come back."

Dalton looked at Presley as if he too were now crazy. Shaking his head, Dalton pushed himself off the wall, stood for another moment taking in the consequences of his sudden change of heart, then yelled for the captain to let him out of the observation room.

Dalton would never be heard from again.

CS⧫SO

"Captain, open up the cell, and let me in," Presley said.

"Can't. Judge's orders."

"I'm not in any danger," Presley said. "I want to be allowed to sit with him."

"You can sit with him right here," the captain said, placing a folding chair next to the bars of the cell.

Presley looked incredulous. *They are really afraid of him here,* he thought, as he watched the captain leave the room.

Mitchell moved his chair over to where Presley sat.

"How are they treating you in here?" he asked, unsure of what to say and how Mitchell would react to any line of conversation. Mitchell started to hum:

In the sun . . .

Presley listened intently. "What are the words from?"

"If only I could remember my name," Mitchell said quickly, as if an afterthought.

He looked at Mitchell for a half-moment, then realized he was stating the name of an album often played when they were young.

"Great album, Mitchell, his best," Presley said. "Do you remember those summers when we were kids, playing at the waterhole?"

Presley's question took Mitchell back. "I do." Staring passed Presley, Mitchell said. "I spoke with my father."

Presley looked at Mitchell with a furrowed brow. He remembered that period in Mitchell's life when his father died.

"I have been having these intuitive, spiritual hikes along the Hassayampa of late," Mitchell said. "They reveal things to me. I have seen us as children playing on the river. I watched as my younger self, and my father, became one. I made peace with him. My life is no longer defined by his lack."

"Yea, that's good Mitchell," Presley said.

Presley remembered Otis, who had lived a long, square life, leaving behind a family filled legacy of hard work and fairness he now understood. The antithesis of Otis' life was now before him. Evil in the world had caught Mitchell, and Presley was struggling to make sense of it.

Images of wickedness paraded through Presley. So much of the world had caught him too—its march of ugly, mindless, twenty-four-hour-a-day news, of largely unsavory social networking, where one kind of evil or another found not only each other, but also a sense of normalcy, through the Internet—exchanging poisons in chat rooms, and other camouflaged, coded, web-based hiding places. Presley thought of the all-encompassing and constant need for stimulation and materialism, and how everything—everything in the world—from utter darkness to toilet paper, was available for a bid. He looked through the bars at his friend, now blinded in heart and mind, by what very well may be this new techno-evil. He thought of a rumor spreading through Prescott and beyond that Red's killer found her through a local publication's Internet website, which contained her picture and their business address. Presley furrowed his brow and thought to himself; *it's a new vehicle for wickedness. It endlessly assaults the soul of humanity, and that assault has taken shape as lines on my friend's face.*

"Are you getting enough to eat and drink in here?" Presley asked.

Mitchell nodded positively then softly repeated the refrain from "Laughing."

In the sun . . .

Presley took in his friend. There were things to handle including a memorial service for Red, and a decision facing Mitchell that he was not going to be able to make; Red's need for cremation.

Presley moved through the process of acting on behalf of Mitchell. He made the tough calls, setting up a memorial service at a local Methodist church, where a small gathering that included Emma, were in attendance. She played her guitar, singing "Fire and Rain." Tears rolled down Presley's face.

Two days later, on another solitary and sad afternoon, Presley walked out onto Mitchell's property, to the oak tree containing the declaration of eternal love from his friend to his departed wife. In its shade he stood, sorrowfully looking at the trunk of the old tree. The inscription had been stretched and faded by time, but he knew through his own living that the inscription's intent still rang true.

Yet he could not bridge the gap between the living referenced on the tree, and the death that unfolded behind him. He thought of Emma and her interpretation of "Fire and Rain." The song's intent moved Presley to his emotional knees at the memorial. It now moved in him again, this time into the richly colored and scented fall of leaves, scattered upon the ground.

He sobbed in his remembrance of Red, and recalled her actions as Mitchell's wife. He watched sadly, from a distance, as his friend succumbed to addiction; cocaine in its wicked fury, was all that could be seen above the water line of Mitchell's troubled life. Mitchell had been saved by love, and that fact now convulsed through Presley. He watched her, over time, remove shame, regret, and indescribable sadness, from Mitchell; all of which flowed from a heartbreaking family heritage that had stained humanity.

He let her death cut him. He looked back at the cabin. Through the roof Presley found images, perhaps imagined, perhaps not, of blood soaking through fabric, of a dying pulse, of a sharp and unyielding blade submerged beneath a woman's skin. Suddenly Presley turned to his side and vomited. At once he cried out loud, anguishing for the soul of Red. He became, in heart, the great vacancy of her life in an evil and cruel world. He was taken by the woman's inspired and disciplined example, and returned to the eternal question of why, crying again to the forest around him, to the flows of water, to the seasons changing, and now to the indescribable grief, that all who knew her, save Mitchell, had endured in the days following the killing.

Presley, in Mitchell's stead, and for him, endured the rage and the loss that was Mitchell's. And now, upon the forest floor, where the Hassayampa River bended, where the elements came together in his life's memory, came an outline of life descending from above, a vision of a woman with flowing red hair, obvious to his eyes, but not his mind—disbelieving what he beheld. Whispering down through time and space was the youthful and beautiful Red, white and still upon the remnants of a sad day. With both hands now on an urn Presley looked about the forest, at the color of the earth, hearing the wind in the trees, and thought of their constant presence in his life. The sky held its bright blue light on him. He held out his hands, turned the urn over, and watched the falling of carbon to earth. Presley delivered Red to what had always been—and to what will always be; the precious passing and understanding of time and how its space, filled with love, is living. He walked around the tree, circling it with the waterless impulses of who Red once was. Presley produced an antique pocket watch. In its rear chamber he placed a small portion of Red's ashes.

Trembling, Presley turned away from the oak. Deep breaths followed him to the cabin, as he numbed his way through a list of chores that needed attention. He, for his friend, ensured that every speck of horror had been cleaned now that the prosecutor was done with the collection of evidence. He, for his friend, replaced locks, straightened furniture, repaired holes, and tidied the different things that had made, and marked, the life of Mitchell and Red.

At dusk, the sun long-set behind the hills west of the waterhole, Presley turned his back to the evening colors, looked at the freshly renewed cabin, and sighed deeply. Putting his hands in his pockets, feeling for the pocket watch, he turned again to the western horizon, put away the sadness, and walked away from the cabin with the thirty foot windows.

Chapter Sixty Six

SEVERAL weeks had past since Mitchell's incarceration had begun. He continued passing his silent hours in song. He was observed often by a psychiatrist—hired by Mitchell's court-appointed attorney. What was observed, was a man going through the various stages of grief. In reviewing evidence and statements made by investigators of the bloodbath, the psychiatrist assessed, and would testify that his client suffered from shock and was temporarily insane—of the kind often found in a soldier after battle, or a wife at the long end of a horribly abusive marriage.

Mitchell still had no recollection of the facts surrounding his killing of the killer. He knew now only that his wife was not with him.

During the weeks that followed the investigation, it was revealed that the killer had attacked and killed before. Through the use of forensic DNA evidence and procedure, the man Mitchell killed had been linked to three other unsolved rape and murder cases in Arizona, and in other states.

Gossip blew. He was hailed as both hero and ruthless blood-thirsty maniac. A local columnist wrote that "pulling a man's femur out of his leg, while the victim was alive and helpless, is as sick and disgusting a vision as anything I have ever read or watched. He needs to be locked up for the remainder of his horrible life."

Mitchell got wind of none of it. He remained removed, yet made good use of his time as a prisoner. Presley brought Mitchell books from the now long-vacant cabin, and he read nonstop. He revisited many of his favorite stories, living in worlds painted perfect in their conception.

Without realizing it, Presley delivered to Mitchell the old man's journal. Mitchell noticed it immediately, and was hesitant to pick it up, sensing the book to be more like a door which stood ajar—letting in wisps of information his five senses could register, but not understand. He overcame his reluctance one afternoon, and read the following passage:

> *The Sea Man looked up at the*
> *crystalloid sky, frozen in its own reach for a*
> *beginning and an end. He looked around to the*

leafless trees and brown grass, and the ground
that held so much of the cycle of life, as it
began, and of death, as it ended in the passing
of time. Ash to ash, *the Sea Man thought.*

Mitchell shut the book tight, squeezing it with both hands in
an effort to force the meaning of the story out of its leather-bound
covers. Straining, he thought of a grave yard. The thought grew into a
view from a hill of the Atlantic Ocean. Spotted about the hill were
grave stones. Mitchell's memory opened up the face of a man dying on
Christmas Day decades ago. Materializing before him was one of the
grave stones. It grew in size and detail to reveal a name; Frank. *Frank,*
Mitchell thought. *Frank.* He knew who it was. It was Red's father. It
was Christmas Day, and he died delivering oil on his day off to a
family freezing in a winter storm. Red had told him the sad story long
ago, about a grave on a hill, in a small New Jersey town: Manasquan.
She was ten. She spoke of the day after Christmas, when she buried
her father. It was the day after the storm. Tears came as he recalled
Red's story of the bitter cold, and a wind that blew through her tiny
shore town. *Black ice.* It was black ice that caused the oil truck to flip
viciously, exploding; a kindness repaid by death.

Black ice. He thought of evil running through veins, of warm
skin under cold blood, drying. He stopped his mind dead in its tracks;
he was about to slip into a hole. For the first time since his isolation
began, scenes not readily available to him, of the immediate past, were
knocking. He looked down at the journal in his hands, and anxiety
grew.

The days that lead up to the trial found an increase in
Mitchell's paranoia; not of the actual trial itself, but of the tugs from
his sub-conscience. There were colors and outlines of shapes that
would flash in the middle of a deep breath, or at the edge of a turning
page, or in the moment just before he fell asleep that spoke to an
appalling horror. All of which would usher in enormous releases of
adrenaline, causing him to sway while standing, or hold his head when
sitting.

One evening, when 'lights out' had been ordered, Mitchell fell
into a deep sleep. Dreaming, a diminutive white room came into focus.
The walls and floor were covered by small, white, glossy, square tiles.
It was cold and quiet. Looking down at his bare feet, Mitchell found
himself, in complete nonchalance, using a hand-held circular saw, to

cut off the front half of each foot. It was done painlessly and easily. Blood began to pulse from each foot, pooling and staining the white-tiled floor.

Presently Red appeared in front of him. They stood together beneath a canopy of oak. Subdued sunlight bent the contrasts of ancient things. At once Red turned, and began to run from him. To his horror he could not follow her. He tried to run toward her ever-disappearing outline, to no avail. His feet, now useless, kept causing him to fall forward. On one final fall to the ground, he looked up to see Red vanish around a familiar bend on a familiar road. He awoke from the dream, and slowly mouthed the question; *what have I done?*

Blood on the white tile walls had manifested into tears on his face. Red's running from him became an ache in his heart beyond any weight love had ever held. He was crushed by her departure. *Where is she? Where did she go? What is around the bend?* These questions left his open mouth softly, and in the dark cold jail cell, were heard only by stone and steel. The tears continued their flow. Flashes of her body, of her skin, her lips, moved in and out of focus just above his head. Her skin, its smell and feel—the way it wrapped itself around her breasts, full and comforting to his head in a morning hug—rifled through him. He could feel her inside of him still. Her eternal perfection—from vision to scent to touch—was in his beating heart. He could not know his life without her, yet she had changed. She was running away, leaving him on the ground, disabled, unable to walk upright, unable to pull her next to him.

His ears had filled with tears. His eyes hurt. He rubbed them and wiped his wet face and ears dry. The moments inside of love leaving had subsided. The grief would end, as he closed his eyes in a dreamless slumber, for the remainder of the night.

⁂

The peace of sleep was broken by a guard informing Mitchell that his big day had arrived. *What day?*

A woman appeared. Mitchell had seen her many times before. She was an attorney; his attorney, and on this day she seemed more agitated than usual. Laurie had very little success in communicating with Mitchell, and was of the opinion that she could not count on him in anyway, during his upcoming trial. She told him that she would try to have his charges reduced, or possibly dropped, but found Mitchell un-communicative. He would ramble, sing songs, and when he

374

acknowledged her, when she established contact with him, his gaze was not into her eyes, but on her bare neck and exposed collar bones. Her frustration could be heard in deep breaths of resignation.

She had both empathy and fear for him. The coroner's report, of the man he killed, froze her breath. His actions reminded her of a lion tearing apart its prey, and she knew that such thoughts were not helping her. His constant staring at her skin gave her the creeps.

Laurie was attracted to him as well. There was a quality in him that she was drawn to, and this attraction flew in the face of his revenge killing. The two pieces of the puzzle did not fit, and the resulting paradox, that of attraction then repulsion, left her bewildered. *How could such a good-hearted person commit such a brutal crime?* Yet when she thought about it further, his actions on that night seemed strangely noble. *He did what he could do to defend his home, his wife, and his life. He was not a victim, and would have defended his wife had he been home. And yet, there he is, staring at my neck again.*

Mitchell's gaze at her skin was not his focus. There was a tug of great solace that possessed him—a memory of divine experience—of something he once knew, but could not know again. He was unable to communicate this to Laurie, and the opposing perceptions remained between the lawyer's paperwork, and her heart.

During one of her one-way visits with Mitchell, he handed to her the old book. It was opened up to a passage and he pointed to it. Laurie put on her reading glasses and began to read:

> *The Sea Man was troubled. Looking out his window, with memories of what was not right in his life, and with priorities that handed to him the short end of the stick, he asked God to help him settle the debts he held in his heart.*

> *He did not like the heaviness in his chest. When under the spell of inequity he found it hard to breath. He found no hope in the sun rising, and fear as the sun set. Bitterness and resentment were the day's bookends.*

> *When under such a shadow, the Sea Man could not see the vision of life God had given him. It filtered the mirror in his soul, seeing only what was evil in the world, and in*

doing so, losing sight of his Blessed Horizon, and the precious momentum built by working his hands and feet in the Current of the Expanding Universe.

The window held no answer for him on this day. He stood up, got dressed for church, and walked through the desert toward the doors that had held insight and wisdom to life's mysteries in the past.

As he walked, the morning lifted winter's frost from the floor of the desert, giving the Sea Man optimism that his darkness would be lifted too. He knew on this morning that words and music would be heard that would help him realign inequity.

He knew that injustice must remain as a constant companion in life. Its utility was found in the contrast it provided. The Sea Man often counted his blessings in the face of it.

Yet on this morning, there were some things that lingered longer and harder in him, things that would not let up in their pressure, cramping him.

He knew, as the church grew closer that he would find peace, that God would provide stability, and show him how to balance the inequities.

He had often tried to ease this pain, through short cuts and short term thinking, and always on terms agreeable only to him. Each and every effort on behalf of an easy way out failed, leaving him further diminished.

Before him on this morning, his eyes were heavy with doubt and self-censure. The feelings that came, through of the actions of others—feelings that smarted from the inside— feelings that lessened God's intentions for him, were the notes that played in his heart.

This movement of thought put him further and further away from his occupancy in God's current, making him increasingly vulnerable to the energy of injustice, thus developing within the boundaries of his life the proverbial vicious circle. He wondered about the source of inequity, and the idea that pre-meditated inequity came from the minds of those afflicted with narcissistic natures, as in the hearts of sociopaths and selfish souls.

He had arrived at the entrance to the sanctuary. Opening the large door allowed a great breeze to blow over him, lifting his spirit out to the sun and blue sky above. He was greeted by several church members dressed in their Sunday best. Their smiles and the bright colors they wore elevated his step, and a simple smile curled on the corners of his lips.

He located his seat, looked over the day's presentations to find a sermon about ten words. The songs were sung. The message was delivered. The words that lingered on after the service were: "I can do all things through God, who strengthens me."

On his way home, he began to recite the words out loud, over and over again. He found a rhythm in the words, and added to them his own context, which described the inequities in his heart. At once he found a 'can do' spirit rise within, and the difficulties in his heart replaced by the hard-earned momentum of faith.

The perfection of nature, in the form of a blessing from God, became the ten words the Sea Man could use, to help air out the faces of selfishness, bringing him peace amidst the bright sun, and its blue ocean of a sky—of an ideal Sunday afternoon.

*"Remarkable," the Sea Man
thought.*

She put the book down on the floor and looked at Mitchell. She knew a soul in trouble when she saw one, and Mitchell was just hanging on by one breath, and then another.

Mitchell saw that Laurie had stopped reading, and slowly brought his gaze up from her neck, chin, cheeks, and finally into her eyes, disarming her, shocked to see his eyes looking directly into hers. "What is it Mitchell?"

He looked down to the floor, reached through the bars of his jail cell, picked up the journal, pointed to the passage just read, and with great sadness asked: "How do I get here?"

At that moment Laurie could see Mitchell; the one Red saw years ago under the spell of abuse and neglect; the one love dusted off and polished, then placed on a pedestal as its only care. She was quite moved by the sight, and through the filter of his sadness, found it significant that such tenderness was still there, still reaching out after humanity's black ice had run its course through him.

"Mitchell, no matter the outcome of this trial, no matter what hangs over you in the form of a jail cell ceiling, or a blue sky, there is one thing I want you to know—you are already there," Laurie said, as she pointed to the journal.

He closed his eyes looking for whatever it was she saw in him, and remembered for a moment that she was right, that he had known once a capacity for love, and an awareness of its abundance, yet there it remained, as something only seen when peering over a cliff. He would not travel too close to the unrevealed edge of why Red was not there.

"I brought you a suit to wear, your trial begins today, remember?"

He had remembered, and was grateful to her for the suit.

"I want you to change into it, and go with the guard down to the courtroom. I will meet you there. Mitchell, I want to say something to you right now that you must understand. The prosecutor in your case is going to go over, in detail, every thing you did the night you killed the killer. You will be forced to look at your actions, but say nothing, don't react. Remember, we are going to go into detail about why you did what you did."

Mitchell heard her say it. He knew that today would be the day he would be forced to listen to the way certain events unfolded. He would hear sheriff deputies talk about what they saw when they drove onto his property. They would talk about his stance, and what he was holding, and how it stuck in his hands. He knew motive and morals would be twisted, one way or another, to prove whatever point needed to be made, to a jury of his peers, by both sides.

Laurie suspected this much about her client; that he would do what he did that night again and again, if called by the horrors of life to do so. As she walked to the courtroom, she reviewed her plan to allow the prosecution its due course, yet she worried that Mitchell would be drawn into a dramatic recollection of his actions. She shuddered at the details of the night herself, often wiping tears from her face, during the many hours spent in review of the evidence.

Laurie turned and walked through the doors of the courtroom. It was filled with the lives moved by the circumstances of her client's case. Some were there that knew women taken by the killer in the two decades prior. Some had their senses bent toward the morbid visions, scents, and sounds of the night Mitchell took revenge. Some were there to report the details of the trial to the press, and others to witness the descriptions of Mitchell's actions, as a reconciliation of their own.

She found the defense attorney's table, set her things upon them, took a deep breath, and faced the door at the side of the courtroom where Mitchell would enter.

When he came out, the rush of celebrity filled the room. He looked out the courtroom windows, seeing the glowing indigo high overhead—a kind moment for Mitchell—the sky reminded him of better days. He remembered walking on the banks of the river, and sleeping under the watchful eye of the cosmos. He remembered his boyhood home, and where it sat in proximity to the Yavapai County Courthouse. The shadows casts by American elms ushered in memories of seasons passed. He took comfort in knowing that the universe had not changed its use of cycles to promote the passing of time, and the filling of space, as life lived on without him. He found Presley in the front row and smiled at him, thanking him for being there. Locating his chair next to Laurie, he sat down with a deep, anxious breath.

∽§϶

At some point after his trial, Mitchell would think of a scale of justice that served quite well throughout the history of man. It was the perfect deterrent to what was considered bad behavior. It was consequence served in swift and potent fashion and set in motion that one reaps what one sows. He would conclude that he believed in the kind of justice that was found at high noon, on a dusty street, in a western town long ago, where dispute and resolution made its peace in clear and concise form; he would think: *an eye for an eye, the holy book says.*

Chapter Sixty Seven

"AND what was it you saw deputy, when you pulled up to his house?" the prosecutor asked the witness.

"I saw him . . ."

"Who? Point to him for the sake of the jury, please."

The deputy looked at Mitchell with some empathy, having realized his own ugly truth, having long ago decided at dinner conversations with his family, and in shop-talk with fellow workers that he, too, would have exacted justice—perhaps not in the same fashion, but with the same swiftness. He pointed his finger at Mitchell.

"I saw him standing in front of a folding chair with what I now know was a bone. I could not tell at first what he had in his hand. I thought it was a weapon of some sort. I got on the PA, and told him to throw it to the ground."

"Describe to the Jury what happened next," the prosecutor instructed.

"Well," the deputy said, knowing that what he was about to say was going to damage Mitchell's case. "The bone was attached to his palm. The blood dried, gluing it to his hand. He couldn't shake it loose right away which alarmed me. I wasn't sure what it was I was looking at."

In an effort to capitalize on what the witness described, the prosecutor asked further; "what do you mean 'it was glued to the defendant's hand'?"

"Just what I said," the deputy shot back. "It wouldn't shake loose."

Laurie looked over at her client. Mitchell was gazing out the windows toward the blue sky. She estimated that he was not listening to the deputy's testimony. The jury also took note of Mitchell's absent countenance. Some questioned the mind of a man who could cut out and hold the femur of a fellow human being, resulting in his death. Others remained cautiously objective, not ready to judge him.

"What did you see next deputy?"

"After the defendant released the object, and his compliance to lie on the ground was met, the other deputy and I got out of our cruisers. I looked over to the right as we faced the cabin. On the ground was the body of a man. The right leg was in an odd position. There were pools of blood everywhere. It was apparent that the body was dragged several feet from the point where contact was first made between the defendant and the victim"

"What do you mean 'odd position'?" the prosecutor questioned.

The deputy hesitated. He remembered the queasiness that came with looking at the right leg of the victim. "The victim was on his back. The left leg was extended out with its foot up. The right leg seemed to be bent forward in a place a leg normally does not bend, about three quarters the way up between the knee and the hip."

The prosecutor quickly placed a poster board on an easel, and turned it around for everyone to see. On it was a larger-than-life, brilliantly-colored photograph of Mitchell's victim. The jury gasped. The crowd blurted out in horror. One of the jury members became sick. Laurie had seen all the photo evidence but still could not adjust to the unfolding testimony.

The prosecutor continued by asking the deputy to read a portion of the coroner's report pertaining to the cause of the victim's death.

As the deputy read the report, Mitchell slowly turned his gaze from the blue sky toward the three-foot by four-foot poster. What caught his attention was not the body, but the appearance of stick men in the photo. Their eyes were cross and the anger in them seemed, to Mitchell, to be directed at the killer lying dead on the ground. His heart began to climb inside the photograph. Soon Mitchell was submersed into what was now a three dimensional world. His pulse increased. His face turned red, and sweat surfaced, then beaded on his forehead. The color in the photograph continued its march into his senses, his memory recalling what his fingers and his sense of smell never forgot.

The coroner's report described that the deceased's hip socket had been split open, due to tremendous pressure placed on the ball portion of the femur; that pressure being applied at the tip of the exposed compound fracture, where the coroner reported finding shoe prints matching that of the soles Mitchell wore that night.

Mitchell registered only, the unrelenting stares of the stick men in the photo, and found he could not turn away from the rich mix of reds, greens, and blues that made up the life-sized photograph. It was the first time he remembered committing the crime of killing the killer.

The judge, jury, the lawyers, the crowd—were all now fixed upon Mitchell's trance. They were witnessing the madness of remorse layered between rage and revenge. He was inside the photograph, killing the killer again. He was angry—blind with motive, and could not control the wild, enraged call to destroy the evil in front of him. The stick men were infuriated, compelling him to move. A desire to butcher the dying man into smaller and smaller pieces sweated through him. He whirled in the smell of bloody revenge. He was caught by evil perpetuating itself—first, from the killer, then into Mitchell, and to the killer's own bloody undoing, then swirling into the cross eyes of the stick men. Mitchell saw cries for mercy leaving the killer's lips, but did not hear them.

Laurie turned to look at him. She saw a man terrified, and the contrast of her client's chaotic and confused face—among the one hundred-year-old wooden walls of order and compliance—startled her. She put her hand on his arm and tapped it, calling his name.

From somewhere among the deep and forbidding parts of his mind, where decay held stick men and rage as one, Mitchell heard Laurie calling his name. He closed his eyes, breaking the spell of the photograph.

"Would you like a glass of water?" Laurie asked.

"Please," he said.

The judge looked at Mitchell and ordered a fifteen minute recess. The crowd filed out, scratching their heads at the spectacle of Mitchell staring into the color poster. The jury too was stunned by Mitchell's reaction, and the prosecutor now questioned his choice to show the photo as evidence.

"Where did you go?" Laurie asked Mitchell privately.

"I remember now," Mitchell said. "I killed this man for killing my wife."

He finally said it—the words left his mouth. He crawled out of the photograph, and could now see himself working at the task of removing the killer's bone, hearing the man plead for his life, cutting away muscle and tendon, then falling backward into the brush—when finally the bone came loose. He put his hand to his backside, feeling the wound suffered when he landed hard on a jutting branch, cutting himself.

Laurie saw in him a face she had not seen before; it was Mitchell making a connection. She saw in him a killer, yet his reasons were that of a husband's fanatical response to evil, a father's bare-chested roar to defend, a mother's instinct to protect. She saw him as a killer, but only as far as the laws of a natural world would dictate—he had obeyed its call—and was suddenly an extension of its process, or perhaps it was the titanic battle between good and evil, where both had exacted their tolls from him, she thought.

The trial had been called to order after the fifteen minute recess. The day wore on. More photos of the killer's body were shown to the jury with a continued description of what Mitchell had done to him.

A behavioral psychiatrist was brought up to testify regarding the state of mind required to torture someone to death. Laurie did little and often nothing in the way of cross-examination. Her strategy was to go into detail about Red's brutal rape and murder. She knew the prosecution dared not venture into it, if it was to win, and put Mitchell away for murder.

As the trial unfolded, Laurie's guess that the prosecutor would not pursue events leading up to the killing of the killer, had come to pass. His goal of revealing only Mitchell's act of revenge, and not the motive for the act, was reached. His plan was intact, but not for long.

One week after the prosecution's case was heard, the defendant's attorney was called by the judge to present her case. She stood up, faced the jury, and reminded them of her opening statement, where she correctly guessed the prosecutor's spin on Mitchell's guilt. He did not go into the reason why Mitchell acted the way he did. Now she would present to the jury those reasons.

Using the prosecutor's agenda of witnesses and evidence, Laurie called to the stand the same deputy used previously. Laurie began her questioning.

She had the deputy begin at the moment he stepped into Red and Mitchell's home with the captain and the other investigators. She looked to her side. Mitchell was about to remember the reason why he acted the way he did on the night he killed the killer. She knew of no other way to secure his release. The jury had to see what he saw.

"The first thing I noticed was the sofa in the living room had been shoved out of place, and an end table had been knocked over," the deputy said.

"Go on," Laurie stated.

"As I turned to make my way up the stairs to the loft, I heard a gasp come from one of the crime scene detectives."

"Describe the gasp."

The deputy paused for a moment, deciding how.

"It sounded like a startled inhaling of air—an expression of horror."

"Objection! Speculative!" The prosecutor blurted out.

"Your Honor," Laurie replied. "I extended to the prosecutor latitude in his subjective questioning of this witness. I expect the same in return."

"Overruled," the judge said quietly.

"And as you moved up the stairs, did you hear anyone else gasp?" Laurie asked, glancing at Mitchell in an effort to monitor his reactions.

"No, I didn't," the deputy said. "But I heard other sounds."

"Like what?"

"Well, one of the CSI's was a woman. I was looking up the stairwell, and as soon as she entered into the loft area, she began to cry."

"So you heard a seasoned crime scene investigator gasp, and another start to cry," Laurie re-stated.

Mitchell started to tremble. He could not breathe under the weight of where the line of questioning was taking him, remembering his own approach to the loft. Angry stick men were everywhere, and he remembered the smell of blood coming down the stairwell, as he went up it.

"Yes, and then I heard the captain say 'oh my god'."

"And what did you say when you finally found yourself in the loft?"

"I couldn't say anything. I was dumbfounded. I couldn't get my head wrapped around what I was looking at on the bed."

"What do you mean, 'head wrapped around,' deputy?" Laurie asked.

"I mean I saw a woman's naked body on the bed, and there was blood everywhere, including bloody sock prints around the bed. It was what was on her body that I couldn't make out."

Mitchell eyes filled with water. The jury turned to face him, as his reaction to the deputy's description became apparent. He was inside his home again, discovering his wife, mutilated and dead, upon their bed.

"What was on her body, deputy?" she asked.

"Her skin," the deputy paused for a moment to clear his throat and to get his bearings. He was becoming visually upset, reflecting Mitchell's own reaction to what was being described.

At that moment Laurie produced a large, poster-sized, color photograph of Red, on the bed.

The judge closed his eyes first, rubbing his forehead at the depravity displayed in the photo. He was tempted to take the photo away from view but could not, extending to the defense attorney the same latitude as was given the prosecution.

The jury was collectively stunned. Horror passed through them as the photograph revealed the truth. Hands covered eyes and mouths. The female jury members all began to sob. The men sat in shock, as the reality of what was before them took hold, pulsing through their heads, feeling their minds run from the terror Red had endured, and then returning to face it with her, with her memory, and with Mitchell.

The prosecutor could not look at it any longer, and put his face to the ground.

From her peripheral vision Laurie saw Mitchell twitch in his chair. She knew what was about to happen and closed her eyes. She knew he was about to suffer the horror of that night again. She could feel his rage grow, and with a burst he could not contain, he rose from

386

his chair and rushed the photograph. With guards clued-in earlier, and at the ready to respond, Laurie gave the signal to subdue Mitchell. All watched as he lost his mind again. He screamed and growled, pushing with his legs one way and his arms another, trying to get to Red, to the stick men, to the photo, and rip it to shreds. The guards forced him back to his chair, hand-cuffed him to it, and then stood over him to ensure compliance.

The judge demanded order. The crowd, too far away from where the picture stood, could not get a good look at what the photograph showed in detail. Word began to pass among them about its contents. Horror struck one person first, and then another. Journalists could not believe what it was they were describing on paper.

Once order was restored, Laurie asked again; "What was on her body, deputy?"

"Holes."

Another large uproar came from the entire courtroom.

"Order!" the judge demanded, slamming his gavel on his desk.

"Where were the holes, deputy?" Laurie continued her questioning in rapid succession.

"They were on her breasts, and the opening to her vagina."

"How did they get there?"

"Besides a knife, they looked like they were made by human teeth," he said.

"Describe for the record what this photograph shows."

"For the record, the photograph shows the front parts of her breasts eaten away, the nipples are gone as are the areola," the deputy said, in as distant a voice as he could muster.

"Continue," Laurie said.

"The photo also shows the entire vaginal opening had been eaten away by human teeth," he said.

Handing the deputy a page from the coroner's report, Laurie asked the deputy to tell the jury whose teeth they were.

"The teeth marks belonged to the man that was killed on the night in question," the deputy said.

"What else does the coroner's report say regarding the victim's cause and time of death?" Laurie asked.

"It says that the victim died of slow but steady blood loss, and that she was most likely alive when the mutilations took place. She was then raped after the mutilations had occurred."

"How was that determined?"

"The coroner found bits and pieces of the victim's vagina in his pubic hairs, and inside her vaginal canal," the deputy said.

Laurie stopped for a moment and looked around the courtroom. She noticed how still it had become. The Judge had turned away from the witness and the photograph. Mitchell sat with his mouth hanging open, his face red, tears rupturing forth. Then she looked at the jury. Most of the jury could not listen any longer. Laurie looked at the prosecutor, who was visibly shaken by the photograph. She immediately went into detail about how a rope was used to hold Red tightly into place, then produced the rope in an evidence bag, stained with blood.

At once she knew the trial was over. She looked at the judge and stated that she rested her case.

The judge ordered closing statements to be made the next day at ten a.m. As the crowd left and the jury removed, Laurie sat down next to Mitchell, who was still too far gone to walk.

"I'm sorry, Mitchell, to have handled your defense this way," Laurie said. "I felt it was best to stun everyone at the same time, including you, with the details of what you saw and reacted to that night. I felt it was the best way for the jury to see how brutal a crime had been committed to your wife and how 'normal' it was for you to do what you did. Killing the killer the way you did was maniacal. After viewing his actions, it almost makes sense, or becomes a normal reaction. At least that's the way I hope the jury will see it."

Mitchell said nothing. He remained numb in the courtroom. He could not still the moving photograph of his beloved as the detail of it made its way into every cold, wet corner of his mind. He sat motionless. When he closed his eyes to shut out the color of the photograph, it made sounds instead. He put his hands to his ears and began to yell, startling the guards and Laurie, who knew what Mitchell was reliving. He stopped yelling for a moment, his eyes still closed, but the smell of the room his wife lie dead in, returned. He was losing his mind and acted so, enough to compel the guards to take him away as he fought off the memories of his wife's murder. He could not bridge the gap between her life and her death; it was only her life that he knew. It was only her touch, her breath, her driving passion, and willingness to love him, her faithfulness, and loyalty, and her ability to put the wind of life into him that he knew. He fully believed all of her was still there, still beside him, still within reach, as tangible as the elements of the earth.

The meaning of Laurie's words to him just before leaving the courtroom surfaced and Mitchell, pushed against a heartbreaking wall, mustered first another tear, and then a full, prone collapse, face down on the floor of his jail cell, in a reverberation of tortured grief, as he recognized the first slices of his life without his beloved.

Mitchell's wailing—his holding of his heart in the fires of loss—was heard throughout the halls and rooms of the courthouse, taking to hell with him, all those who recognized that finally, Mitchell knew his Red was gone.

After Mitchell left the courtroom, Laurie, sitting alone in the fading light of day, walked over to the easel that held the photo, and folded it upon itself without looking at it. It was the most horrific moment she had ever known, letting her senses comprehend the madness that destroyed Red, and how that madness possessed her client through retaliation. She returned to the table and sat down, taking a deep breath. The sunlight had now disappeared from the tall windows above the courtroom. She took another deep breath and trembled as she exhaled. Placing her face in her hands, Laurie began to cry for Red. Tears spilled through her fingers. She cried for humanity and the stain that cannot be cleaned by verdicts or laws. She cried for herself. The darkness of that night had now become a part of her. It had become a part of everyone in the room, from the judge to the aunt, whose niece had fallen prey to the killer long ago.

The collection of souls in the courtroom that had endured Mitchell's madness went to their prospective homes and lives with a burden placed squarely on the shoulders of their sleep. The photo would haunt many of them for years to come, and as the last thoughts trembled across the memories of the day, each person in the courtroom thought of Mitchell and prayed for him, for his soul, that it might rise out of the dim, damp, horrifying places it had gone.

In closing statements, the prosecutor talked only about the law and what it required as punishment for murder. He informed the jury that it was their obvious responsibility to find Mitchell guilty for killing the killer, as he was, according to the coroner's report, still alive and to no one's doubt, pleading for his life. Had he lived, a jury, perhaps even this jury, would have found him guilty of an evil beyond comprehension, and sentenced as such. To allow Mitchell to go free for taking the law into his own hands would send a message out into a law-abiding land that it is acceptable to exact personal revenge and personal justice. He ended his statement, saying that if not for any other reason, Mitchell was insane, and society was not safe with him running free.

Laurie simply asked the jury what they would have done, facing what Mitchell faced, the night he came home to the horror in his home. "Red was someone's mom," Laurie said. Mitchell suddenly remembered Red's daughter, Sian, and whether or not she still lived, and how he would tell Sian of her mother's death.

"She was someone's sister," Laurie continued. "And someone's daughter, and someone's friend. She was all of these things yet to Mitchell, Red was his wife. Red was his life, and to see her taken from him in such a manner reduced him to the very scene that unfolded before him. He became the evil that was lying outside on the ground, injured. Red's loss of life became Mitchell's loss of sanity, and the instinct to exact an eye for an eye, as justice, could not be denied. None of you could have acted any differently. In one way or another, all of you would have exacted the same end, for justice. So many applaud him for having the wherewithal to act on this senseless brutality, and put an end to it, finally. In that book of justice, he was the sword, and is to be respected for it."

With that, Laurie ended her defense of Mitchell's defenseless act. All they could do now was wait to see if the jury would have done the same.

Mitchell was not present for the final statements. He was lost to the outside world; the world without bars and ceilings. While both closing statements were heard, Mitchell was without his mind. He was aloft, floating above the world, looking about his property, taking note of the color of the earth, and the sound wind makes at the tops of trees. The sound was a constant in his life and was, as always, accompanied by the bright blue white light of the sun. It was comforting upon his face. He thought of his own, his one true love, and beheld, on the ground below him, Presley tilting an urn to the ground. Mitchell witnessed the passing of Red, as carbon, from hand to earth, to what had always been, and always would be; *the precious passing and understanding of time, and how its space, filled with love, is living.* He circled around the old oak with Presley, watching the waterless impulses of his wife fall to the ground. He remembered her kisses, her belief in him, and her love—its survival in his arms and around her waist. As the last of the ashes fell, he remembered his luck in her choosing him.

Chapter Sixty Eight

"I know what you did to my uncle," Zac said. "Who do you think you are?"

"Then you know what your uncle did to my wife," Mitchell said. "No explanation of my actions is necessary."

The word, *father,* crossed his mind again.

"You are no different than him," Zac said, looking away from Mitchell in a way that suggested the ruffian was not of the same mold as his dead uncle.

Laurie caught Zac's expression as well. She looked at Mitchell with compassion, as he stood and faced a member of the killer's family. She gave her staff a nod that it may be safe to return to the office; a physical confrontation between Mitchell and Zac may not ensue.

They continued to stand in one another's space; neither one would back down. Laurie looked at Mitchell's profile, as he peered down upon the blood relative of the man he had tortured to death. She moved her gaze toward young Zac, who stared up at Mitchell with questions in his eyes. At last Mitchell broke the silence; "Your name is Zac?"

"What do you care?"

"I don't know, I guess I need to know the name of the punk who's sucking in all the good air I breathe," Mitchell said emphatically.

"I already know yours, you freak," Zac said.

"Thank you for the compliment Zac. Why are you always down here when I am?"

"Cuz you killed the only family I had left," Zac said. "You were the last to see him alive. You have my blood on your hands. That's why I come down here when you are. I don't know why I stare. I don't want to. I can't help it."

Mitchell swallowed hard. The word, *father,* led to the growing list of odd connections he had to the young boy. *He was a blood relative of a man—a killer—who fathered Sian—who was now also Zac's deceased cousin—murdered by the same man Mitchell killed.*

Zac, who now stared passed Mitchell, was, like Mitchell, struggling to fathom the associations between them.

Mitchell breathed deeply, pressured by life's unforeseen circles. Laurie decided to leave the two alone and return to work, feeling removed once again from Mitchell's life. She observed that Mitchell's tragedy had taken on a life of its own, represented by the two souls that now stood facing one another.

"Mitchell, I'm going to leave you here with Zac," Laurie said, sadly and clumsily hugging him. Mitchell grasped Laurie's hand, squeezing it.

"Okay Laurie. I will call you later; let you know how things are going."

She turned to go. Mitchell noticed Zac move his glance finally off of him and onto Laurie, as she moved away from them.

"Listen Zac," Mitchell said. "I'm going to go back to my lunch. You can join me if you wish." Zac looked back up at Mitchell and shrugged his shoulders. "Okay," he said.

It was a long, tongue-tied walk back to where he and Laurie were having lunch. A deep breath was had by both, as they moved lunch from the bench to the tall shade of a nearby elm. A thermal shuffled both heads of hair, cooling lines of sweat found on their scalps.

"Zac," Mitchell said. "Where do you live? How do you know when I am down here?" Mitchell asked.

"I live above that record store with a friend and his mom," Zac said, pointing to the record shop on Montezuma. "I see you out that window; I can see the whole square from there."

Mitchell stopped chewing in mid-bite, and looked over at the record shop, the one in his dreams about Sian. *They were so real,* he thought, remembering Sian's walks back to her apartment from the Dinner Bell. He raised an eyebrow and looked at Zac, aghast at another circle ending where it began.

"Do you go to school?" Mitchell asked. "How old are you?"

"No, I don't go to school. I don't need the crap they feed there. There's enough crap in life already."

Mitchell looked hard at Zac, concerned that such a young boy had too hard an opinion on life. "So what are you, thirteen, maybe fourteen years old?"

"I'm thirteen. I don't have time for school; I've got to make a living. So far the truancy officer hasn't found me. I work at the Dinner Bell as a busboy and dishwasher. That's where I found out who you were. Everyone talks about you, especially when you drive by. There are two old-timers who constantly bicker about you. One says that you are his hero; the other says you belong in jail. Everyone looks when you drive by in that piece of shit pickup truck of yours. No one there knows that the man you killed is my uncle. *No one!* I'd like to keep it that way."

"Yeah, sure," Mitchell said, reeling again through the dreams and visions of Sian. "No one needs to know. You've got quite the record of trouble-making over there you know (Mitchell pointed at the court house). Are you hungry?" Mitchell said, offering the boy apple slices with almond butter. Zac reluctantly took a couple and snapped them in his mouth, gregariously eating both slices, licking the almond butter from the roof of his mouth. Mitchell enjoyed the spectacle.

"Where are your parents?" Mitchell asked.

"I'm not sure . . . but I think they might have been killed by my uncle." Zac's voice broke. "I miss my mom . . . my dad too but mostly I miss her . . . she made everything okay."

"Sorry to hear it . . . ,"

"I can't say for sure," Zac said. "It happened long ago, when I was very young. They were there one day, and then gone the next. My uncle grabbed me, and moved us out here from New Jersey, then disappeared. My friend's mom took me in, and I help out by giving her my pay check and tips from the waitresses."

Mitchell leaned his head back against the tree. He closed his eyes and felt the cool sunlight penetrate his eye lids. He thought of the young boy sitting beside him sharing his lunch. *He has no family,* he thought, *he has no father.* Without going into too much detail mentally, Mitchell was thinking that Zac could use some guidance in his life.

Zac leaned his head back too. It dawned on him suddenly, instinctually, that the person sitting next to him was not going to hurt him; there was something in Mitchell that ran contrary to the gossip flying at the Dinner Bell.

The great, old American elm sensed the presence of two human souls leaning against its trunk; souls encountering a season of change. Through this understanding, the tree then noticed the red-headed, white-winged grace of an angel among its branches, looking down upon the man and the boy, ushering in the winds of change, blowing fallen leaves skyward.

Chapter Sixty Nine

LAURIE and the prosecutor gazed at the members of the Jury. Mitchell's gaze was set upon the azure glass ceiling that could be seen out the large windows high above his head.

The judge conferred with the bailiff and deputies in attendance, instructing them to watch the defendant carefully as the verdict was read. He pounded the gavel aggressively, and spoke directly to the entire courtroom.

"As this verdict is read in my courtroom, I expect each and every one of you to respect the decision that is made here today. I will not tolerate any outbursts from anyone, including the press."

He turned his attention then to the jury.

"Has the jury reached a verdict?"

"Yes we have your Honor," the jury foreman stated.

"Bailiff," the judge said, pointing to the foreman.

The bailiff handed the verdict to the judge, and then waited.

Laurie looked at Mitchell. He was oblivious to the formal procedures taking place—ones that would spell out the remainder of his life. His focus remained on the azure wash high overhead—on a journey back to a memory of himself as a boy—a thermal had lifted his hair and his spirit skyward—rising with the wind.

The judge looked at Mitchell. He saw the defendant slowly smile, as the memory of his boyhood days blossomed. The judge read the verdict and without emotion, returned it to the jury foreman.

Laurie motioned for Mitchell to stand, following her example. She swayed a moment as she did so; she had not slept for the two nights previous.

Mitchell stood up, but could not connect to the moment before him. He was being lifted skyward. He saw for the first time a faint outline of life forming in the firmament. It captured him. The vision astonished him. He faced the light squarely, unable to hear any of the activity in the courtroom; he had only enough room in his senses for what he saw out the windows. It was on the other side. The vision smiled as it moved closer to him. It was a face he knew, one that he thought he would never see again, yet there she was.

"What say you—on the charge of second degree murder?" the judge asked the foreman.

The foreman cleared his throat. He faced Mitchell, and was stunned to see tears of joy running down Mitchell's face. The other members of the jury looked on as well, each reacting in their hearts, as they watched Mitchell move on and out from the dark days of his recent past.

The judge cocked his head sideways to get a glimpse of what Mitchell was smiling at. Laurie looked too, not understanding her client's apparent release from the burdens of an evil world. The moment lingered longer, as everyone in the courtroom strained to see what Mitchell saw.

Clearing his throat again, the foreman said: "We the jury find the defendant . . ." He paused for a half a second, wondering how Mitchell knew what he was about to say; ". . . not guilty."

Laurie fell forward on the desk, stunned that her defense had worked. The judge looked on, past the crowded courtroom, to his scales of justice, and nodded his head in formal agreement. The prosecutor remained seated, stunned too that the vicious attack by the defendant was not punished. The crowd did not contain itself, and roared at the announcement of Mitchell's innocence.

Mitchell remained focused on the face and hair flowing free among the elements of the beyond. It was his beloved. She smiled at Mitchell, releasing him from his black home—his soul from its ache. She had returned to him as the love of his life, to find a home in his heart again. There were no more devils. There was no more dust. He had been lifted by her, shining toward him, when he needed her most. She had come back to his side, to his hope, and she was now his again.

Laurie put her hand on his. He turned his tear-soaked face to Laurie, then to the judge and jury. He could not speak. His wet face communicated to the formal members of the courtroom his gratitude for finding reason and justice in his actions when his heart broke that night.

The prosecutor left without a word to Laurie. She helped Mitchell off his chair, and they walked out together. The four giant walls of the courtroom released him, as he moved through the large wooden doors. Turning left, they walked outside into the light of day. Waiting for them was the sun, and shade, and a breeze that cooled Mitchell's hot face, as his tears dried. Presley came forward out of the crowd and hugged his lifelong friend. Mitchell put his hands on his friend's face in a gesture of thanks.

Mitchell searched for and found his beloved in the roofless and windowless expanse above him. She stayed with him. As he moved, so did she. He had been set free, both physically and spiritually. She remembered him. He loved her without measure.

In this ecstatic state he turned toward Laurie, and suddenly realized his life had been saved through her interpretation of the night he killed the killer. He was indebted to her and found that saying goodbye to her would be odd—he had spent so much time with her. She looked deeply into Mitchell's eyes. The revenge killing of his wife's murderer was a noble act in her heart. In many dark hours, hunkered over evidence and photographs, Laurie slowly aligned her heart to his actions, making them, to her, the only thing he could have done—in the face of what was done to Red. She believed that what he did was just, and Laurie honored her beliefs by defending Mitchell's actions in a court of law. He put her face in his hands too. She was taken by his gentleness. He pulled her forehead close to his lips, kissed it in heartfelt thanks, then quietly said "goodbye."

ଛ୬

Mitchell got in Presley's car, ready to leave behind the time spent as a prisoner and defendant in the Yavapai County Courthouse.

"You have always been there for me," Mitchell said. "At every turn you show up to escort me around the next bend in my life, without judgment, without delay, and without advice, you are just there, as my friend."

Presley looked at him. "What would you like to do right now," he asked.

"I think it's time to go home," Mitchell said.

The sense of 'full-circle' followed Mitchell as they drove from downtown Prescott to the driveway leading up to Mitchell and Red's cabin. Presley stopped the car at the base and the friends got out. Mitchell looked around the very familiar surroundings. He noted the absence of stick men.

"I think I'd like to do this alone," Mitchell said.

"Okay. If you need anything just give me a call."

Presley took a good look at his old friend, sizing up his state of mind. There was no doubt that the trek up the driveway, into the yard where he killed the killer and then into the home where his wife died, would be hard for Mitchell. His gut told him Mitchell would be okay. They shook hands, and then hugged.

"You'll need this," Presley said, handing Mitchell the new key to his home. "Everything is as it was before that night. There is no sign of anything anywhere, even outside."

Mitchell looked at Presley. A hard tear appeared in Mitchell's eye.

"Presley," Mitchell said. "Again, thanks for always being there. Thanks for always being my friend."

"Yea, sure, no problem, you don't have to keep sayin' that," Presley said, in an awkward yet sincere fashion. He walked back to his car and retrieved a box containing what Mitchell recognized immediately as the urn that held Red's ashes, saying "this is yours too."

Each set of hands trembled as the box was passed from one to the other. Mitchell turned to face the old oak. Presley closed his eyes. For a moment life over-whelmed the two men. With deep breaths, each put the moment inside their minds.

"This too," Presley said, reaching into his pants pocket for the pocket watch that contained a small portion of Red's ashes.

"What is this, Presley?"

"I don't know, it just came to me. It's an old watch, at least as old as when our fathers were young. My dad collects these things, and he gave me this one, and others, a long time ago. I thought you'd like to have it, to keep with you, to keep Red with you, as a way to always remember the time you spent together."

Through more trembling hands, Presley showed Mitchell the opening that contained Red's ashes, and how to close it and lock it so they would always be kept safe.

Mitchell saw in his friend something rare in the realm of friendship; Presley had always accepted Mitchell and Red, and could see that his friend was glad the couple had found one another so long ago.

It was time for Presley to go and in their parting, they shook hands one more time. Presley got into his car and pulled away. Mitchell watched him leave. He watched the dust on FR 63 rise, then settle around contrasts of shadow and light thrown long by the setting sun.

Mitchell stood silently, listening to the stillness of his surroundings. He looked down at his feet and then turned them toward the driveway. He took one step toward it and stopped, setting the box containing the urn on the ground, next to their mailbox. Mitchell was being pulled by the flow of water nearby. Walking toward the Hassayampa, he found the spot were he wrote his last words in his journal about his father. He looked above for signs of his beloved. She was there, wrapped in complete joy.

But Mitchell could not rise up to meet her. Without warning black ice began to pour through his veins, and at once he collapsed down onto his knees, falling forward, face first into the rocky bank of the river. A sudden realization—a comprehension so vicious in its form and meaning shuddered through him, making him feel as if he were falling into hell itself. He looked skyward and found her still there, still smiling, reaching out for him, wanting him to know the joy she knew. But Mitchell still could not rise up to meet her. He pushed himself upright, and put his face in his hands, anguishing. Rifling through him, with each beat of his heart, was a new grip on a timeline: *he turned back to finish his thoughts—Red was attacked—he would have saved her*—shredded through him. A horrific cry of madness ensued from his guts. The silence of survival in the wild forest came forward to acknowledge a cruel twist of fate—one where learning a little more about himself that night was at the cost of loosing his Red. *I'm sorry Red,* blasted through him as he looked up to behold the smile of an angel. *I'm sorry I turned around. Oh God Red,* his mind silently screamed, as he put his face back into his hands. Screaming through them he yelled, "I'm sorry . . . I'm sorry Red. Please come back . . . come back . . . come home . . . please come home to me." He looked up. She remained above him in her spirit world, and through her eyes he saw her love and her acceptance of life unfolding as it did. Through her eyes he heard the wisdom of her world; *brutality and evil have no quarter here my love, how could you have known. We all trust the day ahead. We, all of us, hope for the best, and look my love, it has come true. I know no pain here. Our heaven is real, and reflects what we have known in our lives, and this place where I am has come because of who we were as husband and wife.*

Mitchell rolled onto his back. There again, as constant, as eternal as the horizon, floated the image of Red, still glowing with joy. Her presence shifted then stopped, as if to encourage Mitchell to rise to his feet and follow her home.

He did. He followed her face home, and knew that he could not walk up the drive without her. The movement of color through invisible waves, changing unseen light into shapes resembling Red's face told him she was still there with him. Mitchell saw her freckled skin, her perfect nose, her kind brows, thin and perfect above her eyes—eyes that smiled at him. It was a face that moved beyond any earthly hold of pain or evil. Wise and compassionate, Red's face came close to his. The pull to follow her, to reach up to her place in the universe, longing for what was now hers, quivered in his hands.

Mitchell took another step toward the house and, when doing so, he saw again Red move forward with him, then ahead to the A-frame abode that was her earth-bound home. As he came upon the clearing, flashes of the night he killed the killer filtered his view, but for only a moment. Instead of pain or rage, the flashes, those short, sharp creeping memories of madness, now lead to other thoughts; new sensations of peace, not fully understood. Looking up, he saw Red's face surrounding the entire cabin. *Was your murder and what I did in response settled?* He asked her out loud. She smiled; beholding a beautiful universe beyond the reach of evil. For the first time he allowed himself the notion that he did the right thing, not because a jury of his peers said he did, but because in his heart he honored the life of his wife. It did not bring her back to him, but killing the killer told her memory that she was loved. He understood that while she endured the cold blades of cutting steel and depravity sinking into her, she questioned her worth as a human being. Justice gave her the answer. Mitchell's actions told her, as she left her tortured physical form, that the man she loved, loved her; that her integrity and deep belief in a good and natural world would not die with her. These notions filled him as he walked toward the cabin. He knew that what he did as justice kept her spirit at his side, and as he climbed the stairs to the main floor, he knew in his heart that he had honored her life; that he was loyal to the love they held. There was now in him no further remorse for his actions, only the sickening associations to the darkest sides of human existence. He had been called to answer an injustice with justice, to balance the cause and call of paradox, and found through his actions the death of his wife come full circle in symbol and worth, just as his hope in a the blue heaven above, when he was a boy, came full circle in the form and breathing of his beloved Red, as a man.

He walked up the second flight of stairs to the loft. The afternoon light filtered through the prism he had put at the apex of the ceiling years ago. Rainbows were all around. They were on his face and in his eyes as starlight, and they moved freely over their bed when he looked at it for the first time. Their dancing about charmed the spirit of Red, and she joined her husband on the bed when he sat down upon it for the first time. All evidence of the horror was gone. It was spotless and renewed.

Mitchell put his back on the bed and the warm memories of his wife's presence next to him filled him with tears. *How lucky I was.* He closed his eyes, pushing tears out, feeling the heat of his emotion in them as they rolled down his face. *How could living become such a treacherous thing?*

At once, Mitchell heard an answer, and in that answer was the soft, brush-like feel of Red's fingers wiping tears away from his face.

We are a part of a universe that put what happened to me, and my killer, in motion billions of years ago, were the words Mitchell heard as the familiar love and grace in her fingertips brushed the hair on his head.

The Cosmos asks 'what will you do now?' Her voice continued. *I have traveled the length of it, Mitchell, and the question is universal.*

Mitchell looked up and the ceiling, pointing to the heavens above, as a rainbow flashed across his eyes. His staring took him beyond the roof of his home.

I, too, have seen universal things, Red, Mitchell stated in mind. *The blue sky has always been the contrast to your red hair, and here you remain, complete in memory, and in my faith for the love I feel for you.*

Red looked at Mitchell with the innocent ages as her source of peace and said; *then you understand what is true; the only way to keep your love alive is to stir it forward.*

Chapter Seventy

"YOU'RE gonna go live with that sick fuck after all I done for you? I took you in and now you're gonna shame me and leave us high and dry? " was the grilling Zac got from his friend's mom, when he informed her of his decision to take Mitchell up on his offer. He accepted Mitchell's terms: paying his own way, resuming his education, following the rules, treating everything there with respect, and to never disobey Mitchell. He was to do what he was told. Only after an appropriate amount of time, and only then, would Mitchell show him what respect he may have earned. Rigorous honesty would be the foundation for which their relationship would be built, as would zero tolerance for behavior that resembled anything cruel.

Mitchell stood at the door of the apartment above the record store and stared at the woman who damned him. Mitchell cocked an eyebrow while cornering a smile. "Zac," he said, "you ready? You got everything?" He remembered his dream of Sian in the shower, which was visible behind the woman.

"Yeah, I am," Zac said. "I've got everything."

"You'll be just like him," the woman cried. Fear poured from her eyes as she took in Mitchell's gazing through her. "People will feel sorry for you, especially when I tell them who you really are," she threatened. Zac looked at his friend in dismay, who had betrayed his secret to his mother.

Mitchell looked at the friend. "You are an untrustworthy wretch," he said. "If anything happens to Zac because of this betrayal, from either of you, you will have me to answer to." The friend hung his head, looking at the ground in silence. Mitchell observed the ever-present darkness of humanity before him; the fear of fear, and the treachery of false friendship.

The memory of Sian in the shower became another memory of his beloved. He looked out a window at the end of the apartment's entryway, at the blue sky. He missed her so.

You are doing a good thing, he heard her say, as the melding of Red's perpetual youth and beauty in Sian had became part of the eternal memory of his wife. He looked at Zac, and viewed paradox in its full glory; his own life coming around again, in the form of leadership in the young boy's life.

Thoughts of his father on the Hassayampa came and went. He motioned for Zac to go, and through what was now background noise coming from the fear inside the apartment, the man and the boy descended the stairs, and made their way back to Mitchell's old truck. Mitchell looked across Montezuma Street toward the courthouse and saw Laurie waving at him through a courthouse window. Both Mitchell and Zac waived back. The rusted steel doors clanked shut; the strike of steel on steel echoing up and down Whiskey Row, causing some to turn and observe the town nut, and a town punk, drive away together. The old timers Jess and Hartley, from the Dinner Bell were among them, each standing for some time staring, as the truck moved up the hill a half mile south, turning as it reached the apex, toward White Spar Road, and points south and west of the courthouse square.

Chapter Seventy One

MITCHELL sat up on the bed and when doing so, his body moved into the awareness that he was alone. Physically, he was deeply disturbed that although he could see, and hear her, he could not touch her. She was spirit. She had become the energy of love, the outline and the memory of human goodness. She rose with the sun, had graced the sky, and would sit, he hoped, with the moonlight beside his dreams and longings at night.

Yet she was not there. He stood up, traveled back down the stairs to the kitchen, turned on the light, and observed how it illuminated the places where she lived. He fixed a sandwich and poured a soda over ice. These simple tasks remained sources of pain for him.

Out on the front porch, the view presented an ominous dusk—he would be spending his first night alone in their cabin.

The sun set quietly through the trees. Music played. All the doors and windows were open to the coming night. The home began to delicately glow in different areas, as the arc of a day passing, cut through the base of the trees in the horizon.

The evening sprang to life through the startling sound of Mitchell's phone ringing in the kitchen. At first he was reluctant to answer it, wondering who it might be. He wanted to be alone, to feel lonely, and face the feeling of missing his wife. As the phone continued to ring, Heart's "Love Alive," began to play. Among the sounds of singer and guitar, the phone answering machine picked up the call and Mitchell heard Laurie's voice leaving a message.

"Mitchell," Laurie said. "This is Laurie. I was thinking of you. I'm not sure if you are home. I watched you leave today. Thank you for waving goodbye to me. I will miss having you as a part of my day and I am glad this nightmare is passing for you. Well, most of it anyway. Listen, if you'd ever like to have lunch, call me. I hope that your first night out of the courthouse will go well. Call me. Bye."

Laurie's voice, he realized for the first time, was an anchor for him during his incarceration. That was odd too. Red had been his anchor and his steam at the same time. It was Red's voice that had encouraged him through the years. It was her wise heart that had counseled and consoled him. It was Red that held him above her own existence, and it was Red who was honored by Mitchell for doing so. She was his wife in every traditional sense of the word, giving him command of their home, giving him the traditional role of husband and head of their house.

That's right Mitchell, he said to himself, *she* gave *you those things.*

Not one day passed in all their years together that he did not hear an offer for him to make love to her. That fact was uncanny. When done, when laying on his back in complete physical and spiritual exhaustion, she would often hear him ask the cosmos; *what is this life I have been given, where, in the middle of the afternoon of every day, I am offered the pleasures of her heart and its vessel?*

Even on this night, his first alone, he still marveled at her desire to please him. He knew that such a woman was matchless in the world, as a loving and faithful wife. Physically, Mitchell knew he was nothing special, average looks and build. Paradoxically, Red was a physical marvel and could have had anyone, yet she chose him, and by doing so, gave him the all-encompassing love that turned a boy into a man, the kind of man that then becomes irresistible to a loving and faithful wife. Red knew the secrets of being that kind of wife. He scratched his head in marvel of the cosmos pointing its finger at him when Red came through the server isle at the Olive Garden so many years ago.

Hearing Laurie's voice was an odd moment indeed. For her to care about how his first night at home would go, after seeing in colorful detail what he was capable of, surprised Mitchell.

Mitchell stood up from where he sat on the porch and looked out at his property and at the tall stands of wood beyond and found a peace he was not expecting. He looked out at the oak on the edge of the clearing and found at its base the ashes of his beloved. He could not see them, but could feel their call for him to remain in motion in his life. Red said this. She told him not to bring the past or future to bear on any more exhales or inhales. *No more fear,* Mitchell thought. He had heard it all his life; in AA meetings, in the huddles at football games, from the mouths and actions of his friends at the waterhole, in the retribution of Red's life.

He moved inside closing and locking the door behind him, shutting down the living room and kitchen windows, then walked upstairs to his bedroom. Pulling the covers back to lie down, he closed his eyes to find Red right next to him. He put his arms around her and instantly fell asleep, not moving once for the next twelve hours.

Chapter Seventy Two

MITCHELL and Zac pulled up to the open area in front of the A-frame cabin. Zac did not know, as he got out of the truck, that he walked on the ground that held his family's blood. Mitchell would keep it that way. Zac, with a back pack hanging over his shoulders, walked quietly out into the middle of the property and took a long look around. It was odd for Mitchell to witness this. Zac reminded him of his own childhood, and as each day progressed, that notion hung truer in the air.

He felt their lives were the flip side of the same coin . . . of many coins. Youth on one side, experience on the other. Anger—one side, wisdom—the other. Leadership—chaos. Boundaries—cruelty. He saw now that the good side of this collection of coins would be handed down and would replace generational addiction and malice. From a man to a boy, from a father to a son, Mitchell would make the world a better place by bequeathing to Zac, time-honed character. It made sense to Mitchell that such an inheritance was being passed on the banks of the Hassayampa with his youthful self, and his own father, as witnesses. Mitchell saw his placement in Zac's young life as the correction the universe was looking for, and could comprehend further why his life had unfolded as it did.

"C'mon Zac," Mitchell said. "Let's get you moved in and squared away. I've got a room behind the kitchen for you to move into. There is some work to be done. We need to move storage boxes down to the basement and get you organized."

Zac looked at Mitchell and found it a hard moment to feel the hand of discipline in his life. He had handed his life over to Mitchell, and was not really sure why he did. From instinct it was suggested and Zac acted on it. He knew it would be good, but could not nail down just what 'good' was. With difficulty, Zac put one foot in front of the other and proceeded to meet Mitchell at the side entrance of the home.

Mitchell stopped him at the threshold by laying his hand on Zac's shoulder. "This is my sacred home, Zac," he said. "It will not be tarnished by cruelty or deceit. This is your sanctuary from your lot in life, just as it became mine. The woman who lived here and loved me is still here. She, too, welcomes you and you will honor her in both action and thought for she suffered far too much the wickedness that, unfortunately, is your heritage. In time, that will change. You must understand that by walking through this door you are leaving this heritage behind."

Zac looked up at Mitchell. He understood every word. Mitchell could see the comprehension in his eyes, as he did on the courthouse lawn. Mitchell again saw himself in Zac, and knew that he was to raise the boy as his own, and to lead him into a character-driven life.

Chapter Seventy Three

HE was worn at times. The transition from Red's husband to the quiet of his life after her death was deafening. He did his best to cook for himself, but the combinations, tried and true throughout Red's life, of herbs and spices, of details in how to cook things, of shopping at the grocery store, of planning, he had not an inkling. She had spoiled him and he could not seem to get it right in the kitchen no matter how he tried. He could not duplicate how things tasted when she made them, when she brought them to him, waiting on him as if he were a king.

Mitchell sighed. She was gone; yet there still. It was confusing. Her things, things that he had bought for her over the years, remained untouched. He would often take a piece of clothing with him to bed or to the river after he had resumed his hikes. Her smell was found throughout the home and was connected to so many parts of his day. Time had diminished nothing. In the kitchen, it would be oregano that would put her presence in the sunlight. He would play the great Broadway songs and classics that grew on Mitchell over the years— putting her life on recollection road—as the many productions and plays she was a part of—took center stage on the floor of their home.

Sleeping alone was the hardest and coldest change of all. The nights among the woods sat quietly around Mitchell's soul at night, yet loneliness had not taken its toll. He listened to his wife when she encouraged him to move, to breathe, to write, and reclaim what was his to reclaim. He had done so, and found that his sleeping at night was becoming more and more a thing of normalcy rather than awkwardness. Music remained a mainstay in his day. The great rock-n-roll that he had grown up with—spurred him on.

It was well into the second half of Mitchell's morning when he heard a car pull up into the area in front of his cabin. It was a BMW or Mercedes, Mitchell couldn't tell which, but what impressed him about the car was how out of place it looked next to his old pickup truck. The driver's side door popped open and Laurie appeared, in full corporate dress.

"Hello, Mitchell," Laurie said. "You're alive!" she stated emphatically.

"Yes . . . uh, sorry I didn't call you back," Mitchell paused, having all but forgotten about the call. "I . . . uh . . . I've been getting things organized around here, and . . . well . . . uh . . . would you like to come up for a moment?"

"Are you sure?" Laurie questioned, unsure of her un-announced presence.

"Yeah . . . sure . . . it's right there, around the side of the house."

"Oh, okay," Laurie said.

Mitchell stood at the top of the stairs that led from the printing studio to the main floor.

"That's it . . . this way."

Laurie skipped up the stairs rather athletically.

"Do you really use all that stuff down there?" Laurie asked, as she made her way onto the main floor.

"Let's see," Mitchell said. "How does the saying go? I use some of the equipment all of the time but not all of the equipment all of the time . . . something like that," he said, half smiling. Mitchell had shut the business down after Red's passing.

Laurie took note how interesting it was to see Mitchell show any sign of a personality. She could only remember him under the spell of murder and its aftermath. She also took a quick note of how tidy everything looked to her. She was not sure what to expect, especially from one as dark-hearted and mysterious as Mitchell. She got the feeling that everything was quite normal with him.

He asked her to sit down and if he could get her anything to drink. Laurie found her way around the stairwell railing to the large sofa that faced the fire place. Looking around nervously, she picked up the first book she could see, realizing it was the same book Mitchell had asked her to read during one of their exchanges at the jail.

"What kind of book is this?"

"It's a journal, written by the old man who owned this place before us," Mitchell said. "It's the book I asked you to read."

"I remember," Laurie said with interest. She opened it and read a sample of the old man's text. "It has a religious tone to it, doesn't it?"

"Yea," Mitchell said with earnest. "More of a spiritual tone—he talks to God all the way through it."

"About what?"

"About everything I guess."

"For example?" Laurie pressed.

"Well, friendship for one," Mitchell said, reaching for the book. She passed it to him, and he quickly thumbed his way to the page that held a discussion between the Sea Man and God about friendship. He read:

> *"A friend," the Sea Man said to God, "was a wife I could trust. Tested by time and by space, a friend has a heart that has known mine. Tested by changes in paradigm and paradox, a friend was a soul connected to mine through an un-ending grace. Tested by the petty and mundane, my friend, my wife, saw beyond the obvious, and delivered a moment of reprieve when it was called for."*

Laurie cocked her head sidewise and listened intently. She watched Mitchell's mouth move with directness in delivery and understanding of words in sentences. Again—an odd change from an introverted murderer silent and deadly in his own thoughts. To see him show expression as he did the day his verdict was read was a stark contrast to the depressed jail resident—one who would sing songs to himself.

He stopped reading the journal while letting the thoughts of friendship linger a moment longer. Mitchell looked at his visitor and realized for the first time that she was an attractive woman.

They had come upon an odd moment when their presence to one another would change. The moment would find Mitchell reaching out to be of service to her in some fashion, and it would find her accepting whatever offer was to come from Mitchell. The dynamic of their relationship was struggling to cross over from professional to personal—a clumsy endeavor for both of them.

"Would you like some coffee or something to drink?" Mitchell asked. "My well water is wonderful."

"Water sounds great."

"So what brings you out this way Laurie?"

"Well, Mitchell, you," Laurie said matter-of-factly. "You fell off the face of the earth after the trial. I wanted to make sure you were alive."

Mitchell smiled at her, disarming her concern.

"I'm still alive. I've been trying to get my affairs in order. It's hard sometimes. Red is still here, Laurie. In so many ways I can sense her presence."

Laurie again watched with surprise how well Mitchell communicated feeling.

"It was Red that I saw right before the verdict was read," Mitchell said.

Laurie thought back to that moment in the courtroom, remembering her own confusion in the volcano of emotion emanating from Mitchell. He seemed to know what his fate was before it was read to him.

"You saw her?"

"Yes, I saw her coming toward me as I looked out the tall windows in the courtroom. It was the first time I remember seeing her face since the night she died. She was moving toward me and kept saying to keep my heart alive with love, and to keep my breath moving deeply through me. She was saving me from drowning in the ugliness of that night. She reached out and lifted me above the bottom I had fallen into, like she had done so many times before in my life. Regardless of the verdict, I was free of my anger over losing her, as long as I could see her as she had become. She was beautiful, Laurie. Her hair sat deep red against the crystal clear blue sky. Her eyes calmed me. I was gazing into the heart of peace. I was safe from the fates designed by murderers and juries, of prosecutors and judges. Her appearance out the window gave me the same sense of love and acceptance that I have always had from her. It was her love that saved me that day and, with or without the jury's permission, her love had set my heart free yet again . . . and . . . "

Laurie sat mesmerized by Mitchell. She had no idea he was capable of such thoughts, and she realized that she had known only that part of him that responded to evil.

"You must miss her so," she said, with a small tear in her eye.

"The first night was the worst. So much of her is still here in so many ways. Making the switch from her physical presence to her spiritual and emotional presence as memory is tough. When she is near spiritually, I will tear-up, right in the middle of another thought or errand. Boom. There I am crying for no reason. It has been a touch embarrassing at times. I will order a cheeseburger with a tear in my eye."

"You think that her spirit is here with you?"

"I feel her near. She is very, very happy. In dreams at night or in my own passing thoughts, she has told me she knows peace beyond measure. She wants me to feel it too. I tell her that I'm happy she has found it. She tells me it can be mine too. I'm not sure exactly how it's done, but believe me, I do try to find it."

"I have read so many books about this very thing," Laurie said supportively. "They say that a deep loving connection cannot be broken, even by death. Tell me more."

"Well, I don't know what else to say," Mitchell said. "I feel I may be boring you with this. I do have two more passages from the old man's book that help to describe what I had with Red, and what seems to remain because of the great love we shared."

Mitchell opened up the journal and read two separate passages the old man had written about his own love:

> God said, "it was your truth Sea
> Man, it was what you looked for; your life was
> made of the moments that love gave you to live.
> Your life was set with the highest kind of
> existence, when at once you knew who you were,
> and what love was, and you beheld those
> moments under the golden sun, while she waited
> for you at the hearth she had made for you."

"And the second one:"

> The Sea Man replied: "She was all I
> could hope for and I, an old man, would finally

know how to remain grateful for the simple
understanding of who she was as God's
intention in my life.

> *She was my blessing, my return road.*
> *She was my living and breathing, thinking and*
> *playing, cooking and love-making womb. I was*
> *wrapped up by her. I was given a key from the*
> *Maker of Life to a gate that opened up to*
> *God's ultimate gift; our own Garden of Eden.*

> *You took her, and placed her among*
> *the heavenly bodies of an early December*
> *morning, as the waning crescent, floating*
> *through the arcing orbits of Venus and*
> *Mercury, and I know now of no greater*
> *inequity, no greater emptiness, than your*
> *expanding universe."*

Mitchell closed the journal stating: "He lost his wife, too."

"It's very sad and beautiful. Where'd you find it again?"

"Right here," Mitchell said, tapping on the floor of the living room. "I found it when I was insulating the ceiling in the basement below. It was placed up between the joists. When I pulled it out, my face was covered with the dust that collected on it over the years."

"Who is the Sea Man?" Laurie asked.

"I'm guessing it was the owner of this home before us," Mitchell said. "This is a strange coincidence in itself. When Red and I followed the 'for sale' sign up to the front yard, he walked out and greeted us heartily. I ultimately recognized him from another chance meeting decades earlier in another chapter of my life. I still find both of these chance meetings very serendipitous. And now, to find a journal he may have written, one that I refer to for advice, only adds to the intrigue of who this man was."

"What was the chance meeting from earlier in your life?" Laurie asked.

"I was hitchhiking up to a trail I lived near when he picked me up. I wanted to hike to the summit of San Gorgonio Mountain, to try and find a solution to a problem I was having. I believe the old man that we bought this home from was the same man who gave me a lift to the trailhead, and who was there when I returned from my overnight stay at the summit. He asked me, upon my return, if I had found what I was looking for. It was the question that needed to be asked, at that precise moment in my life. It was the one question that needed an answer. Looking back, I believe he asked me that question so that I would find the answer that love is all that any of us are looking for. We all want to be loved."

"I'm surprised to be meeting *you* for the first time. I'd no idea, no clue who you are, and I'm pleasantly surprised by what I see and hear today."

"Thank you Laurie, for your kind words," Mitchell said. "Can I make you something for lunch? You must be hungry."

"No, thank you, Mitchell" Laurie said. "I keep my girlish figure by keeping the calorie consumption down."

He noted that Laurie had come out to see him for another reason other than the one she stated upon her arrival. He could feel the energy she was giving to him. She wanted to change the dynamics of their relationship. She wanted more.

A moment of awkwardness hung between them. Mitchell did not want another woman in his life. Laurie could feel the hesitation and quickly made a comment about needing to get back to work, and then asked:

"Have you ever been to The Rose?"

"I have heard of it, never been," Mitchell said.

"Would you like to meet me there for lunch?"

Mitchell answered awkwardly, ". . . oh, that's very nice of you to suggest, but, I'm sorry, I just can't, I'm still love and miss my Red, and can't seem to lessen what is in my heart, I'm sorry Laurie, I'm just not there yet."

"Okay, I understand completely. I thought it would be nice to do, but no problem, I can see that you are, and will probably always feel the way you do about your wife," Laurie said with a smile in her voice. "I will call you in a couple of months to see how you are doing."

"Okay. Laurie, I want to thank you again for all you've done for me, and for what you did as my attorney, and for checking up on me. I know I'm a lousy prospect, and a guy like me doesn't deserve to have lunch with a gal like you. I appreciate you asking me very much."

"You sure?"

"Yeah . . . I'd be a terrible date . . . all those people looking at us, wondering about your sanity, or if I'm in trouble again."

Laurie got up to go. "Answer your phone, next time I call, okay?"

"I will," Mitchell said, smiling at her.

He walked her downstairs, to her car, opened the door for her and she got in. Mitchell smiled at her and waved goodbye, as she drove away.

What does she want with me? He thought, and headed back up stairs to the quiet world where he lived with his Red.

Mitchell started thinking about de Benneville Pines. A notion of his life was returning, taking root in the quiet moments of his day; that despite the movement of treachery through his life, there was still a call to breathe, and to live, fully, charging through him. Suddenly, the raging, willful beat of The Who's "Live at Leeds," filled his mind. He walked briskly to the stereo and the shelves containing his vinyl. Alphabetically he searched for the plain brown wrapping that was to him iconic of the album. Finding it, he quickly placed the album on the turntable, clicked the ancient remote, and watched with silent appreciation the tone arm and needle alight onto the edge of the record. It crackled and snapped in its familiar and reassuring way. First he heard the drums, then the guitars, then the voice of his youth blast through the large A-framed room. The music rose with the heat and adrenalin flowing through his blood. He grabbed his air-guitar, the same one that made Red smile at him with admiration for the rare and real emotion that rock and roll music pushed through him. He remembered her as the only woman in his life that never judged him, that accepted him as he was. It was Red. She made him feel young everyday. She made him feel like a prince. She just watched him dance, and loved him for his raw and unrehearsed claim on his soul. On this night he again lost himself in a wild spell of rhythm found in the songs "My Generation," and "Magic Bus."

As the songs played themselves out, through the front door and along the tree tops, Mitchell noted the goose bumps that would come and go on his arms and legs. The music defined him still, after all of these years. He was grateful to Red for not letting him forget this. That was her great gift to him. Her love brought him nearer to himself. *What kind of wonderful life did I get to live with her,* he thought as the then twenty-year-old members of the band pulled off the perfect play of a young man's rebellious yell. He still felt it, after all these years, he still felt like a young man. *Red had done this,* he thought. *She had loved me so well that all of my life had been given back to me.*

The needle alighted gently off the record. He lifted the vinyl plate up from the turn table and slid it back to the sleeve, being careful not to disturb the paperwork that was a part of the album's original promotion. He remembered the day as a young boy purchasing the album from Tower Records, and how excited he was when, for a moment, he believed he had scored misplaced documents belonging to the band.

He reassembled the album, put it back in its place on the shelf and recalled how Red teased him about his careful qualities regarding the vinyl and stereo.

The memory clipped him at his knees and he fell to the floor in painful longing. He rolled over to his back, shocked at the intensity of his yearning to have her again. Slowly, he turned his head toward the front of the room, looking out the tall windows to the heavens. At that moment he saw Red saying:

> *No more pain my love, no more longing.*
>
> *I am truly with you, in your heart, in your breath.*
>
> *In your forward motion living your life.*
>
> *I am the love you feel, the colors you see.*
>
> *I am the scents of spirit and the changing melodies of the wind.*
>
> *I am what you made me.*
>
> *I am the white blinding honor of love.*
>
> *I am these things because of who you are.*
>
> *Rise my love, let the crumbling weight of loss be no more.*
>
> *Let my memory lift you into your day.*

Let my love set you tall with the pines.

I am the time and space you have left to live.

Live them my love, live them fully.

Live them without remorse, without regret.

It is your birthright to have this while you yet live among the waters.

It is yours to breathe in, to hear and to see in the running river.

It is yours to behold in the blue sky above.

A life without pain, without fear.

A promise from the Universe and its Source.

You can rise anew, unencumbered by fate, and its ash.

Let your heart survive this moment.

Let your soul fly freely in its honor and love.

Mitchell closed his eyes for a moment, still hearing her words. *Yet were they hers?* She had said them, but were they connected to the background, connected to the canopies of blue behind her outlined face, and her red hair moving in the wind? She had spoken them, yet somehow they seemed not to come from her, but through her. *Was she the messenger? Then who or what was the source?*

Mitchell was again in deep thought of who his wife had really been. She gave to him, as his wife, the kind of love and encouragement she now spoke as the messenger of the blue sky behind her. Now to have her remain as his connection to the message, or to the understanding, or secret to life made it no secret at all. Living life was about the engagement of love in the waking hours. Such a notion was not a secret to him. It was how Red lived her life. It was how she loved him.

He picked himself up off the floor, sat on the sofa and wiped the tears from his eyes. *Will I ever stop missing her?* He took a deep breath and stood up, putting one foot in front of the other in an effort to keep moving forward, to keep on living his life while there was yet honor and light to live it.

೮౿

He looked down the river, watching it roll and swash, rambling where rock and root put it. The conversation he had with the spirit of his father returned to his memory. He had not thought about his dad since the afternoon when both forgiveness, and horror, washed over him. Opening the journal, Mitchell read again these words:

> *Suddenly, before The Sea Man was the hand of God which held a letter from The Sea Man's father. The Sea Man recognized it as one of his possessions. With a postmark on the envelope from decades past, God pulled out the letter. It was a simple one page note with a phrase on it in his father's hand writing. The phrase was no longer complete for the second half of it had been rubbed clean from years of moving and storage.*

> *When The Sea Man looked closer at the phrase he found God's finger pointing to the part that could still be read. God asked The Sea Man to read it out loud to Him. The Sea Man read it and said out loud back to God: "God helps those . . ."*

> *Though the words came directly from the hand of his father, the meaning now came from the heart of God and in this moment God answered The Sea Man's prayer. The Sea Man saw his association with the letter move from one of sadness and longing to one of resolution.*

> *As The Sea Man moved back into the Current, his mind awash in the grace of God's love, he found himself repeating over and over again the phrase "God helps those . . .God helps those . . ."*

> *The Sea Man thought of his father. He saw a moment that long ago marked his father's thoughts to him about effort, come full-circle, with its original intention read again. He saw again the power of grace, made a part of the day by his efforts, and the right of every heart to see its life as God intended.*

Then he wrote in his own journal: *Parents are to bestow, through the great characteristics of courage, compassion, loyalty, and love, the deep-seated notion of self-worth, in their children. Self-esteem be damned. Self-esteem is a hollow existence. Self-worth is where creation finds a home. Self-worth is where love lives in the light of both the sun and moon.*

The day suddenly lifted its time from Mitchell's shoulders, and he was present with the passing of the elements. Nature's beating heart found response in his senses from one sound to the next, from one light-filled occasion to the next, from one passing scent to the next.

The sun had fallen again on another day of simple living, and he breathed deeply the knowledge of his place in the grand design of the universe.

ℰℐℒ

The front porch, and the arc of night approaching, kept Mitchell company, and in the moment. It had become his comfort; the moment. It had come alive. It was magical. And there he remained for the duration of the day's end. Standing up and saying goodnight to the dark blue air around him, he turned to go in when at once he heard Red's voice telling him to let go of the past completely. What unresolved bitterness was there—what injustices held the past, as wind blowing through the trees, must be turned back to the time and place it belonged. Red told Mitchell not to carry on with the past any longer, to bless the spirits of all life, living or living beyond.

Such a waste of another moment in your life, he heard her say. *Please say no more of what should have, or could have been.*

Useless thoughts were zeroing out of his heart like dead pine needles to a forest floor. They hit him hard and deep, cracking against the remnants of old habit and familiar ring. She was no longer keeping time with him. Impressions upon his senses from her effort-filled life had left him. His heart would grasp for things no longer present, out of routine, yet with each breath he found that routine fading. Like a sunset, or a solstice, or a rainbow moving past the brilliance of the moment, she was leaving him.

He put his forehead to the cupboard, resting it in sad recollection. "I can't forget you," he said, looking the small light on the kitchen counter. "I want to always have you with me, my love, always." He turned around and leaned against the kitchen counter putting his hands in his front pockets and his eyes to the ceiling in an effort to still the fall of another tear.

"I know, enough is enough, but do I also have to lose the memories that my senses hold of you?" He said to the interior of his home. "Do I forget the way your nose felt resting against my cheek? Must I lose the sensation of your angelic voice filling our home with song?" Mitchell stopped talking again, wiping his cheek with the resignation of letting another sad tear roll from his broken heart.

He walked over to the sofa and fell upon it exhausted from the day and from another round of letting go. He fell asleep immediately, not waking until the dawn shown brightly on what the morrow would bring.

∽∞∾

The weeks and months idled on. Journal entries were kept, as Mitchell remembered the grace and beauty that Red had given him:

I knew the joy of a boyhood imagination, unbounded by fear, or its proximity near me. I was taken by the texture of bark on trees then, and now by the pitch of the tall roof that covers and protects me.

Once absorbed into the rhythm of creativity, I have become the forward motion of energy in boundless form.

On that bike, or in that tree, my tanned skin was, and is, stained by sap, dirt, and sweat.

It was not about understanding the definitions of courage and faith, but then and now, acting as such. It was about being a boy, armed with the hands of compassion, and the fleet feet of loyalty, found in the breath of each moment.

I understand the message in the smile and eyes of my wife's courage, coming face-to-face with me as a direct connection to the spirit of young, growing, thriving things, in God's great universe.

It was, and is, about fearlessness—of knowing my place in the cosmic order and loving that place—my hands on the handlebars of that bike—my life in the branches of every tree I have ever climbed.

I knew, and know, the unbounded lack of fear—and clarity in the moment—the energy that burned, and burns, through me.

I knew, and know, what is not obvious in living in this world—it was, and is, so simple—to not let the march, from ash to ash, consume this simplicity. Let the rendering a moment upon a bike—or in a tree—be perfect in living a life.

At once and from out of the blue heaven above, Mitchell thought of Red's daughter, recalling the late night conversation in an Olive Garden many long years ago. *Sian.* He wondered if she still lived and if there was a way to find her, and let her know about her mother's passing.

❧❧

The day was at an end. Mitchell faced a quiet fire and the night air making a home next to it. Without much thought, he extended his hand toward the end table and opened the old man's book. He read:

> *Mercury and Venus sat above the very last waning moon, as the dawn broke on a December day. The Sea Man sat in his window watching again the rise of the sun over the desert. The morning's picture of the planets and moon was stunning, leaving The Sea Man with a sense of being something tiny and insignificant in the universal scheme of things. He dearly missed his wife.*
>
> *The planets of Mercury and Venus held in the Sea Man the finest memories of love—his wife's spirit burned brightly in the heavenly scene.*
>
> *The orbs were always together in the morning before dawn. Sometimes nearer, sometimes farther, always inseparable in relation to the view the Sea Man had of them. Yet in this view of love something was out of balance in the relationship between the two celestial bodies.*
>
> *One light always burned brighter than the other. One seemed to stand in front with her back to her lover. The other seemed distant and alone as if the separation in their relationship hurt her deeply. In their relationship, the Sea Man saw a love unequal in its parts, a love unreconciled in its pain—as a widower standing alone over a gravestone.*

The celestial bodies were a statement to him—symbols of his own journey through life.

He turned his attention to the waning moon. The morning was cold and crystal clear, and the crescent could be seen in its entirety, with the sickle of light below, and the dark blue shades of the sphere above. Above the sickle beacon rested the two lights, one forward and present, the other distant and diminished—as hands grasping for one another, yet beyond their longing to do so.

The Sea Man thought of the words in a sermon once told. It spoke of giving love, and not expecting any in return, and equated this unequal love as the Messiah's love, a higher love, where much had been given over the millenniums, and very little returned.

He saw this un-equal love represented in the lights above the sickle moon and could not, at times, bare the sight of it, as the sun's light rising from below washed clean his wife's presence in his life —again.

Of the Higher Love and his own reach for it, the Sea Man felt there was more to say. He felt there would always be an imbalance of love in his relationship with God because the Sea Man still, especially in early December, before the dawn, allowed too much anger—and its resulting pain, in his life.

"Will the anger and pain I feel toward you ever cease? Does the pain you feel over the tortured death of your son, your great love, ever end?" the Sea Man asked, not expecting God to answer. "Will the remainder of my life ever find a balance?"

"My love knows balance Sea Man," God said. "My love continues to grow in its depth and width as the Current of My

*Expanding Universe moves toward its Blessed
Horizon. The love I have for you is not un-
equal and transcends your definition of what
love is. I came into this higher love, which I call
a perfect love, by forgiving your transgressions.
In doing so, I am able to love like I do, where
love is perfect and balanced in it's giving, not
looking to be loved in return. This kind of love
fuels and renews itself, where the making and
giving of such love sustains the soul and
nourishes My Universe. The closest experience
you can come to this kind of existence Sea Man
is to make forgiveness the foundation on which
you build love. Doing this diminishes your
expectation of a return. Forgiveness pushes out
fear and resentment, freeing up the space they
rested in, allowing the breath of life to clean the
air, making crystal clear why a forgiving love is
made and given in the first place. This
'unequal' love brings peace in this life and a
place at My table in the next."*

*The Sea Man looked up at Venus
and Mercury seeing again his own experience
with love. The sun rose further, wrapping its
all-encompassing light around the two planets
and sickle moon, overwhelming their presence in
the heavens, and the great emptiness they
symbolized in the Sea Man's heart, as the
memories of his love moved among them.*

Mitchell put the book down, stood up and stretched, feeling
the exhaustion of a day well spent catch up with him. He made his way
upstairs to a bed he still shared with Red. In his dreams she would find
him. In his dreams she would play with him, talk to him, listen, hope,
cry and excite him. In the blanketed warmth, and by letting the day go,
his last thoughts were of floating on his back in the waterhole as a boy.
He smiled and drifted into the cosmos unencumbered.

Chapter Seventy Four

THE remaining days of the season put a spell on Mitchell's life. He was open to the times he spent walking the length of the Hassayampa, walking often to the waterhole, finding there the childhood peace that had eluded him as a young man. He had learned on the river, and through his wife, that it was his birth right to feel joy, and to be happy without the prerequisites of a culture already too fat with material wealth to be healthy.

One afternoon, after agreeing to Zac's requests that he be home-schooled, and to reopen the printing business on a part time basis, so that he might learn a trade, Mitchell headed out to the old oak.

He found a spot under the oak's branches, leaned back, and found the ever-present image of his beloved, looking down upon him. He opened his journal, and recited these words:

"My Red. So this is it then. This will be my earth-bound life. I am to travel through it without your hands in mine; to remember, but not know—the scents flowing freely from your hair and skin; to desire, but not have—your sweet breath upon my neck; to cry for, but find no relief—in the desperate wish for the ash beneath me to become what it once was; to be resolute, but see no end—in my ache for everything that was you. I see that your death has made me a Sea Man—one without anchor or foundation—floundering lost in a desert—rather than in the home he was born to know and love—a man of the endless horizon—bound now by rusted barbed wire fences—blocking his arrival to the seashore.

My beloved, I love you now more than ever. How can that be? And now I will always search the heavens for you, or perhaps in those stretches of grass, salt, sand, and shore where you might be waiting for me. My beloved, I love you now more than ever, I ask you again, how can that be? How can that be?"

The question rolled down Mitchell's face; the tears now joining Red's ashes underneath him.

Zac looked out the tall windows, across the clearing, to the old oak, and watched Mitchell grieve again for his lost wife. Zac tried to understand the depth of Mitchell's sorrow, and how one man could destroy the lives of so many. Zac stepped back from the windows, to prevent Mitchell from observing him—however empathically—the pain flowing out like roots in the ground.

అ⌘

On a stretch of river found between his property and the waterhole, the world of his boyhood wealth, Mitchell could see who he had become in the reflection of the water tumbling by his feet. Zac sat with him. He beheld with great confidence what living his life had brought to him, and knew clearly what he would give to this boy as a leader in his young life. He had become a man who understood the fine working of love. There was no room in the reflection for the kind of car he drove or for the size of the house in which he lived. He did not behold diplomas and accolades from other men or corporations as important. He looked only to the actions of his life—the movement of his hands and feet—as a reference for who he was. He hoped this way of life might help Zac unfastened the legacy his uncle had given him.

"You know I saw you and Red come into the Dinner Bell a couple of times," Zac said. "She was known to the staff as never eating much but always being a great tipper, I mean, both of you . . . you guys always left a great tip. I guess that's why the news of what happened out here was so wrong; what happened to you guys couldn't have happened to two nicer people."

Zac suddenly realized his conversational tone about that night's events might have not been received well.

"Yeah, the only thing she ever ordered there were French fries—she liked 'em well done, no spice. And she always ordered just a hair more than she could finish. French fries were her treat. And I always said that she was a 'cheap date,' because she was. Most of any check, any where we went to eat, was made up of my meal. She loved Tab. Can't always find it you know."

"Tab?" asked Zac.

"It's a cola that still has Saccharin in it"

"Saccharin?"

Mitchell gave Zac a sidelong glance. Zac returned it.

With some lightheartedness, Mitchell splashed some of the Hassayampa upon Zac saying: "you don't know Tab, you don't know Saccharin, what *do* you know?"

"It was probably Red that was the good tipper," Zac retorted, giving Mitchell a shot back of river water.

"You're sassy kid." Mitchell paused. "You remind me of my boyhood friends. That's a good thing."

Zac had heard many of the stories, but was still very interested in Mitchell's childhood reflections.

"On our first visit to the waterhole, Presley went to the highest ledge, and without hesitation, jumped into the unseen bottom, screaming as loud and lively as he could, as if it were his last breath. If his father had seen him do that, it would have been the end of him"

Silence.

"Can we try to find my parents? I'd like to know for sure what has become of them."

"Of course. Maybe Laurie could help us with that."

"Do you like her?" Zac asked.

"She's a good egg Zac, I just don't have the heart for another girl in my life."

The man and the child each gave way to more private thoughts about Red, letting the quiet of the river take hold of both of them.

The water was soothing as they slipped in barefooted. They took in the sunshine and the sky blue expanse, and breathed deeply the breath of their lives. Mitchell reached over his shoulder into his pack, pulled out the old man's journal, and decided to read aloud whatever page would fall open, with the aid of the breeze that kept them company on a fine afternoon. He read:

The Sea Man remembered:

> *Suddenly, the moment stood white*
> *and still. Nothing moved. From deep within*
> *him, to the stretch of the curving earth, beyond*
> *the blue heavens, there existed the calm,*
> *smooth, motionless passing of time.*

Mitchell thought of the passage's paradox when, on one evening, he extolled justice for the one he loved. Who he had become, through the illumination of a great woman's love—had made him act in faith and to fight for and protect that which he loved—knowing in his bones that he would act again, to fight for, and protect, the young boy sitting next to him—if life asked that of him. He read on:

> *The Sea Man looked skyward to*
> *mentally record what preciously remained*
> *before him.*

Mitchell understood well the words in the old man's story. Being a man was in equal parts courage, and compassion. One without the other had left him diminished in his life in so many ways. He knew these characteristics both as a boy at the waterhole, and again later, as her husband. He got up and motioned to Zac to accompany him downriver, toward the waterhole. Once there, Mitchell found his spot in the old man's story:

> *In transition between musical notes,*
> *the peace presented itself to the desert. He*
> *listened.*
>
> *He closed his eyes to feel the sensation*
> *of falling back, like slipping into a spiritual*
> *gap that cradled his hands and feet perfectly.*

Mitchell at last knew peace as a man in a chaotic world. Leaderless in his young life save his friends examples of love and friendship, he had flailed dramatically through his early days as a man. This would not be Zac's fate.

> *Illuminating his mind, the peace*
> *around him became visible through the lids of*
> *his eyes, and the filter of oxygen-rich blood,*
> *bending the reddish white glow from a warm*
> *winter sun into an abstract of sincerity*
> *unknown in his life before.*
>
> *The tall Saguaro contrasted daylight*
> *and shadow across the Sea Man's face, making*
> *him keenly aware that the very simplest of life's*
> *moments are found between the changes of the*
> *day—where peace maintains its quiet domain.*

Mitchell saw the cosmos; a chaotic place that ran two parallel universes of good and evil, in constant contact with one another. For so long, he had been a product of that friction. Love had changed that.

The Sea Man took note of how the winter sun had furthered the textures and contrasts of all living things. He was a part of something perfect and beautiful. He took a deep and quaking breath—an effort to will from his heart concealed truths—found in the gaps between what is, and is not registered in his senses.

Mitchell looked up again at the blue expanse of heaven and realized that being a man was about the grasp, and utility, of paradox.

The Sea Man found his will no match for the truth—a truth already evident—one that accounts for an infinite and universal love—one both scientific and spirit-filled—one known in the sun's light or the moon's shadow—one that will forevermore present itself to those who allow it to be known.

He came to know it. The winter's sunlight opened around him, contrasting the petty spells the he was normally accustomed to, whispering . . .

. . . white and still.

White and still, the Sea Man thought.

"White and still," he said out loud to himself, allowing the syllables and their inflections to become something more than a spoken thought in an insignificant and ordinary world.

The old man's story calmed Mitchell.

"White and still," spoken, became a message that stirred, then flurried about the Sea Man.

"White and still," spoken, rolled into moments that pounded the Sea Man's heart.

Mitchell spoke the words out loud. "White and still," he said softly, feeling the words roll from his tongue, and onto the water gathering around his feet.

> "White and still," *spoken, moved to the forefront of the Sea Man's thoughts, as the three words presented further notions of forgiveness and acceptance in his life.*

> *White and still was the love he had known from the heart of his wife, giving flight to thoughts of God and his request that a free will would choose goodness, following in His dying child's example on the world's ever-growing cross.*

Mitchell thought of sacrifice, and the laying down of one life for another. He thought of a soldier's call, and what great love it took to be courageous. He looked down at Zac, who was lost in a boy's day dream; the smell of water evaporating off of blue granite in a winter's sunlight, lifting an imagination skyward.

> *All this in a moment shared with the winter sun, a symbol of the love God gave to the souls of His Expanding Universe, by the birth of love billions of years ago.*

> *All this in a moment taken by the heart of a man who had not taken such moments before. A man who had not known love in light. A man who had not known love in shadow. A man who had not known love in the moments in-between.*

Mitchell recalled the moment he found the old man's story hidden in the floor of his living room.

> *Behind the obvious. In front of what was in easy reach. What had always been there if sought—was the peace and presence of God.*

Mitchell remembered the first time he opened the book and the movement in his gut, as he read the opening pages, that he and the Sea Man were one in the same.

> *Although not obvious and not within easy reach, the Sea Man opened the gifts of*

*acceptance and forgiveness, and in doing so, was
defined by what was white and what was still in
God's beautiful Universe.*

The cycle of hardship and sorrow moved through him, and his understanding of how the movement of this cycle through his life, had made him a better soul in the eyes of the universe.

*Stilled and illuminated by the light of
God's morning, the Sea Man could see what
forgiveness and acceptance gave to him and his
world; a peace beyond what any moment or any
sense could contain. It was a peace not of the
world of which he was a part. It was
participation, presence, a belief in the calm,
smooth, motionless passing of time, where a
mortal man could place his very sparks at the
steps of Heaven's gate, therefore, turning the tide
of what remained in life as important, as valid,
as the sum of living in the Current of God's
Expanding Universe.*

*The Sea Man heard at last, what had
long abandoned him during his struggle in living:
there, out his window, was heard the great roar of
the ocean—and reaching for Heaven was the
tallest lighthouse he had ever seen—its beacon as
bright as an early morning December love. His
desert had become his sea—and at last—he had
found his way home.*

Mitchell closed the book. He remembered the old man. He shook his head at the timing and immenseness of the words he wrote. From that time in history to the moment before him in the present, Mitchell marveled at how the secrets of the universe unveiled themselves to those who would will effort to know them.

To the trees and blue sky, to the water flowing downstream, to all the elements of the earth Mitchell spoke. He thanked Red for loving him. He thanked God for the comprehension of paradox, and of what living in the universe asked of him, and for the boy who now walked beside him.

They placed one foot in front of the other and as he began his walk with Zac up the Hassayampa one more time, he noticed the embodiment of Red moving with confidence and grace toward him. Mitchell stopped for a moment, rubbing his eyes, feeling the cold water run past his legs. Around Red's embodiment was heard a choir from the heavens above—her songbird voice layered in multiple keys—her eternal hope and faith for him, coming through in song. He looked again upstream and found the image move from memory to the present. She walked past Mitchell, taking with her all of Mitchell's pain and sorrow, freeing him to live again. He watched as Red moved through him. She looked back at Mitchell, and said: *always look for me, my love, I am out there, where the tall grasses meet the ocean-borne breezes,* and then continued her journey downstream, to that point where the Hassayampa returned to the earth.

THE END

Appendix A

COWBOY MOVIE

LAUGHING

AS THE RUINS FALLS